MERCENARY

As a favour to a CIA officer, maverick elite operative Stratton agrees to carry out a routine task in Central America. Burnt out after months away from home, he parachutes into the jungle for the op – and encounters a group of rebels planning to bring down the region's feared and hated leader, Neravista. Against his own strict principles, Stratton becomes embroiled in the rebels' plight and joins the popular uprising. As he helps them with the coup he finds himself falling for Louise, the beautiful daughter of their leader. But Stratton doesn't know what he's got himself into. The fight is not only against the vicious local government, but, chillingly, the CIA itself. He is in way over his head and the consequences are explosive . . .

Books by Duncan Falconer
Published by The House of Ulverscroft:

THE OPERATIVE
THE PROTECTOR
UNDERSEA PRISON

DUNCAN FALCONER

MERCENARY

Complete and Unabridged

CHARNWOOD
Leicester

First published in Great Britain in 2009 by
Sphere, an imprint of
Little, Brown Book Group, London

First Charnwood Edition
published 2010
by arrangement with
Little, Brown Book Group, London

The moral right of the author has been asserted

British Library CIP Data

Falconer, Duncan.
Mercenary.
1. Stratton, John (Fictitious character)- -Fiction.
2. Intelligence officers- -Great Britain- -Fiction.
3. United States, Central Intelligence Agency- -
Fiction. 4. Central America- -Politics and government
- -Fiction. 5. Suspense fiction.
6. Large type books.
I. Title
823.9'2–dc22

ISBN 978–1–44480–039–5

Published by
F. A. Thorpe (Publishing)
Anstey, Leicestershire
Set by Words & Graphics Ltd.
Anstey, Leicestershire
Printed and bound in Great Britain by
T. J. International Ltd., Padstow, Cornwall

This book is printed on acid-free paper

To Louisa
To David
wherever you are now

PART 1

Prologue

Washington DC, Christmas Eve

Stratton checked his watch and, using the car's side and rearview mirrors, looked in every direction along the street. He was sharing the dark, lamp-lit residential road with several other parked cars but no other people seemed to be around. Many of the apartment buildings overlooking his position had a Christmas light or illuminated decoration in the window but otherwise there was little sign of life.

He had an uncomfortable feeling. It had built gradually since he stepped off the plane. Put simply, he was nervous. This was unusual for him while he was on a job, but he knew why he felt that way. This mission wasn't for the SIS. It was private. Personal. That made the risk he was taking different from those he was used to. He was going to kill a man that night — with luck — and Stratton would be high on any subsequent list of suspects. He was going to punish another for that most primitive of reasons: revenge. This time he would have no safety net. No one would protect him. He was there on his own account and would be treated as a common criminal if he was caught. His plan

1

was high-risk and he could end up in jail for a very long time.

Stratton clenched his jaw at the thought of the chance he was taking. 'Screw it,' he muttered resolutely. It was worth it. In fact, he could hardly wait.

It had taken several years to get the information he needed to plan the operation. In that time Stratton had continued with life as a British military-intelligence asset, using his privileged position to keep a weather eye out for that one piece of data, the clue that might allow him finally to set the trap.

The opportunity had eventually fallen into his lap thanks to Sumners, his immediate taskmaster and SIS human-resources officer. It wasn't altogether surprising that Sumners had led Stratton to his target. The SIS man was tangentially connected to the individual Stratton was after although, luckily for him, he had played no part in the incident that had caused Stratton to embark on this personal mission. Stratton was convinced that Sumners didn't even know what had happened all those years ago. If he *had* known he would never have been so careless as to leave lying around the clue that had put Stratton on the warpath.

The target was a high-ranking CIA operative, which was why he had been so difficult to track down. As a matter of routine his powerful employers went to great lengths to protect him. The man had a similar background to Stratton's. His core expertise was in Special Forces, the American variety and, as with Stratton, his

2

country's pre-eminent intelligence agency utilised those skills from time to time.

Over the years Stratton had worried that something might have happened to the man before he himself could get to him. There were no doubt others who had the same aim as Stratton. The man was evil and had plied his trade for many years all around the world. But, much as Stratton wanted him dead, it was more important that the man knew that it was Stratton who was going to kill him because then he would know why.

The clue that Stratton had been waiting for came in the form of a discreet invitation mailed to Sumners from the USA. It was lying on the SIS officer's desk one day when Stratton arrived at the MI6 building beside the Thames to discuss an upcoming operation. The card's succinct inscription cordially invited Sumners to attend a rare gathering of the 'Black Pigs Association'. The only other wording was the date, time and address of the venue. Leaving the card exposed was a significant slip — or so Stratton prayed when he read it, since it might not necessarily have come from the person he sought. But, even so, there was still something about it that excited him. His instincts had tingled and even though there was an element of unavoidable doubt he was as undeterred as a heat-seeking missile homing in on its prey. At worst it might lead to another clue.

Stratton had heard the phrase only once before, from Sumners's own lips, the very next time he had met his boss after returning from that fateful mission all those years ago.

'Are you a member now?' Sumners had asked him, his tone sardonic and superior. 'Black Pigs?'

Stratton was in no mood for one of Sumners's characteristic petty jibes but he did his utmost to disguise his feelings. He felt filled with hate: he was desperate for retribution and Sumners represented his only chance of ever finding the elusive agent. If Sumners had had the slightest idea what had gone wrong on that operation he would have clammed up about the subject. But it was clear from his light-hearted reference to the man who had masterminded the task that he knew nothing about what happened. And as long as Sumners was not suspicious his guard on the subject would be low. The SIS officer was, by nature and vocation, a very secretive man.

'What's the Black Pigs Association?' Stratton had asked.

'It's the nickname of a certain group of CIA operatives and their select foreign allies,' Sumners had replied, pausing to allow the inference to sink in that he was one such 'select' individual. 'Men from a certain era who were involved in certain unmentionable things in certain places . . . But if he didn't tell you about that then you were not invited to join,' he added smugly.

Stratton left it at that. Sumners was not the type to elaborate any further once he had finished with a subject. And any attempt to get him to open up more would only arouse his suspicions. Stratton would not risk that.

It had taken several years but Stratton's

4

patience had paid off eventually. He was well aware that his target might not even be at the gathering but the point was that he could be. Stratton would not miss the opportunity, because one might never pass his way again. The date gave him a few weeks to organise the task and secure the necessary equipment, which was minimal and uncomplicated to acquire. He could plan practically the entire operation from the UK using satellite imagery and the internet.

Eighteen hours before the hit Stratton boarded a flight, arrived in Washington DC, picked up the car and equipment, carried out a detailed reconnaissance of the target location and with time to spare sat back to gather his thoughts and imagine the moment he had been waiting for for so long. He no longer even bothered to consider the possibility of the man not being there.

Tears began to form in Stratton's eyes. He blinked but did not wipe them away. They rolled down his cheeks, over his lips and to his chin, from where they fell to his chest. His reason for being there, the images of those moments that had led him on this campaign of revenge, filled his head. It seemed as if the execution of the plan had reopened the wounds of that day, the last time he had cried for her.

Stratton wiped his face on his sleeve and tried to put the thoughts aside. He pulled the hood of his heavy fleece over his head, smoothed the thin leather gloves around his fingers and climbed out of the vehicle. The icy air gripped his face and his breath turned to steam. He was pleased it was so cold because of the advantage it gave him: projectiles travelled more true in freezing air.

He walked around to the boot of the hire car, took out a backpack, which he placed over a shoulder, hit the remote that secured all the car's doors and made his way along the street, head down in case there were any CCTV cameras.

He turned the corner and walked along a busy road which he cut across to enter a dark alleyway dividing the block. He weaved around overflowing garbage dumpsters and bags of trash, scattering foraging vermin that had been taken by surprise at his silent approach. At the end of the alley he broke into a jog to cross a brightly lit road and to avoid an oncoming car and disappeared into another quiet street.

Halfway along it he turned into the entrance to an underground car park, headed down a steep incline, ducked under an unmanned barrier and walked calmly into a low-roofed, cavernous and dimly lit enclosed space that amplified every noise. A tyre screeched somewhere below as a car turned a tight corner. Stratton speeded up to a fire exit and pushed his way in through the door as the vehicle appeared.

He paused to listen inside a concrete stairwell that zigzagged tightly upwards. The car drove off and the only sound that remained was a gentle hum from the stairway lighting. Stratton took the first flight at a brisk pace he could easily maintain and carried on to the top.

The stairs ended abruptly at a heavy metal door. Stratton paused to catch his breath and listen before easing it open to reveal a spacious flat roof in darkness, crowded with ducts and airconditioning units. He stepped out into the icy breeze, closed the door quietly and crossed the familiar roof to a spot between two fan housings. The edge of the building was only feet away.

He removed the parts of a professional crossbow from his pack and quickly assembled the weapon, placing a foot in the stirrup and levering back the string that rolled through pulley wheels on the ends of the prods until it was locked by the trigger mechanism. The final component was a sophisticated telescopic sight that he locked into place.

Stratton opened a narrow plastic box to reveal three lethal bolts, their tips viciously barbed, their fletchings painted orange and with long slender green quetzal-bird tail feathers attached to the nocks by a line of gut. These were symbolic rather than a flight aid and an important part of Stratton's message to his target.

He placed one of the bolts in the bow's launch groove, inched forward to where he could see the street far below, rested the bow beside him and focused a pair of binoculars on the ornate entrance of a building opposite. Stratton could make out the partial figure of a man standing inside the glass entrance, illuminated by the colourful lights from a Christmas tree. A doorman or a security guard. With the party scheduled to end at midnight, in just over an hour, it was time for the old waiting game. An activity with which Stratton was more than familiar, particularly in the cold and holding a pair of binoculars with a weapon close by.

Stratton watched for more than an hour before the first men sporting dinner jackets walked out into the chilly air and down a flight of steps to the pavement. The flow of guests, all men, was intermittent, their breath turning to vapour as they came outside.

One of them paused at the top of the steps to pull on a coat. He looked familiar. Stratton scrutinised him through the binoculars. It was indeed Sumners, buttoning up his coat and looking back though the glass doors as if waiting for someone.

Stratton put down the binoculars, picked up the crossbow and balanced the stock in his hand. He made sure that the quetzal feather was neatly tucked behind the bolt and brought the tiller tight against his shoulder. He focused the cross-hairs of the scope on Sumners before moving them to the glass doors.

A group of four men came out. In their middle, holding court while fastening the buttons of his own coat, walked the one that Stratton had been waiting for. It was difficult to miss him, unfortunate perhaps for a man in his business — covert operations. He had a full head of thick white hair and he was also burly — not fat, just robust. He stood out in a crowd. Stratton had not seen him for several years but the last time was etched indelibly in his mind. The man had been standing on a cliff and looking down on Stratton hundreds of feet below, a gun in his hand. Their positions were

8

now reversed: a poetic irony.

The target picture was perfect. The man had paused halfway down the steps to press home a point he was making, much to the amusement of the others. Stratton aimed the cross-hairs at the centre of the target's torso and eased them closer to one of the man's shoulders. It was important that he should drop him with the first bolt but not kill him. That was difficult to ensure because of the steep angle. He had to avoid the heart, of course, but also the main arteries leading from it or the man might quickly become unconscious.

Stratton exhaled. As his lungs emptied he steadied his grip on the crossbow and took first pressure on the trigger. The weapon jerked as the prods straightened, sending the bolt at four hundred feet per second towards its mark.

It struck the man with the force of a horse's hoof, hitting him in the chest. The tip must have cut through his spine because his lower limbs folded instantly and he dropped like a dead weight, his heavy frame rolling down a couple of steps before he came to a stop on his back. The other men froze, except for Sumners who moved to the cover of the doorway.

None of them went to the man right away. He stared up at the night sky, an expression of utter shock on his face as he struggled to understand what had just happened to him. He fought to breathe and his hand quivered as he tried to find the object that was burning his chest. He was aware that his body had been pierced by something that was not a bullet. It occurred to him that perhaps something had fallen on him.

But as his fingers found the end of the bolt and explored the fletching he realised it was an arrow of some kind. The quetzal feather moved in the breeze and through his fingertips and when he realised that it was attached to the arrow's nock a memory worked its way into his thoughts. He had seen such a thing before. He inched up his head, forcing his chin towards his chest in order to look at it, but he was unable to raise his head far enough.

One of the other men finally dropped to his knees beside the wounded man. 'Call the police!' he shouted in the direction of the doorman. 'Get an ambulance! Hurry!'

'I want to see it,' the wounded man rasped, grinding his teeth in determination. 'I want to see it!'

His colleague seemed unsure what to do. But he put his hand behind the man's head to help raise it up.

The man grimaced with the pain but he had never lacked grit or tenacity. When he saw the fletching and quetzal feather he knew its meaning straight away and relaxed his neck muscles as if there was nothing more to be done. His helper lowered his head back onto the step.

The man knew only too well the significance of the arrow. He squinted at the rooftops high above, hoping to see who had launched it. He could make out nothing but blackness, not even stars, but it didn't matter. He knew who was there and that his nemesis had not yet finished with him.

A thin smile began to form on his lips but it

faded as the vivid images of what he had done those years ago filled his head. If he could have said a final word to his executioner it might have been an apology, for it was the only awful deed in his life that he regretted. At the time it had all seemed necessary to him but even his black heart had been touched by the vileness of his actions. He wondered how long he had before the end.

A second bolt struck him in the throat, cutting through his larynx and smashing a chunk out of the concrete behind his neck. The man went still and blood trickled from his mouth, his open eyes glazing over as the life went out of them.

PART 2

Six Weeks Later: Central America

Harris looked exhausted. He sat on a rotten log, taking a breather, his safari clothes covered in a patchwork of sweat, his trousers muddy up to the knees. The narrow track they had come along had dried since the climb out of the valley and the trees had thinned. The sun — and the air — were welcome. He dug into a breast pocket and pulled out a stick of gum, unwrapped it, tossed the paper onto the jungle floor and pushed it into his mouth. 'Gum?' he asked his young assistant who was photographing some kind of insect on the ground.

'Thank you, no,' Jacobs replied, with a cheerful smile. Jacobs was as dishevelled as Harris but he did not look as tired as his boss.

Harris hardly knew Jacobs. He was a new guy on the team, fresh from the factory, an Ivy League graduate who had spent barely a couple of years stateside before getting a transfer to the Centrals. Rumour had it that his family was well connected. As far as Harris was concerned, apart from both of them being in the same business they were worlds apart. 'Where's he gone?' he asked.

'The soldier?'

'No. I was suddenly worried about Elvis. Of course I'm talking about the damned soldier!'

'He went into the bushes.'

Harris looked up and down the goat track that disappeared into the forest in both directions. 'Are you screwin' with me?'

Jacobs looked a bit startled by his boss's apparent bad mood. 'No, sir. I'm sure he — '

'I know he's in the goddamned bushes somewhere because there's nothing else around here *but* bushes!'

A short South American Indian man wearing a grubby khaki army uniform stepped from the jungle, clutching a bunch of lush green leaves and chewing something. He had a single chevron on his jacket sleeve and carried a battered old rifle slung over his shoulder. He offered some of the leaves to Jacobs who accepted them with an appreciative nod, shoving them into his mouth.

Harris stopped chewing his gum, his mouth falling open as he watched his assistant munch the leaves into a pulp. 'Jacobs?'

'Sir?' the assistant replied, looking at him.

'Do you know what that is?' Harris asked like a disconcerted parent.

'Uh-huh.' Jacobs nodded.

'Jacobs . . . We're FBI. We don't do cocaine.'

'This isn't exactly cocaine.'

'That's coca leaf, right?'

'Yes.'

'It's an opiate, for Christ's sake . . . How long you been chewing that stuff?'

Jacobs shrugged. 'Since a while back.'

14

'Well, at least that explains why you've been bouncing along like Peter fuckin' Pan.'

'It helps take my mind off the discomfort.'

'That's how it starts . . . Do you mind? If I have to place you under arrest it's only going to complicate matters right now.'

Jacobs looked hurt.

'Spit it out,' Harris snapped.

The younger man did as he was told and wiped his mouth.

Harris sighed. 'That's gonna be a story for the guys when I get back,' he muttered. 'Whenever the hell that'll be.'

Once again he wondered who was behind this mission that had brought him into such a hell-hole. The order had reached his small office on the second floor of the US embassy in Salvador, coming directly from the top of the FBI tree without any of the usual bureaucratic diversions. Alarmingly, he thought he had detected that familiar sinister whiff of the CIA about it. The Agency was happy enough to get the Bureau to carry out some of its dirty work and to a man of Harris's experience this job had some obvious indicators. A search in this beaten-up and backward country, which had suffered guerrilla conflicts for decades, for the murderer of a US Special Forces colonel suggested that the victim had in some way been involved in the country's past troubles. Harris knew there had been no *official* US presence in the country during its most recent conflict, which indicated that he had been employed by a covert intelligence outfit, the CIA being the most

15

likely candidate. That particular rebellion had ended a couple of years ago and the only comparable danger these days came from bandits, which was why the local governor had supplied Harris with just one highly trained bodyguard . . . currently out of his tree on coca leaves, along with Harris's assistant.

Harris got to his feet, banged any crap it contained out of his hat, put it on his head and looked out through the trees at the stretch of country that they had covered since dawn. The lush tree-canopy stretched like a rolling ocean, reaching towards a line of craggy hills that marked the horizon. He would have appreciated the landscape's natural beauty more if he knew how much more of it he had to cross.

He hoped that he would find out more about this mysterious scenario when he got to the damned village that they were headed for, otherwise this nightmare trip that had so far taken three days' trek from Salvador was going to be a waste of time.

'If this was such a high-priority task why wasn't there enough in the budget to book a goddamned helicopter?' Harris muttered to himself.

'What was that, sir?'

'I was talking about flying there, but then I guess I'm the only one who isn't . . . Since you're so pally with our military escort here perhaps you could ask him how far we still have to go.'

'Oh, less than two kilometres,' Jacobs replied

16

matter-of-factly, taking a close-up snapshot of a flower.

'You know that for a fact?'

'He told me.'

'And when were you gonna let me know?'

Jacobs put down his camera and shrugged while smiling politely.

Harris nibbled his bottom lip as he adjusted his pack on his back. It hurt wherever he put it. 'Let's go,' he said, facing the soldier and looking at him accusingly.

Barely a hundred metres further on the track joined a wider one with wagon-wheel ruts in it. A kilometre later they broke out of the dense foliage to find themselves facing a hill whose slopes were covered in small mud and wood huts. The dwellings were packed tightly together, the roofs a mix of straw, corrugated metal sheets and colourful plastic tarpaulins. Hundreds of smoke spirals rose skywards. The immediate impression was of a shanty town.

The first villagers to notice them paused long enough to register that they were foreigners and then went back to harvesting beans in the fields at either side of the track. The children reacted with more liveliness. They cheered, gathering around the two Americans as they entered the village. The kids' grubby little hands, as filthy as their bare feet, tugged at the men's clothes. The soldier made a useless attempt to shoo them away but soon gave up when he realised that Jacobs was enjoying the attention. Instead he approached

17

one of the local adults in order to ask for directions.

Jacobs tried to engage the children in conversation, asking their names and using sweets to tempt any of them who came forward. Harris didn't mind since it kept them away from him.

The soldier thanked the villager and beckoned Harris to follow him.

'Jacobs — let's go,' Harris called out as the soldier headed for a narrow path between some huts.

Jacobs dealt out the last of his sweets and hurried to catch up.

The track wound steeply uphill between dilapidated dwellings. Some children followed but as the path became steeper they ran back down noisily, leaving the group alone.

The path reached the summit where it levelled off and the houses gave way to a small wood where it was noticeably cooler. The small group came to a stony clearing in the centre which was occupied by a handful of goats and scrawny chickens. The soldier stopped and pointed to the far side.

A solitary hut stood there, its wooden porch shaded by a bright green awning that flapped easily in the breeze.

The sky had darkened and Harris decided that a cloudburst was imminent. He approached the hut.

Clay flowerpots dotted the porch and windowsills, brightening the otherwise drab surroundings. An old Indian sat to one side of

18

the front door on a low wooden stool. He was clearly absorbed in some task and did not look up at them.

The soldier plonked himself down beneath a tree, his mission completed — this part of it, at least. He took a roll of magnolia leaves from a small sack and unfolded them. Inside were several maize *pupusas* filled with pinto beans, which he tucked into.

The old Indian looked different from the locals they had encountered so far, as if he was not from the region. His frame was larger and he was far more powerfully built. His facial features were broad, his hands and bare feet wider. He was peeling calabazas and using his toes to hold the small pumpkin-like vegetables while he pared them with a knife. Harris realised the man was using his feet because he only had one arm. He wondered if the man had other handicaps: he appeared to be unaware of the two strangers now standing in front of him.

Harris removed his pack, took out a waterproof folder and examined a photograph of a man. He was pretty sure the Indian wasn't who he had come to see but he wanted to be certain.

'Por favor,' Harris said after clearing his throat, wondering if the man might be deaf.

The Indian paused and looked up at him with hound-dog eyes, as if waiting tiredly for Harris to continue.

'I'm looking for François Laporte.'

The Indian stared at Harris blankly as though he had not understood a word.

'Fran-çois La-porte?' Harris repeated, emphasising each syllable.

The Indian put down his knife and got to his feet. He turned his broad back on the two men, opened the front door and went inside the hut.

Mumbled words came from inside and a moment later the Indian returned, leaving the door slightly ajar. He sat back down on his stool and picked up his knife.

Jacobs stepped closer to Harris. Both men craned to look through the small opening but it was too dark inside to make anything out. There was movement and a second later a man stepped into the doorway.

At first glance he appeared to be quite old, a slight stoop adding to the impression. On seeing the two men he straightened up and regarded the strangers with squinting eyes. It was more an expression of curiosity than a reaction to the light.

Harris recognised him immediately as the man in the photograph, although his skin was darker and his features were craggier. The date of birth in the file gave the man's age as forty-six but he looked ten years older. His face was scarred in places, old scars, and he had a weariness about him, as if he was ill or had been through an intense physical struggle.

'Can I help you?' the man said in a thick, distinctly French accent.

'François Laporte?'

'My name is Victor,' he said.

Harris was not put off. He knew this was his man. 'I'm Walter Harris. And this is Tom Jacobs,' he said with a contrived politeness intended to put possible suspects at their ease before he delivered his next sentence — which usually had the opposite effect. 'We're with the United States Federal Bureau of Investigation.'

Victor eyed the two men's sweat-stained and muddy clothes. 'Are you lost?' he asked.

Harris maintained his polite smile, noting that the man had a sense of humour. 'I don't believe so, no.'

'You're a long way from home,' Victor said wearily, showing no outward sign of surprise.

'Not really,' Harris said. 'This is part of my patch.'

'A patch,' Victor echoed. 'Yes . . . that's about all this place has ever been to America.'

'Aren't you a visitor yourself?'

Victor looked a little annoyed. 'I live here.'

'Aren't you French? You were born in the Dordogne — as François Laporte.'

'I was born in a small village called Masseube — near the Pyrenees, actually. And my name is Victor. At least your trip was not entirely wasted. You now have my name and place of birth correct.' Victor stepped back into the hut and closed the door.

Harris continued to smile, appreciating what he took to be the man's bravado. 'Mr Laporte . . . Victor,' he called out. 'I've come a long way just to ask you a few questions.'

The door remained closed.

Harris waited patiently, his smile fading.

Jacobs looked at his boss. 'What do we do now?'

21

Harris ignored the question and stepped forward onto the porch. As the FBI man reached for the door the old Indian came to life. He jerked his head up and looked at Harris who froze as the Indian pointed the knife at him.

Jacobs was unnerved. He wasn't used to this. He glanced over at the soldier, hoping that the man might help. But the little fellow was sitting back, his eyes closed, slowly munching his food and oblivious to everything else going on.

Harris stood his ground. If Victor's watchdog got to his feet he would back off. 'Did you know that Colonel Steel was dead?' he called out. 'He was murdered. In Washington DC.'

The porch awning flapped gently in the breeze. Harris began to wonder if this was a waste of time. He couldn't force Victor to talk. He had been aware that Victor might not have been at home but he hadn't thought that he'd find him and then be ignored by the man.

Harris looked back at Jacobs in the vain hope he might have a suggestion, but the young agent's expression was vacant. Harris stepped back off the porch. He had no intention of giving up yet, not after the damned slog to get here. But this was beginning to look a little tricky.

'What do we do now?' Jacobs asked.

'Is that all you can say? Why don't you try coming up with a suggestion now and then instead of acting like some stupid schoolkid?'

Jacobs wasn't offended by the insult. 'We could offer to pay him.'

'What?'

'Pay him.'

'You're suggesting the FBI starts paying for interviews?'

'No. Just this time. We've come a long way. It would be a shame to go back empty-handed, that's all.'

'A shame? Are you still high?'

There was a sudden crack of thunder so loud that it unsettled both of them. Seconds later the heavens opened up and it started to rain heavily.

'This is just great,' Harris grumbled as the downpour instantly soaked him.

Just then the hut door opened and Victor stepped onto the porch. He looked confused. 'Did you say Steel was dead?' he asked.

Harris glanced down at his feet as the ground around them flooded quickly. 'That's right.'

'You think it was me,' Victor said, a grin livening up his face.

'You haven't been out of this country since you arrived here ten years ago,' Harris said above the noise of the rain.

'I willed it to happen. Every night before I went to bed I prayed,' Victor said, looking up at the sky. 'And every morning I woke up I prayed. God finally heard me. The Antichrist is dead. My wretched life is finally complete. I can die in peace.' Victor's eyes suddenly narrowed. 'You wouldn't be joking, would you? That would be in very poor taste.'

'I'm not very good at telling jokes. I certainly wouldn't have come all this way to tell one.'

Victor looked down at the old Indian, smiling. 'Did you hear that, Yoinakuwa? The great beast and slayer of innocent women and children is dead.'

The Indian held his gaze for a moment, his dour expression unchanged, and went back to peeling his vegetables.

Victor's smile faded as he remembered the old man's pain and how it could never be eased even by such glad tidings.

'Can we go inside?' Harris asked. 'We've come a long way.'

Victor did not appear to hear, lost in his memories, and stepped back into the hut. Another thunderclap shook the air and the volume of the rain seemed to increase. Harris walked onto the porch, keeping an eye on the Indian.

Jacobs was uncertain if he should follow but he took a step towards the door anyway. The Indian remained focused on the *calabazas*.

Harris stepped into the doorway and looked at the interior of the hut. A fire crackled in a grate on the far side of the cramped little room. One opening led to a kitchen area and another to a bedroom. It was basic, to say the least, well lived-in and cluttered. The air inside smelt like a mixture of tobacco and mildew but it was not an entirely unpleasant odour. The room had only one window, partly covered by a grubby curtain; the lack of light added to the impression of musky dilapidation. A table stood against a wall and two old leather armchairs on either side of a crate that acted as a coffee table faced the fire. Various items adorned the walls and shelves, mostly old Indian weapons and pictures. There was something strangely cosy about the place. Perhaps it was nothing more than the atmosphere created by the crackling fire and the sound of the rain beating on the roof.

Victor lit a twisted cheroot from the flames of the fire and blew thick smoke at the ceiling before slumping down into one of the armchairs. 'Please, sit,' he said.

Harris put down his backpack and eased himself into a chair. Jacobs looked around the room as if it were a museum. He stowed his own soaked pack and sat on one of the creaky chairs while studying the knives on the wall.

'Would you like a drink?' Victor asked.

'That would be great.' Harris shrugged.

'Yes. We should celebrate such good news. Yoinakuwa!' Victor called out.

A moment later the Indian stepped into the doorway.

'Some wine,' Victor said, his gaze resting on Harris who was slow to catch on. 'Visitor's treat.'

'Oh. Right,' Harris said, digging into his pocket to produce some notes. 'Dollars okay?'

'Of course,' Victor said. 'Where is the Yankee dollar not welcome?'

Harris held out several dollar bills, unsure how much to offer. Yoinakuwa took them all and walked away, closing the door behind him and muffling the drumlike noise of the rain hitting the awning.

Harris and Jacobs exchanged glances. The younger man looked vindicated.

'Did you change your name or is that our mistake?' Harris asked Victor.

'I was born François . . . François Laporte. When I found myself embroiled in the local politics here I decided it was . . . well, politically uncomfortable. 'François' sounded too much like Franco . . . as in Francisco Franco, the fascist general — Spanish Civil War.'

'Yes, I understand.'

'We were in the middle of a revolution and I thought Victor was more victorious-sounding.'

'A scientist turned revolutionary. That's quite a switch.'

'Is it? Surely scientists are revolutionaries by nature. An FBI agent turned revolutionary, now that would be fantastic. If that's why you're here by the way, you're too late to join up. The revolution's over.'

Harris smiled politely.

'So. If you have come all this way just to tell me that Steel is dead then I'm flattered,' said Victor.

Harris took a moment to collect his thoughts. 'What can you tell me about Steel?' he asked. 'How did you know him?'

Victor shrugged. 'Steel worked for the CIA. Did he not?'

'I'll be honest. I don't know who he worked for. I've come here to ask you some questions, that's all. It's just a small part of a larger investigation.'

Victor shrugged. 'That much was obvious, I suppose,' he said. 'Steel came here to help the rebellion because at the time it suited American foreign policy in the region. He was a clandestine operator. He had no papers of authority. But he

26

had money, weapons — he could provide lots of both. He supported us, or at least gave us the impression that the United States supported us. And why should they not have? We were democratic liberals prepared to risk our lives to kick out a bunch of fascist pigs. It was a classic enough story. The Neravista government was nothing more than a corrupt, despotic dictatorship of the worst kind. They were a darkness, a blight on the land, and Neravista himself was an evil man with the blood of children on his hands.'

Harris wanted to avoid any political stuff and paused to let the moment pass. 'How often did you see Steel?'

'He came now and then. He would appear out of the blue, without warning.'

'Over how long?'

'A year, maybe. You see, we believed he was our friend. Maybe he was for a time. I'm sure he began by following orders. It seemed as though the Americans supported us in the beginning. Why would they have merely pretended to? But Steel changed his mind at some point, or his bosses did. Or we were sidelined by something that became more valuable to them. I don't know. I was not privy to that information.'

Harris took a notepad from a pocket and opened it. He jotted down a comment before underlining his next question. 'Did you know an Englishman named John Stratton?'

Victor stared at the fire, smiling thinly. 'Stratton. Yes. I knew him.'

'Do you know who he worked for?'

27

'He worked for Steel, at least in the beginning. He seemed to be his own boss. You didn't ask people like him where he came from or who he worked for . . . It was obvious what he was.'

'What was that?'

'What else could he have been? He was a mercenary.'

Harris nodded as he made a note. 'Steel left behind a letter to be opened in the event of his death. It included a list of names, people who should be suspected of his murder if he died in suspicious circumstances.'

Victor chuckled as he took a long draw on his cheroot.

'Why do you find that amusing?'

'I'll bet you don't have the list with you.'

'No.'

'That's because you could not have fitted it into your pack. There were many people who wanted to kill Steel. I knew a few thousand myself.'

'I suppose Steel meant those who would have had the skill to find him as well as kill him. After all, considering the line of work he was in . . . Stratton was on that list.'

Victor shrugged as if he had no idea why.

'In an excerpt from Steel's report on the rebellion he wrote that Stratton had betrayed him.'

Victor shook his head, as though he was denying a statement he'd heard often before. 'What do you know of the rebellion?' he asked.

'Not a lot. There was a popular rising against Neravista's dictatorship. It lasted several years and the government succeeded in putting it down.'

'So many suffered for so long. So many died and you describe it all in a couple of short sentences.'

'I didn't mean to make light of the conflict. There's hardly a country in this part of the world that hasn't gone through a painful change of government costing many lives in the last forty years.'

'I suppose it was a small rebellion compared with most. This is a small country. Around here it's still called Sebastian's Rebellion. It was the rebellion of many but it bears the name of one man. And rightly so . . . You heard of him?'

'I understood that he was one of the rebel leaders.'

'There were several leaders, true, but Sebastian was the main one. He was the most intelligent, the most powerful, the most determined to finish what he essentially began . . . I was his second in command, you know . . . his last one . . . Through the course of the campaign some of us lost our way. Doubt set in. Ideologies altered. Then came confusion, lies, corruption. By the end just about everyone had betrayed someone in some way. Not Sebastian, of course. He never wavered from his course, to the very end. Stratton's only betrayal was of himself. He betrayed his own code of survival. We all lost in the end.'

A flash illuminated the room through the window and a second later an enormous crack of thunder sounded as if it had detonated just outside the door. Water began to drip through the reed roof onto the floor. 'What was Stratton's part in the rebellion?' Harris asked.

'He got caught up in things he never expected to . . . He was not an ordinary man. He did not try to lead but men wanted to follow him anyway. He did not try to impress others but others wanted to be like him.'

'My report describes him as a trained killer. Is that how you yourself would describe him?'

'Would you describe a gentle breeze as a killer? But a tornado is also just a wind . . . Stratton was like a welcome breeze most of the time. But he could also become a tornado.'

'How did he come into it?'

Victor grinned. 'In a spectacular fashion,' he said, taking a final drag from his cheroot before tossing it into the fire. 'He arrived the same way he left . . . Like an eagle . . . '

1

A Hercules transport aircraft thundered low over the jungle, gracefully following the contours of the rolling peaks and troughs of the forest canopy as dawn broke over the distant horizon. The plane's sand-coloured fuselage, free of any identifying markings, was not as old as the paint job made it look. The propellers purred robustly as it banked easily onto a new heading and levelled off towards the rising sun.

As the tailgate motors whined the two large doors separated, the upper one folding into the fuselage, the bottom one lowering to form a level platform.

Stratton, wearing camouflage clothing, with a holstered pistol on his belt and a parachute on his back, stepped from inside the dark interior onto the ramp. The wind tousled his unkempt dark hair and he looked down at the jungle speeding past several hundred feet below. The dense forest spread beneath him like a vast undulating carpet, with distant rocky hills on one side and a series of table-top plateaus on the other. He tried to clear his mind and enjoy the spectacular view but he couldn't. There was too much to think about.

He hooked the butt of a short black M4 carbine to a clip at his shoulder so that the barrel pointed down and secured it to his waist with a bungee. Meanwhile the crew extended a section of parallel rollers that looked like a large ladder from inside the cabin to the end of the ramp and quickly clamped it to the floor. The loadmaster, wearing headphones, strode out to Stratton and put a hand on his shoulder. 'One minute!' he shouted.

A crewman handed Stratton a helmet while another placed a heavy camouflaged backpack at his feet. Stratton buckled on the helmet, turned the pack upside down, stepped through the shoulder straps, pulled the pack up in front of him and clipped it to his belt harness. He took a deep breath and exhaled slowly to help ease his growing tension. It was always the same, he thought. The only time he remembered ever being totally indifferent about a jump had been when he was doing half a dozen a day, and only then by around day three of the jump schedules. Otherwise every time he'd pulled on a chute and stood on a ramp ready to go he had experienced butterflies to some degree. Stratton wasn't the daredevil type but then again, if the odds of survival were in his favour and, most particularly, if the reason for jumping was good enough, he would go for it. But he had every excuse to feel a tad uneasy about this jump. It was a LALO — low altitude, low opening — and it was above jungle. That would never become routine.

A heavy crate one metre wide by two metres long emerged from the hold on the rollers and was brought to a stop on the edge of the ramp where a block prevented it from falling off. Strapped to its top was a large chute with a static line attached. Half a dozen similar containers were rolled out behind it.

'We gotta standby!' shouted the loadmaster, his voice echoing over speakers throughout the hold.

Crewmen took up their positions alongside the crates. A plastic bag shot out from somewhere inside the cabin and spiralled away in the slipstream.

'Secure that trash!' shouted the loadmaster.

A series of bright red lights flashed on around the ramp. The crewman on the end of a safety line crouching by the lead container, his clothes flapping furiously in the turbulence, gripped the restraining block.

One of the men leaned close to Stratton. 'You're one crazy son of a bitch!' he yelled.

Stratton ignored him. He fitted his goggles and braced himself for what was coming next. The guy was perfectly correct but not in the way that he meant. He probably thought Stratton was looking forward to the jump. He was wrong. Stratton was looking forward to being on the jungle floor, sure — but not to getting there.

'Goin' up!' shouted the loadmaster, grabbing a firm hold of the side of the ramp.

Each man braced himself as the pilot powered up the engines to maximum and pulled the nose of the aircraft up into a steep climb. The view out of the back was suddenly all green. The containers shunted against their restraining blocks and everyone hung on to their handholds as gravity tried to suck them out.

Stratton could smell the exhaust from the engines, a sweet odour that tickled the back of

33

his throat that was now dry. He looked down to see a large clearing in the jungle appear directly below. It was the drop zone and he could only pray that they were on target.

The red lights changed to green. Stratton's nervousness suddenly peaked and then fell away sharply as the climactic moment drew near and his concentration intensified.

'Go! Go! Go!' shouted the loadmaster.

A crewman yanked free the first restraining block and the heavy crate rolled on, tipped off the edge of the ramp and plunged into the slipstream where it was grabbed and ripped away in an instant. The attached static line went taut and dragged from the chute pack a long stream of pink nylon that inflated into a massive mushroom shape that slammed the brakes on the container, which swung violently in response. The other crates followed in quick succession.

Stratton took a deep breath, turned around and shuffled backwards to the edge of the ramp, keeping an eye on his feet to make sure that he didn't fall off prematurely. He looked through the gap between the ramp and the bulkhead to see they were still over the clearing and then watched as the remaining crates rolled towards the edge of the ramp. The seconds to his jump were ticking away. He could not turn back now. At that moment it felt as though his mind was processing a million thoughts, not all of them helpful. He gripped the pilot chute and looked for the jungle again. The end of the clearing came into view. That was not good. He felt a sudden rush of concern. A glance to the other side revealed the last container slipping off the tailgate platform. Stratton ignored a warning from inside his head to abort and threw the pilot chute out behind him. He braced himself for the part of the jump that he hated most.

The pilot chute sprang open as it sailed out on the end of a long bridle that wrenched a deployment bag from Stratton's parachute pack. He braced his shoulders and pressed his chin against his chest in preparation for the inevitable whiplash as the main chute deployed. It felt like he'd been standing there for an age although in reality it had been less than a second. The chute cracked open, yanking Stratton off the ramp like a rag doll, and for a few seconds he had absolutely no control. He tried to wrap his arms tightly around himself, as if to stop his limbs from being torn off.

As the aircraft levelled out the crew shuffled to the edge of the tailgate ramp to watch the progress of their payload. Stratton's chute was a bright green nine-cell square with a red blotch across its top which, when the chute was fully deployed, became a large fire-breathing dragon.

'That is one crazy bastard,' someone shouted as Stratton recovered to make a tight turn barely a couple of hundred feet above the jungle.

'He ain't gonna make it to the edge of that clearing,' the load-master mumbled into his headset.

'Don't matter,' said a big man in civilian clothes and with a thick head of white hair who was standing behind him. He was wearing his own headphones. It was Maxwell Steel, a colonel in the US Marine Corps. 'He's just the pizza boy. As long as they get the pizzas.'

The loadmaster looked around at the man who was running the show. The crewman did not try to conceal his contempt as he walked away to operate the machine that pulled the flapping static line cables and deployment bags back into the aircraft's hold.

As the aircraft banked steeply away Steel took a last look at the man he had hired to deliver the load. He couldn't understand what all the hoo-ha was about. If you made it you made it, if you didn't you didn't. That was his philosophy.

★ ★ ★

It took only a second for Stratton to confirm his fear that he was not going to make the clearing. If he'd been as certain of it when he'd been on the ramp he would have cancelled the jump and asked to go around again even though that would have pissed off everyone, especially Steel. The drop had started three seconds too late. That meant hundreds of metres in this business. Most of the bundles had landed inside the clearing but not all of them. He saw one strike the outer edge of the surrounding trees, the parachute ripping into the branches as the heavy bundle dropped between them. Not that he gave a monkey's. He had his own problems.

Stratton's square had a seventeen-foot horizontal gain to a one-foot drop. The wind was light and not a huge factor. Hitting the trees was. That could mean broken bones and getting hung up in a branch, and, depending on the extent of the injury, that might be the end of it. He had to find a way through — and quickly. A swift turn presented a choice of several gaps big enough to slip through. There was no way of knowing the obstacles he'd encounter inside the darkness, of course. He would find that out the hard way. His immediate task — one of many — was to sort out the angle of approach.

Stratton selected a hole directly beneath him. He soared out for some distance before turning back around. His experience told him that the trees were very tall and umbrella-like, and most of their branches would be near the top. If he could get past those then below would be mainly tree trunks — not that easy to steer through either.

Stratton concentrated on the dark opening, deftly pulling and releasing the toggles to adjust the chute's glide path. He had to drop in perfectly or he would overshoot and that would be that.

The closer he got the deeper inside the hole he could see, but there was still no clear route through. At the crucial moment he pulled down on both toggles to remove much of the chute's lift. As he plunged inside the gap it went dark and his eyes took a moment to adjust. He dropped rapidly and released the toggles to regain some lift. But as he did so a dense array of tangled branches appeared and he yanked down fiercely on one side to turn away, using what little control he had left. The chute's fabric scraped against branches as Stratton swung in a tight arc. His legs struck them hard and they clung to him like grabbing hands. The reduction of weight took the air out of the cells and the parachute threatened to collapse. A violent and desperate kick released him but not before the chute had almost dropped level with him. He fell and for a moment was unsupported, but as he swung beneath the canopy his weight snapped the risers taut once more, the cells reinflated and he sailed on inside the jungle.

He was through the worst part of the descent but the dangers were not over. The tree trunks stood like vast pillars in a cathedral, the spaces between them barely wide enough to turn in. Littered across the jungle floor lay the decaying remains of past generations of trees. He pulled and released the chute's toggles, using all his concentration and skill to weave between the massive columns.

The parachute flapped noisily as Stratton kept the speed as low as he dared without stalling, making the turns like a slalom skier, sometimes grazing a tree trunk.

The ground rushed towards him and as a small clearing appeared he lined it up. He released the toggles in order to eject his back-pack, which he kicked off while he grabbed for the controls again. The pack dropped several feet before it jerked to a halt at the end of a line that was secured to Stratton's harness. He took the lift out of the chute to stall it. The backpack hit the ground as his forward momentum ceased, and he dropped onto his toes beside it as if he was stepping down from a chair.

The parachute collapsed and once Stratton had unclipped it he slumped down to recover. One near-disaster after another within seconds was more than he had bargained for. He looked up at the hole in the almost solid roof of jungle, wondering how the hell he had managed to get through. If he'd ever needed a reminder that he'd been born lucky, the last few minutes had been it.

The sheer beauty of the forest was captivating. For as far as Stratton could see the trees stood majestically, higher than telegraph poles. In places the sun's rays broke through to light up patches of the jungle floor. The air smelled sweet and tangy and he could practically taste the moisture in it. It was eerily quiet too but that was only to be expected. Every creature in the area would have scattered when he crashed through the jungle canopy and they were probably now silently watching him from cover.

Stratton would have been content to sit where he was for a while and even make himself a brew but he didn't have the time. This was hostile country and a multi-bundle drop could have been seen for miles around. On top of that the intended recipients would show up at some stage, he hoped. The rendezvous procedure he'd been given was terrible. 'You'll know 'em when you see 'em,' Steel had said. When Stratton had asked for a little more info, the American had replied sarcastically, 'On one side are soldiers and on the other side are rebels. Don't give 'em to the soldiers. And if you do, make sure they pay for 'em.' He'd amused himself, at least. It

39

had heightened Stratton's suspicion that this was a cowboy operation. So had missing the drop zone by several hundred metres. The good news was that as soon as the rebels showed up he would have one small task to do and then he could get out of there.

He unclipped his M4, untied the line to his pack and took a walk to check out the immediate area. Satisfied that he was alone, he leaned his gun against a tree and removed his chute harness. He took a nylon bag from his pack and folded the chute into it, then removed a smaller pack that contained a semi-automatic pistol, a change of clothing and boots, medical equipment, some money, a passport, GPS, a bottle of water and some rations, all inside a waterproof bag. He dug a hole between two large roots at the base of the tree, placed the small pack inside and covered it up. He pulled his knife from its sheath, cut a large triangle into the bark at head height and stood back to memorise the tree's characteristics. He used his compass to note the bearing from the clearing, which he could see through the trees, and felt confident that after he had paced the distance to the edge of it he would be able to find the tree again, in daylight at least.

Stratton secured the parachute bag to the top of his pack, heaved it onto his shoulders, grabbed his gun and started to march to the clearing, counting the paces as best he could while stepping over dead trees.

As he reached twenty steps his senses screamed out a warning and he stopped dead. He was being watched. He was not a hundred per cent certain — he wasn't psychic — but he was experienced enough never to ignore such warnings.

A glance around revealed nothing and he eased the pack off his shoulder, lowering it soundlessly to the ground.

As Stratton turned he saw a young man, an Indian by the look of him. The youth wore only a pair of trousers that were cut off just below the knee and he held a bow in one hand, with an arrow placed lightly against the string: his fingers gripping the nocked shaft in readiness to pull it back. A quiver filled with more arrows hung by his side. Stratton guessed that he was about sixty metres away. The Indian would have to be good to get him at that range, especially if he was moving. Stratton needed to know if the youth was alone so he turned slowly. Directly opposite the young man, about the same distance on the other side of Stratton, stood a near-duplicate figure who was watching him with the same calm intensity, a bow and arrow in his hand too. Stratton had to respect their ability to get so close to him, and from opposite directions at that. So much for his keen senses, he thought. Defending himself against two bowmen who'd bracketed him like this would be that much more difficult. Cover from one would be exposure to the other. And if their shooting skills were anywhere near as good as their stealth technique, Stratton was in trouble. But they had not yet drawn back their bowstrings. With any luck, he thought, they did not mean to hurt him. He suspected that he would already have a couple of arrows in him if they did.

Stratton rested the M4 on his pack and held out his open hands, a smile spreading across his face. 'Hola,' he called out.

The young men did not move, their hawkish stares fixed on him. Stratton swivelled his own gaze from one side to the other, keeping them both in view. They didn't appear to want to communicate in any way. It was all a little weird. As he pondered his next move a sound that grew louder by the second came from the trees. It was the unmistakable noise of people moving through the undergrowth. He could only hope it was the men he was supposed to meet and that these Indians weren't working for the other side. If it was government forces he didn't think they would allow him to leave. In that case he would have some explaining to do.

Stratton kept his hands in view as he looked in the direction of the new visitors. Another half-naked Indian appeared but this one was older and stockier and carried his bow across his back. The heavy trudging sound came from behind him — it sounded like there were a lot of men.

The next man to appear was not an Indian but a dark-skinned Latino wearing military fatigues and carrying an AK47. Behind him walked half a dozen others and when they saw Stratton they stopped to allow two more men through. The one in front looked similar to the Latinos but seemed seriously intense. He walked as if he expected someone to shoot at him any second and looked like he was ready to fire back. The man just behind him was short and stocky, in his forties and with European features. He wore a multi-pocket fishing waistcoat over his camou-flage shirt, a floppy hat on his head and the only weapon he appeared to have was a pistol in a holster on his hip. His dress and bearing alone singled him out from the others. It appeared that he was the one in charge. Stratton would have been surprised if he turned out to be a local.

The man in the fishing jacket said something to one of the others who walked back towards the main group shouting at them to halt. The order was repeated for some distance back into the jungle. His intense-looking colleague stopped to let the leader pass. The man eyed Stratton as he approached. When he stopped a few metres in front of Stratton he took a good look around, in particular up at the trees. Stratton maintained a pleasant smile. He felt sure these were rebels and not government troops.

'My scout says you came through the canopy?' The man's accent was distinctly French.

'Yes,' Stratton replied in a tone that conveyed regret.

'I would have thought that since this time they were also dropping a man they might make an effort to hit the clearing.' The group's leader looked and sounded irritated. His face had not seen a razor in days. 'I've been up there too so I know what it's like. It was difficult enough in a balloon. By parachute I would have said it was suicidal.'

Stratton could only puzzle over what he meant about the balloon. 'It wasn't by choice,' he said.

43

'Did they push you out of the plane?'

'Good point,' Stratton conceded.

'I hope they're paying you enough.' The man scrutinised him more closely. 'You're English?'

Stratton nodded, wondering what his story was and how he came to be here.

The man remained moody but he seemed to become less stand-offish. 'My name is Victor,' he said by way of introduction.

'Stratton.'

'I am Sebastian's second in command.'

Stratton knew nothing about the conflict nor did he know anyone's name, thanks to Steel's terrible briefing. But he smiled politely and nodded as if it was all quite clear.

'Did any of it reach the clearing, do you know?'

'I think most of it did.'

'If you would lead on, then,' Victor said. 'Neravistas are in the area. We must assume they saw the drop.'

Another snippet of information. Neravistas were obviously the bad guys. Stratton picked up his pack and weapon. Someone called out the command to march and the shout was repeated several times, echoing back for some distance.

Stratton had already walked several metres before he remembered that he was supposed to be counting paces. He made a rough estimate of how many he'd taken so far and as they headed up an incline he looked back to see a long snaking line of men and burros. He could not see the end of the column.

They came to the first container. It was

hanging several metres above the ground, dangling from its shredded parachute which had snagged in the upper branches of a tree. The crate had broken open and several large plastic boxes lay on the ground.

Victor was incensed. 'If those idiots only realised that it takes valuable time to retrieve these. We must get these boxes loaded as soon as possible!' he called out over his shoulder.

Orders were shouted and a group of men set about gathering the container's contents. Stratton continued on. The undergrowth grew taller and thicker as they approached the edge of the clearing and men came forward with machetes to clear a path. They all looked like they had been living rough in the jungle for a while. They were unwashed and grubby, and most of them had long hair and beards. Apart from their camouflage gear, which seemed to have come from several different sources, they didn't look like soldiers. But there seemed to be a solid enough rank structure and the discipline was there. Stratton wondered about their soldiering skills, though. Not all the weapons he could see looked in good condition.

The men soon cut through to the clearing where the bundles lay scattered over a wide area. Stratton took a count.

'That's it,' he said to Victor. 'They're all here.'

Victor nodded to the serious-looking officers, who barked some orders and the rebels hurried into the clearing with their burros in tow. There must have been over two dozen animals and a hundred men.

Stratton made his way to one of the pallets to inspect a plastic container that had fallen out of the crate and had been damaged. He opened the lid and lifted a sponge cover to reveal a couple of dozen green tubes marked with black stencilling.

'Rockets!' exclaimed one of the men who saw them. Within seconds several rebels surrounded the box, removed some of the launch tubes and inspected them excitedly.

Stratton watched one of the men holding his tube up the wrong way round. When he began pushing in the rubber firing button, even though the device was not armed at that stage, it was evident he had no idea how to use it. Stratton watched other rebels beginning to do things with the tubes that were definitely inadvisable. He was suddenly alarmed.

'Whoa, whoa, guys,' he called out. 'Stop. Just a minute. Hold on. You, don't do that . . . Listen in!' he finally shouted.

They stopped talking and gave him their full attention.

Stratton looked at the men, most of whom were a few inches shorter than him. At six foot he wasn't particularly tall, neither was he noticeably muscular, though he was athletic. But he was quite big compared with most of the rebels, this bunch at least. 'Does anybody here know how to fire these weapons?' he asked calmly.

A barrel-chested man held his launcher confidently as he stepped from the group. 'You just pull this bit here and then — '

'Stop, stop, stop,' Stratton asked, holding out

46

his hands. 'Don't pull *anything* . . . Do you know what kind of a rocket this is?'

There was silence. 'It's the kind that blows things up,' someone called out, much to the amusement of the others.

Stratton smiled along with them. 'That's good. You're right. It's the kind that blows things up. And if you're not careful you'll blow us all up right here and now.'

'So show us how to fire it,' one of the rebels said.

'Yeah, show us,' another man echoed.

'Well . . . I didn't exactly come here to — '

'What are you people doing?' Victor interrupted, calling out as he strode through the undergrowth towards them. 'Get this stuff loaded! Or are you just waiting for the Neravistas?'

The men put the launch tubes back in the box and hurried to the task.

Victor looked to the sky worriedly, wiping the sweat and grime from his brow before inspecting the rockets. 'What are those?' he asked.

'Sixty-six-millimetre rockets.'

Victor appeared to have mixed feelings about the weapons.

'You didn't ask for these?'

'We never know what we're going to get. I think they send us whatever they have a surplus of. Last month we got two hundred pairs of chemical-and-biological warfare over-boots and a dozen gas masks . . . Are they simple to use?'

Stratton looked down at the tubes. 'Well, yes — when you know how.'

47

'You can show us?'

'I came here to show you how to set up the claymores.'

'The what?'

'They sent you several boxes of claymore anti-personnel mines. I was told to show a couple of your men how to set them up and then I'm on my way.'

'Is it such a big deal to show the men how to fire these rockets as well?'

'No. If you've got time,' Stratton said with some reluctance. He had set his mind on getting going as soon as possible in the hope of making it to the border before the following evening.

'We'll have plenty of time when we get back to the camp,' Victor said, walking off.

'Hold on . . . excuse me,' Stratton said, following him.

Victor stopped to shout at several men tying a box onto the back of one of the burros. 'Quicker, you people. We need to leave.' He turned to Stratton to hear what he had to say.

'My task was to show your people how to set up claymores, but I was supposed to do that here at the drop. I'm leaving as soon as you guys do.'

'We don't have time to do any training here. We must pack up and go as soon as we can. What do you people think this is? We're at war. Didn't they tell you anything?' Victor walked away.

'Actually, no,' Stratton muttered to himself. But he wasn't going to give up so easily. He caught up with Victor who was chastising a group of men who were having problems with one of the burros. 'If we move away from here a couple of kilometres and take a break, I can run some training then.'

'We don't take breaks. We have to go as quickly as we can. It won't be safe until we reach the camp,' Victor said, walking away to resolve another crisis.

Stratton watched Victor go, realising that it was pointless to continue with the argument.

He had a decision to make.

He walked to the edge of the clearing, sat down and rested his carbine across his legs. He took the GPS from his pocket and turned it on. The decision he faced was either to follow the rebels to their camp as Victor had suggested, do the training and then leave, or to bug out right there and then. He could slip off into the jungle and probably no one would notice until they were ready to go, by which time he would be a couple of miles away.

But even as Stratton considered the options he knew that he would never be able just to walk off. Although he didn't know anything about these people and would never see any of them again, he couldn't leave as long as he knew there was a chance of someone getting hurt or worse because he wanted to get home a day earlier. He wasn't happy about it but he would have to stay — for the time being, at any rate.

The GPS beeped. He logged the location, turned the GPS off and put it back in his pocket. Then he realised there was probably no point in leaving his emergency pack at this location if he was going to the rebel camp. It would be wiser to conceal it closer to their base.

Stratton shouldered his rifle and went back into the forest. Within a few minutes he was back with his emergency pack, which he tucked away into his large backpack.

Despite the obvious hardships they'd suffered the rebels seemed a happy enough bunch. He wondered how far away their camp was. On the flight he had studied a map of the country and had worked out that he could probably get to the border from the clearing in under two days, bearing in mind the terrain. Even if the rebels' camp was a day further away it wouldn't be such a big deal. Once he crossed the border it would be a simple case of dumping his kit, putting on civvies and travelling like a backpacker to Panama and the airport. He felt a little better about it now that he had adjusted the plan. It would be fine, he assured himself.

Stratton wondered why Sumners had offered him up for this job in the first place. It was nowhere near the level at which he was used to operating. Perhaps there was nothing else on at the moment, although he found that hard to believe. MI5 and MI6 were always busy. Maybe it was another effort by Sumners to keep him on the outside. The problem was that the man despised him. It was a deep wound and there was nothing Stratton could do to heal it, not that he particularly cared to. He had no respect for Sumners and all he could hope for was that the man would soon get moved on to another department — or, better still, another country.

Stratton would have loved to know the

connection between Sumners and Steel. They were so different in just about every way. Both of them were arrogant and condescending, of course, though Steel was far worse. He probably knew nothing about Stratton's past or his qualifications but that was no reason to sport such a disdainful attitude. It didn't feel personal, though. Steel was probably an arse with everyone. Stratton was no more than a delivery boy to him. With luck he would never have to meet the man again.

Despite the combination of abuse and encouragement from Victor and his second in command, the intense-looking officer whose name was Marlo, it took the men half an hour to secure the loads and form up the burros ready for departure. At one point a quarrel broke out over the division of the parachutes but Marlo solved the dispute by ordering that the chutes should be sliced into panels and distributed among the most energetic packers.

Stratton checked the time, compared it to the location of the sun to get a rough directional guide and joined the line that was trudging at an easy pace back towards the forest. A passing burro was not as loaded as the others and Stratton hooked his parachute bag onto the wooden frame across its back. He kept his pack in case he needed to bug out.

As he neared the trees he picked up the sound of a distant drone. He thought initially that the C130 had returned for some reason. The rebels who heard it stopped to search the skies, looking concerned.

'Into the forest!' Victor shouted. 'Quickly!'

Most of the rebels were already inside the jungle but half a dozen burros and a dozen men were still out in the open. The men yelled and beat the animals to get them moving quicker. The rebels were clearly worried about something.

As the sound grew louder it became tinny and nowhere near as powerful as that of the engines on a Hercules. But as with any aircraft not easily visible and flying close to the ground, especially over woodland, it was difficult to judge where it was.

The plane burst into view right over them, only metres above the forest canopy. It was a light single-engine aircraft, two or four seats at most. Its noisy appearance frightened the burros, one of them bolting into the jungle while a couple headed across the clearing.

'Quickly!' Marlo yelled. 'Get those damned animals under cover!'

The craft banked steeply to make a tight turn.

'He's seen us!' Victor cried. 'Hurry. Get those animals under control. Everyone into the trees!'

The men did not need encouraging. But no amount of shouting and beating could move one particular burro. Loaded with bundles, it sat on its backside and stubbornly refused to budge.

As the plane made a wide turn around the clearing Stratton was startled by several shots close by. It was Marlo, firing rapid bursts of automatic fire from his AK47. Although the aeroplane was a relatively slow-moving craft, a hit at that distance would still have been lucky.

Other men joined in and a sustained volley of fire crackled around the clearing.

The aircraft held its course, flying in a wide arc until it disappeared over the forest.

'He'll be back!' Victor shouted, agitated. 'Move that animal!'

Several men struggled with the burro, one of them beating it severely with a branch, but still it would not move.

Marlo and his group remained alert, their rifles aimed skywards as they waited for the aircraft to return.

It appeared at the far side of the clearing, heading directly towards them.

'Here it comes!' Victor cried as he ran over and kicked the burro in frustration. 'Get this animal up or I will shoot it!'

Marlo and his men fired at the plane.

As Stratton watched the aircraft he saw something sticking out of its side window. When the plane closed in he realised it was the co-pilot's arm and he was holding something. Stratton's instincts warned him to find a tree to get behind.

The men did not stop firing as the aircraft flew right over them.

The co-pilot released the object.

As the plane disappeared over the tops of the trees the ground shook with the force of a violent explosion.

The bomb had landed not far from the stubborn burro and the animal went berserk, jumping to its feet and kicking out wildly. One of the rebels had been wounded by the blast and was kneeling, inspecting his bloody abdomen, when the donkey struck him hard with both its back hooves, sending him flying. Blood poured from the animal's flank as it bucked and neighed madly.

One of the men went to the aid of his comrade who had been kicked, only to discover that the wounded man had died.

A shot sounded and the stubborn burro dropped to the ground, its legs still kicking. The rebel fired another round into the animal's head, finishing the job.

'If a bomb hits those boxes we'll all be dead!' Victor shouted in frustration.

The men grabbed up the boxes and ran with them to cover. A couple more picked up their dead comrade and followed.

The aircraft appeared again, turning around the outside of the clearing. The men feverishly herded the remaining burros into the jungle. As the craft came at them once again, they fired on it.

Halfway across the clearing the aeroplane veered sharply as if it had been struck, but it righted itself and the co-pilot poked his arm from the window once more. Stratton suspected that the bombs were mortar shells, ideal for dropping from light aircraft.

As the plane flew overhead the man released the bomb and this time everyone flung themselves to the ground. The missile fell short of the group, exploding noisily but failing to injure anyone. By now every man — except Marlo's anti-aircraft team — was inside the forest. They could hear the plane but couldn't see it, and it continued to buzz around the area, perhaps hoping to catch a glimpse of the column through a gap in the jungle canopy. An explosion some distance away perhaps signalled the enemy's frustration. It was followed by silence.

While the rebels regained their composure, some of them wrapped the dead man in a poncho and secured the body to the back of a burro. The group was soon snaking through the forest at a steady pace.

Stratton joined the men near the rear. He hadn't seen much of the Indians since that first meeting and assumed they were scouting ahead. So far it had been an interesting morning. These people really were at war. The aircraft could have radioed the column's location and if the government forces were in any way organised the rebels could expect another contact of some kind. It was clear that Stratton was going to have to keep alert.

He still felt annoyed at being with the rebels despite having settled for a revised plan of escape. The problem he had was the reason for him being there. He was a salaried member of Her Majesty's forces and this was a half-arsed job for a US Special Forces colonel. The US and the UK were allies, sure, but this was essentially a covert operation. He was beginning to think that Sumners might not have had the authority to send him. And why hadn't Steel used one of his own boys? That was a bit odd, to say the least.

Stratton had considered all that before the

jump but since the mission was supposed to be nothing more than a drop, a quick lesson in explosives and then a trek back home, he hadn't given it much more thought. Now he was growing concerned. What would happen if the other side caught him, for instance? Steel had sketchily covered that by telling him that he had friends on both sides and that Stratton would be fine. Stratton was no longer confident that would be so. The urge to bug out and leave these people to their own war grew in him again but he held it at bay. He decided to take things one phase at a time and reckoned that if the situation changed significantly he would quit and go home. He ran his fingers through his moist hair, scratched a small bite on the back of his neck and trudged on.

For the first few kilometres the terrain was fairly level but after crossing a shallow river it began to ascend. The forest canopy also thinned beyond the river and the sun shone down on the column. Within a couple of hours they had gained a lot of altitude and the ground became rocky. The view of the roof of the forest they had walked through was stunning.

In the late afternoon the sun went behind dark clouds that promised a deluge and the humidity increased notably. Eventually rain pelted down and slowed the column's progress as the steep terrain grew slippery. Victor kept the men marching with only a few short breaks. The rebels ate on the move.

The rain finally ceased as they were traversing a steep hillside and shortly afterwards the column came to a stop. Stratton sat down on a rock and had a sip of water. He did not feel as fit as he would have liked, not yomping fit at least. It was always the same. A man could go for as many runs as he liked and do all the gym training he wanted. But when it came to a good long trek carrying a heavy pack there was no better preparation than yomping itself.

The front of the column had disappeared into a dense wood and some movement ahead turned out to be a runner making his way back down the line. He was informing each man of something and as he passed Stratton he whispered a single word harshly. 'Neravistas!'

Stratton watched the man reach the rearguard and after a brief chat all but a handful of men, left to watch the burros, hurried past him up the line towards the front. The tension among them was perceptibly high.

Stratton instinctively studied the surrounding terrain, looking for places that offered cover from any gunfire and for potential escape routes. Any firefight involving these people would be a very good reason to get out of there.

Yet after several inactive minutes his curiosity got the better of him. He picked up his pack and rifle and headed up the line of burros. As he reached the front of the column he saw why it had halted. A dozen men hung by their necks from various branches. The ghoulish expressions on the faces were horrifying: their eyes bulged, their tongues hung out of their mouths, their necks were elongated and broken. One noose held only a head — the body lay on the ground

57

beneath it. Thousands of flies crawled over the bodies, concentrating on their eyes and mouths. The smell of death and decay was overpowering.

Stratton had seen his share of dead bodies but he would never get used to sights like that. The smell alone was enough to make anyone vomit and he moved upwind of the macabre display.

All the rebels except those minding the burros were huddled in a group just below the crest of the hill. Victor, Marlo and a handful of others squatted to one side and appeared to be arguing heatedly in low voices.

Stratton kept his distance and sat against a tree to watch what was going on, ready to take off at the slightest sign of trouble. There seemed to be some indecision among the rebels about what they should do. He couldn't tell if the warning about the Neravistas was that they were nearby or that they had already been and gone.

The discussion was interrupted by the arrival of one of the young Indians who went directly to Victor. Whatever he said caused more discussion, which continued after Victor sent the Indian back the way he had come.

One of the rebels from the large group saw Stratton and decided to come over and sit close by. He was a young man who, despite the excitement, had a casual air about him. He took a piece of dried meat from a breast pocket and offered some to Stratton.

'No. Thank you,' said Stratton.

The young man, who was quite skinny, had piercing dark eyes below a greasy jet-black fringe. 'They are unable to agree on whether to attack or not,' he said, taking a bite of the meat and tucking the rest into his pocket.

'Attack what?' Stratton asked.

'There is a Neravista patrol heading our way, the other side of this hill,' he said, pointing towards the crest. 'The scouts say they do not know we are here . . . They may be the ones who did this,' he said, indicating the bodies.

'Who are they?'

'They're from Bajero's brigade. The one with his body separated from his head, he's Altorro, Bernard's cousin,' he said, jutting his chin towards a strong-looking young man with long hair and a beard on the edge of the group who was looking towards the dead rebels with a forlorn expression on his face. 'I knew him too,' the young man added.

'Why'd they hang them?'

'That's what they always do to us when they capture us. It's their policy. It's a good incentive to fight to the death, no?' he added.

Stratton had to agree. 'What do you think is going to happen?'

'Now?'

'Yes.'

The young man did not seem very sure. 'Marlo wants to attack but Victor thinks we should let them pass. Marlo is always aggressive and Victor is always cautious.'

Stratton looked over at the commanders. 'Who do you think is winning?'

The young man shrugged. 'Marlo believes we should take every opportunity to strike at the enemy. Victor is arguing that we are not an

59

attacking force at this moment but a resupply column. He says our responsibility is to get the supplies home safely. Marlo is arguing that we are a guerrilla force that must adapt to opportunities and that we must revenge those men. We can become fighters when it is time to fight and then change back to a resupply convoy after we have won.'

'Isn't Victor in charge?'

'He's in charge of the supply column but he is not a soldier. Marlo was once an officer in Neravista's army and is technically in charge of any fighting . . . My name is David,' the young man said.

'Stratton.' He held out his hand and David shook it. 'What do you think?'

'I don't think it's such a good idea to have two commanders.'

'Yes,' Stratton agreed, liking the young man. 'What do you think they should do?'

David took a moment to consider his response. 'I would make my decision based on the number of enemy. If we are more than them maybe we should attack.'

'Have you ambushed Neravistas before?'

He shook his head. 'Not like this. But I have taken part in some attacks.'

'How well armed are they?'

'They have more weapons than us. Better weapons. More machine guns, usually. They have grenades. Sometimes they have mortars.'

'What about artillery or air support?'

'They can't get their big guns into these mountains. There are no roads for them to get close enough . . . You've seen their air force.'

'Are there likely to be other patrols in this area?'

'It's possible. But communications are difficult in this region. We blow up their radio masts whenever they build new ones.' David looked at Stratton, eyeing his sophisticated weapon and other equipment and the ease with which he seemed to take the threat of conflict, as if this was nothing new to him. 'What do you think we should do?' he asked.

Stratton shrugged. 'I'm inclined to agree with Victor. But then, I just got here.'

David nodded thoughtfully as he looked over at his commanders.

'You're an officer?' Stratton asked.

'No,' David said, with a grin that displayed a full set of badly stained teeth. 'I'm hardly a soldier. I'm a teacher.'

Stratton had not given the rebels much thought as individuals but the young man was a reminder that rebellions like this one were fought by ordinary people. 'How long have you been with the rebellion?'

'Only a few months,' David said, looking down at his hands in thought.

'Why did you join up?'

'My father was accused of supplying the rebels with food. He was a farmer. They came one day and shot him . . . and then they shot my mother. Why they shot her also, I don't know.' As David said this it seemed to affect him deeply. 'I had nowhere else to go, I think.'

'How is it going?'

'The rebellion? I don't know. It's hard to tell. We keep fighting, they keep fighting. We hope Neravista will one day give in to us . . . You will have to ask Neravista, maybe.'

The older Indian arrived at the crouch and reported to Victor who immediately appeared disappointed by what he heard. Marlo, on the other hand, became suddenly enthused and moved away to talk hurriedly with the men. David left Stratton to join his colleagues. After a quick briefing a couple of the men headed back to the column while the main group made its way to the crest.

The young teacher hurried over to Stratton. 'The scouts report less than twenty soldiers. That was the number agreed between Victor and Marlo. If there were more we would let them pass. We will attack.' He left again to catch up with his colleagues.

Stratton watched the ragtag group of individuals go. They wore expressions on their faces that ranged from unease to resolve as they checked their weapons and adjusted ammunition pouches. There was scant sign of any military expertise about them but they seemed determined enough.

Once again Stratton considered getting out of there. He was ready to leave but the motive to do so, the impulse that would push him over the edge and make him go, was not yet sufficiently compelling. He wanted at least to see the men's preparations for the ambush.

He moved to where he could watch the rebels making their way down the steep slope as silently as they could. The tall trees that provided a patchwork canopy continued down the hill. The ground was stony with little undergrowth, making it advantageous to the ambushers on the high ground since it provided them with a clear view below. The slope would also make it difficult for the Neravistas to charge once the ambush had been sprung. So far the position looked good and Stratton decided to wait.

The men formed a line a short way down from the crest, lying or kneeling behind what little cover there was. Silence descended as they settled into position. Marlo moved along the back of the line, whispering words of encouragement.

Two men came over the crest from behind Stratton and made their way towards the far end of the ambush line. Their rifles were slung over their shoulders and they were each carrying one of the newly delivered 66mm-rocket launch tubes.

Stratton wondered whose idea that had been. As he understood it, the rebels didn't know how to fire them. He looked around for Victor but he was nowhere to be seen. The two men moved out of sight beyond the trees and, unable to resist seeing what they might do with the rockets, Stratton followed them.

The two rebels joined the end of the ambush line, where Victor was craning his neck to see down the slope. On seeing the weapons he spoke to the men briefly. One of them extended his rocket tube, which readied it for firing. Perhaps he did know how to use it, Stratton thought. He seemed to have convinced Victor that he could because the Frenchman allowed him to take up a firing position.

Stratton took cover beside a boulder a few metres behind Victor who had gone back to looking for the enemy. The rebel leader suddenly jerked back behind his tree as if to hide. He made a hasty signal to those nearby that suggested he had seen something.

Down the slope Stratton saw the top of a tree move. He eased himself up in order to get a better look. A man in camouflage gear and carrying a rifle was leaning against the tree, digging something out of the top of his boot. He removed the offending bit of debris and continued on through the wood, more interested in watching his immediate footing than his wider surroundings. He was followed by another soldier and shortly afterwards half a dozen more men ambled into view. They chatted casually, rifles slung over their shoulders. More followed, one with a pack on his back that had a long whip antenna protruding from it. Their voices filtered up to the ambushers, each soldier clearly unaware that they were being observed so closely.

One of the rocket men lay on his belly, facing down the slope. The tube rested along his back and he pressed his cheek against its side so that he could look through the sight. The other man was having difficulties with the catch that had to be released for the tube to extend and he tugged at it in frustration.

Marlo had positioned himself in the centre of

the ambush line and kept the men from firing until the enemy was in the kill zone. He raised an arm. When he dropped it he cried, 'Fire!' The sudden volley, a combination of single aimed shots and wild automatic fire, shattered the silence.

Victor moved back from the line a few feet: with just a pistol for a weapon he was not going to get involved. Stratton saw the imminent danger and leapt forward. He sprinted down the hill and as he grabbed Victor by the scruff of his neck and yanked him out of the way the rocket fired.

The missile shot out of the tube with a deafening roar as a long tail of fire erupted from its rear. The rocket struck the ground with a glancing blow, bounced skyward at a steep angle and hit a tree halfway up its trunk, which the massive explosion shattered. Burning wood splinters rained down. The top half of the tree, a large mass of heavy branches, came crashing down in front of the ambush line.

The bushes behind the man who'd fired the missile burst into flames — and so did his backside and the heels of his boots. He leapt up screaming, then fell to the ground rolling over and over furiously in an effort to put out the flames. The other rocket man immediately abandoned any plans to fire his own weapon — his partner's fate was a dramatic warning.

Victor lay staring at a burning bush near where he had been kneeling and thought of the horrific consequences if Stratton had not pulled him out of the way.

A handful of guerrillas kept firing but most had left their positions because of the explosion and the falling timber.

The government troops returned a few rounds before they fled, shooting wildly behind them as they ran.

Marlo yelled at the few rebels who were still shooting to cease fire.

Victor got to his feet, shaking with rage as he looked for the rocket-firing rebel who had by now managed to put out the flames but whose clothing was still smouldering heavily. 'You idiot!' he shouted. 'You told me you knew how to fire it.'

'I did, but not how to aim it.'

Marlo stormed over, his face flushed with anger. 'Who fired that rocket?' he demanded, looking from Victor to the man.

Victor was not a vindictive person and although he was indeed angry with the rocket-firing man he wanted to protect him from Marlo who had a dark soul. 'Shouldn't we be more concerned about a counter-attack?'

'The enemy have scattered!' Marlo shouted. 'But they should all be dead! Who fired the rocket?'

The smouldering rebel was beating his boot heels with his cap to stop them from bursting into flames again. 'It was me.'

'You damned fool!' Marlo shouted, taking an aggressive step forward. The guerrilla, a proud peasant and former farmer with heavily muscled arms and shoulders, stood his ground and looked Marlo coldly in the eye.

'It was my fault,' Victor said, moving between them. 'I am responsible. I said he could shoot the rocket.'

Marlo stared into Victor's eyes. 'Then *you*'re the fool,' he said, a dangerous edge in his voice. The Indian scouts arrived and Marlo faced them. 'How many did we kill?' he demanded harshly.

The old Indian held up three fingers as he looked at Marlo coldly. He obviously did not like the man's tone.

'*Three?*' Marlo shouted as he moved away. 'We should have killed *all* of them. I have joined an army of idiots. And that makes *me* look like an idiot,' he said, pausing to look back at Victor. 'I don't like that.'

From at least one angle the attempted ambush had been a farce but from what Stratton had seen the rebels had been a match for the government troops, who were not professional soldiers, either. But Marlo was right. Had it not been for the misfired rocket they would have killed a good number of them. The men hanging in the trees would have been avenged.

The rebels did not take long to reorganise themselves. The hanging corpses were placed in a single unmarked shallow grave. There were too many to take back with them and, according to David, they came from another camp too far away for them to be transferred. David also told Stratton that if the grave had been marked and any Neravistas came across it they would simply dig it up and hang the bodies again or maybe mutilate them even more brutally.

As the column started on its way again, Stratton stood to one side, his parachute bag in his hand. Considering all that had happened he was still uncertain whether or not he should leave them. According to his GPS they had covered twenty-three kilometres as the crow flew. He'd heard the rebels say that they would be at their camp by nightfall, which was only a couple of hours away. Having come this far he decided he might as well see the camp at least. Then he could give the guerrillas their weapons training and be on his way by mid-morning the next day.

This was a good enough place to hide the emergency pack and Stratton found a tree whose appearance and position looked sufficiently easy to memorise, buried the small pack at its base and cut a mark at eye level with his knife. He hit the waypoint mark on his GPS, which would get him within three metres of the tree, and typed in a name.

He hooked his parachute bag to a passing burro and joined the column.

Victor was subdued for the rest of the journey. When night fell the column continued moving with the Indians, who were adept at their task, guiding the rebels through the darkness. After a steep climb, traversing for more than a kilometre, they reached the summit of a hill and the glow of a hundred campfires could be seen in the distance. It was quite a sight. The sky was clear and the stars were exceptionally bright. It had been a long day: Stratton was looking forward to lying down and closing his eyes.

2

Stratton followed the column of men and burros into the rebel camp. Two large sandbag-and-log defensive emplacements at either side protected the entrance, and two more were set back thirty metres, providing defensive depth. All of them were protected from the rain by a mixture of natural materials and canvas and were manned by a couple of men, each with M60 belt-fed machine guns. Half a dozen armed men policed the entrance, which appeared to rely on the familiarity system. If a stranger's friendly intentions could not be verified they would not easily gain entry.

The main thoroughfare into the camp was broad and muddy, with stones and logs filling the deeper ruts. Judging by the number of cooking fires the main living quarters, a sprawling township of tents and tightly packed dilapidated wooden and corrugated-iron huts, were arranged in one huge mass in a central lower area. It bustled with activity, and music wafted from somewhere along with the sound of many voices.

The sentries eyed Stratton suspiciously as he approached but Victor was waiting to escort him. Stratton unhooked his parachute bag from the burro and gave it a pat on the rump by way of thanks. A bunch of barefooted children ran past through the mud, chasing a partially deflated football; a woman shouted for one of them to come home.

'I'll show you to your quarters,' Victor said.

The Frenchman looked preoccupied as he led the way along a narrow muddy track that was shrouded in darkness. Stratton supposed he was still unsettled by the day's activities and stayed a few metres behind him to give him his space.

The sounds of the camp died away as they approached a dense patch of jungle. Up ahead a large bonfire illuminated a collection of log cabins. A dozen or so men were gathered at a large wooden table made from split tree-trunks. Some sat while others stood close by. All were listening soberly to a man who was speaking in authoritative tones.

Victor stopped far enough away from the group to hear what was being said but not so close as to become a part of what was obviously an important meeting. Stratton waited behind him. The tension in the air was palpable.

'This is an opportunity for peace,' boomed the speaker, a large, bear-like individual who stood at one end of the long table. He wore clean olive-green fatigues with a long brown shawl draped over his shoulders and tucked under a thick mane of hair that only served to augment his imposing appearance. 'This time we must consider the offer that has been placed before us,' he went on. 'I don't remember anyone ever saying we wanted an endless, sustained guerrilla war. Our plan was always to fight until we could influence the government, to become a voice that

70

would be heard and respected. Then the fight would continue. But not with guns. With words — words backed by the respect that we have won.'

'You have arrived at a most interesting time,' Victor said to Stratton, keeping his own voice low. 'I think this could be a pivotal moment in this rebellion. The man speaking is Hector. He will either bend us in a new direction or we will snap and break apart. He is head of the Fifth Brigade . . . and he is as formidable as he looks. But these days he would rather be a politician than a soldier.'

'I have told Neravista's representatives that we are ready to discuss terms,' Hector continued.

'You had no right to speak on behalf of everyone.' The new voice was soft yet strangely piercing. Everyone turned their heads to look at a white-haired older man who was sitting at the opposite end of the table. The look in his eyes revealed a deep inner strength.

'That's Sebastian,' Victor said.

Stratton studied the man. He looked the oldest in the group, the only man with white hair, but he was not frail. He was also the only one not wearing military-style clothing. But what really distinguished him from the others was an aura of clear superiority that was inherited, not learned. He had an aristocratic air about him that seemed quite out of place in this grubby jungle setting.

'And you had no right to bring in these new weapons without consulting the council,' Hector retorted. 'Yes, I know about the rockets and special mines.'

'We are still at war,' Sebastian replied coolly. 'It is each brigade leader's duty to maintain armaments.'

'It's your timing that I am most concerned about. By bringing in these new arms now you are sending the wrong signal.'

'I do not accept any terms offered by Neravista, therefore my signal remains the same as always.'

'That is not your decision to make. We are five brigades held together by a democratic union. It is the council that makes the decisions, not any single member.'

'We are not a democracy, Hector. Not yet. That is only our ambition.'

'We have been fighting for peace and this is an opportunity to achieve it.'

The older man shook his head slowly. 'We did not begin this fight for peace. We already had that. But it was Neravista's kind of peace, where whoever threatened his dictatorship was imprisoned or murdered. It was peaceful only for those who did not challenge him. You are not going forwards, Hector. You're throwing this struggle into full reverse.'

All eyes went to Hector as Sebastian's words made their impact.

'I want Neravista's leadership dismantled now as much as I did when I began this fight,' Hector countered, undeterred. 'But it is time to change our strategy. We can still achieve our goals. For three years we've fought. Many have died. I don't want to spend the next twenty years burying my people who've died in the fighting. There is more than one way to win this struggle.'

Stratton noticed out of the corner of his eye someone over at the entrance to what appeared to be the main cabin. A young woman in jeans and a leather jacket walked from it towards the group. Her long dark hair was tied back in a ponytail and she stopped behind Sebastian, near the table, where everyone noticed her. Hector was distracted momentarily by her arrival.

The glow from the fire revealed her youth as well as the noble confidence of her solemn expression. Stratton found her stunning to look at. But something else about her, apart from her beauty, struck him.

'I warn you now,' said Sebastian, speaking slowly and deliberately, 'I will not be a part of this ridiculous parley. It's an insult to everyone who has fought, and in particular those who have actually given their lives, for this struggle. And if you go ahead with it I will continue the fight without you.'

'And I hand the warning back to you,' Hector said, leaning forward on the table as if to enforce his point. 'I will not allow you to destroy this opportunity.'

'I always understood an opportunity to be a moment of favourable circumstances,' the young woman said. Her voice was confident and clear. 'While we fight Neravista there will always be the opportunity to talk.'

Victor smiled. 'Sebastian's daughter,' he said softly, the pride in his voice unmistakable.

73

'With all respect, Louisa,' Hector said, 'this is a meeting of the council. You are not a member.'

'I can do what I want. I'm a rebel,' she retorted.

Several of the men found the comment amusing, including Hector.

Louisa remained solemn in contrast. 'My father provided you with opportunities greater than any that Neravista will ever give you. He began this revolution. You all followed him. He has always been the backbone of this great cause. Why is it that you no longer trust him?'

'No one here denies Sebastian the respect he deserves. I will break the neck of anyone who does not show him any,' Hector said, looking around darkly at the others to reinforce the threat. 'But it is time for a change of direction. If Sebastian cannot see that then perhaps it is time for him to step back as . . . as our spiritual leader.'

'What makes you think you are qualified to take his place?' Louisa asked, a frown creasing her brow.

Hector's tightening expression revealed his growing irritation at her effrontery. 'I am not alone,' he said. 'I have the support of the rest of the council.'

'Sheep,' she muttered, loudly enough for those the comment was aimed at to hear.

'That's enough, Louisa,' Sebastian said curtly.

Hector might have been fuming but he seemed unable to sustain his anger. His stare softened and, if anything, reflected a certain

74

admiration and, perhaps, desire for the outspoken girl.

Victor took a deep breath and stepped decisively towards the group. 'I am not a member of the council either, but I have a say too,' he said in a raised voice.

Everyone looked towards this new intruder.

'This matter is beyond the brigade leaders and council members alone,' Victor continued. 'We are all a part of the rebellion, every man, woman and child in this camp and the others. I am under Sebastian's banner as your lieutenants are under yours. But Sebastian does not own me. We are not a conscript army marching at the behest of ambitious officers. We are individuals, egalitarians expressing our beliefs and willing to put our lives on the line for them. This is a critical time in our adventure and we all have the right to say what we believe.'

The speech was met by mixed reactions among the rebel leaders. Louisa did not hide her evident fondness for Victor.

'And so what is it that you believe, Victor?' Hector asked with more than a hint of contempt in his voice.

'I do not believe that when you have your sword against the throat of your adversary you remove it in order to negotiate with him — certainly not with one like Neravista.'

'But you can't expect a straight answer from a man with a blade at his throat,' the big brigade commander replied. 'I believe it is time, not to give up our weapons but to keep them with due vigilance in our hands while we try to work something out. Neravista wants to discuss terms. We should give him the space to do so.'

'Have you forgotten what kind of animal he is?' Sebastian said, getting to his feet. 'He has murdered thousands of our people, many of whom died at the hands of torturers such as his own brother. Those people lost their lives simply because they wanted a change, a fairer, more just alternative. We began this fight to remove Neravista. But all you want is to join him. Do that and you will only share the blame for the blood he has on his hands.'

'Be very careful, Sebastian,' Hector growled.

'There is no negotiating with Neravista!' Sebastian insisted. 'He has to be destroyed. And we cannot allow another dictator like him to take power. We have to wipe this country's political slate clean. We must begin again. We will build a government based on liberal democracy. Freedom. That cannot be negotiated with Neravista. To him, the words 'liberal' and 'democracy' are like a crucifix to a vampire. He will fight to the death of everyone in this country to hold on to his power. He has no choice. He knows he will die otherwise.'

Most of the rebel leaders paused for thought at this. One of them, sitting beside Hector, whispered in his ear.

Hector looked at Stratton. 'Who is that man?' he boomed. 'Since when are strangers invited to listen in on our council meetings?'

'He works for Steel,' Victor said.

'Why is he here?'

Victor was about to speak when Hector

interrupted him. 'Let him speak for himself.'

All stares focused on Stratton. 'I'm just the delivery boy,' he said.

'Ah. The weapons,' Hector surmised.

'He's our guest,' Victor said. 'There's no need for this.'

'I know why you brought these weapons here, Sebastian. Not to destroy Neravista's army but to destroy this opportunity for peace. That decision was made by you and you alone. Is that the kind of liberal democracy you are fighting for, Victor? I'm beginning to wonder if we might not just be exchanging one Neravista for another.'

'How dare you?' Louisa snapped, stepping forward aggressively.

Her father put an arm out to halt her.

Hector was aware that he had gone too far and directed his ire elsewhere. 'Leave,' he said to Stratton.

'Stay where you are,' said Victor.

Stratton was rapidly growing uncomfortable with the situation. He did not like the way things were heading.

'Don't dare to counter my command,' Hector shouted at Victor. He looked at Stratton. 'Get out of this country,' he growled at him.

Stratton did not move, more out of indecision than stubbornness. Lines were clearly being drawn in the sand and whoever he obeyed would score a point. Right then, he felt like siding with Sebastian but he reckoned he should leave his options wide open. The only thing he was certain of was his regret at not getting out earlier.

'You either leave on your own or I will have you tied behind a mule and dragged,' Hector said, taking a step from the table towards him. Several of his men moved their hands to their pistols, staring malevolently at Stratton.

The Englishman had suddenly become a political football in this overheated debate. Since he was not one of the rebels his death could be an acceptable symbolic insult to the Sebastian faction that no one would actually be obliged to avenge. Stratton thought of his M4 resting on the pack behind him and wondered which way he should run when he grabbed it.

'He is our guest,' Victor repeated defiantly, straightening his back. 'You will stop this childish bullying.' His determination to stand up to Hector was clear for all to see.

Hector was a short-tempered bear who was unused to being disobeyed and Victor's attitude served only to enrage him. He reached beneath his jacket and took out a glistening machete. 'You dare to give me orders, and in front of the council! I'll show you what I think of your guest,' he said, striding towards Stratton. 'Run, little dog, or I'll cut you in two.'

Stratton appeared to have only one ally and it looked as if he was not going to be enough. The Englishman watched the big man step closer, his mind racing through his very limited number of choices. If he stood his ground and defended himself he would lose whatever sympathy the others might have for him. If he took off, their hostile feelings might not be intense enough for them to want to pursue him. It was a case of saving his skin or his pride. Staying alive was the wiser choice and he decided that if he could depart at a walking pace it might at least leave him some pride. He raised his hands in a soothing gesture and was about to step back when Victor stepped in front of him to face Hector.

Sebastian's second in command tightened his jaw as Hector neared them.

'Don't challenge me, Victor. Step aside.'

Victor did not move.

Hector continued to advance. 'I said step aside.'

The Frenchman clenched his sweat-soaked fists at his sides. It was clear to everyone that he was not going to get out of Hector's way.

The big man stopped an arm's reach from him, keeping his machete level. 'This is the last time I will ask. Stand aside.'

'I will not.'

Hector grew conscious of the many stares that were fixed upon them. In his anger he had gone further than was wise. He had made threats that he had not expected to have to carry out. The gringo was supposed to run away and Victor was not supposed to challenge him in this way. There was now only one way out of this. If he backed down, even though everyone would know it was out of pity for Victor, he would lose face. Sebastian's poodle would have won. There was too much at stake. The parley with Neravista was more important to him than the chastisement he would receive for killing the Frenchman. He was going to have to wound the man, at least. 'You go too far, Victor,' he said raising the machete.

As Hector drew back the weapon in readiness to strike, an arrow shot from the darkness and slammed into a wooden post a few feet from him. Its fletching was painted orange and attached to the nock by a small piece of gut was the long slender tail feather of a quetzal bird. Another arrow followed quickly, striking inches away, its long shaft quivering before it grew still.

All stares went to the arrows and to Hector who was frozen to the spot. Everyone at the table knew the missiles' significance. From the darkness the old Indian stepped into the glow from the fire. He did not have a bow in his hand, just a spear, but behind him, moving deliberately, the two young Indians emerged, their bows drawn fully back, fresh arrows levelled, the firelight highlighting the subtle circular tattoos on their hairless arms and torsos. The icy look of total commitment filled their eyes.

One of Hector's lieutenants moved a hand to his pistol. The first young Indian pointed the tip of one of the arrows in the taut bow towards him and the man let go of his weapon. No one present doubted that the slightest aggressive move by Hector or his men would end lethally for them.

'Call off your Indians,' Hector hissed angrily.

'Please don't move,' Victor said rather nervously, glancing back imploringly at the Indians. 'I don't have as much control over them as some people think.'

'I said call them off!' The commander was incensed. Not only had he been stopped in

80

mid-blow but he had been forced to stand there looking like a fool, unable to move. Like everyone else, he was well aware of the Indians' complete fidelity to Victor.

'Put down your blade,' Victor said, stretching an arm out towards the Indians. 'Slowly'.

Hector lowered his arm and stepped back. He faced Sebastian. 'This is a black day,' he growled.

'Don't let your injured pride take control of your judgement,' the old man advised.

'I will give you time to reconsider your position. But not long. I urge you to think it over carefully. We can end this war together. Or you can continue it alone.'

Hector marched away, his men following. The other brigade leaders nodded respectful farewells towards Sebastian and headed away into the darkness.

Sebastian left the table and walked to the main cabin. Louisa followed him.

Victor breathed out noisily, relaxing visibly as the strain eased. He looked back at Stratton. 'Why didn't you just run?'

'Why didn't you let me go when I asked?'

Victor conceded the point.

Stratton picked up his rifle and slung his pack over one shoulder. 'Well, thanks very much. I'll be on my way, unless there's anything else.'

'There's no point in you going now,' Victor said.

'Is that French humour?'

'You'll be okay for tonight. I'll arrange an escort in the morning. They'll take you to the

81

border. No one will bother you any further, I can assure you.'

Stratton looked around at the Indians and tended to believe him.

'You can stay in the cottage,' Victor added.

Stratton shrugged his agreement. 'Thanks for stepping in, anyway,' he said.

Victor rolled his eyes at the comment as if Stratton had no idea of the problems that it had created. 'I could do with a drink,' Victor decided, heading towards the cabin furthest from Sebastian's.

Stratton followed, looking back at the Indians who were watching him. He gave them a wave which was not returned.

'I owed you,' Victor said. 'The rocket. I repay my debts.'

'Is that the only reason you stood up to Hector?'

Victor paused at the door of the cabin, glancing at Stratton as if he had broached a delicate subject. 'I would have done it anyway.'

Stratton found the answer curious. 'Why?'

'You no doubt suspected there's a history between Hector and me. It's true. There is. But it's all on his side. I would have stepped in front of him anyway, like I said, but I'm not entirely sure why. Ask them,' he said indicating the Indians.

Victor pushed the cabin door open and walked inside.

Stratton glanced back at the Indians, who were talking among themselves. None the wiser, he followed Victor into a large room that was lit by a hurricane lamp. It was open-plan, equipped with a small kitchen, a dining table and several chairs, a couple of them facing a cold grate filled with fresh logs. The room seemed to be used for storage. All kinds of boxes were stacked around, most of them marked with US military stencils. A flight of stairs led up to an open mezzanine half the length of the cabin with a balcony that overlooked the ground floor. Under the stairs was a collection of very large glass bottles in woven baskets with corks the size of fists sealing their necks.

'Hector has always been antagonistic towards me,' Victor said as he inspected the contents of a collection of well-used cooking pots on the stove. 'Resentful is probably a better description,' he corrected himself, feeling inside one of several clay pots on a shelf and producing an onion. 'I think it's just a strategy on his part. I'm another way of getting at Sebastian,' he added, searching a box on a shelf for more ingredients and a variety of local vegetables.

'Are there many foreigners here?'

'We've had soldiers of fortune from other parts of the world come through over the years. We don't have the money to pay them. Some have stayed anyway. A few, like me, are here on principle. I'm not a soldier of fortune, I hasten to add. There are some Spaniards in the Fourth Brigade, a handful of Americans in the Second.' His nose wrinkled in horror as he sniffed the contents of one of the pots. 'You're probably not fussy about what you eat, are you?'

Stratton was used to people assuming that

because he was a soldier he was uncultured. He would have been the first to admit that he was a long way from sophisticated but neither was he a total slob. 'I'll have what's on offer,' he replied.

'I have become used to poor cuisine,' said Victor, sniffing a piece of meat on a muslin-covered plate. 'It is probably the greatest sacrifice I make by staying here and the one least appreciated by my comrades.' He took a glass jug off a shelf, shook it upside down to remove any dust and held it out to Stratton. 'Fill that, please,' he said, indicating the bottles under the stairs.

Stratton inspected the tops of the huge bottles and found one that had already been opened. It was almost full and too heavy to lift easily so he tipped it onto the side of its wicker base and poured some of the velvet-red contents into the jug. He replaced the cork and brought the jug over to Victor who handed him a clay mug which he filled with the wine along with one for himself. 'I suppose you don't care what you drink, either.'

'I know when a wine is corked,' Stratton replied. 'I just don't mind drinking it.'

'Ah. An honest Englishman.' Victor was about to propose a toast but paused thoughtfully and scratched the several days' growth on his cheeks. 'I don't know what to drink to. Today's unforgettable past or tomorrow's uncertain future . . . Let's keep it simple. Santé.'

'Cheers,' Stratton said.

They took healthy swigs. Both men grimaced as they lowered their mugs.

'That's an interesting grape,' Stratton offered, clearing his throat.

'You think it's made from grapes?' Victor said, sarcastically. 'My taste buds are ruined.' He went back to preparing the food. 'I was born not far from a vineyard that was overlooked by the Pyrenees. When I was a young boy I would sometimes sneak in and eat the grapes until I could hardly walk. I would lie and stare at the mountains and daydream of being an adventurer. They were Tannat grapes and when I grew up I preferred to drink the wine that was made from them. All my life I could recognise the smell of a Madiran from across a crowded room ... I don't think I could tell the difference between it and a glass of acid today.'

Stratton looked out of the window. The fire, left untended, was growing dim. The three Indians were sharing a meal at the big table. 'What's the story with them?' he asked.

'The old one is Yoinakuwa, and Kebowa and Mohesiwa are his sons,' Victor said as he chopped vegetables. 'They've been following me around for over three years now. I can't get rid of them.'

'That sounds like a complaint.'

'It is and it isn't, of course. Today was not the first time they've changed someone's mind about attacking me.' He put the vegetables into a pot. They sizzled immediately.

'They just follow you around for no reason?' Stratton asked, wondering what the rest of the story was.

Victor seemed reluctant to elaborate and

drained the mug. Stratton refilled it and Victor continued with the story. 'I came to this country five years ago as a jungle-canopy research scientist. You ever heard of the Nerugan nature reserve?'

Stratton shook his head.

'It's a hundred kilometres north-west of here, near the border. I was the station director. Yoinakuwa led the tribe that lived in the reserve. He was a king of his people. It wasn't a huge tribe but big enough to have a king. King Yoinakuwa,' Victor emphasised. 'I like the way it rolls off the tongue.

'A year or so before we built the facility, which was a couple of years after we began raising funds for the project, gold was discovered across the border. The subsequent frenzy spilled over into the reserve. We petitioned the government not to award any licences to mine the gold in the reserve and at first it looked as if we'd been successful. But we were naive. We should have guessed that if there was no official mining company it would leave the place wide open to illegal miners. They began coming in and setting up small camps all over the place. It didn't affect us, not right away. But it wasn't good for Yoinakuwa and his people. The miners had no respect for the land. They hunted anything and everything, placing crude traps all over the place, competing with Yoinakuwa's people for the food. That's when we . . . when I became more involved. I found Yoinakuwa a legal representative. My plan was to get the Indians to make their own claims to the land they had occupied

86

for thousands of years. My naivety was only just beginning.

'The illegal miners came up with a plan of their own, a rather simple and terrible one. Knowing it would take a long time for the Indians to legalise the claim they decided simply to wipe them out. Kill them. The depth of human depravity is beyond measure. After the first few killings Yoinakuwa and his people got ready to defend their land and hunting grounds from these foreign invaders. But they had no idea what they were up against. They had bows and spears but the enemy had rifles. And they were prepared to pay men to come in and use them. Yoinakuwa's tribe quickly became the hunted. I tried to attract international attention to the illegal gold mining that was causing genocide. Guess what?'

'The miners came for you.'

'Exactly. That's when I learned there was no limit to my naivety . . . The strategy against us was more subtle. But not *too* subtle. They began by destroying our equipment and intimidating our guards. When that was not enough they murdered two of them. And when that was not enough they tried to kill me. I was operating our COPAS one afternoon — '

'COPAS?'

'Canopy Operation Permanent-Access System. It's a large helium balloon with a basket suspended below that allows you to move vertically and horizontally on a system of wires through the treetops.'

'Ah. The balloon in the canopy,' Stratton said,

87

recalling Victor's comment when they first met.

'Those were my favourite times. I could spend all day up there. It was like being in a different world that had its own laws of nature, a microcosm of life practically independent from the ground. It even had its own weather. Those bastards shot at the balloon while I was in it. They burst it and it crashed to the ground. I was lucky to survive. They thought they had killed me and tried to cover up my supposed murder by burning down the facility and making it look as if the Indians had done it. When they realised I had survived the bastards came to kill me again. I managed to escape into the forest and went in search of the only allies I had. I arrived at Yoinakuwa's village just as the mercenaries that the miners had hired were mounting their attack. They destroyed every hut and hunted down and killed nearly every man, woman and child. I found Yoinakuwa lying unconscious beside his dead wife and daughters. His two sons were making a last stand beside him. I had a rifle that had belonged to our security guards. I held off the mercenaries long enough to get Yoinakuwa and his boys out of there. They killed everyone else, every member of Yoinakuwa's tribe. The miners' aim was to destroy the Indians so that none of them would ever be able to challenge the invaders' rights to the mines. And they succeeded . . . or as good as.

'Yoinakuwa and his sons are the last of their line. It's bad enough for a man to have to bury his wife and children. No man should have to bury his entire history. Since then they have

88

never strayed far from my side. I truly don't understand why. I know it's partly because I saved their lives. But I have told Yoinakuwa many times that he owes me nothing. I even told him that I was largely to blame for everything by stopping the licensing of the miners in the first place. It made no difference to him.'

'Are they the reason why you don't leave?'

'Ha! An interesting question. It's true that I have often thought about leaving. You lose heart at times. It's also true that I could not bring myself to say goodbye to them. Maybe I'll take them back to France with me one day. I just don't see them stacking shelves in the local supermarket, though. Obligation is a terrible thing, to be sure. I hope I wake up one morning and find they have gone. With luck that's the way it will be.'

Victor placed two plates on the table, along with a pot containing his gastronomic creation. He found some bread in a wooden box on the table, broke a piece off to test its freshness and placed a lump in front of Stratton. 'Eat,' he said as he spooned the food onto the plates. 'This is as good as it gets around here.'

While Victor poured them both more wine Stratton tasted the concoction. 'Not bad,' he said.

The scientist shrugged. 'From a man who enjoys corked wine that's not much of a compliment.'

Stratton smiled.

Victor could not help liking the Englishman. He held up his mug. 'Thanks again for the

89

rocket thing. That was a natural act of chivalry. You can't be all bad.'

The door opened and Stratton reached swiftly for his M4 a few feet away.

Louisa stepped into the cabin. 'Oh,' she said, pausing in the doorway. 'Hello, Victor.' She closed the door behind her.

'Louisa,' he said, greeting her.

She stopped at his back and rested her hands on his shoulders. 'You've had a long day, and a very unfriendly homecoming.'

Victor enjoyed her show of affection. 'I have cooked some food,' he said.

Louisa looked into the pot, dipped a finger in and tasted the contents. Her expression showed her approval. 'I'll take some for Sebastian.'

'Be quick before my English friend eats it all.'

'You are friends already?' she asked.

'We have both lived and died today,' Victor said. 'I don't know what that means but we are certainly not enemies.'

Stratton could not take his eyes off Louisa. She was even more beautiful close up. 'Hi,' he said, getting to his feet and wiping his hand against his side before offering it. 'I'm . . . ' he began. But Louisa walked away to the kitchenette and took a jug off the shelf.

'You're making quite a collection of people who owe you their lives, Victor,' she said as she filled the container from the bottle under the stairs. 'Now you have a mercenary.'

'I'm not a mercenary,' Stratton said defensively. He wasn't actually offended. He was too thick-skinned for that. But he wanted to avoid the word's negative connotations.

'Perhaps he just needs to look up the word,' Louisa said to Victor as she took a bowl from a shelf and spooned some of the food into it. 'Okay. So what are you if you're not a mercenary?' she asked, turning to face Stratton.

'You wouldn't call the Fedex man a mercenary.'

'Why not? He delivers anything to anybody who pays.'

'Don't bother,' Victor said, interrupting Stratton before he could reply. 'You will never win with her.'

Louisa collected up the food and drink and went to the door.

Stratton opened it for her.

'You have made an enemy of Hector tonight,' she said, looking at Victor. 'That was unwise.'

Victor shrugged. 'Maybe you can put in a good word for me.'

The thinnest of smiles formed on her lips. 'The Save the Victor club just keeps on growing.'

'You can't have too many members,' he said, scraping the last contents from his bowl and sucking it off the spoon.

'See you tomorrow,' Louisa said. She glanced at Stratton holding the door open for her and although her instincts and breeding required a thank-you she could not bring herself to voice it and walked out without saying another word.

Stratton closed the door and sat back down in his chair.

Victor took a black cheroot from a pocket. 'There's a bunk upstairs,' he said as he lit up. 'I'll try and get you out of here before the sun comes up. Hector has spies here. I don't think he'll pursue you but it's best to take the safer option when you can.'

Stratton felt suddenly tired. The thought of lying down sounded very good. He stood, picked up his pack, parachute bag and carbine and walked up the stairs. 'Thanks for dinner,' he said.

'My pleasure,' Victor replied.

Stratton dumped his pack beside the bunk, unzipped the parachute bag and tipped the contents out onto the floor. He began to unravel the chute, picking out twigs and other debris from the material. Then he hooked the harness around the banister ball at the top of the stairs and walked the suspension lines to the far end of the room, untangling and stretching them out.

Victor came to the top of the stairs to see what he was doing. 'We don't have any planes if you're planning on parachuting out of here.'

'I'm drying it out.'

'You are a professional, aren't you?' Victor asked, his tone rhetorical.

Stratton looked up at him. The comment was correct, but not in the way the other man intended.

'I'll see you in the morning,' Victor said and headed back down the stairs. 'I like to sleep below. The rats that live in the thatch irritate me.'

Stratton glanced up at the reed ceiling. His back suddenly ached from the day's activities — a combination of the jump and the long yomp. He was looking forward to lying down and hurried to finish cleaning the chute.

★ ★ ★

Stratton had a fitful night's sleep, waking up at every sound from inside and outside the cabin. The most annoying disturbance came from the family of rodents — or rats, as Victor had described them — that was living in the reed roof. They kept scurrying about, causing bits of thatch to fall on him, which eventually prompted him to erect his mosquito net. No sooner had he done that than the rain came down heavily. It got rid of the rodents, only to replace them with another irritation: a constant cascade of drips that the net could not shield him from. After shifting his wooden bunk around the floor more than once he eventually found a drip-free zone. Then, just as he thought he was finally dozing off, he heard one of the stairs creak. It felt like he had been asleep for barely minutes but when he opened his eyes he could make out objects in the room by the early morning light coming through gaps in the roof. He watched the top of the stairs, resting his hand on the stock of his M4.

Victor's freshly shaven face appeared. 'I see you did not trust my hospitality,' he said.

Stratton did not understand and sat up.

'You slept with your boots on,' Victor explained.

'Oh,' Stratton said. 'An old habit when I'm in a new place.'

'I spent the first year of the campaign sleeping in my boots. And with good reason. We always seemed to be running away . . . You want some coffee?'

'Sure,' Stratton said, scratching the stubble on his chin.

'Do you wash?'

Stratton thought it was an odd question. 'When I get the chance.'

'It's a choice one makes in these circumstances. I'll put some water on the stove,' Victor said, going back downstairs.

Stratton opened his pack, removed a small bag and dug out a toothbrush and some paste. He went downstairs to the sink, which had no taps, and searched around it, looking inside a couple of jugs.

'I just realised I used the last of the water. I'm going to get some more,' Victor said, picking up a bucket. 'Use the coffee.' He held out a mug to Stratton.

The soldier took the advice, brushed his teeth and rinsed his mouth with the coffee.

'Oh. I've just remembered — you're not going anywhere today,' Victor said as he reached the front door. 'Sebastian wants you to stay and train the men as planned.'

Stratton choked back his impulse to tell Victor in crude terms that Sebastian could think again if he thought Stratton was some kind of serf who had to do what he was told. Exercising considerable restraint, he asked merely, 'Don't you think I might have some say in the matter?'

'I thought it was just a job to you,' Victor said, a hint of apology in his tone.

'Haven't circumstances changed just a little?'

Victor nodded, more to himself than to

Stratton. 'Is that okay by you?'

Stratton had grown used to the idea of getting out of this place as soon as he could and once again he found himself undecided about delaying it further.

'If you refuse I will understand,' Victor said, waiting politely for an answer.

Once again Stratton felt unable to say no. He reasoned that a few hours more was no big deal. By the afternoon he would be gone. 'Okay,' he said.

'Good. I told Sebastian you did not seem the type to frighten easily.'

Stratton headed back up the stairs to pack his parachute and kit ready to go.

'After breakfast I'll show you around the camp,' Victor called out. 'Have you had burro steaks before?'

'Donkey?'

'Yes.'

Stratton was out of Victor's sight so he felt free to make an expression of distaste. 'One of my favourites,' he called out.

Victor smirked at the sarcasm he detected and removed a muslin-covered bundle from one of his pockets. 'Hey!'

Stratton appeared on the balcony.

Victor threw the bundle up to him. 'Why don't you get the frying pan hot?'

Stratton opened the bundle to reveal two large bloody steaks, both with rinds that had long grey matted hair growing from them.

'It's almost as good as horse,' Victor assured him as he left and closed the door.

★ ★ ★

It was a bright, clear morning as the two men walked across the compound. On the far horizon a thin line of dark clouds seemed to be waiting to roll in but for the moment the air was a perfect temperature with hardly any humidity.

The ground was slippery, unable to absorb the constant rains, and the path to the main camp area was peppered with deep pools of mud. Everything was mud-coloured except for a sprinkling of green and blue plastic sheeting on the roofs of the habitats, and the lines of laundry. Smoke rose from countless cooking fires to form a grey cloud that hung in the windless air. There were people everywhere — women doing morning chores, men in fatigues hanging around smoking and chatting, and children running in and out of the huts and playing in the open field.

Victor and Stratton crossed the higher ground away from the main camp and walked along the side of a gentle hill, until a long wooden hut came into view at the top. It had a circular corral in front of it in which a white horse was trotting around.

'The stables,' Victor pointed out. 'They are just above the cabins. We've come around in a semicircle.'

They walked across the slope and approached a small isolated wood. Several men were gathered around a smouldering fire to one side of an entrance guarded by a sandbagged defensive position. They acknowledged Victor with a nod as he approached.

Victor led the way into the wood, which concealed several rows of pallets covered in tarpaulins and camouflage netting. The cooler, damper air beneath the low canopy of branches smelled of a mixture of rotting foliage and gasoline.

Further along the path lay a line of boxes that Stratton recognised.

'We keep some of our stores here,' Victor explained. 'There are other caches around the camp — away from the living quarters, of course. These are your weapons.'

Stratton noted that there was only about a third of what he had delivered. 'Do you have a training area? Somewhere we can fire a sixty-six?'

Victor pointed up ahead where a narrow path cut through the wood. He led them back to within sight of the sentries and the stables on the hill. 'We use this area for weapon testing. You can fire in that direction. Beyond those bushes the ground drops away to a cliff, above a river. Nobody goes there. Will it do?'

'It's fine,' Stratton said, looking around and thinking how he might organise things.

'What else will you need?'

'Half a dozen guys smart enough to be able to teach others what I teach them.'

Victor nodded. 'Is this afternoon okay?'

Stratton sighed to himself. Yet another delay.

'The men have work this morning,' Victor explained as if he had sensed Stratton's disappointment.

'Sure,' Stratton said, forcing a smile.

They both looked up as a horse and rider appeared, speeding across the top of the slope and silhouetted against the blue sky.

'Louisa,' Victor said. 'She rides like an insane person.'

'Is she from here ... I mean, from this country?'

'She's second-generation. Sebastian was born here. His father came from Spain when he was twelve.'

'She wasn't brought up here?'

'Until her early teens. Then, apart from the last few months, she's been in the US and Europe. Living life as a young person should.'

'Why did she come back?'

Victor looked as if he disapproved. 'She says she wants to be with her father. I think there is more to it than that. She majored in some political subject. She's one of those youngsters who knows everything and has experienced nothing ... She loves her father. She also believes in him and the struggle.'

'She's friendly to you.'

The scientist chuckled, as if he understood how Stratton thought she felt the opposite about him. 'She thinks I'm a romantic idealist, and an old one at that. If I was ten years younger I would sweep her off her feet.' He noticed Stratton staring at her and thought he could read the soldier's thoughts. 'A mercenary would have no chance, my friend.'

'I'm not a mercenary.'

'Well, you look and act like one, and that's enough.'

They watched Louisa pull her horse to a spirited halt when she reached the stables and dismount lithely. Sebastian came out to greet her and after a brief exchange she led her mount into the stable. Sebastian went to the corral and leaned on the fence. The white horse strolled over to him and he stroked its cheeks.

'When I first met Louisa I thought she suffered from the classic syndrome, a daughter wanting to be like a son to her father. But it's not the case. She's a perfect woman. When she returned from abroad Sebastian was happy to see her . . . at first. Then she told him she was staying. It was completely against his wishes but that woman does not take orders from anyone, not even from Sebastian. She told him she had completed her education, as he had wanted, and that he was no longer going to rule her life.'

A smile formed on Victor's craggy face once again but it faded as darker thoughts clouded his mind. 'He's right, though. These are not good times. Not that they were ever great. But they are worse than ever now. She should not be here. She will become a pawn in this game. She is Sebastian's only weakness. I suppose it's fortunate that Hector is in love with her. He's rash. But she mellows him. Not enough, perhaps, as you saw last night. In some ways I feel bad for him too. He loved Sebastian, admired him above all men. Hector would not go against Sebastian and certainly not against Louisa for any other reason than his political convictions. He would like to convince her even more than Sebastian that what he is doing is the best for the people, and for them both.'

Stratton was beginning to understand some of the complications. They fascinated him. Louisa fascinated him. 'What's his story?' Stratton asked.

'Sebastian's?'

'He looks more like an aristocrat than a general.'

'He comes from a long line of both.'

'Did he fall out with Neravista?'

'Most of the aristos in this country stand alongside Neravista. Sebastian is one of the few who went against him. Like many Latin American countries this one is ruled by the landowners. Most of the wealth and all of the power is controlled by a small group of people. By turning against Neravista, Sebastian was following a long line of noble rebels in his own family. His grandfather lost out in a rebellion against Franco in Spain before the Second World War. Sebastian doesn't want that failure to run in the family.' Victor checked his watch. 'He wants to see you.'

Stratton looked at the Frenchman. 'Why?'

'Maybe he wants to talk you into staying. I don't know. He's more pragmatic than Louisa. When you're in a fight, make friends with fighters, no matter what their motive.'

Stratton was getting bored with the endless insinuations that he fought only for money. But it was obvious that the rebels had fixed views about him and nothing was going to change them. He had no fears that Sebastian was going to talk him into staying, not even for another day. He was leaving the camp at the end of the day's training and that was final. Even if it was dark by the time he left.

He was about to set off when Victor stopped him.

'Tell me something. Be honest with me. Do we seem foolish to you?'

Stratton was not sure exactly what the Frenchman meant.

'You must have come across people like us before. I would understand if you find us amusing.'

'I've never done anything like this before.'

'You don't look new to this kind of work.'

'What I mean is, I've never delivered arms to a bunch of freedom fighters before.'

'What kind of things do mercenaries do these days?'

Once again Stratton ignored the label that Victor was trying to pin on him. 'There's nothing foolish about fighting for political change. It's dying for it that doesn't make any sense to me.'

Victor nodded. 'Spoken like a true mercenary.'

Stratton shook his head wearily and walked off up the slope.

Sebastian was stroking the horse and speaking softly to it as Stratton arrived and stopped a few paces away.

'What do you think of him . . . my horse?' Sebastian asked.

'It's a beautiful animal.'

'Are you familiar with horses?'

'No.'

'But you have instincts. You're a warrior. That

101

puts you closer than ordinary men to animals like this. Tell me what you see in him.'

Stratton studied the animal before stepping up to the fence and reaching out to touch it. The horse did not move as Stratton stroked its cheek.

'Kindred spirits, as I said. He comes from warrior stock himself.'

The horse turned its head slightly to look at Stratton. It was a powerful and stalwart-looking beast. 'I see pride. Dignity. He seems content.'

The old man nodded. 'He's a true white, as resolute as they come. There has always been a white in our family. Tradition is important, don't you think?'

Stratton could agree with that. There was none in his family but he had learned the meaning of the word — the concept — while serving in the British military.

'Tell me,' Sebastian said. 'Why have you chosen to stay here when your life is in danger?'

'Because I was asked politely.'

Sebastian allowed himself a rare chuckle. 'And the real reason?'

Stratton had to think about it for a moment. 'To be honest, I don't really know.'

'Then examine what did not drive you away. Fear could not, because you're unafraid. Self-interest was not enough. You came with Victor and his men to finish the job — so you are altruistic. You saved a stranger's life, which makes you empathetic. Forgive the examination. I am interested in the instincts of animals but even more so in those of men. In times of confusion instincts are all we have to rely on

. . . Have you seen much of the camp?'

'Victor showed me some of it.'

'You need to see it all. Louisa!' Sebastian called out.

His daughter stepped out of a stall. Her expression went blank when she saw Stratton. 'Yes, father?' she said as she walked over to them.

'Would you show our guest around? Give him a horse.'

Louisa did not look overjoyed at the prospect. If Sebastian noticed her lack of enthusiasm, he gave no sign and faced Stratton, looking him in the eye. 'I'm glad you're here,' he said with true sincerity.

Stratton watched him head down the path towards the log cabins. The man was without doubt a member of a rare breed. Some people were born with an exceptional aura and Sebastian was one of them. He had begun and was now holding together a national rebellion by sheer force of will.

Louisa was looking at Stratton as if she'd won a booby prize.

'I take it you don't fancy being a tour guide today,' he said.

'You're very intuitive.'

'I've had enough compliments for one day, thanks.'

She gave him an insincere smile.

'Maybe some other time,' he said, turning away.

Louisa would have been happy to let him go but she was mindful of her father's request. 'Wait.'

Stratton did not respond.

'Can I say something?' she asked.

He slowed to a halt and looked around at her tiredly.

'You're my father's guest. If he wants you to be shown around I will oblige him.'

'Hey. Don't put yourself out on my account.' He continued down the slope.

'Look . . . ' Louisa began. But Stratton was marching off at a stubborn pace. She gritted her teeth, turned away from him and stormed back to the stables.

Stratton worked on suppressing his annoyance. He could usually tolerate disrespect, choosing the diplomatic thick-skinned option that would prevent conflict and let him get on with the job. But every now and then bad manners and insults got to him. Louisa had managed to needle him more easily than another person might have and the reason for that was obvious enough. His ego had been chipped. She was beautiful and he wanted to be attractive to her but she saw him only as a lowlife.

Stratton decided that the best course of action was to avoid the woman altogether. She was only going to wind him up whenever they met. Staying out of her way for the next few hours should not be difficult.

He tried to focus his thoughts on the upcoming weapons training but Louisa had well and truly got under his skin. There was something about her that he could not shake. Stratton had avoided meaningful relationships with the opposite sex for years. It had been a rule of his, and her attitude should have made it easy to sustain. Having a love interest in his line of work was pointless. In his early days in the SBS he had had a girlfriend and there had been some great times but the difficulties and eventual heartbreak had not been worth it. The strains of maintaining a relationship when both parties were often apart for long periods only really became clear after he'd tried it. Sure, he was looking forward to getting home — but only because he didn't want to be here. If he was offered another job by the time he got to Panama he would take it. And he wouldn't have to make a difficult phone call to explain, in effect asking for permission not to come home until God only knew when. His pride might have taken a knock but he had to get on with the job in hand.

The sound of hooves thundered behind him and he turned to see Louisa charging his way on her horse with another one alongside her. She passed him in order to turn the snorting animals and bring them to a halt across his path.

She steadied the beasts, taking a moment to compose herself. 'I was rude,' she said. 'It was unnecessary.'

Stratton knew he should have simply insisted that she forget the tour since he was leaving in a few hours but he couldn't bring himself to.

'After last night you had every reason to leave,' Louisa continued. 'You did not, which . . . it's to your credit. My father wants you to stay and train the men. It was wrong of me to act the way I did.'

She had said her piece but without actually

apologising. Stratton decided to hold out for it.

It was as if she had read his mind. She turned away so that he could not see her rolling her eyes. 'I'm sorry,' she mumbled, avoiding his gaze.

'I couldn't hear that,' Stratton said. 'What was that last thing you said?'

Louisa clenched her jaw and flashed her eyes at him. 'I'm sorry,' she repeated, tersely.

He decided it was the best he was going to get and smiled victoriously at her.

'Can you ride?' she asked coldly. 'This one's a little feisty but she has a good spirit,' she said, holding out the reins to him.

Stratton had been on horseback a few times in his life but he would not have described himself as a confident rider. He didn't think in any case that a tour of the camp was essential. But he found that he was suddenly enjoying Louisa's company in a weird kind of way.

'I'm assuming you can sit in a saddle — but then, you don't look the type to have been in the cavalry,' Louisa said, clearly baiting him.

Stratton slung the M4 across his back, took the reins, held them fast on the saddle's horn while he placed his boot into the stirrup and pulled himself up. He made the move successfully but sitting on a saddle felt alien immediately.

Louisa did not wait for him to settle in and she headed across the field at a trot. Before he could do anything his horse set off after her. Stratton was not in control of the animal but if it was happy to follow hers then he supposed that was good enough.

106

'What were you talking about with my father?' she asked as he came alongside her.

'We were talking about instincts. He's a perceptive man. I suppose that sort of thing can skip a generation.'

'Oh? I also figured you were vulnerable to flattery,' she said. 'Starved of it, more like,' she muttered, but loudly enough for him to hear.

Stratton wasn't used to verbal jousting with a woman and immediately felt vulnerable. He decided to back off.

'Did he ask you about your family history?' Louisa asked.

Stratton grew cautious, aware that she was not done with him yet. 'No.'

'Your boss, Steel? He told Sebastian that his father fought with the Lincoln Brigade during the Spanish Civil War. It's the sort of thing my father would respond to. I think Steel's a liar. Don't suppose *your* grandfather was in the Spanish Civil War, by any chance?'

'No, but I'm told my grandmother wore puttees and wanted to join the Gurkhas.'

Louisa looked at Stratton as if he was strange. He remained poker-faced. 'I'm glad you have a sense of humour,' she said as she spurred her horse into a canter. His animal followed automatically.

The ground sloped steeply away before them, providing a breathtaking view that stretched for miles. The jungle unfolded into the distance like a series of huge overlapping waves. Louisa's horse eased into a spirited gallop down a slope covered in knee-length buffalo grass. Stratton's beast responded in kind and they quickly reached a speed that was a new experience for him on horseback. He focused all his efforts on staying on the animal's back. His only thought was that if the horse tripped they would both probably die.

Stratton leaned forward and gritted his teeth, remembering an old adage: the only way to deal with speed was to want to go faster.

Louisa's ponytail came loose and her hair flowed behind her like a cape. She gradually became lost in the rush as she pushed her animal to the maximum.

The ground seemed to disappear a few hundred metres ahead, the jungle becoming visible again only in the far distance. Louisa eased her horse's head to one side and they leaned into a wide turn. Stratton's horse did the same. He was far from being at ease but a part of him was revelling in the experience. The power of the animal thundering beneath him was extraordinary. It conjured feelings of ancient warriors and what it must have been like to charge into battle on horseback.

Several rebels crossing the high ground stopped to watch the pair tearing across the landscape below them. David was among them and he called out to Victor, who came over to see what was going on.

Stratton expected, or at least hoped, that Louisa would slow down as they arrived at the edge of the dead ground but she suddenly turned her beast sharply to run along it. Stratton's horse made the same adjustment, which he was very soon most thankful for, his heart skipping a beat when he realised why the animal had swerved. The dead ground was in fact the edge of a cliff. But it was not the last surprise that the young woman had in store for him.

Any enjoyment he had previously managed to get from the ride was replaced by fear as they galloped along the top of the precipice, barely metres from its edge. Louisa did not let up and seemed to be moving ever closer to the void as if trying to see how near to it she could ride. Stratton's horse followed directly behind hers as if unable to think for itself.

The ground had levelled out, the cliff curving outwards in a gentle arc towards the jungle in the distance. An odd clump of bushes suddenly appeared up ahead a couple of metres from the cliff which Louisa passed on the cliff side. Stratton's horse followed, cutting so close that the foliage clipped his foot. A quick glance revealed that his horse's hooves were inches from the edge. Stratton tugged the opposite rein in an effort to turn the animal away but it had no effect. Yet another odd clump appeared up ahead, this time even closer to the cliff. To Stratton's relief Louisa passed it on the outside. At least there was a limit to her risk-taking.

The good news was that they were closing on the point where the jungle met the cliff and the daredevil ride would have to head inland at least.

Victor watched from the hilltop with growing interest, well aware of an obstacle ahead that was not yet visible to Stratton. He wondered what

Louisa was planning. She didn't appear to be slowing down and he shook his head, hoping Stratton had some equestrian experience.

A small fold in the ground up ahead disguised a narrow slice into the cliff, a chine that reached inland a dozen or so metres. The first time Louisa had seen it was when she'd been riding at a gentle trot and she had stopped in front of it. After an inspection from both sides of the cut, paying particular attention to the soundness of the edges, she had trotted back the way she had come, turned her horse around and broken into a fearsome gallop. That first time she'd made the jump she'd chosen the middle where the chine was a couple of metres wide. The following day she had returned for another go, this time leaping its widest point close to the edge for an added rush. It was not the longest jump she had ever made but with the added degree of difficulty, namely the abyss below, it was one of the more exhilarating.

Louisa spared only a moment to consider the dangers to Stratton, knowing that his horse would follow hers. She had time to avoid the chine and for a second she was undecided. But the devil in her forbade her to show any sympathy for the mercenary. She reckoned his type were fond of regaling their chums with exaggerated accounts of their adventures. Well, he could add this one to his repertoire. She did not mean him harm, not physically anyway. It was an opportunity to scare him and hence too good to miss. His horse was a sturdy beast that had made the jump many times. And though

Stratton had no riding form to speak of he did have something of a natural seat. If he lost his nerve he might try to pull up or turn aside, though. That could be a problem.

The chine came into view through the taller grass and Louisa rose up in the saddle to take some weight off her horse's neck. With perfect timing the animal made the leap. The thunderous sound of his hooves ceased as he took to the air. They struck the ground and the thunder returned. Louisa eased back on the reins as she turned to look behind her. When she saw Stratton she suddenly grew concerned that she had gone too far.

Stratton had not yet seen the chine but he had not missed seeing Louisa's horse take to the air. By the time he spotted the jagged cut in the cliff it was too late to do anything, even if he could have. His horse was the master of the moment. All he could do was hold on tight.

Time seemed to slow for him at that point. The sound of his horse's hooves grew muffled as every metre of ground ahead came into sharp focus. The horse jolted as it prepared to jump. Stratton loosened the reins to allow the animal the freedom to do what it needed. As the gap approached Stratton's feeling of tension soared. The horse brought up its front legs and Stratton's head went down alongside the animal's neck.

As they jumped Stratton found himself looking down into the void. He was aware only of a vast emptiness below.

The horse landed hard and threw Stratton

further forward. He almost lost his seat but regained it as the horse's rear quarters dropped, its legs sliding beneath it, its hocks hitting the ground. Stratton grabbed its withers instinctively but could not keep his grip. Indeed, his instincts warned him not to. He slid off the horse's side as the beast bounced back to its feet and he struck the ground hard, rolling a couple of times before coming to a stop.

The animal trotted off, shaking its head and snorting irritably. For a moment Stratton lay where he had landed, wondering if he had sustained any damage. He sat up slowly and removed his carbine from where it was slung on his back. Earth filled its muzzle where it had dug into the ground and he gritted his teeth irritably as he knocked the soil out.

Louisa walked her horse up to him. 'You okay?' she asked. 'You did well.'

He looked up at her as he got to his feet, scowling angrily. But she just laughed at him.

'You think that was funny?'

'Yes, I do, actually.'

Stratton felt the anger beginning to well up inside him. His treasured composure was cracking. He did not like to be laughed at. 'You stupid prat.'

Louisa, stopped laughing but kept a broad grin on her face. 'Temper, temper.'

'I suggest you take a closer look around you and appreciate where you are. You're a long way from your high-class college, playing your silly girly games.'

She tried to hold her smile but Stratton's

words stung. 'You're not just angry about falling off your horse?'

'No, I'm not. I don't appreciate being mocked by an immature princess like you. You're in the real world here — one of the darker parts of it, at that — where actions and words can have serious consequences. Do yourself a favour and grow up.'

'You think I don't know where I am?' Louisa retorted, her own anger surfacing. She jumped off her horse, stormed over to a heap of brush like the ones along the edge of the cliff that they had dodged around and pulled a section away to reveal a large wooden crate. She removed the heavy lid with some difficulty to uncover a huge coil of knotted climbing rope.

'This cliff acts as a boundary for almost half the camp,' she said. 'We can only be attacked from one direction. But if we had to escape, the cliff would make it difficult for us. This rope reaches to the bottom. There are over a dozen of them.'

'Whose idea was that?'

'Mine,' she said, looking smug.

'You plan to get a couple of thousand people down a dozen ropes during a gun battle?' Stratton asked as he stepped over to the chine to look down.

'It's only intended as a last-ditch escape route.'

'Six hundred feet?'

'At least some of us could get away.'

'In the rain, at night? What about the women and children? The elderly? The wounded? And you think the men will leave without their families?'

The confident expression left Louisa's face.

'You set a camp with its back to a cliff you'd better plan to stand and fight,' Stratton said, walking away. 'Stick to ironing your father's shirts.'

Louisa clenched her jaw, wanting to protest against his last comment, but for once she didn't know what to say.

She climbed back onto her horse, took hold of the reins of the other one and trotted them up the hill the way they had come.

Near the top she saw Victor watching her and steered towards him. 'You angry with me too?' she asked as she halted her horse.

'You could at least wait until after he has instructed the men before you try to kill him. Just because you don't approve of him doesn't mean you can act like that,' Victor added.

'Okay,' Louisa said, as if she'd had enough preaching for one day. 'But today he helps us, tomorrow he helps Neravista. That's the problem I have with him.'

'How do you know that?'

'Victor, you are as bad at judging people's characters as my father is. Look at the man. Look at what he does.'

'Before he came here perhaps he would have done the same for Neravista. But I don't think he would now.'

'He's won your trust easily.'

'Does my opinion no longer count with you?'

'You know that's not true.' Louisa sighed

heavily, wanting to change the subject. 'I'm worried, Victor.'

'You mean about last night?'

'Is Sebastian going to lose control?'

Victor did not have an answer for that question. 'It's going to be different from now on, I think.'

'What do you think will happen?'

'I think you should leave. Go back to America or Europe.'

Louisa rejected that advice with a dismissive gesture. 'If my mother had not died this rebellion might never have begun when it did. Did you know that?'

'Your mother died long before the uprising.'

'It took Sebastian several years to make his plans. He didn't begin making them until after she died. She gave him her blessing on her deathbed. She fought against it while she was alive but she knew that was all he would live for once she was gone and so she made it easier for him. He would have succeeded had she been alive.'

'You talk like it's already over.'

'I'm afraid for him.'

'You think you can take the place of your mother?'

'Is that so ridiculous?'

Victor did not know how to answer.

'I can't leave him, whatever happens. Tell me, why do *you* stay?'

Victor thought for a moment. 'I believe in destiny, that I was put on this earth for a purpose. It wasn't until I came here that I knew what that was. You see, I have always believed that the world was headed inexorably towards peace and contentment for all, no matter what evil existed. I never expected that it would be achieved in my lifetime but that didn't matter. Anything I did to help would not be in vain. Others not yet born would take my place to continue the struggle. But one day I realised there was a flaw in that belief. If it was inevitable, then I was not essential to it. The world doesn't need me.'

'So why are you still here?'

He shrugged. 'For something less noble. Recognition. I want it for myself.'

'That's not so bad a reason, Victor. It's part of what distinguishes us from other living things. It's only normal.'

Victor smiled, but what he could not tell Louisa was that he had begun to doubt himself. He feared it would lead to self-betrayal which might eventually become something far worse. He also feared he was not the only one who was changing.

3

Back at the stables, Louisa dismounted and handed the reins of Stratton's horse to a stable boy. As she unbuckled the saddle of her own horse she noticed a man whom she didn't recognise standing by the corral looking at her. He wore the usual grubby military fatigues of the rebels. He took a piece of paper from a pocket, jammed it into a gap in the fence and walked away, glancing back to make sure she had seen what he'd done.

She watched him as he went down the path that led to the cabins and then she retrieved the note. When she looked back he was gone.

Louisa opened the note and read it, then screwed it up and leaned on the fence. The white horse walked over to her and she stroked his cheeks without focusing on him. He muzzled her hand and moved closer, demanding her undivided attention. 'Are you feeling neglected today? Be thankful that is the worst of your problems,' she said softly. 'Remember one of father's sayings? It's your life-changing decisions that give life its meaning . . . That goes for you too'.

She kissed the white horse on the nose and walked away to her own animal, buckled up the saddle again, mounted and set off at a trot, quickly breaking into a canter across the open ground towards the edge of the jungle.

Louisa walked her sweat-covered horse along a shaded jungle path lined with the peeling trunks and branches of eucalyptus trees. She had covered several miles and now she peered through the trunks in search of a hut in a small clearing that she knew was somewhere close by. A sudden roll of distant thunder made her horse uneasy and she patted its flank to calm it. 'Easy, Merlin. It's only the rain coming.'

A patch of brightness ahead signalled the clearing and the hut soon came into view on its far side.

A saddled horse was tethered to a hitching post outside the hut. She stopped alongside it, dismounted and tossed her reins around the same wooden bar. Thunder crashed across the skies once again, this time preceded by a flash across the sky.

As the sound of thunder reverberated into the distance, she looked around the surroundings before facing the door of the hut. It was ajar and, mustering her courage, she walked inside.

Hector stood on the other side of the sparsely furnished dusty room, looking out through an opening, aware that he was no longer alone. The only furniture was a rickety table leaning against a thick wooden pole — which held up the centre of the ceiling — and a couple of chairs.

He turned to look at her, his face sombre. But a second later it lit up with a broad smile. 'Louisa,' he said, walking over to her and wrapping his heavy arms about her to hold her in a grizzly-bear hug. She almost disappeared inside his embrace before he held her out at arm's length to take a look at her. Her response was cold but he was not dismayed, as if he expected it. 'You were so beautiful last night you took my breath away.'

'Spiritual leader?' Louisa asked him sternly. 'That's how you described my father.'

'I didn't mean it in quite that way,' Hector said, letting go of her. 'I was trying to control the conversation. It was politics.'

'What do you know about politics? You insulted him in front of everyone, suggesting that he's been little more than a guide through this damned rebellion.'

'I had to bring him down a peg or two.'

'You ever thought about trying to elevate yourself instead?'

'I'm forever glad he doesn't have your kind of debating skills.'

Her expression stayed unchanged.

'Louisa. Please. He has been like a god to us. I needed the others to see him as a mere man . . . one who makes mistakes.'

'And what about you?'

'Come on. I thought you took a degree in politics. It's a game . . . Okay,' Hector then added quickly, regretting the comment. 'It's not a game. I retract that. I'm not as eloquent as you. I don't have your education. But you know what I mean. Of all people, do I have to explain myself to you?'

'What makes you think you're right? Why are

119

you so sure you're not the one making the mistake?'

'I'll tell you why I know I'm right. Sebastian operates entirely on passion. His kind of passion is the fuel that ignites rebellions. I could not do it. I admit that. He is remarkable. But passion is blind, Louisa. It does not know when to pause and inspect the wreckage created by its own fury.'

'And you're the new voice of reason and sensibility, I suppose.'

'Is that so hard to believe?'

'You're out of your depth.'

'You think so?'

'We're not dealing with honourable people. Neravista is a murderer. Amoral. A liar, cheat, thief, a torturer of men, women and children. For God's sake, Hector. He's playing you like a fish.'

'Not a fish, a shark. And I'm in the pool along with him.'

Louisa rolled her eyes. 'One of my lecturers used to warn about using metaphors in a debate since even the dullest wit can recover.'

'Thank you,' Hector said, trying to convey hurt in his tone.

'Neravista can't afford to lose power. If he loses this country he loses everything.'

'You're making my argument for me. Of course he cannot afford to lose. That's why he has to make a deal.'

Louisa shook her head in frustration. 'He's not going to agree to anything that reduces his power.'

'Don't be so sure.'

'He's offered you autonomy?'

'It's a most important part of the agenda.'

'Guarantees?'

'We're not at that stage of the negotiations yet.'

'Dear God, Hector. You want a completely different form of government from him. You think he's even going to consider that possibility?'

'Once we get our foot in the door I'll kick it wide open. Small steps, Louisa. But peaceful ones. Can we talk about something else for a moment?'

She knew what he meant. 'There's nothing more important than this.'

'There is something of *equal* importance, though — to me, at least. I want to talk about us.'

'There is no us, Hector.'

'Tell me one thing. Be honest with me. What if I am right? If I win? What about us then?'

'To win, Hector, you would have to try. And the cost of trying would be far too much for Sebastian to pay.'

'I'm in love with you, not with Sebastian.'

'When you talk about Sebastian's future you talk about mine.'

'But that's like asking me to choose between my politics and you.'

'You just said your politics and your feelings for me were equal. You have to have a good memory to be a politician. They have to lie all the time.'

'Is that what you're suggesting? You and Sebastian instead of politics?'

'No, Hector. I'm asking you not to split the rebellion. Have you even tried discussing this with Sebastian?'

'You heard him last night. He will not hear any of it.'

'Because you pushed him into a corner before you made your intentions clear. I believe that was your plan all along.'

'Rubbish. I don't need Sebastian to deal with Neravista — and yes, Sebastian would have made it more difficult, even impossible, as he is trying to do. But I did not try and shove him aside. Not the way you describe it.'

'I applaud you, Hector. And I apologise for being wrong about you. You've taken to politics very easily. You lie with such conviction. Goodbye.' Louisa turned her back on him to leave.

He made it to the door a fraction ahead of her and placed his arm across it, barring her way. Hector would not have been so bold with a woman like Louisa before that day. He had started his adult life as a goat herder in the eastern provinces and he remained aware of his humble beginnings, especially in her presence. He was the youngest of five brothers, of whom three had left their parental home when Hector was still an adolescent to start their own families while two had already died in infancy. The village he'd grown up in had had no doctor, the nearest one being a walk of two days or more away. Usually, if someone fell ill, they pulled through or they died.

Hector's opportunity for an education presented itself with the arrival in his village of an American non-governmental medical aid agency. One of the volunteers was a student from New Mexico who spoke Spanish and English. When Hector showed an interest in his books the student took it upon himself to teach the boy the basics of literacy. Hector's appetite for learning was unquenchable and the student was soon teaching Hector how to read during just about every spare waking hour either of them had. Six months later, by the end of the student's contract, Hector could read and write just about as well as any boy his age. The day the student left Hector asked if he could accompany him as far as the capital where he intended to get a job and continue studying. And that was precisely what he did. He rushed home to say farewell to his mother and asked her to tell his father out in the fields that he was leaving home. He tied all his earthly possessions into a bundle no bigger than a football and jumped aboard the NGO bus.

The student let Hector stay in their offices for a couple of days until Hector got himself a job as a waiter in a hotel restaurant. Within six months he had risen to a position in lower management. In that time he also witnessed the injustice of the Neravista government and, thanks to some of the better-educated staff at the hotel, he developed a more than mild interest in local politics. After suffering a severe beating at a peaceful demonstration for better conditions in a local hospital, his patience for passive campaigning withered. He gravitated towards those who wanted a militant approach. Yet none of the leaders of any of the political parties inspired him until one day he went to a meeting outside the city.

Several hundred people from all walks of life attended, something Hector had not expected since news of the meeting had circulated clandestinely. He was surprised to see how many of them appeared to be well-educated members of the middle class. But what really impressed him was the main speaker, Sebastian. When he talked everyone listened intently. He was so incredibly subtle. If Neravista himself had been there he would have heard the call for armed rebellion loud and clear but an inspection of the transcript would not have revealed a single direct reference to weapons or force.

The other sight that for Hector almost overshadowed the impression left by Sebastian was that of his daughter. Louisa stayed very much in the background, quite literally. Few people probably noticed her standing in a far corner. For the would-be revolutionary she stood out like a beacon. To Hector she was a vision sent from the gods.

Several months later there came another opportunity for Hector to visit Sebastian's estate to hear him talk. On the journey Hector and his companions boldly discussed open revolt but by the time they arrived he could think of just one thing. From his place at the back of the meeting he searched in vain for Louisa. As Sebastian's turn to address the gathering came, the young rebel's expectations rose. When the proceedings came to an end and she had still not showed herself he asked a member of the household staff where Sebastian's daughter was that day. She was away at school, he was told.

Hector was very disappointed, but on his way out of the house he happened to see a framed photograph of Louisa. The face that he had been longing to see for months was even more beautiful than he remembered. The picture sat on a dresser along with a hat and scarf that he recognised as those she had worn that first time he'd seen her. He glanced around to check that he was alone and without a second's hesitation he wrapped the frame in the scarf, stuck it inside his coat and walked out.

Hector waited a long time before he saw Louisa in the flesh again. By the time the call to arms came and Sebastian had set up his first guerrilla encampment in the mountains she had already been sent away to America.

Hector's enthusiasm brought him to Sebastian's attention early on in the forming of the various rebel companies and he was given command of a special reconnaissance unit. The other companies soon came to rely on him for vital operational information and his reputation was born. He matured quickly into a fine, positive commander known for leading his men from the front. By the end of his second year he had been promoted to brigade commander in the ever-expanding rebel army that was by then receiving funding and supplies from America as well as secretly from private investors and governments in Mexico, Brazil, Argentina and other Latino countries. At the start of the third year of the campaign Sebastian formed the inner council and Hector was elected a member.

His experiences in those years altered Hector. He grew hardened in almost every way. And he was aware of it. Some called him callous, others were even less kind. But it was not until he once again saw Louisa that he realised there were parts of a man's heart that could never change.

When Sebastian introduced his daughter to Hector he had to remind himself that she did not know him. He tried to act accordingly and, in particular, to prevent his desire for her from becoming obvious. When she shook his hand she looked into his eyes and said she remembered him from her father's first address all those years ago before she had left for America. Hector was stunned. He had hardly taken his eyes off her that day and she had not so much as glanced in his direction. For her to remember him after all that time could mean only one thing.

His brigade was several hours' ride from Sebastian's encampment and it was weeks before he could find an excuse to make another visit. In that time he daydreamed about how their love would blossom. Yet when he did finally manage to visit Sebastian he found that Louisa was never alone. The only physical contact he ever had with her was when saying hello and goodbye, when he held her hand for longer than might have been considered polite.

But despite the lack of intimacy Hector believed there was a place in her heart for him. Whenever their gazes met, at dinner for instance, he could see a tenderness that he felt was more than just comradeship or respect for his rank. Bizarrely, and he could scarcely even admit it to himself, his desire for her was part of what pushed him obsessively towards the peace talks. He could never factor it into his calculations but there were many things that would change if the fighting ceased: one of the most important to him would be a more stable environment in which he could court her.

But as Hector held his arm across the door in front of Louisa that day the look she gave him filled him with dread for their relationship. 'Don't go, not like this,' he begged.

'I don't have a choice, Hector,' she said softly. 'I'm Sebastian's daughter. There's still a choice for you, though.'

Hector had hoped deep down that she did not agree completely with her father and was merely being supportive out of family loyalty. He was shocked at how badly he had misjudged her. He lowered his arm and she left.

Hector listened to Louisa climb onto her horse and ride away. He felt a sudden chill.

The rhythmic sound of footsteps heading towards the hut brought him out of his reverie. Hector walked to the other end of the hut to await his next visitor.

Ventura stood in the doorway, wearing an all-knowing smirk. He was a short man, compact compared with Hector, sophisticated, well-groomed and wearing a full-length tailored raincoat that tastefully matched the expensive riding suit beneath. His black moustache was a thin line in a 1930s style and he had an air of confidence and self-importance that came from his membership of the upper class. He was accompanied by several thuggish armed men, also in civilian clothes, who remained outside as he stepped into the hut and closed the door behind him.

'I can't say I'm inspired with confidence by that meeting,' Ventura said, looking with distaste around the simple dwelling.

'When Sebastian realises he is isolated he will reassess the situation,' Hector said flatly.

'I wonder if you know Sebastian as well as you think you do. You appear to have misjudged his daughter somewhat.'

Hector felt his anger rise but choked it back even though he could not hide it completely from his expression. 'I have control of the council. That is the important thing.'

Ventura seemed pleased with his ability to rile Hector easily. 'I'm not so sure. As long as Sebastian commands his brigade he remains a threat. He has a gift for bringing men round to his way of thinking.'

'You talk as if you and I are on the same side. We are not, Ventura. Just remember that.'

'Your ambitions confuse me, Hector. Surely we're converging forces.'

'Perhaps. But we all have to change — make compromises — if we are to achieve an

128

understanding. That includes your boss Neravista. I don't want peace at any price. Just remember that.'

'Of course. And Neravista understands that too. But we can't wait on your reassurances for ever. The lull in our military activities is purely to give you the time to take control. We are prepared to renew our offensive — and vigorously — if you fail. And what about these new weapons that Sebastian has just received? They do not help matters. Some of my colleagues think you are merely playing for time in order to consolidate and rearm.'

'The arrival of the weapons at Sebastian's camp is your fault as much as anyone's. The Americans know our position but you were too slow in making them aware of yours.'

'They know it now. But they have the luxury of being in a position to play all sides until they have what they want. We believe we can satisfy their demands.'

'If Sebastian can be made to change his mind the weapons will no longer be a factor.'

'We talk in circles, Hector. It all comes down to one man. The question is, can you handle him? If you can't we will have to find someone who can.'

The brigade leader flashed him a look. 'Don't toy with me, Ventura. And don't try to go behind me. I am the one you deal with now. And I decide how to deal with Sebastian, and killing him is not an option. Defy me on that and you can suffer the consequences.'

'We're not the only ones who want Sebastian

out of the way. The rebel movement has never been as fragmented as it is now, thanks to you. The divisions are firmly along the lines of Sebastian and the rest of you. Many who used to support Sebastian would now like to see him gone . . . Don't tell me you haven't considered killing him yourself. Wasn't it you who said that peace for all is more important than any individual? You have commanded men in the field. You understand the need for sacrifice. Perhaps you have doubts of your own that you're not telling us.'

'I don't have doubts,' Hector growled.

'*I* have one. *You*, Hector . . . I'm beginning to doubt that you're the man to bring this rebellion to an end.'

Hector moved close to Ventura, looming over him.

Ventura was not fazed by Hector's size. 'Don't be under any illusions about our position,' he said. 'You came to us looking for a solution to end this rebellion. We listened and sympathised. But there is a limit to our patience and our belief in you. If you cannot deliver the conditions required for these negotiations to take place we will recommence hostilities and punish you. You know what needs to be done. I know you have the courage to do it. I'm not sure if you have the will, or the intellect.'

Hector gritted his teeth, his anger boiling over, but Ventura did not stay long enough to face his glare.

★ ★ ★

Stratton headed up the track from the log cabins, passing the stables on his way to the training area. He felt a little stiff in places after his fall from the horse and he had a few painful bruises on his arms. He put it all behind him by working out his schedule in his mind. He estimated that he could be on the road by around late afternoon, which would give him a couple of hours of daylight to get some distance from the camp. With luck he would make the border on the morning of the second day. He could pretty much imagine the rest of the trip, in particular the last stretch: the train journey from Waterloo Station to Poole and then a pint in the Blue Boar with some of the lads, if any of them were in town. He was looking forward to sleeping in his own bed in his own house, and to making dinner in his own kitchen and watching a good movie and enjoying a glass of good wine. It seemed like a million miles from where he was at that moment but in three or four days he would be there. Just the thought of it made him feel better.

A group of men were waiting for him as he headed down from the top of the rise near the corral. They sat around enjoying the sun and chatting light-heartedly.

When the men saw Stratton approach they got to their feet. The young teacher, David, was one of them, the others Stratton recognised from the supply pick-up — particularly the two who had nicked the rockets for the ambush.

Stratton nodded to David and greeted the others. They seemed unsure how to treat the

131

mercenary, as he was known around the camp: the man who was not one of them and who held no rank. But it was obvious to all of them that Stratton was an experienced soldier, and no ordinary one at that if the parachute drop was anything to go by, a feat beyond any of them. There was also the way he conducted himself generally, the ease with which he adapted and how he carried himself and his weapons. They didn't know much about him but enough to believe anything he had to say about soldiering.

'What's your name?' he asked the one who had fired the rocket the previous day.

'Miguel,' the man replied somewhat sheepishly.

'How're your burns?' Stratton asked.

'Okay,' Miguel said, ruefully indicating the bulge of the bandaging under his trousers to the amusement of the others.

Stratton looked at the other man who had tried to fire a rocket.

'Umberto,' the man said, with a grin.

'Would you like to learn how to fire a rocket correctly?'

'Is there something else I can learn?' he asked. 'I don't like those things.'

The men laughed again.

The next man in line was powerfully built with a more sombre demeanour than the others. 'Carlos,' he said.

Stratton nodded and looked at the next.

'Eduardo,' he said.

Stratton nodded again and walked a few paces to where he could face them all. 'The plan is to show you how to use the rockets and the claymore mines effectively,' he began. 'Then you're going to become the teachers to everyone else. Do you think you can manage that?'

They all nodded.

'They're not complicated. The big issue, apart from being able to use them effectively against an enemy, is to make sure we don't hurt ourselves or our buddies. So listen to everything I have to say, ask all the questions you want and, above all, make sure you understand everything about the weapons concerned. When I'm gone there'll be no one else to ask. Okay?'

They nodded enthusiastically.

'Good. Let's go see the toys.'

'Er, excuse me,' Miguel said. 'What do we call you?'

'He's called the mercenary,' Eduardo said to Miguel as if he should have known that.

'Stratton will do,' Stratton said.

'Stratton?'

'That's right,' he said, heading down a track. Eduardo hurried ahead and led the way into the small wood Victor had shown Stratton earlier. On reaching the pallets the men stood back to let him select the boxes.

'Let's start with that one there,' Stratton said, pointing to a box on the top of a pile. David and Carlos lifted it to the ground. Stratton unclipped its latches and swung the lid open to reveal a moulded plastic cover which he removed. Inside lay neat rows of hand-held rocket launchers. He lifted one out and, with a snap, deftly pulled it open into the armed position.

133

'Wow,' Umberto exclaimed, taking a step back.

'Don't worry,' Stratton said, taking a long, slender dart-like object from inside the lid of the box. 'This is a trainer. It has a non-explosive head. It's what you had at the ambush — not like Miguel,' he said.

The others laughed, much to Umberto's dismay.

'Let's take a look in those two there,' he said.

Miguel and Eduardo hauled down the two boxes concerned and placed them in line with the first.

'Open that one,' Stratton asked as he closed the launch tube and replaced it in the box alongside the others.

Miguel opened the box to reveal rows of claymore mines in their canvas sacks. He reached to touch one.

'Stop,' Stratton said sharply. 'First rule of this lesson. Touch absolutely nothing unless I say so. Is that understood?'

The men recognised the seriousness of his words and acknowledged them.

'Especially this,' Stratton said, lifting out a black plastic box the size of a milk carton. It had a thick red tape around it with warning signs emblazoned on all sides. 'These are the detonators that fire the claymores. They're highly sensitive. You get these wrong and you won't need to worry about getting anything else wrong ever again. You got that?'

They nodded.

'Open that box,' Stratton said, indicating the next one.

Miguel reached for the clips on the side of the box, unfastened them and pulled the lid back. He gripped the edge of the plastic moulding and as he raised it there was a metallic pinging sound and something flew out of the box into the air.

Stratton's mind raced, desperate to remember what the sound meant. He had it before the object landed at his feet. He knew what it was even before he focused on the curved piece of pressed alloy three inches long and spoon-shaped at one end. It was still rolling on the muddy soil as he turned on his heels and yelled 'Grenade!' as loudly as he could.

The others did not react as fast. A second had ticked away before the horrible danger struck them and they began to turn away — all except Miguel. He stared in disbelief at the grenade nestled in between the tightly packed rows of military explosives. Only when it smoked and hissed as the fuse that ran down its centre began to burn towards the detonator did he make any effort to get away. His right foot slid on the soft ground as he planted the other heavily.

Stratton counted the third second instinctively in his head, straining to put as much distance between himself and the boxes as possible. Before the end of the fourth second he knew he had to be close to the ground. There was a tree only metres ahead of him and he threw himself down beside it. As he hit the ground he grabbed the base of the trunk and his momentum slung him around the back of it.

The explosion was massive — its force scooped Stratton up bodily and threw him through the bushes. His world lit up like a supernova and before he could come to a rolling stop he started to scurry madly along on his belly, knowing that there was more to come. One after another, deafening blasts whipped at him as he thrashed his way through the dense undergrowth, the shock waves slamming into him like hurricane-driven concrete blocks. Something struck him in the back, burning like crazy, but he fought his way onwards. A huge ball of fire ignited the foliage around him. The heat was intense. Yet he knew it was time to get to his feet — if he still had them.

Stratton pulled his legs beneath him and, keeping low, thrust forward like a sprinter. He punched through a thicket, clawing at the ground in desperation as he went. Another series of explosions went off like a firework display, projectiles whistling through the air in every direction. As he burst from the bushes he rolled down an incline that took him out of the direct line of fire and when he came to a stop he curled into a tight ball to weather whatever else was to come.

Stratton lay there, breathing heavily, wondering if he was going to live or die. Being conscious right now was not necessarily proof that he would survive. The explosions continued. He could feel the heat from the blazing wood but the blasts were no longer coming directly at him so he uncurled to take a look.

His clothes were smouldering but his limbs appeared to be intact. He had all his fingers although they were lacerated. He felt his head and face, his nose and ears and teeth. They were where they should have been as far as he could tell. He felt his stomach and his sides and when he looked at his hands again they were wet with fresh blood from somewhere.

The shock wave from yet another ground-shaking explosion tore through the foliage and shot over him. Debris rained down everywhere. Something heavy, a piece of a pallet, hit the ground close by. He felt a sharp pain shooting through his back near his shoulder blades and he reached around to feel something sticking from his flesh.

Stratton ignored it and forced himself onto his knees as he wondered what had happened to the others. There were shouts coming from the sentry post and men were running in every direction. He staggered a little as he got to his feet and headed back towards the burning wood. A fresh blast sent him to the ground once again and he wondered how many more explosives were left. The wood, what was left of it, continued to burn. Smoke was everywhere, making his throat and eyes as sore as hell.

Through it he saw a man kneeling and made his way towards him. Another man lay on his back beside him. Both had blackened skin and at first glance were unrecognisable.

'You okay?' Stratton shouted.

The kneeling man looked at him, breathing heavily, the whites of his eyes stark in his blackened face, his hair mostly burned away, blood streaming from his nose and a cut on his face. It was David. The other man too was obviously in a lot of pain, cradling his arm.

'Have you seen the others?' Stratton shouted, realising that his ears were ringing.

David was in a state of shock but managed to understand enough to shake his head.

There was a chance that the rest of them could be alive. Every second counted. A series of bangs went off, sounding like small-arms ammunition exploding. Stratton ignored them and headed back to the edge of the wood, pausing to look around. There was no sign of life and he pushed his way back in through the burned branches. He had not gone far before he saw something moving in the ash. The man lay on his side, shaking involuntarily, and Stratton carefully turned him over onto his back. He could not tell who it was. 'You're going to be okay,' he said as he quickly checked him for any obviously serious wounds such as wholly or partially severed limbs. The man looked badly burned — his clothing was stuck to his flesh in places. Stratton knew from experience that the greatest threat to life from burns came after the immediate trauma, with dehydration and infection. But at that moment the most important thing was to get the man out of any further danger.

Stratton shouted for assistance and several men came towards him to help. He continued on into the wood despite the flames that now played around him. The smoke slowed him down and he was forced to squat low to the ground in order to search for the missing men. He saw another one lying still up ahead, a flaming branch across his body. Stratton hurried to him on his hands and knees, coughing violently as the acrid smoke filled his lungs. He yanked the branch away, burning his hands, grabbed the man under his arms and began to drag him back. But the lack of oxygen was taking its toll and he began to feel dizzy. He made one last effort, inhaling the hot ash-filled air, and as his lungs convulsed again he pulled the body backwards for several metres. As he dropped to the ground hands grabbed him and Stratton let them haul him away, unable to help any more.

Stratton felt himself being placed on the ground. Although he was now in clean air, all he could do was cough and hack harshly. As the spasm passed he rolled onto his front, panting heavily, black saliva drooling from his mouth. He opened his watering eyes to see the charred figure of a man lying beside him. The man's face was unrecognisable and he lay motionless, his mouth wide open.

A voice cut through the noise of the growing crowd, shouting for people to get back and out of the way. Victor arrived and surveyed the carnage.

He went to the surviving men, talking to them briefly, assessing their injuries. Another body was carried out of the wood and placed on the ground. Victor stood over the survivors, horrified at their condition.

He came across to Stratton and squatted down beside him. 'Are you okay?' he asked.

Stratton pushed himself up onto his knees. 'I can manage,' he croaked.

'Lie back down,' Victor ordered.

Stratton knew that the man was right but he needed to prove to himself that he was going to live and to do that he had to get to his feet. He struggled to stand upright but then the light faded and he fell back to the ground, unconscious.

4

Stratton opened his eyes, feeling drowsy and disorientated. His mouth and throat were so sore and dry that he could not even swallow. After finally managing to focus on the straw ceiling he turned his head on the pillow to see his backpack beside the bed. He realised that he was on the mezzanine floor of Victor's cabin.

He was stiff from head to toe. As he made an effort to roll onto his back a violent pain shot through his shoulder blade. He lay still, taking short sharp breaths to ease the stinging, trying to take everything in. But his thirst was unbearable and another look around revealed a jug beside the bed.

As he stretched an arm towards it he heard footsteps on the stairs. Victor came into view, smiling unconvincingly. 'How are you feeling?' he asked.

Because of the constriction in his throat Stratton was unable to answer him. He grappled for the sheet, pulled it away and, mustering all his strength, rolled onto his side, ignoring the pain. As he fought to sit up and lower his feet to the floor Victor helped, knowing it was pointless to try and stop him.

'Why are you always wanting to sit up when you should be lying down?' Victor asked.

The movement had been painful and Stratton lowered his head to ease the dizziness. He focused on his bare feet and arms. Most of the ash and smoke-soot had been washed off but his skin was still dirty. He realised suddenly that he was wearing only his shorts.

'You'll probably fall back down again in a minute.'

Stratton wanted to say something but the sides of his mouth and throat felt as if they were stuck together. He mimicked drinking from a cup.

'Yes, of course,' Victor said, reaching for a mug that was beside the jug and handing it to Stratton. 'Drink slowly,' he advised.

Stratton tipped enough water between his lips to wet his tongue and repeated the process until the vital liquid was flowing down his throat. He tried to say something but his larynx was still too dry so he filled his mouth with water and tilted his head back before swallowing.

'How are the others?' he rasped, his voice barely audible.

But Victor understood him. 'Miguel is dead. So is Umberto. Eduardo is badly burned. The doctor gives him a fifty per cent chance of survival. Carlos is not quite as bad. He has a broken arm but the doctor thinks he will be okay. David will be fine, as will you be. The doctor removed a piece of metal from your back. He said it did not penetrate your lung cavity.'

Stratton thought about the information, saddened by the loss of the men even though he had not known them. He emptied the mug of water into his mouth and handed it to Victor to refill.

Victor obliged. 'Do you know what happened?' he asked.

'Have you asked David?'

'Not yet. I wanted to hear it from you first.'

Stratton cleared his throat. He was starting to feel better now that he could swallow again. 'It was a booby trap.'

Victor's mind raced. 'You're sure?'

'A hand grenade, set to go off when the box was opened.'

Victor looked disturbed. 'We've never had sabotage before, not like this.'

'Where're my clothes?'

Victor indicated a pile of fatigues on the other side of the room. They looked like those worn by the rebels. 'Yours were too badly burned,' he said, pointing to a charred pile of material on the floor. 'Your carbine is under the bed, along with your pistol. I don't think the carbine will work any more, either.'

Stratton leaned down, pain stabbing his back, and pulled the guns out from under the bed. The M4 was a mess, its plastic stock and butt brittle and broken in places. The magazine was gone and when he tried to pull back the breech it didn't budge. He dropped it to the floor and checked the semi-automatic pistol. The grip was a little charred but the magazine slid out easily enough and, yanking back the top slide, he found that the mechanism was working smoothly when a round flew out of the chamber. He put the pistol on the bed to deal with later.

Stratton got unsteadily to his feet. 'Well,' he

143

said, stretching his back and ignoring the pain. 'I don't think I can take any more of your hospitality.' He went to the pile of fatigues and looked for a pair of trousers and a shirt that might fit.

'I understand, of course,' Victor said, noticing that the dressing on Stratton's back was bloody. 'We'll need to change your bandage before you put your shirt on.'

Stratton pulled on a pair of trousers that were long enough in the leg but big around the waist. 'My boots?' he asked, looking around.

'Yours are no good. Try those,' Victor said, pointing to an open box filled with jungle boots of various sizes.

Stratton went to the box and rummaged through it, checking the sizes, pulling out a boot attached to another by its laces. He noticed that his wristwatch was broken. 'I don't suppose you have a box of watches around here too?'

'I'll see what I can do. They're not a common resupply item.'

'What is the time?'

'Almost six p.m . . . It happened yesterday,' Victor informed him.

Stratton looked at him quizzically.

'The doctor put something in your drip to keep you asleep.'

Stratton checked his forearms to find the tell-tale puncture made by a drip-feed needle.

The Frenchman went back to the top of the stairs. 'I must go. I'll be back later.'

'Victor?'

Victor paused to look back at Stratton.

'Can you get me to the border? I want to go home to heal.'

'Oh.' Victor looked disappointed.

'What?'

'I thought you would want to find out who did this to you.'

'No. I just want to go home.'

Victor nodded. 'I'll arrange something for you,' he said, starting back down the stairs.

'Why are you trying to make me feel bad about going? This isn't my fight.'

'It's a struggle between good and evil. I thought that was everybody's fight.'

'It's not the only one out there.'

Victor nodded. 'True enough.' He continued down the steps and out of the cabin.

*   *   *

Stratton sat heavily back down on the bed and lowered himself onto his side. He lay there for some time, fighting the urge to sleep. Fearing that he would lose the battle he sat up, got to his feet and collected together the various items of clothing he'd selected. As he finished threading the laces through the eyelets of the boots he heard the door of the cabin open and close and footsteps on the stairs.

'You're going to have to check every one of those boxes,' Stratton said. 'I'll show you a way of doing it safely before I go.'

When he looked up it was not Victor at the top of the stairs but Louisa. She looked different. The coldness in her eyes had gone. She was

145

staring at him in silence as if unsure what to say or do.

Unable to think of anything either, Stratton picked the shirt off the bed to put it on.

'Don't do that,' Louisa said, walking over to him. 'Victor said your bandage needed changing.' She was holding a couple of packets of medical lint, a roll of surgical tape and a pair of scissors.

He put the shirt down and held out his hand for them.

'You're a talented man but I doubt even you could change that dressing on your back by yourself.' She walked around the other side of his bed. 'You were right, what you said earlier. I'm not a whole lot of use here really. But I have learned how to change a dressing. I spend a few hours most days helping out in the clinic. It also allows me some interaction with the people. Sit down, would you, please.'

Louisa's voice was gentle and sincere. Stratton found it disarming. He sat down and she knelt on the bed behind him, gently placing a hand on his arm to steady herself. Her touch was soft and he had no control over the sudden rush it gave him. The contact weakened him but in the most pleasurable way. Her proximity, the brush of her shirt against him, her breath, they were all sensual to him. He tried to block the feelings, fighting them, but it was like refusing water while dying of thirst. She placed her hands on his shoulders and he quivered.

'I'm sorry. My hands can be cold even in this part of the world.'

146

'It's okay,' Stratton said, clearing his throat. 'Go ahead.'

Louisa picked gently at the corner of the bandage and started to pull it away from his skin. The wound began to throb but he welcomed the pain as an aid to neutralising the other feelings.

Her hands began to tremble and she paused. 'I'm sorry. I don't do blood very well.'

'You're not hurting me,' he lied.

As she peeled the rest of the dressing away a trickle of blood rolled down Stratton's back. She deftly stopped its progress with a piece of lint and cleaned the rest from his back. 'Our medic stitched it very well,' she said. 'You'll have a scar to match the others. I thought you would have more.'

'And you were being so nice.'

'I can't seem to help it with you, can I?'

He could sense she was smiling.

'I don't mean it any more, though,' Louisa continued, her voice soft and sincere. 'You risked your life to save people you didn't even know, people I thought you couldn't care less about. I knew Miguel. His wife just had a child. A little boy. I helped deliver him . . . I went to see her last night. He's the first person I've ever known who's died. I mean, someone who I've talked to and laughed with. I keep seeing his face. I haven't been here long enough to have experienced that before. I thought I would be tougher. Will I get tougher, do you think?'

'No. You'll build walls around yourself. You'll

make yourself harder to get to, but you won't get any tougher.'

Louisa felt unable to respond in case she began to cry, which she did not want to do. But she lost control and a tear escaped to roll down her cheek and drop onto his back. 'I'm crying on you.'

'Don't wipe it off,' Stratton said in a low voice. He immediately regretted how the comment had laid him open.

She looked at the back of his head through tear-filled eyes. 'I don't know you at all.'

'Yes, you do. Take away all those things you thought about me and have a look at what's left.'

Louisa smiled at the thought. 'I don't know what I'm looking for,' she replied. Without being conscious of the effect she was having she gently pushed her fingers into his hair to remove a piece of ash.

Stratton closed his eyes as he felt her fingers on his scalp.

She suddenly realised what she was doing and took her hand away in order to finish tending the wound, placing a fresh piece of lint over it and taping it securely.

'There,' she said. She picked up his shirt and held it up behind him. 'Your shirt.'

He snapped out of his reverie and pushed his arms into the sleeves. She moved closer to wrap the garment around his chest for him to button it up, keeping her arms there for a second too long. He touched her hand as if by accident while he buttoned his shirt.

Then, as if realising that she had gone too far,

148

Louisa pulled back and climbed off the bed. A confused stream of emotions ran through her.

Stratton could sense her retreat and he did not look at her.

'I'll leave you those,' she said, putting down the remaining lint and tape.

He got to his feet to tuck in his shirt as she headed for the stairs.

'Are you hungry?' Louisa asked, pausing at the rail.

'I am, actually.'

'My father asked if you would like to come to supper, if you were feeling well enough.'

Despite his hunger her presence was the only reason he would go and Stratton thought that perhaps it was not such a good idea. 'Thanks, but I'll find something here. Maybe you could tell him I'm still resting.'

Louisa seemed to accept his answer and was about to walk down the steps when she paused, wrestling with a thought. 'I'd like it very much if you did come. I'd like you to leave with a better impression, of all of us. Victor will be there.'

Her words were enough to persuade him. 'How can I say no?'

'See you in a while, then.' She continued down the stairs and Stratton sat back on the bed as the door of the cabin closed. He wondered what had just happened. It was as if they had skipped an entire chapter in their lives. But wars had that effect on people. It made them less diffident. There wasn't the time to be otherwise.

Weariness took hold of him and he lay down on his side and brought his feet up onto the bed.

This time he did not try to stop the wave of sleep from enveloping him.

★   ★   ★

It was dark by the time Stratton walked along the path towards Sebastian's cabin. The stars were unable to penetrate the heavy clouds that hung low in the sky, threatening rain. A group of rebels on guard duty clustered around the defensive position on the other side of the courtyard, sharing cigarettes and conversation.

Stratton stopped at the door of Sebastian's cabin. The anticipation of seeing Louisa grew and he shook his head at the strangeness of the situation. He had never experienced feelings quite like this. How ridiculous, he thought. There he was on the other side of the world, in a country that he would be leaving in a few hours, never to return — and he goes and meets Louisa.

He knocked on the door. A moment later it opened and she stood in front of him, looking as if she knew now that there was a secret between them.

'I thought you were standing us up,' she said.

Stratton walked in, feeling self-conscious. Victor and Sebastian sat at the table. They had already eaten. 'I'm sorry. I fell asleep and . . . I don't have a watch,' he explained.

'The transformation is complete,' Victor announced. 'He wakes up a new man, with a new wardrobe and a new reputation.'

'Please. Come in,' Sebastian said, gesturing for

Stratton to take a seat.

Victor reached into his pocket and pulled out a small box. 'Before I forget, this is for you.'

Stratton opened it to reveal a wristwatch.

'It's my spare,' Victor said. 'The one I'm wearing will go on for ever, anyway.'

Stratton accepted it. 'Thank you,' he said, removing it from the box and putting it on.

'How are you feeling?' Sebastian asked.

'Better than I should,' he said. 'I'm sorry about the others.'

The old man nodded and they all observed a solemn and quiet moment. Victor broke the silence by reaching for a jug of wine and filling the glass in front of Stratton. 'There. That's the best medicine you can have now. It must be good for you. It tastes so goddamned awful.'

Louisa brought a plate of food to Stratton who felt suddenly famished and dug into it.

'Tell me. Are you from generations of British folk?' Sebastian asked.

'I've never traced my family tree. But I remember my father seemed to think that we had ancestors who fought at Waterloo.'

'Which side?' Victor asked.

'The winning one . . . sorry, Victor.'

'No need to apologise. I wasn't there.'

'I don't suppose you know if any of them fought in the Spanish Civil War?' Sebastian asked.

Stratton gave Louisa a surreptitious look and caught a hint of a smile on her lips. 'Not that I know of, sir,' he replied.

'The British were a great help to my

grandfather during the Spanish Civil War. Do you know much of the fight against the fascist, Franco?'

'Not much,' Stratton said, wanting to carry on eating but feeling that he should be polite.

'You should read about that war. You would find it interesting. Almost two and a half thousand of your countrymen volunteered to fight in it. Men and women. All ordinary working-class people. Almost five hundred of them were Jewish. That was before the Second World War had even begun, remember.'

Victor could not ignore the way Louisa was looking at Stratton. He detected a new connection between them. There was certainly none of the conflict that had existed before.

A large painting on the wall caught Stratton's attention. It was a battle scene, a panorama of explosions and of men on horseback.

'It's from one of the battles of the Jarama Valley,' Louisa said as if reading his thoughts.

Stratton shook his head, none the wiser.

'The painting belonged to my father,' Sebastian said. 'He was there . . . not fighting, of course. He was only six years old. Some say it was the last great cavalry charge in Western Europe. You see the white horse in the centre?'

Stratton nodded as he studied the painting more closely. The horsemen were led by a man on a powerful white horse, all charging towards a river with defensive positions beyond.

'That was his father. My grandfather. Louisa's great-grandfather. My father watched him die that day. He led five hundred horsemen. Flesh and blood charging tanks and machine guns. It was described as a foolish act by many. They rode without the support of artillery. Sixty per cent of them were cut down before they were even halfway to their objective. My grandfather was not one of the first to die even though he was at the head of the charge. All those around him were killed or wounded but he rode on alone, regardless. Who knows why? Perhaps it was the madness of battle. I like to think it was an act of defiance, a message to the Nationalists. He wanted them to know they would not take the valley while men like him still held it. He was right in that, at least. The Republicans had lost many battles in that war but they denied Franco the valley and, in so doing, Madrid too. We lost the war but not our pride.'

There was silence while everyone saw obvious parallels between that war and this.

Sebastian got to his feet. 'I have work to do so I'm going to bid you all goodnight,' he said.

'Goodnight,' Stratton said, getting to his feet and offering his hand.

Sebastian took it as a final goodbye and smiled. 'I hope to see you again,' he said. He shook hands with Stratton and left.

Silence hung in the air only to be broken by the sound of a sudden downpour outside.

'This chicken is very good,' Stratton said as he sat back down.

'I thought it was rabbit,' Victor said.

'It's guinea fowl,' Louisa stated.

Victor raised his hands in disgust at his lost

ability to recognise a taste. 'I am no longer French.' He took a cigar from his pocket and lit it, blowing the smoke at the ceiling. 'Marlo has left us,' he said matter-of-factly.

Louisa saw the implications of the news immediately. 'Are you sure?' she asked.

'With his two lieutenants, Carlo and Fernandez.'

'When?'

'Yesterday. After the explosions,' Victor said.

'Why?'

Victor shrugged. 'He does not confide in me.'

'But you must have your suspicions.'

'Marlo is the kind of man who would jump from a ship if it was taking water before going below to see if he could fix it.'

'Do you think he had anything to do with the booby trap?' Louisa asked.

Victor shrugged again as he drew on his cigar. 'My gut reaction is no. Marlo was never really one of us but I don't think he would do anything like that.'

'Where would they go?' Louisa asked.

'Perhaps they are waiting to see what happens.'

'I didn't trust him anyway.'

'That's not the point,' Victor said. 'He was respected by many of the men as a good field officer. It will affect morale. Many have had cause to lose confidence these past few days.'

'Have you told Sebastian?' Louisa asked as she removed some plates from the table and took them into the kitchen.

'I was going to tell him tonight. I'll leave it

until tomorrow. It doesn't make much difference. We are set on our course. People will either come with us or get off the bus.'

There was a loud knock on the door.

'I'll go,' Victor said, getting to his feet.

As soon as he opened the door a jovial voice boomed 'Victor!'

Victor was mildly shocked. 'Colonel Steel.' He stepped back to let the man in. 'This is a surprise.'

'Good to see you again. How've you been?' Steel asked as he walked in, his hat and poncho dripping all over the floor. He was a big man and looked even larger in his cloak and headgear. He removed his hat to reveal his thick head of white hair. 'Louisa!' he cried, grinning broadly as if he was a much-missed uncle. He reached for her hand, pulled her towards him and gave her a kiss on each cheek.

Louisa smiled politely while trying to disguise her discomfort. 'This is indeed a pleasant surprise.'

'You look even more beautiful, if that's possible.' When he saw Stratton, Steel did not look remotely surprised at the operative's presence. 'You still here, Stratton? I thought you'd be on your way back to good old Blighty by now.'

Stratton forced a smile of his own.

'Well, this is all nice and cosy. Do you mind if I join you?' Steel asked, tossing his hat on a chair by the door.

'You know you're always welcome,' Louisa said.

'And I come bearing gifts, as usual, but this time of the edible kind.' Steel dumped his poncho on the chair too. A leather bag hung around his shoulder. He opened it and took out a bottle of red wine which he handed to Victor and a brown paper package that he gave to Louisa. 'Cheese,' he said. 'I don't know what kind but they served it after dinner last night in the city and I had to bring some for you because it tasted so good.'

Victor inspected the wine label and, none the wiser, set about opening it.

'Christ, it's raining buckets out there,' Steel declared, vigorously warming his hands at the fire. 'I tell ya, I've been in some deluges before but I swear this country takes some beatin' when it comes to surprise cloudbursts. Where's the old man?'

'He's retired for the evening.'

'Retired? Well, get 'im up. Steel's here. And if that's not a good enough reason tell 'im we got things to talk about that can't wait till morning.' Steel had a huge grin across his wide face as he sat down. 'Mind if I help myself?' he asked, looking at the food. 'Been a long road,' he said, reaching for a hunk of bread and some meat and filling a glass from the wine jug. 'I got a ride along that highway a dozen klicks east of here. Then I got myself a mule the rest of the way. I hate walkin' if I don't have to and I haven't had to in a while,' he said, laughing as he filled his mouth. 'Excuse my appetite but I haven't had a good meal all day.'

Victor found the wine palatable. 'The

156

government troops patrol that road,' he said.

'Sure do. Not as well as they should, though.'

'What do you tell them when they stop you?'

'Hell, I'm an American tourist.' Steel laughed. Then his face took on a slightly more serious expression. 'They know who I am, Victor. You think I don't talk to them too? Just remember, it's you people I'm behind.'

He looked around the room, stopping at the painting of the Jarama Valley battle. 'Sebastian tell you about his grandpappy?' he asked Stratton.

'A little.'

'Did he tell you that's somethin' we have in common? In the Spanish Civil War my grandpa was a member of an American volunteer force, the Abraham Lincoln Bridgade — fought alongside Sebastian's grandpa. Hell, we got our asses well and truly handed to us at that party. Lost more'n half our men. My father told me something my grandpa once said about the Jarama Valley scrap. When it was over, those who survived said they figured out why their brigade was named after Abraham Lincoln. Because he got assassinated too.' Steel burst out laughing.

Stratton tried to smile politely. But there was something about Steel that he just did not like and the more the man talked, the stronger his hostile feelings became. He could not believe Steel was so thick-skinned that he did not know when people were uncomfortable around him.

'So. How they been treatin' you?' Steel glanced only briefly at Stratton as he asked him the question. 'How's the training comin' along? I thought you'd be done and gone two days ago.'

'Stratton's lucky to be alive,' Victor said.

'Come again?' Steel asked. He looked worried but there was no way of knowing if his expression was genuine.

'A box of your weapons was booby-trapped. Two of my men are dead, one may not make it and another is seriously hurt.'

'I don't believe it!' Steel exclaimed. 'When'd this happen?'

'Yesterday,' Victor said.

'Holy cow. You okay?' Steel asked Stratton, scrutinising him in case he had missed any obvious physical injury.

'I'll be fine.'

'You said booby-trapped. How?'

'Classic grenade set-up,' Stratton explained.

'You're shittin' me. Do we know who did it?'

Victor shook his head.

'Did we lose everything?'

'We still have sixty per cent of what you sent us.'

'Wow,' Steel muttered, getting up to take a turn around the room and looking as if the news had sickened him.

Stratton watched him, wondering if any of his reactions were genuine. He looked like a ham actor who was doing an unusually fine job. It was hard to tell since he did not know Steel well enough. But the display of concern seemed out of character.

The door at the end of the room opened and Sebastian stepped through, together with Louisa.

'Colonel Steel,' Sebastian said. 'Good to see you again.'

Steel turned on the charm. 'Sebastian.' He walked over and gave the rebel leader a bear hug. 'It's good to see you too. You're looking great. Hey, I just heard about the explosion yesterday. That's crazy. We've never had anything like that before. Are we looking at government infiltration or something else?'

Sebastian turned away and sat in his chair. 'Sit. Please.'

Steel sat opposite him.

'It was probably inevitable that something like this would happen,' Sebastian said. 'I'm surprised it did not happen sooner — '

'Wait a minute,' Steel interrupted. 'Sebastian. Excuse me, but I need to be clear on one thing first. Was this internal politics or not?'

'I don't know. It's possible.'

'Hector?'

'I would not point a finger at anyone right now,' Sebastian said.

Steel sat back and stared thoughtfully at the older man, his thoughts appearing to run in several directions. 'I wanna summarise where we are right now. Do you mind? I need to get my bearings back about all this. You've got problems. That means the rebellion's got problems. There's a power struggle going on. It looks to me as if you're being isolated. Would you say that was fair?'

'I would not argue with that assessment. But it lacks depth.'

'I know. Sorry. I'm just trying to synopsise it.

Before we can come up with a strategy we have to be sure of the ground and the threat. Look, I'll be honest. I knew a lot about these issues before I got here. It's part of the reason I'm here. I didn't know about the attack, though, the booby trap. But it falls in with the symptoms.'

The others were all watching Steel without interrupting him. He was an assertive, overpowering individual, but it wasn't just that. Any implied or open criticism of what he had to say would simply provoke a diatribe in which he would insist that his personal support and that of his country was the key to the rebellion's success and that therefore whatever he said was gospel. To be spared that tedious rhetoric people tended not to question him. Yet there was no denying that he did provide substantial aid and political leverage and so he could not be ignored. An air of suspicion hung about him like a mist, nonetheless.

'Can I throw a theory out there?' Steel asked.

Sebastian gestured to him to go ahead.

'Okay. This is classic. You know it, I'm sure. It's how I see it, anyway. You have five powers, all supposedly equal, your five brigades. They remain even, more or less, because of that balance, that equality. So how do you get rid of one of them, for whatever reason? Say you don't like a particular commander any more. Doesn't matter why. He doesn't like you, you disagree on policy — whatever. This strategy goes back to the Wars of the Roses and beyond. How do you get rid of him without the others punishing you for stepping out of line? The answer's simple. You need them on your side against him. To achieve that you get them to fear him. One way to do that is to make him stronger than you and the others. It's difficult for him to resist as well. I mean, everyone wants to be top dog. But it upsets the balance. And what happens? The others turn on him. They band together in order to be able to destroy the one who's become the strongest. And the one secretly manipulating everything, well, he gets what he wants, which is to get rid of him. I think that's what's happening here. Someone made you a threat to the others. And now they are banding together to bring you down.'

'Hector?' Victor muttered.

'If the cap fits,' Steel said, sitting back and looking pleased with himself.

Sebastian, Louisa and Stratton sat silently watching Steel.

'Look, it's just a theory,' Steel said, taking a bite of food. 'I'm full of 'em.'

'I take it you have solutions for your theories?' Louisa asked.

'Yeah, I got solutions. But usually the more difficult the situation the more difficult the solution.'

A quiet descended on the room.

Steel interpreted it as despondency. 'Hey, don't let it get you down, guys. My money's on you. Has been since day one and I'm not about to change. None of those other commanders can pull this rebellion off. That includes Hector.'

Sebastian's curiosity was piqued. 'How would you disrupt this plan to isolate me?'

161

'Well, I personally believe the concept of five equal brigades was flawed anyway,' Steel said, getting into it. 'I'm a soldier and, as you know, direct. They're not equal. Honeros has half the men Hector does. I don't trust Bajero. Sandina, well, he'll go along with whoever has the loudest voice. My point is that there needs to be a stronger brigade for the others to follow and look up to. Don't forget, it's the voices of the men in those other brigades that rule, not the brigade commanders. So if they want to isolate you, let 'em. But take advantage of the moment and let's go do something big. Shit, you got the weapons. You're halfway there. Your toys are bigger'n theirs. Use 'em.'

'You're talking about an independent attack?' Victor asked.

'Course I'm talking about an independent attack. It's not the first time you've carried out your own ops, is it?'

'No, but we always consult with each other.'

'Then this time you don't tell 'em until it's over. Upset the apple cart. Send a message to Hector. Wreck his little parley with Neravista. Remind them all who you are. The voices in the brigades will speak and their leaders'll have no choice but to join you.'

No one said anything, until Sebastian asked, 'You have something in mind?'

'I sure do.'

'Something you already had in mind before you came here?' Sebastian added.

'Yep. Look, Sebastian. I came here to tell you it's time to turn up the volume. This rebellion has gone stagnant. It's dragging its feet. I'll be blunt. You got to get this horsey moving along or else. My people need to know you're the one to back. They want to see some returns on their investment.'

'Or you'll invest elsewhere.'

'This is a high-stakes game, Sebastian. Frankly, my administration is losing confidence in you. Our next presidential campaign starts in a few months. We've got a lotta open boxes lying around the Oval Office. We need to close some of 'em up and put 'em away. This is one of 'em. And it ain't just us. Your neighbours are also getting tired of it. They want to see some stability or at least the possibility of it — and soon. If you can't offer it they'll look to someone who can. It's that time.'

'You mean they'll look to Hector?' Victor asked.

'No way,' Steel said in a tone that suggested the scientist was completely on the wrong track. 'Neravista.'

Louisa and Victor looked concerned.

'What did you think, guys?' Steel asked as if they were all naive. 'That this could go on for ever? That's Neravista's strategy. He knows all he has to do is drag this out, make you guys look like a bunch of terrorists screwing up the country and your supporters will eventually move on. You won't last long without them. You'll never win, that's for sure. It's time to make a noise. A big one. Tell everyone you're here and you intend to win.'

Sebastian looked lost in thought but it was

163

obvious that Steel was getting through to him. Victor and Louisa watched him, also inclining in favour of the American despite their personal doubts about the man. He was making sense.

'What did you have in mind?' Sebastian asked eventually.

Like a storyteller, Steel held them in suspense while he gathered his thoughts. 'How would you like to take out Neravista's brother, Chemora? He's head of the special police, right? Chemora has the blood of thousands of your countrymen, including women and children, on his hands. Everyone knows he's a lowlife. No one will miss him . . . except Neravista, of course. What could be better?'

Victor watched Sebastian, who had not reacted. 'He never leaves the capital,' he said. 'The city falls under Hector's brigade, anyway. We have logistical difficulties in mounting operations in large urban areas.'

'What if he was planning a trip into the countryside in a couple of days? What if you knew his destination and precisely where you could hit him? Would you be interested?'

Sebastian took his time answering. Victor had a drink and lit up another cigar. The storm was getting worse outside and a gust blew open a window and almost extinguished the hurricane lamps, plunging the room into near-darkness. Louisa closed the window and the lamps flickered back to life.

'Yes,' Sebastian said finally.

Steel smiled. 'Give me some room here,' he said.

164

With help from Louisa and Victor they cleared much of the table. Steel opened his bag, took out several maps as well as a collection of satellite photographs and brought a lamp closer to illuminate it all. 'What I'm about to tell you doesn't leave this room,' he said sombrely.

Stratton remained where he was. He wondered why Steel had made him a part of this secret meeting but reckoned there was good reason. He would no doubt learn soon enough what that reason was.

'Now . . . here's your camp here. The army is planning an operation in this western region here. What's that, fifty, fifty-five kilometres?' Steel said, moving his finger across the map. 'They know the area is vital for food to your brigades. They're gonna cleanse it, of food as well as people. That means rounding up hundreds of farmers, villagers — anyone who they suspect of supplying the rebels with food — destroying farms, crops, livestock, you name it. He's gonna switch off that area.

'Chemora plans to set up an interrogation centre somewhere here. Now you guys know his MO better than I do. First he likes to go out and collect a couple dozen people of any age and gender and hang 'em by their necks along the route to the interrogation centre. It's what the sick bastard calls psychological softening. By the time his victims have walked the line of dead men, women and children they're about ready to spill the beans on anybody.'

Louisa was disgusted at the very thought of it.

165

Steel produced the satellite photographs. 'I asked my people to shoot these a couple days ago.'

Sebastian leaned forward to take a closer look at them. Victor moved to where he could see the photos better. Louisa preferred to watch from where she was at the end of the table. Stratton watched Steel.

'The army has already established base camps here, here and here,' Steel continued. 'They're setting up a cordon around Chemora's interrogation centre which we believe will be in these huts and tents here. As far as Chemora is concerned he's heading into a secure zone. You guys don't normally operate this far west. There are a couple of choice locations to ambush him. My favourite is this bridge here. You take out Chemora, you not only score a major point in this rebellion by getting rid of one of the most evil bastards in it, you save the lives of hundreds of your people. Neravista will have to postpone the operation without his brother, or even cancel it.'

'There will be reprisals,' Victor said.

'You get into a fight, you don't hold off striking your opponent for fear of getting struck back. That's why you're there. Move the people out of that area after you've hit it,' Steel suggested, standing upright and putting his hands on his substantial hips. 'If that don't earn you the respect of the other brigades I'll eat this map.'

Sebastian got to his feet and walked slowly around the table, sunk in thought. 'An ambush

166

like that would require a lot of people,' he mused.

'Not at all. You have claymore mines and rockets. You could do this with a handful of men.'

'What about the ordnance? The rest of it could be booby-trapped too,' Victor said.

'What do you reckon?' Steel asked Stratton who was sitting quietly. 'You said it was a grenade. Someone had to put their hand in to pull out the pin and close the lid. All you need to do is the reverse.'

'Jesus,' Victor exclaimed softly at the thought. 'But even if we were to learn how to blow up that bridge, could we do it?'

The smell of the lure that Steel was using to entice the rebels was beginning to stifle Stratton.

'Nope. But *he* can. There's your man right there,' Steel said. 'Stratton'll do it for you. Won't you, boy? You'll help out.'

Steel and Stratton locked stares.

'When I heard you were still here I put in a call to your boss. I was curious to know whether you were up to a little action or not. Was I surprised when I took a look at your résumé! You people've got a regular action superstar here. Stratton's quite the one-man army.'

Stratton could see more complications with the operation than anyone else in the room. Steel was probably aware of some, but he was not the type to give a damn anyway. He was too independent for Stratton's liking. The main issue for Stratton was his status as a British military operative. He had been permitted to deliver

167

weapons to the rebels and to teach them how to use them. If anything went wrong within those parameters — if, say, he was to be captured while entering or leaving the country, even if his mandate was exposed — the diplomatic hurdles that he and his employers would have to jump over would be manageable. It would be no worse than being caught selling arms to the enemy of another country, something that might not be welcome to the politicians but would be within the bounds of diplomatic acceptability. However, for Stratton to become physically involved in a conflict, to provide military expertise in order for one side in what was essentially a civil war to achieve a notable success, was definitely *not* acceptable. Stratton would be screwed if he got caught. If the Neravistas wanted to hang him the British government wouldn't be able to do much about it. Steel had to know that much and the fact that he had not first discussed it in private with Stratton and then made it clear to everyone else who was involved made him even more of a louse.

Steel waited for an answer.

Stratton got to his feet. The cold expression on his face said enough. 'Thanks for supper,' he said to the others as he strode to the door and walked out into the rain.

Steel watched the door close behind him. 'I didn't have Stratton pegged as a prima donna,' he said.

'Isn't that unfair?' Louisa said. 'It sounds like a dangerous operation.'

'Oh, Stratton ain't afraid of any operation. Not

168

that guy. This is a walk in the park for someone like him. It's me that he has a problem with. He's got his feathers ruffled. I wasn't exactly cordial to him when we first met. I was busy, had a lot on my mind. Truth is I didn't know a whole lot about him then. Let him cool off. He'll come around.'

'He's leaving in the morning,' Victor said.

Steel collected his maps and photographs and put them back into his bag. 'Let's wait and see.'

'If he won't do it, is there any other way we can?' Victor asked.

'Let's talk about that later,' the American said. He picked up his poncho and hat and left the cabin.

Sebastian got to his feet.

'If we could, would we do it?' Victor asked him.

'Kill Chemora?' Sebastian said, his expression reflecting revulsion at the mention of the man's name. 'I'd drive a stake through his black heart as soon as look at him.' He headed for his room, pausing at the door to look back at Victor. 'What do you think of Stratton?'

'I think he is honourable.' Victor shrugged. 'But he has his own path. He said it isn't his fight.'

'It wasn't his booby trap either but he went back into the burning wood to get those men,' Louisa said.

'His mind rules his heart,' Victor said. 'He's brave, of course, but he would have calculated the odds on his survival before going into that fire.'

'I don't agree with you,' Louisa said.

Sebastian left them alone, closing the door to his room behind him.

'One day you're trying to kill Stratton and the next you look as if . . . well, you're different with him,' Victor said.

Louisa went back to clearing up the table. 'I was wrong about him, that's all.'

Victor went to the front door and looked back at her, a smirk on his face. 'I'm still French, you know.' He winked and walked outside.

★ ★ ★

Stratton sat stripping his pistol and placing the parts on the dining table. Water dripped from the roof of the cabin into several pans he had placed on the floor. The door opened, the draught almost blowing out the candles on the table as Steel hurried in to get out of the weather.

'Goddamned rain,' he cursed, shaking the water from his hands.

Stratton went back to his weapon.

Steel put down his bag and took off his coat, glancing all the time at Stratton as if trying to figure him out. 'You mind if I have some wine?' he asked, looking inside a jug on the table that was empty.

Stratton ignored him.

'Come on, Stratton, lighten up,' Steel said, going to the wine casks and filling up the jug. 'We got off on the wrong foot, that's all.' He brought the jug to the table and filled two mugs, holding one out to Stratton. 'We could be of help to each other. I've got a lot of connections in our business, on your side of the pond as well as mine.'

Stratton decided to humour the man and see how far he would go. He took the mug.

Steel smiled and tapped Stratton's mug with his own. 'To the revolution,' he said, taking a good swig.

Stratton took a sip.

'Sumners, your boss back in London — he's no big fan of yours, is he? He's never said as much but I can read between the lines. It's kind of why I was the way I was with you in the beginning. I got the impression he didn't rate you too highly. Let's face it, this job is way below your skills grade. What is it with you guys?'

'As you say, he doesn't like me.'

'Yeah, well, that's between you both, I guess. If you're wondering how he feels about you getting involved, I spoke to him last night, told him we were considering an op that might require your expertise. I asked if there were any issues. He had none.'

Stratton was not surprised. Sumners would love to hear that Stratton had been caught, or worse.

'You know,' Steel continued, 'if you plan this right it's a stand-off attack. You could trigger it and be miles away from there before anyone turned up to see what had happened. What do you say? Any comment at all?'

'No.'

'Are you at least thinking about it?'

Stratton said nothing.

171

'I need to know one way or the other. If you don't do it I walk out of here and, well, hell, this rebellion's over. They can't do this op, not without you. I know it's a heavy load I'm puttin' on you, I mean, you having to be the one who calls in the rebellion. But, well, that's the way it is sometimes. More often than not the biggest decisions in war come down to just one man. Kind of funny really. Neravista and those people in there think they control this war, when, right now, it's all down to just you and me.'

'What are you going to do when you leave this business, Steel? Sell second-hand cars?'

The Marine colonel found the comment amusing, but there was a darkness to his chortle. 'I like you, Stratton, you know that? You're a funny guy. Tell you what,' he said, finishing his drink and collecting up his stuff. 'I'll let you sleep on it. But come morning I want an answer, and no answer means no.'

As Steel stepped back out into the rain, Stratton put down his mug. It was possible that Sumners had given the man permission to make use of Stratton but he would bet everything he owned that the conversation had not been recorded. If Stratton was caught both men would deny having anything to do with him and his mission, he was sure of that. They would say that he had done it off his own bat. He had become involved.

Stratton began to clean the various parts of his pistol and put it back together.

5

Stratton got up as the sun's rays broke over the treetops and started packing his gear. His gut instinct was to get out of there as soon as he could but he had woken feeling all over the place. Steel's statement that the rebellion would falter without the attack had got to him, despite his efforts to dismiss it. He felt guilty, in spite of the clumsiness of the American's manipulation. Then there was Louisa. She was the least of the reasons he had to stay and should not have been one at all. But he could not deny that she had a greater influence on him than anything else. It was crazy. The sooner he got away from the camp the better.

Stratton picked up his pack and parachute, left his charred clothes and unusable M4 on the floor and walked down the stairs.

He dumped his kit on the table and decided to make himself a cup of coffee. While waiting for the water in the old percolator to boil he mulled over the ramifications of getting involved in the rebellion and London finding out. It soon became confusing and he wondered why he was even considering it.

The percolator bubbled and he turned off the heat, checked inside a mug for bugs and half filled it with the hot black liquid. The coffee was strong.

The front door opened and in walked David,

Victor and another young rebel soldier carrying two large plastic ammunition boxes between them. Panting with the effort they lowered the cases heavily to the floor, grabbing their aching arms after releasing their load.

'Whose idea was it not to rest until we reached the cabins?' Victor asked.

'Yours,' David replied, out of breath and inspecting his palms where the ammo-box handles had cut into them. David's hair was short all over to minimise any contrast with the patches that had been burned away. His face and arms were already beginning to peel.

Victor noticed Stratton's backpack. 'I see you're ready to go.'

'What are those?' Stratton asked, knowing the answer.

'One box of claymore mines, one box of rockets,' Victor replied curtly.

'Is that wise, bringing them into the house?'

'Is that fresh coffee?' the Frenchman asked, ignoring the question. He poured some into a mug and took a mouthful, savouring it. 'I was hoping you might show us how to operate them before you go.'

Stratton looked at him as if the man had lost the plot.

Victor unlatched one of the boxes, snatched it open, then shouted in a pantomime fashion, 'Oh my God! What have I done?'

Stratton watched him as if bored.

Victor burst into a cackling chuckle. 'I'm sorry. I could not resist. I checked them for grenades as Steel said. I opened the box just

174

enough to slide my hand in and felt around.'

'You did them all?'

'Are you crazy? Just these two. I'm not doing any more. I almost had a heart attack. I was up all night thinking about it. But I had to. You brought them all this way. You should at least finish what you came to do . . . This is Bernard, David's cousin.' Victor introduced the young man.

Bernard nodded a polite hello.

Stratton nodded back, remembering him from the ambush. He was the one whose cousin had been among the hanging victims.

'We'd like to know how you would use these to . . . well, to blow up a bridge.'

Stratton studied the man who was making a pathetically obvious job of baiting him. 'There's no way I can teach you how to blow up a bridge in a few hours and you know it.'

'We are not so stupid,' Victor insisted. 'Tell us how to prepare them, at least, and we will work out the rest.'

Stratton simply stared at him.

'Make a sketch. I can work from diagrams.'

'You don't know the specifications of the bridge.'

'Oh,' the scientist said, feigning deep thought. 'So, we would need an expert at the bridge to show us how to place the explosives once he had examined it?'

Stratton took a sip of his coffee.

'I'm not trying to talk you into doing anything, if that's what you think,' Victor insisted. 'No, no, no. You'll do whatever you feel you should, I

175

know that.' He faced David, hands on hips and wearing a serious, thoughtful expression. 'We need to find an expert.'

'Where do you think we can find one?' David asked, playing along pathetically.

'Oh, for God's sake,' Stratton interrupted. 'I can't do it and that's that.'

Victor looked into Stratton's eyes and finally believed the Englishman. 'You mean it, don't you?'

'Yes. I'm going home. I think I've come closer to dying more often here and in the shortest space of time than anywhere else I can remember and I'd be stupid to test my luck any further.'

Victor nodded and lowered his gaze to the floor. The fight seemed to go out of him as he wandered to the other side of the room, unsure what to do. When he turned around his face was determined. 'Fine. We'll do it without you. Just show us how to explode these damned things.'

'You can't,' Stratton said.

'Don't tell us we can't!' Victor shouted, his face turning bright red. 'Do you see any experts here in anything to do with war? David's a teacher! Bernard's a farmer! I'm a conservationist! Go out there and find me a born soldier and you'll be looking all day! You'll find a lot of shopkeepers, tailors and cooks! We've even got a university professor and a circus clown! Don't tell us we can't because we all wake up every morning and have to tell ourselves one more time that we can! If you want to preach to those who can't, go to our cemetery, it's filled with those who tried. Now. If it's not too much trouble, would you mind showing us how, please?'

He stood red-faced and shaking but his expression was resolute.

'You're serious, aren't you?'

'You're damned right I'm serious. We leave before midday. This is our fight and we're here to fight it. Just tell us how to explode these bombs, then you can go and get on with that other struggle against evil you were talking about. Ours is here.'

Stratton looked at them all. They were no longer playing. He sighed heavily. This was going to be hugely problematic. Poole suddenly seemed a long way away. 'Get me the maps and the satellite photos,' he said, finishing his coffee and putting the mug down.

'You don't need those to show us how to explode the bombs,' Victor said.

'Let's get one thing straight from the start,' Stratton said, his expression toughening. 'You never question me, or anything I tell you to do. And you do it immediately. Is that understood? Now get me what I just asked for.'

Victor was suddenly hopeful, his eyes lighting up. 'You're coming with us?'

'No. *You're* coming with *me*.'

The Frenchman's face broke into a broad smile. 'He's coming with us,' he said to the others. 'I mean, we're going with him. I'll be back in two seconds. Don't go anywhere,' he said to Stratton, hurrying to the door and leaving the cabin.

177

Stratton lifted one of the cloth claymore bags out of the box and checked the contents. Apart from the mine itself it contained the hand dynamo, cabling and a complete booby-trap system including trip-wire, plus pressure and release switches.

He had hoped that agreeing to do the task might settle his mind but it had not.

★ ★ ★

Hurrying to Sebastian's cabin Victor saw Louisa walking nearby and went towards her.

She looked up as he approached.

'You look lost,' he said.

'No. Not lost.' She sat on the edge of the long table, picking at the wood.

'You're waiting to say goodbye to Stratton.'

Her smile was genuine if a little sad. 'I know, the perceptive Frenchman in you.'

'Do you think you could prepare a horse for him? We will be leaving in a little while.'

Louisa nodded and got to her feet lethargically.

'He's not leaving . . . well, not to go home, at least. He's going to do the ambush.'

She stopped in her tracks to look at him.

'We're going to get Chemora,' Victor said, looking pleased. 'I don't know what it is about that man, but when he says he's going to do something, well, you know what I mean? No, you probably don't. It's an instinct thing.'

Louisa took a moment to absorb the information. 'Who else?'

'Me. David. Bernard. I must go,' Victor said, heading for Sebastian's cabin. 'We'll be gone a few days, I expect. But we're going to get Chemora. I know we are.'

Louisa's mind whirled as she watched him walk away. She headed up the path that led to the stables.

★ ★ ★

In Sebastian's cabin Steel sat at the table, wearing a pair of glasses and reading a document while sipping a cup of coffee.

'Can I have those satellite photos and maps?' Victor asked, confidently.

Steel looked at him over the rim of his glasses. 'Why?'

'Because we're going to do the job, of course.'

'Who's 'we'?'

'What would you say if I told you that I and some of the men were going to give it a try?'

'I'd say forget it,' Steel said, getting back to his papers.

'And what would you say if I told you that Stratton was coming along too?'

Steel looked back at him. 'I'd ask if you were telling the truth.'

'I am.'

Steel smiled thinly, put down his coffee, dug the maps and photographs from his bag and slid them across the table. 'Have fun,' he said casually as he went back to his reading.

Victor picked up the maps and photographs and left the cabin. When the door had closed behind him Steel put down his document, removed his glasses and began to think of his next move in earnest.

★ ★ ★

Stratton climbed onto his horse. David winced as he lowered himself into his saddle and adjusted it.

'You okay?' Stratton asked.

'Yes. And you?'

'I'm fine.' The dull throb in Stratton's back was constant but manageable. Otherwise, apart from a sore throat and feeling like he'd smoked a hundred cigarettes the night before, he felt okay.

Bernard led three burros from around the back of the stable, their backs loaded with supplies.

Victor cut a piece of plastic-coated wire from a drum and offered it to Stratton. 'Is this good enough?' he asked. 'I hope so because I have a thousand metres of the stuff.'

Stratton nodded. 'It'll do. What about batteries?'

Victor showed him two six-volt motorbike batteries. 'I checked that they're fully charged.' He pulled an AK47 off his shoulder and held it up to Stratton. 'Your new rifle . . . Okay, so it's not new but it's the best I have.'

The soldier took the weapon and checked it over. Victor handed him a magazine pouch which he slung over his shoulder and the weapon across his back.

'You look like a proper rebel now,' Victor said.

180

'Which ensures I'll be hung as one if I'm caught.'

'True enough,' Victor said, grinning as he climbed onto his horse and looked around. 'I was expecting Louisa to see us off.'

Sebastian walked around the corner of the stable towards the corral where the white horse walked up to him. 'Good luck,' he said to them as he reached out to pet the animal.

'Thank you, Sebastian,' Victor said. Then, to the others, 'Shall we?'

The group moved off, the three burros bringing up the rear. Victor urged his horse into a trot and the others followed.

They slowed to a walk as they entered the jungle. A few metres in they came to a defensive embankment, essentially a shallow trench reinforced on the outer side with logs and sandbags. It was the camp perimeter and a handful of rebels sat around, acting as sentries. The group crossed a removable gangway and headed down a steep slope the other side.

They emerged from the trees a short distance later onto a track. It was wide enough for a couple of horses to walk abreast and Victor moved alongside Stratton. 'When I was a kid my favourite story was d'Artagnan's adventures with the Three Musketeers. Finally, I feel like I'm living the part.'

The Englishman gave him a sideways glance. Victor did look quite proud, it was true.

They had not gone far when Victor and Stratton slowed to a stop. Behind them David and Bernard looked ahead to see why and also

181

stopped. All of them were surprised.

Louisa sat on her horse dressed in the same camouflage clothing and jungle boots as the men, with a pair of plump saddlebags across the animal's loin. She stared coolly back at them.

'What do you think you're doing?' Victor asked, moving forward.

'What does it look like?' she replied.

'It looks as if you are planning on a long ride somewhere. But I can't imagine where to.'

'Shall we dispense with the childish badinage? I'm coming with you.'

'I don't think so,' Victor said firmly.

'I spent the last few hours going over the pros and cons of why I should and should not go. I also went through every argument I could expect you to make to dissuade me. Nothing I could think of was convincing enough to suggest I should not come and so I'm here.'

'You are a stubborn woman, Louisa, but this is one debate you are not going to win.'

'You're going to hear me out whether you like it or not,' she said, her jaw tightening. 'And if you insist on riding on without hearing me I will simply follow you.'

Victor did not doubt her. 'Okay. Say your piece. But you're just wasting our valuable time.'

'I have as much right as you to be on this mission. I was born in this country, my father began this revolution. I can't continue to witness this struggle from within the camp. I don't want to be a fighter but I have to understand what it's like. You said you would be long gone by the time the government soldiers reacted to the

182

ambush. So why can't I come? I'm a better rider than any of you if we have to move fast.'

'I think Victor is concerned about the unseen dangers,' Stratton cut in. 'No matter how simple an operation looks on paper there are always things that can go wrong.'

'The only reason you're stopping me is because I'm a woman.'

'No,' Victor corrected her. 'You're Sebastian's daughter. What do you think he would say if he was here right now?'

'You think I would say anything different to him?'

Victor sighed irritably. 'Why do you really want to come? This doesn't make sense, Louisa, and you've always been a sensible woman.'

'Okay,' she said, taking a moment to compose her answer. 'Since I was young I've always listened to my father's talks on freedom and revolt. I was fascinated and inspired. I went to America to study law and politics. When I returned it was not just to be by my father's side. The battle for liberty won't end with the vanquishing of Neravista. There will always be others like him. I'm going to be a part of this country's political future. When men like you have brought the killing to an end I'll take up the fight in the halls of government. But I'll want people to know that I played a part in this struggle. When people hear me fighting for their rights they'll know that I understand the meaning of those words as well as any soldier. I want to be known as the woman who rode with you to destroy

Chemora and help bring down Neravista.'

Victor looked confused. 'That's it?'

'Yes. I'm asking you to give me my future.' Louisa looked serious and they all realised she was probably more determined to go on the mission than any of them.

'And what if something happened to you?' Victor asked. 'What about your future then?'

'If I don't do this, I'm going to do something else. You might as well let it be this, with you, and get it over with,' she said.

Victor looked at Stratton for help but all the other man could offer was a lame shrug. 'I would not be able to face Sebastian. Does that matter to you?'

'Victor, my life is here now, with my people. I'm a part of this. You might as well get used to it.'

He hated the way she could get him to change his mind. His meagre persuasive arsenal was exhausted. 'I'm all out of words,' Victor said to Stratton. 'I cannot stop her. But this is your operation.'

Louisa looked at the English soldier, aware that he was a different proposition. She could wrap Victor around her little finger and ultimately do what she wanted but that would not be the case with Stratton. If he said no it would be over for her. Ultimately, she would not jeopardise the mission for her own needs. Stratton would know that too.

Stratton's only consideration was Louisa's lack of combat skills. But she wasn't going to get any experience sitting in the camp. If she was going to stay with this struggle then her best chance of survival was to learn how to fight. She might even discover this really wasn't the place for her. 'You'll do nothing without my say-so and that means nothing, even going to the latrine. If you disobey I will gag you and tie you to that horse until we return. Is that understood?'

'It is,' Louisa replied, looking him sternly in the eye.

Victor shook his head and flicked his horse's reins to make it walk on. 'I'm in so much shit,' he muttered.

'Ride in the middle of the group,' Stratton told Louisa as they moved off.

She pulled her horse around behind his as he moved alongside Victor.

'Wasn't there a fifth musketeer?' Stratton asked.

'That was the king — not the king's daughter,' Victor said, not amused.

'I don't think this group has quite finished growing,' Stratton said, looking through the trees on the sloping ground above them.

Victor followed his gaze. Kebowa and Mohesiwa were running, carrying their bows and a small leather back-pouch each. They were dressed as normal, wearing their knee-length trousers, with their long black hair tied back.

'I never told them I was going anywhere but they always seem to know,' Victor said, impressed. 'Yoinakuwa's not with them. He must know we're going a good distance. Is that okay, them coming along?'

'Why not?' Stratton said.

185

Victor rode ahead to greet them as they came down to the track.

Stratton looked back at Louisa. She looked solemn and held his gaze only for a second. He wondered if he had seen a trace of fear in her eyes. Despite the dangers, he could not help feeling pleased that she was there.

★　★　★

The group rode off the plateau, using goat tracks and stream beds, all the time heading due west. The Indians decided that one of them would remain near the party while the other scouted ahead. They often swapped places. The brothers were very similar yet Stratton had begun to notice slight differences between them. Mohesiwa appeared dominant although the two discussed everything. He found their dedication to the revolution bizarre in a way. They did not seek any payment except food. They didn't stand to benefit much no matter what heroics they performed. The only explanation that Stratton could think of was that they now felt they belonged to a community once again. Having lost their own tribe they had found another.

The group went easy on the horses because of the time they were expected to travel with little rest. It was fifty-five kilometres to the ambush site as the crow flew but the map did not show any contours so the real distance was difficult to estimate. Once off the plateau the terrain became rocky, with patches of open ground where Stratton felt exposed. Yet crossing them was a calculated risk if they were going to make it to the ambush site on time. According to the GPS they were making good progress, using the most direct route. The map showed some woodland further south, but it would take much longer that way. Stratton was relieved when eventually they entered primary jungle and visibility could be measured in metres rather than kilometres.

On the journey he learned why David and Bernard had been chosen for the operation, despite David's injuries. Victor told him how they knew the western provinces, since both of them were from there. But there was more to it than that. Although David's immediate family were gone he had other relatives in the area, as did Bernard. The mission was even more important to them yet neither young man had said a word. Stratton realised that the more he learned about his companions, the more he was gradually becoming involved, whether he liked it or not.

The first day went slowly. A coral snake spooked the burros during a water stop. Mohesiwa deftly trapped the venomous creature's head, using the end of his bow. He picked it up, walked it a safe distance away from the group and released it. By nightfall Stratton had a better estimate of their speed. As long as the ground ahead was similar, which David assured him it was, and they continued through the night, they could rest the following day. Then if they waited until last light before moving they would make the ambush site around midnight, giving them a few hours of darkness in which to prepare.

The going was much slower and more dangerous in the dark. The trees looked black, and on some of them barbs grew. They pointed out from trunks and branches at odd angles and looked like spears. A few had grown to several feet in length and had tips as sharp as javelins. Travellers had been known to impale themselves. Poisonous manchineel trees also grew in the forest. Simply touching them or breaking a leaf and releasing their sap could cause lesions. Slashing a branch with a machete would create a spurt of poisonous milky liquid that could blind someone if it struck their eyes.

By midnight the moon shone brightly, lighting their way through the rare patches of open ground, but under the forest canopy it stayed black. At one point the cover was so dense that they had to dismount and lead the horses in single file. David was clearly not fit enough to spend an entire day on a horse and he seemed to be in great discomfort much of the time though he did not complain. The walking came as a relief to him. Victor tripped over several times and, cursing heavily after one particularly heavy fall where he bashed his head and almost lost his hat, he got out his flashlight. Stratton told him to put it away, explaining that soldiers used lights only to check maps, make signals and to figure out how to dismantle a booby trap if it could not wait until daytime. Victor put the light away, muttering something about not being in the British Army.

As dawn broke through behind them they arrived at the edge of the wood and Stratton called an end to the march. They removed the equipment and saddles from the animals and provided them with food and water where they were tethered. They did not light a fire, since it could easily have been spotted by patrolling troops. Everyone was too tired anyway and set about preparing their beds.

Louisa came over to ask Stratton if she could go for a pee. He looked at her poker-faced as if considering it but could not help breaking into a grin. 'Get out of here,' he told her. 'Just don't go too far.'

Victor cleared away the fallen twigs and leaves from his chosen spot, placed a blanket on the ground, lay on it and shuffled around to smooth the surface as much as possible before draping his poncho over him. David and Bernard prepared their sleeping places in much the same way but with less fuss.

Stratton looked for the Indians, wondering what their sleeping arrangements might be, but they had disappeared. He pulled a bundle from his pack and unravelled a thin Gore-Tex sleeping bag designed for the jungle, cleared a selected spot and rolled it out. Without removing his boots he pushed his way inside and rested his head on his pack, his assault rifle beside him.

Footsteps signalled Louisa's return and Stratton watched her prepare her bed a few metres away. Holding her blanket, she took a moment to work out the best way to go about setting up the bed. A glance at Stratton's

189

revealed no lesson to be learned there and she looked at Victor's. She spread the blanket on the ground and searched inside her pack for a poncho, which, it quickly became evident, she had forgotten to bring. Unperturbed, she lay down and pulled the blanket on top of her, resting her head on her pack and closing her eyes as if blissfully comfortable.

The Indians returned, carrying several large banana leaves as well as some of the tree's fruit and quickly set about erecting a small shelter against a tree. Stratton suspected they had some inkling about the weather and studied the small patches of sky that he could see through the forest roof. He couldn't see any stars. He sat up and unravelled a green lightweight nylon canopy from a pocket of his pack. It was a large rectangle with string attached to the corner and mid-length eyelets.

He climbed out of his sleeping bag and as he tied the first corner to a tree a tapping sound from above signalled rain hitting the jungle foliage. He secured the other three corners and a couple of the sides, pulling the canopy as tight as a drum. The final touch was to secure the line attached to the centre of the canopy which he tossed over a branch directly above, pulling it tight to give the canopy a pointed roof. The rain started to drip from the highest branches onto the forest floor, making a drumming sound that gradually became louder and faster when it hit Stratton's cover.

Stratton ducked beneath his new shelter, lay on his sleeping bag and watched Louisa to see how long it would take for her to react. He did not have to wait long. She had fallen into a deep sleep but the large raindrops striking her face soon dragged her back out of it. She sat up and looked around as her mind came back into focus.

She looked over at Stratton to see him watching her. He shifted to one side and indicated the space beside him. Louisa did not waste any time dragging up her blanket and saddlebags and scurrying beneath his canopy. Within seconds she was lying back down with her blanket draped over her. She wriggled a little to get comfortable.

'Thank you,' she said.

Stratton climbed back into his sleeping bag. 'First time camping?' he asked.

'Yes, actually. I missed out on the Girl Scouts.'

He looked at the water dripping off the edges of the nylon sheet. 'I always find this nostalgic, lying beneath a piece of canvas in the rain.'

Drips hit the side of Louisa's blanket and she moved her bedding closer to him, her back against his side.

'You take to camping naturally,' Stratton observed.

'I prefer this to a caravan, pulling into some commercial campsite and plugging into an electricity and water supply.'

'Good for you.'

'I suppose this is the best way to start. Get stuck straight in.'

'Your first camping experience or your first ambush?'

Stratton's words were food for thought to Louisa. 'That hasn't even hit me yet. I can't even begin to imagine what that will be like.'

Stratton could foresee clearly most of the action that he had planned. He did not need to imagine the outcome, either. He had countless previous examples to draw on and could hear in his head the explosions and see the terrible destruction the claymores would wreak. 'You'd better prepare yourself. You're going to see and hear people die and in a bloody awful way.'

'I thought we were going to be well away from it when it happened.'

'Haven't you learned that Steel is little more than a salesman? If we want to ensure that it's done right we have to be there.'

Louisa should have felt more nervous after hearing that. But she could not properly prepare herself emotionally for something she could not even imagine. 'Have you ever thought about having a normal life?'

'Sometimes. Just before the ambush I probably will. Definitely immediately after it.'

'You're different from any man I've ever known. The men react to you in a way I've not seen before. They don't fear you, yet they know you're someone to be feared. They want to be like you but they don't want to be you because they know they cannot.'

The rain fell harder, the drumbeats on the canopy now a constant roll. Louisa turned onto her side to face Stratton, her cheek touching his shoulder. 'Why is it that I feel safe with you?' she asked sleepily. 'I hated you when I first saw you.

You represented the worst form of capitalism I could think of. What's strange is that even now I don't see anything different about what you do. All that's changed is how I perceive your motives . . . You're not interested in money, are you?'

'No.'

'I bet you don't even know what your motives are.'

'No, I don't. Not completely.'

'I should study you more closely,' she said, drifting off. 'I'd like to know why you're like you are and why you do what you do.'

A strand of her hair fell against Stratton's face. He could smell her. It was pure delight. Her breathing changed its rhythm as she dropped into unconsciousness. Only then did he close his eyes and allow himself to follow her.

⋆ ⋆ ⋆

When Stratton awoke the rain had ceased. Louisa was snuggled close to him. He looked for a moment at her beautiful face inches from his.

He eased away from her, slid out of his sleeping bag and got to his feet. The other men were still asleep and one of the Indians lay rolled in a ball beneath the banana-leaf shelter. There was no sign of the other.

Stratton walked to the edge of the wood and looked at the valley that spread out before him. The blood-red sun at the far end was setting in a magnificent blaze of colour. He sensed something to his side and turned to see Mohesiwa watching him from a distance. Stratton waved

193

and, to his surprise, the gesture was returned.

He went back to the group and stood over Victor who was still sound asleep. 'Victor,' he said, nudging him with his toe.

Victor opened his eyes and within a few seconds remembered where he was. 'Everything okay?' he asked quietly as he sat up.

'We should get going. By the time we get the animals loaded the sun will be gone.'

Victor hawked to clear his throat, spat out the phlegm and got to his feet. 'I would love a cup of coffee right now,' he said. 'I was dreaming of a little café I used to go to in Pau. You know Pau?'

'I do. I used to parachute there.'

'Well, I used to drink wine and coffee there, a more civilised occupation but no less dangerous. It was where I met my wife. And where I divorced her. That town had everything.' Victor got to his feet.

David stirred, yawned and reached across to give his cousin a shake. Both young men got up.

Stratton dismantled his shelter without waking Louisa. He crouched beside her and gently pinched her nostrils together. Her eyes flickered open and he withdrew his hand. 'You just saved me,' she said.

'I did?'

'I was having the most bizarre dream about the president of Mexico — who I've never met.' She sat up. 'He asked me to marry him. He was repulsive and started to chase me.'

'It must be these woods,' Stratton said, closing up his pack. 'Victor was dreaming about his ex-wife.'

'I heard that,' Victor called out as he saddled his horse. 'I was dreaming about drinking coffee in the town where my ex-wife lives. She was a beautiful woman, actually. And she truly loved me at one time. Love is one of life's gifts that few really experience. I hope you discover what I mean one day,' he scoffed.

The group ate a light breakfast of bread, bananas and wild canistels, an eggfruit that the Indians had supplied, and within a short while they were mounted and heading out of the forest into the valley.

They were soon in complete darkness, following a winding goat track up the side of a steep, rocky hill that Victor had referred to as a 'goddamned mountain' when he first saw it. But the size of such things is always deceptive at night and within an hour they had reached the top.

Stratton halted them short of the ridge line in order to find a place to cross over without exposing their silhouettes. A road ran along the valley floor on the other side and they had to assume that it was patrolled by government soldiers.

They followed the ridge for some distance before Stratton ordered a dismount and they passed through a narrow cut, emerging the other side to find themselves overlooking another and much larger valley. They could see none of its features in the darkness but according to the map a small river meandered along the bottom alongside a tarmac highway.

They weren't far from the ambush site now

and they stayed on foot down the steep, rocky incline, Kebowa and Mohesiwa sticking close by. The group had not gone far when a light appeared at one end of the valley. They stopped to watch what was obviously a vehicle on the road. As it drew closer the gentle rumble of its engine could be heard. The headlights suddenly began to flicker, strobe-like, as they passed behind something. At the same time the sound of heavy-duty wheels driving over a metal grid drowned out the noise of the engine.

'The bridge,' Victor said.

The truck's red tail lights glowed as it headed down the valley and disappeared out of sight.

The group continued down the slope without another word. A large dark patch near the bottom of their side of the valley turned out to be a small wood, an ideal place in which to hide the horses until the sun came up. As they neared it they discovered a small rise between the wood and the river, which made it an even better place of concealment. The ground was arid and peppered with shrubs and stunted trees.

The moon shone as brightly as it had the night before, more so than Stratton would have liked.

Stratton ordered the equipment unloaded and the horses and burros unsaddled for the time being. He spread his shelter canopy on the ground while the Indians stood by, watching him. Stratton removed one of the claymores from its pouch and laid it on the canopy along with the roll of wire, the twine and a couple of wire-cutters.

196

When the others had completed their tasks they returned to see what Stratton was up to.

'Sit in a line,' Stratton said, slipping naturally into instructor mode. 'I'm going to run through the ambush set-up. If at any time you don't understand what I'm telling you, just ask me to go through it again.'

'I feel like I'm back in school,' Victor said.

'You are. The difference is that if you screw up this lesson we may all die.'

The Indians moved closer to look at the strange devices that the soldier was holding.

'The plan is quite simple,' Stratton went on. 'The bridge is our ambush point — our killing zone. All we're going to do is wait for our target vehicle to drive onto the bridge and then we'll blow it. You're happy with how to wire up the detonators like I showed you yesterday?'

Victor nodded.

'David, Bernard?' Stratton asked.

The two young men nodded.

'Show me again, quickly,' Stratton said. He tossed Bernard a claymore and the wire and placed a detonator in front of him.

Bernard confidently unscrewed the detonator-terminal cap from the top of the claymore. He stripped the plastic coating off the ends of the wires with his teeth, picked up the detonator with care, unravelled the wire that was factory-wrapped around it and connected the bared ends, twisting them together. He finished by tying the join in a knot to prevent it from being pulled apart. He inserted the detonator into the claymore and screwed the terminal housing home.

'That's good,' Stratton said. 'Do I need to see you two do it?' he asked the others.

'If you want,' Victor said. 'But I've never been more sure of something in my life.'

David nodded in agreement.

'Good. Victor, your job will be to roll out the wire from the bridge all the way to here, which will be the firing point. Put the batteries there but keep them in the bag and nowhere near the ends of the wires.'

'Of course,' Victor said.

'We'll prepare all the mines here, then take them to the bridge. I'll lay them out. You boys,' he said, looking at David and Bernard, 'will tie them into position and connect them to the main wire which I will lay. Any questions?'

'What if a car comes along?' Victor asked.

'Kebowa and Mohesiwa will watch from the rise. If they see anything one of them will come and warn us. We'll have plenty of time. Anything else? Okay. Let's go.'

The men began preparing the claymores.

'What can I do?' Louisa asked.

'You're going to be my gofer.'

'Your what?'

'My go-for-this, go-for-that.'

'Oh. I see.'

When all was ready the men divided up the mines between them, hanging the canvas bags over their shoulders. Victor handed the twine to Louisa.

Stratton paused on the edge of the rise to

observe the general area for a moment. They all stood silently watching and listening, allowing their senses to acclimatise to the sights and sounds of the landscape.

Stratton set off and they headed down the slope to the edge of the river, which was as wide as a main road. Bernard was first in after declaring that it was not deep and he went to the middle, where it reached his waist. They walked out on the other side, the road now a stone's throw away, and Stratton followed the river bank around a sharp bend where it went beneath the bridge.

They paused to observe the decades-old large iron structure. It was a truss construction, a skeletal design made up of straight girders formed into triangular frames and riveted together. The sides were high enough to allow a lorry to pass beneath where the cross-beams joined over the top.

'Give us your mines,' Stratton said to Victor. 'Tie off the end of the cable at the left base of the bridge. Allow enough to reach the top of the bridge. Then run it back through the river to where we crossed and on back to the mound.'

Victor shared his mines out between the others, including Louisa, and hurried to the base of the bridge with the wire spool.

Stratton led them up the steep bank onto the road. The tarmac came to a ragged stop where it met the bridge's grid-metal road surface. 'Put all the mines here,' he said, pointing down. 'Bernard. Up you go to the top.'

Bernard started to climb up one of the bridge's girders.

Stratton took a slow walk across the bridge, examining the top and sides as he went. Louisa and David watched him until he was almost at the far end, nearly out of sight in the darkness.

'You nervous?' she asked David.

'Not right now. But I think I will be later.'

'I'm nervous now. I'll be exhausted later.'

David smiled at her and went back to watching Stratton. 'He's a good man, Stratton, don't you think?'

'Yeah, I think he's a good man.'

Stratton made his way back, inspecting the cross-bars above. 'David. Climb up. I'll pass the mines to you and you pass them to Bernard.'

David scurried up. Stratton climbed behind him but stopped only a couple of metres above the road. He stretched a hand down to Louisa. 'Hand me one mine at a time. Stop when you get to ten.'

She passed him one of the bags. Stratton handed it to David who hefted it up to Bernard who was lying on his belly on top of the bridge.

'That's it,' she said when she had reached ten.

'The wire and then the twine,' Stratton said. Louisa gave them to him.

'Shall I come up?' she asked.

'No. I might need you down there,' Stratton replied as he climbed up to join the others.

The three men stood up carefully on the top span that ran the length of the bridge. It would have been wide enough to walk on comfortably if it had been lying on the ground but it was unnervingly narrow so high up.

Stratton walked along it to examine the cross-struts and check his calculations. Louisa followed below, hardly taking her stare off him. The long spans that ran parallel with the road were connected by ten cross-struts.

'One mine under each strut pointing down at the road,' he called out from halfway along.

'In the centre?' David asked.

'Yes. Let's do the first one and see how it goes.'

David knelt down and stretched out along the top of the cross-strut, which was narrower than the main spans. Bernard removed a mine from its bag, straightened the ends of the detonator wires and handed it to him. A length of twine followed and when the mine was secured David tied the ends of the detonator wires on top of the strut in readiness for the main wire.

'Let's get them all in position first and wire them up after,' Stratton said, taking the spool, securing the wire to one end of the long span and allowing it to unravel as he walked to the other end.

He climbed down the angled girder at the end and jumped onto the metal road, wincing at a painful twinge in his back. He had forgotten about the wound.

'Where are you going to put those?' Louisa asked, indicating the remaining claymores.

Stratton placed one in the well of one of the

201

vertical I-beams that ran along the sides of the bridge to see how noticeable it was. 'That should finish it off,' he said, more to himself than to her. 'Throw down some twine!' he called out to Bernard.

Louisa picked it up and brought it to Stratton. He used a length to secure the mine.

'How do they work?' she asked.

'Each mine contains six hundred steel ball-bearings the size of a pea,' he explained as he placed the detonator wire in position. 'They're packed against a thick sheet of plastic explosive. Each one is the equivalent of about a hundred shotguns, but each shotgun's ten times more powerful than a regular one.'

Louisa looked up at David attaching a mine above her and tried to imagine what it would be like when they all went off together. 'Now that I'm here I don't know if I approve any more.' She looked at Stratton for his reaction.

'Bring those others, would you?' Stratton asked her as he crossed the road.

Louisa fetched another mine and handed it to him. 'Does that disappoint you?'

'Of course not.' He stopped what he was doing and looked at her. 'Do you want to cancel it?'

'Would you, if I asked?'

'Yes,' he said.

'Why?'

'Because I'm not doing this for myself.'

Louisa looked up at Bernard and David who were attaching another mine. 'You're doing it for them,' she said. 'If I stopped you I would be doing it just for myself.'

Victor climbed up onto the road and walked to the bridge, carrying the remainder of the wire on its spool. He looked around at what had been done so far. 'What shall I do?' he asked Stratton before realising that he was interrupting a serious conversation.

'Well?' Stratton said, looking at her and waiting for the answer. She seemed to waver.

'Leaders sometimes have to make tough decisions — life and death decisions. It's your call. Do we destroy Chemora? Or do we leave it and walk away?'

Victor realised what this was all about. David and Bernard stopped what they were doing and watched Louisa.

'There's nothing wrong with changing your mind as long as you believe it's the right thing to do,' Stratton said.

Louisa looked at the others. They stared back at her, waiting for her to make a decision.

A distant shout interrupted them. It was Kebowa, charging down alongside the river. He pointed up the valley.

'Trucks!' David said from his vantage point.

'How many?' Stratton asked quickly.

David took a moment to be sure. 'I think three . . . yes, three.' He looked down at Stratton. 'One, possibly two could be locals. Three will be Neravistas.'

'How far?' Stratton called.

'A minute,' David decided.

'You and Bernard clear the hanging twine away and then stay there. Lie flat, look away

203

from the trucks. Victor. Up there,' Stratton said, pointing to higher ground.

Victor set off at a run, pulling his rifle from his shoulder.

'Hide everything,' Stratton shouted to Louisa. He ran to collect the mines at the end of the bridge.

Louisa ran along it, picking up bits of wire and twine, any evidence they had been there.

The vehicles' headlights caught the top of the bridge. David and Bernard dropped to their bellies and lay still.

Stratton hurried along the embankment, dropped over the edge and dumped the claymores. He looked back for Louisa. She was still on the bridge. 'Louisa! Come here!'

A gentle curve in the road hid the vehicles from view but their engines grew suddenly louder as they came round the bend.

Stratton knew they had just seconds before the trucks were on them. He sprinted up onto the bridge, grabbing Louisa as she leaned down to pick up the last piece of twine. The vehicles rounded the curve and their headlights lit up the entrance to the structure. Stratton manhandled her through a narrow gap in the bridge's struts. The river bank was invisible below them but if they did not move immediately they would be exposed. 'Jump!' he urged her.

Louisa didn't hesitate. Stratton followed, landing hard, colliding with her on the rocky slope. He grabbed her and held her close to stop her from sliding down the slope.

The first truck bumped over the edge of the

tarmac onto the metal surface of the bridge's roadbed, the wheels grinding as if they were crossing a cattle grid. The second vehicle was bigger and Stratton made out the back of an open truck, a couple of dozen soldiers inside it. The last vehicle was a jeep of some kind. Before long all three were off the bridge and heading away down the road.

'You okay?' Stratton asked Louisa.

She felt one of her wrists and nodded. 'I'm sorry,' she said.

'For what?'

'I didn't realise they were so close.'

'It's difficult to tell at night. We were lucky,' he said, getting to his feet and helping her up to the road. 'They still heading away?' he called up to David.

The sound of the trucks' engines had already died away but their headlights glowed in the distance. 'All three are still going,' David said.

Stratton was satisfied and breathed a sigh of relief, his gaze resting on Louisa. 'You were saying?' he asked.

She simply looked at him.

'Are we going to finish this or not?' he reminded her.

'I know what you meant,' she said.

The others waited in silence.

'Chemora should not be allowed to do what he does,' she said. 'Let's do what we came here to do.'

'No doubts?' Stratton asked. 'We don't undo this once we've wired it up.'

'No doubts,' Louisa said, her expression grim.

'Start wiring these together like this,' Stratton said to Victor, who arrived a little out of breath. He placed a claymore in the recess of an I-beam. 'Keep the cable behind the struts and out of sight.'

Victor walked to the end of the bridge and began his task. Bernard and David got back to theirs.

Stratton scaled the side of the bridge, clambered on top and began wiring the claymores together. It was a laborious job in the dark and he had to rely most of all on his sense of touch.

As the horizon began to lighten Stratton climbed down and walked the length of the bridge, carrying out a final inspection.

'It will rain soon,' Victor warned, looking up at the heavy clouds that were now just about visible in the dawn sky.

'It won't affect anything,' Stratton said. 'I think we're good to go.'

The three other men filed past him and down the embankment to the river. Louisa waited beside Stratton, looking at their handiwork. He gazed at her and grinned broadly.

She realised he was watching her. 'What's so funny?' she asked.

'I can't imagine any other circumstance where you would follow a man so obediently.'

'Neither can I,' she said, a softness in her voice.

It began to rain, small droplets at first which rapidly grew in size and intensity until they came down hard, soaking everything. The air rang with the metallic plinks of drops hitting the bridge. But Stratton and Louisa did not appear to notice.

'Do you have any particular sentimental feeling when you're standing in the rain?' she asked.

'I do now,' Stratton said, watching the water trickle down her face. Without thinking, he reached out his hand to touch her cheek. He wanted to wipe away the rain, obviously impossible under the circumstances, but the feel of her skin blurred all thoughts but one. He leaned towards her and she did not shy away. He wrapped his arms around her and held her tightly to him. Her hands cupped his face as they kissed.

Victor looked back to see what was keeping them and stopped when he saw what they were doing. He blinked against the rain, unsure quite what he felt about it. A part of him was happy for them both. Love affairs were indeed beautiful things. But another part of him was troubled.

6

The saddled horses and burros stood quietly together, soaked to the skin, their bodies steaming. The rain had stopped but brooding clouds remained in the sky, scraping the tops of the surrounding hills.

Bernard and Victor sat on their ponchos on the slope from where they could see the road at both ends of the valley. Victor munched gloomily on a piece of dried meat. Now that everything lay ready and the waiting had begun his nerves were feeling the strain. He began to see the things that could go wrong. His main concern was how they were going to get away once the ambush had been sprung. It would take precious time to get back up the steep slope to safety beyond the ridge line and they would be vulnerable during that part of their escape. He would have preferred the ambush to take place at night but then they would probably not have been able to identify Chemora's vehicle. In the early-morning light his lined face looked careworn.

David was on watch, lying on his belly and looking through Stratton's binoculars. The Indians squatted under one of the stunted trees, keeping an eye on the rear, and Louisa sat on the empty claymore box watching Stratton sort out the rocket launchers.

Each weapon came with its own shoulder

strap that Stratton was pulling out to its full length. Louisa was curious about the part the devices would play in the ambush. As time went by she was becoming more afraid. She had fought off voicing her doubts, but the thought of the ambush itself, the noise and the destruction, made her ill at ease. 'Why do you think nothing has come along this road since last night?' she asked eventually.

'I have no idea,' Stratton replied, loosening another strap and checking the weapon.

'I would have expected an army vehicle, or a horse and cart at least.'

'Maybe the army have locked down the area.'

'You don't think it's because they know we're here? Perhaps they saw something when they crossed the bridge last night.'

He straightened up to ease a pain in his back and scanned the surrounding hills. 'It's possible. But I doubt it,' he said.

'Why?'

'Just a feeling.'

'What if they don't come?'

Stratton shrugged. 'We wait.'

'For how long?'

'What do you think?'

Louisa frowned. 'I think that ever since I mentioned my political ambitions I've been on some kind of leader-apprentice course. I didn't say I wanted to be Alexander the Great, you know.'

'Strategy plays a part in everything, including politics. The clue to the answer is in our limitations.'

'Like food? Kebowa and Mohesiwa could probably find some. Maybe until someone falls ill. Seriously, how long would you stay here?'

'Until I felt it was time to leave.'

Louisa rolled her eyes. 'That's a real grasshopper answer,' she said, throwing a twig at him.

Victor stopped chewing and began slowly to rise without taking his gaze off the end of the valley. 'I think I see something,' he said.

Everyone looked in that direction.

David scrambled down the slope. 'Stratton,' he called out.

'Easy, David,' Stratton said, calming him.

'No! Look!' David pointed towards the bridge.

Stratton hurried to where he could see the bridge clearly.

'One of the mines has come loose,' David said, handing the binoculars to Stratton.

Stratton focused them on the struts above the road. David was right. A claymore had come loose from its binding and was hanging like a lantern by its wires. Anyone using the bridge would see it.

He hurried back into the wood and to the burros to get the twine.

'Those are definitely trucks coming,' Victor called out.

Stratton grabbed his AK47 and slung the magazine pouch over his back. As he turned away from the burros he was met by Bernard and David.

'I think it's one of mine,' Bernard said, looking ashamed. 'I'm sorry.'

'Don't beat yourself up about it,' Stratton said. 'These things happen. What we have to do now is fix it.'

As he walked around them they moved to block his way. 'We can do it,' David insisted. 'If they are coming you must be here.'

Stratton knew they were right.

'It looks like a convoy,' Victor called out. 'Someone pass me the binoculars.'

Stratton studied the men's determined faces. 'Quick as you can,' he said. 'Secure the mine and get back here.' David nodded as he snatched the twine. He was about to go when Stratton grabbed his arm. 'If you can't make it back here without being seen just get well clear of the bridge.'

'We'll do it,' David assured him. The two men set off as fast as they could.

Stratton joined Victor and looked through the binoculars. There was indeed a convoy on the road. 'Ten, eleven vehicles,' he said.

'Chemora,' Victor said, the tension in his voice obvious. 'It has to be.'

Stratton moved up the rise to where he could see both the bridge and the convoy. David and Bernard were running like hell into the river.

'What if they don't have enough time?' Victor asked.

Stratton was thinking exactly the same thing. 'It's going to be tight, maybe too tight,' he muttered.

'Should I send one of my boys to get them back?' Victor asked.

'No.' Stratton was calculating something.

211

Victor was growing anxious as it began to look like the convoy would reach the bridge before David and Bernard could complete their task.

'Go get your Indians.'

The scientist was about to question him when he changed his mind and hurried away.

'Louisa! You stay there.'

She nodded, clenching her fists with the tension.

Victor whistled at the Indians as he reached the edge of the small wood and beckoned them to follow him.

Stratton headed down the slope towards the road.

Victor reached the side of the rise, saw Stratton and broke into a sprint towards him.

Halfway to the river Stratton turned to walk parallel to it, away from the bridge and towards the oncoming convoy.

He squatted in some foliage and studied the road while Victor caught up. 'Which one of your boys is the best shot?' he asked when the Frenchman arrived out of breath.

Victor shrugged. 'They're both good.'

'Then we'll use them both. I need this convoy stopped well short of the bridge,' Stratton said. 'They have to shoot out one of the tyres of the front vehicle.'

'But Chemora's men will see the arrows sticking out of the wheel,' Victor argued. 'They'll know that someone has attacked them.'

'They'll see a couple of Indians' arrows. What are they going to do, call in an air strike? Get out of there as soon as the arrows hit the tyres. If

212

they can't see you they won't come after you.'

'You're so sure?'

'No. But who's going to chase a couple of crazy Indians around the countryside when there're places to go, things to do?'

Victor's breathing was rapid, adrenalin coursing through his veins. He realised Stratton was studying him. 'Why are you looking at me like that?'

Stratton had been wondering if Victor was up to it but he smiled to reassure the man. 'You're a good guy, Victor. I'm glad you're here.'

'You just want my company when they hang us,' the Frenchman said, making light of the matter to disguise his concern. He looked from the convoy to the bridge. 'I don't suppose we have any other choice.'

'Or any more time,' Stratton added.

Victor understood. He faced the two young men and explained what he needed of them. A moment later all three set off towards the river.

'I'll be back at the firing point,' Stratton called out.

'I'll see you there,' Victor said, hurrying to catch up with Kebowa and Mohesiwa.

Stratton gave the convoy a last look before heading back, this time at the crouch, conscious that the slope would soon be in visual range of the lead truck's passengers.

When he reached the rise Louisa was crouched behind the ridge from where she had been watching him. 'Can I ask what we're doing?'

'We need to delay the convoy to give David

and Bernard more time.'

Her nervousness grew. The ambush had begun in earnest and there were already complications.

'Still glad you came?' Stratton asked.

'Don't make fun of me. You're so comfortable in your world. I'm glad I'm seeing it. In some ways it allows me to understand my father a little better. I often saw the planning and the aftermath but never the dreadful deeds themselves.'

Louisa watched Stratton remove the magazine from his assault rifle, pull back the working parts to extract the bullet that was in the chamber, give the mechanism a quick check and reload the weapon. He then gave his pistol an equivalent once-over and replaced it in his holster.

The gap between the lead truck and the bridge was closing. David and Bernard were scaling the side of the bridge.

'Steel said the rebellion depended on the success of this ambush,' Stratton said. 'Right now that success depends on the arrows of a couple of Indians.'

★ ★ ★

Victor followed Kebowa and Mohesiwa at a crouching run through the sparse brush. He had never done anything as dangerous as this before. His natural inclination was to worry about what could go wrong but he forced the thoughts out of his head. There was no point to them any more. He was going to carry out the crazy task. The rest of the operation depended on it.

He was suddenly concerned that they were getting too close to the road and worried that the Indians had misunderstood the plan. He made a series of mouth clicks and whistles in order to halt them. When they stopped he sought their assurance that they had understood what was required. Victor had never become fluent in their language and neither had they in his. But there had never been a more critical moment where they could ill afford to get it wrong. They explained with a combination of words and gestures that such a shot was not as easy as Victor might think. They had to hit a moving target and not a very big one at that.

The sound of the trucks' engines grew louder as the convoy approached and Victor peered through the foliage to get a look at the lead vehicle. It was a truck filled with soldiers. The repercussions of screwing up suddenly became even more scary. He visualised the men leaning over the side of the vehicle and shooting at them like hunters in a gallery.

The Indians wanted to get even closer and crept forward to the river bank where the vegetation ended. They had a quick confab about something that Victor gathered was to do with crossing the river to ensure an even cleaner shot. A glance at the convoy warned him that they did not have the time and then, as if the Indians had come to the same conclusion, they both placed arrows to the strings of their bows and trained them on the approaching truck. It was a long shot and for the first time Victor began to doubt their skills.

The vehicle behind the lead truck was an open jeep carrying four men. Behind that came another truck but in the middle of the convoy one vehicle caught his attention. It was a highly polished black Mercedes sedan with a small flag flapping on top of the front wheel arch.

Victor swallowed with nervousness. Getting caught by these animals was a horrifying prospect. The stark reality of the situation struck him: if this went wrong his life would end here in this valley. He saw himself being hung and then realised that there was no tree tall enough which meant he would more than likely be shot — unless they hung him from the bridge, of course. That would probably be the result, he decided.

He hoped he looked as calm as the two Indian boys did and wondered if they were frightened at all. They drew back their bows as they brought the arrows up on aim in perfect sync. Victor practically stopped breathing. He wondered what he might do if the arrows missed. If the convoy drove onto the bridge, would Stratton allow it to pass unhindered or would he detonate the explosives, thus killing David and Bernard? It was pointless to wonder. He *had* to succeed. Victor gripped his AK47 and rested his forefinger on the trigger.

As the truck moved directly in front of them, Victor's gaze flicked between the Indians and the target tyre. The wait was excruciating. He almost cried out for them to shoot. Then one of them loosed his arrow and before it had landed the other followed. Both struck the tyre either side of the hub.

The wheel continued to turn with the arrows sticking out of it and for a painful moment Victor's worst fears seemed to come true. He brought his gun up against his shoulder and swallowed hard. He moistened his lips, levelled the AK47 against his cheek and lined up its sights on the tyre. As he began to squeeze the trigger the sight picture changed and the tyre burst.

The truck's brakes squealed noisily and the heavy vehicle came to a stop. Victor lowered his assault rifle and began to breathe again.

The convoy slowed to a halt as the driver of the lead truck opened his door and jumped to the ground. He paused when he saw the two arrows, uncertain if his eyes were deceiving him, and moved closer to inspect them.

He called out to the men in the jeep behind.

Victor tapped the Indians on their backs and signalled them to get going. They followed as he scurried away from the river as low to the ground as he could.

Stratton saw the strike through his binoculars and turned his attention to David and Bernard crawling along the bridge's top span towards the dangling claymore.

When Stratton looked back at the convoy the men from the jeep were at the front of the truck with the driver who was pointing at the arrows. They were all wearing army uniforms and were no doubt officers.

Stratton searched the ground for Victor and

saw him and the Indians making steady progress back towards him. A shot suddenly sounded and the three men dropped to their bellies.

Stratton hurriedly aimed his binoculars back at the truck to see one of the officers aiming a pistol in Victor's general direction. The man fired again. There were two trucks full of soldiers and Stratton feared the men might clamber out and cross the river. If so it would mean a hasty retreat for everyone who could get to the horses in time.

Stratton nearly told Louisa to get ready to run to her horse but decided to hold off for a moment longer, wondering why the officer was not using his troops if he could see Victor.

One of the other men from the jeep pointed elsewhere and the one who was shooting followed his suggestion and fired in that direction. It was evident that they had not in fact seen Victor or the Indians and the officer with the pistol was simply shooting at random.

The driver of the Mercedes climbed out and went to the passenger door behind him. He opened it and a man got out and stood by the car. Stratton studied him through the binoculars. He looked to be in his fifties and wore smart civilian clothes.

Stratton held the binoculars out to Louisa. 'You know what Chemora looks like?'

'I met him once when I was young,' she replied, taking the glasses and looking through them. 'He came to our house. I'll never forget the way he looked at me. He was disgusting . . . That's him,' she confirmed.

Chemora surveyed the scene calmly as one of

218

the officers hurried down the line of vehicles to him. They had a brief conversation and Chemora climbed back inside the sedan.

The officer blew a whistle and waved towards the back of the column as he called out some orders. This was followed by shouts and gesticulations from the other men. Louisa focused the binoculars on a truck near the rear of the column. People were climbing out of the open back but they were civilians — not just men but women and children too. Soldiers were gesturing for them to move quickly towards the front of the convoy.

'My God,' Louisa gasped.

Stratton took the glasses from her and had a look for himself. 'Civilians?'

'They must be his first batch of victims,' she said. 'The ones he's going to hang.'

A soldier herded the peasants along the length of the convoy towards the truck with the flat tyre. The driver opened a box on the side of the truck and the peasants took tools from it. Some set about placing a jack beneath the truck while others unscrewed the bolts securing the wheel. The soldiers inside the truck watched them.

An old man removed the spare wheel from beneath the tailgate and rolled it along the side of the truck. He got a swift kick from an officer and lost control of the wheel which ran over the boot of another officer. The officer who had kicked the man went ballistic and he set about the peasant, kicking and slapping him. He begged for mercy while trying to protect himself. The officer was obviously not getting enough satisfaction and reached for his pistol but it got stuck in its holster. The old peasant panicked and, realising his likely fate, made a run for it. He leapt down the embankment towards the river.

One of the officers cried out something that caused laughter among the other men, which served only to enrage the angry officer further. He finally managed to get his gun out of its holster and took a shot at the man, who by now was almost at the river. He missed, and the bullet struck the water, causing more laughter among the soldiers.

A shrill scream followed as a woman broke from the group to go to the old man. As he waded across the river the angry officer took a steady aim and fired again. The old man fell beneath the water but surfaced immediately and lurched on.

Another officer decided to show his colleague how it should be done and, taking a rifle from one of the soldiers in the truck, aimed it and fired at the woman as she reached the water. The sound of the shot was much louder than the noise made by the pistol, the bullet far more powerful in its impact. It struck her in the back and blood exploded from her chest as it went right through her. But it did not kill her outright and she staggered forward.

The other officers joined in the entertainment, pulling their pistols and sending bullet after bullet into the couple until they both went still, face down in the water, blood oozing from the holes in their bodies.

This inspired another witty comment from one of the officers that was greeted by laughter from the others.

Louisa buried her face in her hands, horrified beyond belief.

Stratton put an arm around her and she clung to him. 'What kind of people are they?' she asked as if it was not possible to reach such depths of inhumanity.

'The kind that aren't going to see another dawn,' Stratton said grimly.

Louisa looked into his face. His expression as he stared at the officers was as cold as ice, the resolve in his eyes absolute. It was frightening and she let go of him. 'You can't set off those explosives now,' she said. 'What about those people?'

Stratton turned to see Victor coming up the rise at a crouching run. Kebowa and Mohesiwa remained below, looking at Stratton as if awaiting their next order.

Victor dropped onto his back beside Stratton, panting heavily from the effort. 'Did you see those bastards?' he growled, inspecting the cuts and grazes on his hands. The knees of his trousers were torn and spotted with blood.

Stratton focused on the bridge. David and Bernard had fixed the mine and were sliding along the top spar back the way they had come. Another check of the convoy showed that the punctured wheel had been replaced and the nuts were being tightened.

'I asked you about those people,' Louisa said to Stratton, her voice firm.

Victor had not thought of that. 'Perhaps it would be more humane than what awaits them,' he said.

'You can't be serious,' she hissed.

Stratton removed one of the batteries from the bag and placed it beside a stick that had been stuck into the ground and that had the end of the command wire that led from the bridge wrapped around it. 'I want you to stay here,' he said to Louisa.

'What about those people?' she demanded again.

'You agreed to do what I said without question. Nothing's changed. Don't move from this spot. Look for me at all times. When I wave my arms at you, you'll touch both wires to the terminals and blow up that bridge. Do you understand me?'

Louisa stared at Stratton, her jaw clenched tightly.

'Trust me,' he said, looking deeply into her eyes. 'Victor,' he said, breaking off and heading down the rise.

Louisa watched him go and stared at the wire and the battery.

Victor stared at her and could only imagine what was going through her mind.

'Victor!' Stratton called out impatiently.

'Dear God,' he said, squeezing Louisa's arm for reassurance before scurrying down the rise after Stratton.

By the time the Frenchman had caught up with him Stratton had slung half a dozen rockets on his back. 'Pick up the rest,' he said as he headed back the way they came. Victor clumsily hitched them over his shoulder. The Indians had followed him and moved to help. 'No,' Victor said. He didn't know Stratton's intentions but rockets and Indians certainly did not mix. 'You stay here and wait for me,' he said before hurrying off.

Stratton crouched at the bottom of the rise to observe the convoy.

Victor squatted behind him. 'What is the plan this time?'

'I haven't worked it out yet.'

'What are the rockets for?'

'With some situations you start with how you see the end and work back. You confident enough to fire one of these?'

'I had a terrible feeling you were going to ask me that. I've seen a bad example. Maybe if you show me a good one.'

Stratton removed one of the tubes from his back and held it by either end in front of Victor so that it was parallel with the ground. 'Hold it like this and pull,' he said. He pulled the ends and the tube smoothly telescoped open until it locked. The action caused the rear sight to pop up out of its housing. 'This is the safety catch,' he said, pulling a sprung lever. He put the tube on his shoulder beside his cheek. 'Just like a rifle, you look through this, line up the front sight on the target, and squeeze down on this,' he said, indicating a rubber button. 'There's hardly any kick.'

'And keep the back away from my arse,' Victor added as his nerves began to tingle once again.

'After the first one you'll wonder what all the fuss was about.'

'What am I shooting at?'

'Nothing until I tell you,' Stratton said, looking hard at the lead truck.

A soldier pulled the jack from beneath the truck and two of the peasants replaced the tools in the locker on its side while the others were herded back to their vehicle. The driver gunned the truck's engine and a dense cloud of black smoke belched from its exhaust, enveloping the officers who were by now back in their jeep. Unable to tolerate the fumes, the jeep's driver swung out into the road and accelerated past the truck towards the bridge.

Stratton looked now for David and Bernard. They had jumped down onto the road and, keeping low, slid down the embankment to the river.

Stratton looked back at the jeep. 'It's about that time,' he muttered and moved off towards the bridge.

They jogged at a crouch through the low bushes towards the sharp bend in the river before it went under the bridge. Stratton stopped in the tall grass at the river bank and knelt where he had a clean view of both ends of the structure.

The jeep slowed as it approached the bridge in order to negotiate the shift from tarmac to metal on the road surface.

There was no sign of David and Bernard but Stratton had to assume they had taken cover.

He placed the rockets at his feet, putting the

224

one he had already prepared to one side and made ready another, all the time keeping an eye on the jeep as it drove across the bridge.

Stratton levelled the rocket on his shoulder while Victor watched the rest of the convoy.

'Victor?' Stratton said without looking behind him.

Victor looked at him and realised with a start why Stratton had called his name. He was looking into the back of the launcher. 'Oh, shit,' he cried as he threw himself out of the way.

As the jeep reached the far side of the bridge the truck approached the other end and slowed to negotiate the hump, the rest of the convoy close behind.

Stratton pressed his face to the tube and looked through the sights, his finger on the firing button.

The jeep bumped onto the tarmac.

Stratton placed it in his sights and followed it along the road that curved back almost towards him. His peripheral vision kept track of the truck now on the bridge. Stratton was not so much waiting for the jeep to be in a particular place as he was the truck. As it reached the end of the bridge and slowed to ease its wheels over the hump there, Stratton pressed the rubber trigger button.

The roar shattered the silence and the rocket shot from the end of the tube, a fiery blast belching from its rear to set fire to the grass behind Stratton. The projectile left a trail of white smoke to mark its track and struck the jeep, exploding and turning the vehicle into a fireball that continued to move forward, the burning bodies limp in their seats. Not surprisingly, it failed to take the bend in the road and plunged down the embankment to hit the river bank, jettisoning its cargo of flaming corpses.

The truck about to drive off the bridge slammed on its brakes.

Stratton dumped the spent launch tube, picked up another, and swivelled through ninety degrees to find the vehicle directly in front of the truck that held the peasants. Smoke from the burning grass wafted around him but not thickly enough to interfere with his aim. He fired. The rocket streaked across the river and struck the vehicle, which exploded, turned sharply and rolled onto its side. One of the soldiers crawled out and got to his feet, screaming as he staggered, unable to see. His clothes, hands and hair were ablaze and he dropped to the road, where he did not move and continued to burn.

The truck carrying the peasants stopped now, the people inside shrieking as they flung themselves down onto its floor in terror.

Stratton glanced at the bridge. Much of the convoy had stopped on it, bumper to bumper. The most important vehicle, the black Mercedes, was in the centre.

Stratton got to his feet and faced the rise. 'Louisa!' he shouted as he waved his arms.

Louisa had seen the devastation that the rockets had caused, realised what Stratton had achieved, and knew that at any second he would call upon her to administer the *coup de grâce*.

She'd already gripped the wires even before Stratton had called her name and was now holding them over the battery. If she'd been asked to pick up a gun and fire it she might have hesitated, lacking the confidence to pull the trigger and deal with the subsequent recoil and noise. But to touch the battery terminals with the ends of the wires was simple. She had come to terms with the guilt of sending so many souls to their deaths. Seeing the old man and the woman who'd tried to help him gunned down so callously only minutes before made it easier.

She touched the wire to the terminals and noticed a little spark, but was not even remotely prepared for the thunderous boom that followed. The explosion was tremendous, rocking the ground beneath her, and she covered her head as she slid down the slope.

Stratton grabbed Victor and together they hit the ground as the shock wave roared over them, punching them viciously in their backs as it passed.

Thousands of steel ball-bearings had been unleashed at bullet speed against the vehicles. The small metal spheres shredded the men sitting in the backs of the trucks, pulverised their skulls, tore their limbs away. No one inside escaped. Glass shattered. Every surface was peppered with holes. The vehicles dropped as their tyres burst. Fuel tanks erupted in flames and the bridge struts to which the mines had been tied buckled skywards.

Above the noise of the explosion's echoes countless ricochets could be heard as the claymores' steel balls hurtled furiously in all directions.

As the massive blast reverberated around the valley and began to subside debris rained down from the sky. A chunk of smoking metal hit the ground not far from Stratton and Victor. The steel balls came back to earth, splashing into the river and all around.

Stratton covered his head as several fragments of hot shrapnel landed painfully on his torso. As soon as the deluge of metal began to subside he was on his feet and grabbing up the remaining rocket launchers. It was not over yet.

A pick-up truck containing several soldiers behind the peasant's truck began to turn.

'Find a target, Victor,' Stratton called out as he snapped open a launch tube. He placed it on his shoulder and a second later fired. The rocket covered the distance in a second and slammed into the pick-up. The explosion lifted it off the road as it burst into flames.

Stratton dumped the empty launch tube and picked up another. He was operating on full automatic, locked into total kill mode and not giving the enemy a second to recover.

Several soldiers scurried from a largely undamaged truck near the bridge and took up firing positions. Victor snapped open his rocket launchers but as he fiddled with the safety catch a boom nearby signalled that Stratton was ahead of him. The rocket hit the truck and the vehicle disintegrated.

Victor finished preparing his weapon — he was determined to fire the damned thing.

The peasants had at first remained in their truck for fear of being shot while trying to flee. When the nearby vehicle went up they panicked and scrambled over the sides in an attempt to escape the carnage.

Several shots came from around the only vehicle that had escaped destruction other than the peasants' truck. Victor put the weapon on his shoulder, peered through the sights and pressed the trigger button. The tube shuddered as the rocket shot out to miss the target by inches and thud into the far embankment, showering the soldiers with dirt and shrapnel. Seconds later half a dozen of them walked out of the smoke with their empty hands in the air in the universal gesture of surrender.

Victor was stunned at the power of the device. He marched down the slope towards the river.

David and Bernard appeared, running along the river bank, guns in their hands.

The Indians crept towards the bridge, utterly stunned by the scene of destruction.

Victor crossed the river, keeping his launch tube aimed at the soldiers. 'Anyone moves and I shoot!' he shouted.

Stratton passed behind him on his way to the bridge. 'The tube's empty,' he said quietly.

Victor kept the weapon on his shoulder anyway. 'They don't know that,' he replied.

David and Bernard were buzzing with excitement and amazement as they joined their comrades.

'David!' Stratton called out. 'Go round up

your people,' he said, referring to the peasants. 'Bernard.'

Bernard was helping Victor cover the enemy soldiers and looked over at him.

'Collect their guns before they realise how few of us there are.'

Stratton climbed the embankment onto the road and walked towards the bridge. The smoke rising from the wreckage was mostly black because of the burning tyres. Ash floated in the air. Every metal span that a mine had been tied to was buckled or shattered.

The bridge creaked and groaned loudly and Stratton wondered how badly weakened it was. He stepped over wreckage to get to the side where he could pull himself up a few feet onto a span for a better view. The vehicles were misshapen wrecks, peppered with countless small holes. Their interiors were laid bare, windows shattered, roofs crushed, engines exposed. The bodies inside were almost unrecognisable as having once been human. Not a single piece of them was untouched by a ball bearing or the blast itself. Some body parts were identifiable — a foot, a hand, a boneless face lying flat on the ground. The rear door of the Mercedes hung open on one hinge and a large piece of flesh, the remains of a man but without any limbs or head attached, lay across the back seat, flopping out onto the road. Only DNA analysis could prove that it was Chemora, but Louisa had seen him. He had been in the Mercedes, and nothing in the car could have survived.

The smoke irritated Stratton's throat and he

jumped down and backed away. He slid down the embankment and crossed the river, heading for the rise, his thoughts now on Louisa.

She had not moved and sat near the crest staring at the bridge, unaware of him, a gentle breeze playing through her long hair.

'You okay?' he asked as he came up to her.

Louisa glanced at him and nodded. 'You did it.'

'We,' he corrected.

'Tell me something. And please be straight with me.'

'I've never been anything but.'

'When did you decide that I would be the one to blow the bridge?'

She was distant. It was only to be expected. 'It just worked out that way.'

'As long as you didn't do it.'

'I always hoped to avoid that, but I would've, if I'd had to.'

'That's right. You came here just to teach . . . We owe you an apology, don't we? We abused you.'

'Maybe Victor was right. This is everybody's fight.'

As Louisa watched the peasants gathering together, the women clutching their children, tears formed in her eyes, spilling forth to roll down her face. 'Why does it have to be like this?' she asked softly.

'We're still growing up.'

'We'll always be like this. There'll always be those willing to destroy in order to get what they don't deserve.'

'I don't agree. I can't agree. Otherwise what would be the point in fighting them? I'd just look for a place on this earth to wait out my life. We'll win in the end. Some day.'

Louisa did not look convinced and she got to her feet. 'What shall we do with them?' she asked, looking at the peasants.

'What do you want to do with them?'

She got his point. 'We'll take them back with us.'

'What about the soldiers?'

Victor and Bernard were stripping them of any weaponry, while Kebowa and Mohesiwa kept them covered with their drawn-back arrows.

'We'll let them go,' she said. 'They can tell the story of what a handful of revolutionaries can do.'

Stratton began to walk away down the rise.

'Legend will, of course, include a shadowy Englishman. But no one will really know who he was and why he came here. He was called The Mercenary, but that couldn't have been true. He took no payment for his work. And then he left as mysteriously as he arrived.'

Stratton continued walking.

Louisa watched him go.

★　★　★

The rebels were strangely quiet on the homeward journey. Even Victor did not say much. But they were not really subdued, not in their hearts. What had happened at the bridge had simply made them more serious. In part

232

they could not believe what they had done or, indeed, that they had all survived — and with hardly a scratch, at that. What was more, they had saved a dozen souls. As Victor had said, it was the stuff of legend.

He believed Neravista would be so shocked by the death of his brother that it could take him weeks to react. That was not due to any emotional debilitation, he was quick to point out. The man was incapable of such a thing, even when it came to his own family. Neravista would have been knocked back by the sheer audacity and fury of the assault.

Those adult peasants unfit to walk rode on the horses and burros with the children. The group travelled during the daytime and rested at night even though there was a possibility that government troops would be mobilised to find them. Stratton decided that the risks of serious injury to the women and children moving at night were far greater. By late afternoon of the third day they reached the plateau and the familiar approaches to their encampment.

Louisa had not given the reunion with her father much thought. But the smell of the campfires seemed to revive the guilt she had originally felt about leaving him, knowing how much he would have worried.

Victor suggested entering the camp the same way they had left, by the rarely used route direct to the stables to avoid the main entrance. It was more than likely that the entire camp already knew about the death of Chemora. News like that travelled fast. Whether or not it was known who precisely had undertaken the task remained to be seen.

As the group approached the stables Yoinakuwa came out to greet them. Victor never ceased to be amazed how that man knew about things before anyone else did. His sons ran to him and after embracing they walked off together, the sons evidently gabbling on about the explosion they had seen and the carnage it had caused.

Louisa lifted off the children who'd been riding on her horse and saw that they were escorted to the main camp. As she unbuckled the animal's saddle she noticed the white stallion running around the corral in an agitated fashion, which was most unlike it. A sudden fear coursed through her — the horse was Sebastian's and such animals were sensitive to a much-loved master's feelings.

As she walked to the top of the track Stratton sensed her concern and watched her. Suddenly she broke into a sprint, and he hurried after her towards the cabins. Sebastian's had a large hole in the side with burn marks around it and the roof had been badly charred.

Louisa reached the front door, pushed it open and hurried inside. The room had been almost destroyed by what appeared to have been a blast of some kind. 'Father?' she shouted, clambering over broken furniture to the room at the back. She pushed open the door to find it looking normal other than the bed being dishevelled. The maid always made it up while her father had his breakfast.

Panic gripped her heart and she ran out of the room and back to the front door as Stratton arrived. She hurried past him and raced outside, filled with dread that something had happened to Sebastian. Reaching the door of the smaller cabin she flung it open. Sebastian was seated at a table, calmly writing something. 'Father!' she cried. He got to his feet and she fell into his arms. They hugged tightly.

'I was very worried about you,' Sebastian said.

'I'm sorry. I shouldn't have left you,' Louisa said. 'Are you all right?' she asked.

'I'm fine,' he said, happy to see her. 'What about you?'

She nodded, almost overcome with relief. 'I'm fine too.'

They laughed and embraced again.

Stratton stepped into the doorway and, seeing them together, turned away as Victor came running over. 'Where's Sebastian?' he asked with urgency.

'He's in there. Everything is fine,' Stratton said, taking Victor's arm to lead him away. 'Give them a moment together,' he said.

Victor understood and exhaled deeply as his tension eased. He looked back at the main cabin and the damage that had been done to it. 'They tried to kill him. I'm sure of it.'

★ ★ ★

In their cabin Stratton and Victor ate a meal by the light of a hurricane lamp and some candles.

Victor was lost in thought and stared at one of the candle flames.

He looked at Stratton, who also appeared to be deep in thought, and held the wine jug over the Englishman's mug. Stratton did not react and Victor started to pour before realising that Stratton's mug was still full. 'You're not drinking tonight?' he asked.

Stratton shook his head.

'What are you thinking about?' Victor asked.

Stratton did not say.

'I think I know. You're going home tomorrow, for sure this time.'

'For sure.'

'Maybe you'll be lucky and something else will stop you.' Victor inspected the palms of his hands. 'Can I ask you something?'

Stratton didn't seem to care either way.

'If you knew something . . . maybe I should say, if you strongly suspected something that no one else did, and you wanted to reveal it, but if you did it would mean risking ridicule, would you still say it or would you stay silent?'

'What are you talking about?' Stratton asked tiredly.

'I know. It doesn't make sense. But I can't say anything without saying what I don't want to say. Ah, forget it.'

Stratton felt a twinge of guilt about not being of help to the Frenchman. 'I suppose that would depend on how important it was.'

'It's very important. Life-threatening.'

'Then why would you be ridiculed?'

'Because people don't take me seriously. Have

236

you ever wondered why Sebastian made me his second in command? Everyone else does.'

Stratton had too but didn't want even to hint at it.

'I was not Sebastian's first second in command, nor even his second or third. Those men had all been soldiers, selected for their military skills as well as for their leadership. They were strong-minded men who had firm opinions about how things should be run. On occasion they would act on their own initiative, often to Sebastian's consternation. He wanted to control everything himself. He came to see those strong-minded men as obstacles. When I arrived he must have decided I was perfect for him. I was educated, I had management skills and I didn't know a damned thing about soldiering. I was also not very assertive. Oh, I can stand up for myself, but that's not the same. I would not obstruct him. But I did begin to question things.'

Victor took a long sip of his wine and went silent.

'Do you have proof?' Stratton asked.

'Of what?'

'This thing you know, or suspect, that no one else does.'

'Of course not. I would not be ridiculed if I could prove it.'

'Is there proof? Can you get any?'

'There must be. But I don't know how to get it.'

'Can you influence a change?'

'What do you mean?' Victor asked, showing interest in the suggestion.

237

'I don't know. Only you do. I'm trying to help you out, that's all.'

'No, no. That's an interesting question,' Victor said, looking thoughtful. And then just as quickly he lost confidence in himself. 'But I don't think I'm strong enough.'

'In what way? Physically or mentally?'

'Both.'

'I think you're too hard on yourself.'

'If that's a way of saying I'm tougher than I think, thank you. But I know myself well enough.'

'That's what they all say. I've spent my entire adult life in wars and conflicts. They have a habit of changing everything about a man. People either change to survive the violence, escape it, or they change to fight it. Maybe you weren't the most perfect second in command when you took the job. But maybe you're a lot more like those other guys now than you think.'

Victor thought about this as he took another sip of wine. 'And you, my friend. How have you changed?'

Stratton shrugged.

Victor smiled as if he knew something. 'Have you ever been in love before?'

Stratton didn't want to hear that particular question. He reached for his mug of wine.

'Come on. Why don't you lower that wall just for once in your life?'

Stratton held on to his mug and stared at the candle. 'I thought I had been, until now. I would have run away the day I got here if I'd

238

known it was going to be like this.'

'Then you have not changed at all. Anyone can fall in love. The change for you would be holding on to it.'

Stratton glanced at Victor, feeling the sting of the comment. He got up and went to the fire that burned vigorously in the grate. A large cauldron of steaming water hung on a chain above it. 'You want this first?' he asked, dipping a finger in it just long enough to discover it was hot.

Victor emptied his mug and got to his feet. 'I had a bath last week,' he said, picking up his hat and jacket and walking to the door. 'I will not be back tonight,' he said, looking resolute about something. 'If you can change, well, I can too.' He opened the door and paused to look back at Stratton. 'In case I don't get a chance to say it later, it's been an honour.'

The two men held each other's gazes for a moment. Victor stepped into the darkness and closed the door behind him. Stratton could only wonder what was on the Frenchman's mind.

A large metal bath hung from a nail on the wall. Stratton lifted it off and placed it in front of the fire. He wiped a finger around the inside to discover that it was coated in dust. 'Which week was that, Victor?' he asked softly.

He rinsed out the bath with some cold water and set about emptying the cauldron into it.

★ ★ ★

As Victor left the cabin he noticed the flames of the courtyard fire. Half a dozen armed rebels were gathered at the wooden table, talking, smoking and drinking coffee. The night had a distinct chill to it. All of the men wore jackets or woollen jumpers.

Victor gave them a wave that was returned with more enthusiasm than he had noticed before. Those who had taken part in the Chemora attack had been elevated to heroic status. Victor could not help feeling inspired by the achievement as he headed towards the smaller cabin.

He knocked on the door, which was opened a moment later by Louisa. 'Victor. Come in,' she said.

Sebastian was at the table, finishing off a meal. 'Good evening, Victor. To what do we owe the pleasure?'

'I was wondering if I could have a brief word with you. Something has been on my mind and I have to discuss it.'

'We cannot have things weighing heavily on minds if they can be lifted,' Sebastian said.

'I'm going for a walk,' Louisa said. 'Don't wait up for me.' She smiled a goodbye to her father and Victor and left the cabin.

Victor faced Sebastian and took a deep breath as if to strengthen his resolve. 'I'm troubled,' he said. 'It has to do with this assassination attempt.'

Sebastian waited patiently.

'The one person I least trust in all of this is Steel. At least we know Neravista. We know what he wants.'

'We all know not to trust Steel.'

'Yes, but we all have different ideas of how far to trust him. You trust him enough to let him into this camp, for instance. I do not. I would not be surprised if he had something to do with the attempt on your life.'

'Where is your evidence?'

'I don't have any.'

'Then this notion is a product of your imagination.'

'That's not all. I think Steel has allegiances to others — stronger than to us. I do not discount Hector's involvement in this.'

Sebastian's gaze turned cold. 'Please don't try to manipulate me, Victor. I expect more from you.'

'Do you?' Sebastian did not miss the flash of new tough-mindedness in Victor's tone. 'I came here to give you my views. As second in command I think I am entitled to air them.'

'If I wanted those kinds of views I would have someone with a background in military intelligence as my adviser.'

'It doesn't take a soldier to see such things. Call it intuition if you want. I'm not a soldier but I have plenty of experience of life.'

'And what do you propose we do about these intuitions?'

Victor was not sure. He had not thought that part through thoroughly. 'Perhaps we should be frank. Let's confront Steel with our concerns and see what he says.'

Sebastian looked suddenly irritated with Victor. 'If you have no stomach for this fight any more then you are under no obligation to stay.'

Victor was stunned by the comment. 'After all that I have sacrificed, this is what you say to me, for expressing my opinion?'

'I've been living by my wits my entire life. Things change, Victor. People change. Perhaps we no longer follow the same path.'

Victor was furious. Frustration welled up in him. He felt as if he had been mortally wounded. 'I have learned something about change tonight. And that is not to be afraid of it.'

Sebastian did not react. Victor went to the door and left the cabin.

He closed the door and stood in the darkness, the emotional wound stinging intensely. But instead of skulking away to drink himself to sleep he straightened his back and gritted his teeth. He was not going to let this one go. If he was at a crossroads with this revolution then it was time to do something other than what he had been doing.

To keep out of sight Victor decided to take the back path between the cabins that led to the stables. When he got there he saddled his horse and led it out of the stall. As he climbed onto the animal's back Yoinakuwa stepped from the shadows, startling him.

'Will you stop doing that,' Victor said, clutching at his chest. 'One of these days you're going to give me a heart attack.'

Yoinakuwa looked him in the eye, his question plain enough.

'I have to go somewhere,' Victor said. 'I will be

fine on my own.' Then he had an afterthought. 'But if I am not back by morning you may find the answer in Hector's camp.'

Victor rode away into the darkness. Yoinakuwa watched him go.

7

Stratton placed his clothes over the back of a chair, stepped into the metal bath and lowered himself gingerly into the hot water. He immersed himself gradually, sliding down until the liquid was up to his neck, taking a moment to get used to the heat before sinking beneath the surface.

He held his breath, relishing the sensation of the hot water all around him. As he resurfaced slowly and opened his eyes the door of the cabin opened. His gaze flicked to his pistol a foot away on the chair and he moved his hand towards it.

Louisa stepped in stealthily and closed the door behind her quietly, keeping her back to it as she looked around the room.

When she saw Stratton lying in the tub looking at her she broke into a giggle. 'I'm sorry,' she said in a soft voice. 'I didn't knock because I didn't want the guards to see me.'

'Did they?'

'I don't think so.'

'Some guards.'

'They're not meant for you.'

'I'm not worth protecting any more?'

'You don't need protecting. Anyone with any sense would be afraid to come in here.'

'You're here.'

'There's nothing in here that I'm afraid of.'

Stratton smiled at the innuendo.

'Can I lock the door?'

He raised his eyebrows questioningly.

Louisa ignored him and drew the bolt across. 'How's your back?' she asked, walking over to him. 'I neglected to change the dressing. I've been a terrible nurse.'

'I understood that was because you'd moved on from nursing.'

'We have to win the revolution first. Let me see it,' she asked, walking behind him.

Stratton leaned forward in the tub as she crouched down. He felt her fingers on his back, touching him gently. Then her palms spread out and covered an area much larger than the wound. 'You heal well,' she said as she dipped a hand in the water. 'You like your bath hot.'

'Not usually. But it's been a while.'

'Can I wash your back for you?'

'You're very kind.'

Louisa was about to pick up the large slab of brown soap on the chair next to his pistol. Then she gave it a dismissive look. 'You can't wash your skin with laundry soap,' she said. 'There's a box of shampoos and gels somewhere.' She stood up and walked away.

Stratton listened to her rummaging through some boxes.

'Victor looked disturbed tonight,' she said.

'He seems to have a lot on his mind.'

'Did he tell you?'

'No.'

'He's having a private talk with my father, just the two of them. That's unusual for him. The ambush has changed him — made him more daring, perhaps.'

The sounds of Louisa searching through the boxes ceased and Stratton waited for the sound of her boots on the floor as she came back. But there was nothing other than the crackling noise of the fire. He heard a soft sound close by and remained still, wondering what she was doing.

He looked down to see her bare foot dipping into the water. The other followed and she lowered her naked body into the tub behind him, stretching her legs out either side of him. She held his lower back tightly between her thighs.

Gently, she took hold of his shoulders and guided him until his back was resting against her breasts. She placed a hand on his forehead and pressed his head back until it was nestling on her shoulder. Then she laid her cheek against his.

'That was pretty sneaky,' Stratton said.

'It's called strategy. It's not just used in war, you know. I was told that you can use it in anything. Even love.'

'That's a wise teacher you have there.'

'Well, he knows his stuff on the battlefield. I don't know what else he might be good at, though.'

It was the most delicious gauntlet that had ever been thrown down before him, Stratton thought.

'There's something I have to ask you,' Louisa said.

'What?'

'Did your grandmother really want to be a Gurkha?' she smiled.

'No. Of course not. Not after three years in the Foreign Legion.'

'Idiot.'

'I don't blame her, really.'

'Stop it,' she laughed.

They lay in silence, bathed in the orange glow from the fire, both of them staring at it and lost in their thoughts.

Finally Louisa spoke. 'Let's not talk about anything beyond this moment. No futures. No dreams.'

'I can't control my thoughts,' Stratton said.

She kissed his cheek. 'Maybe *I* can, for a little while.' He turned his head to look into her eyes and their lips met softly. He reached an arm behind her waist and lifted her around to sit on him. Their kisses grew more passionate, more urgent.

★　★　★

The entrance to Hector's camp looked more threatening than Sebastian's. A tree-trunk wall filled the long gap between two rocky outcrops. It had an immense gate in the middle with a smaller entrance to one side. As Victor approached, looking as haggard as his horse, he saw two earth-and-sandbag machine-gun emplacements, with others on top of the rocky hillocks. Half a dozen heavily armed guards stood outside. One of them recognised Victor and sent a runner to deliver his message to Hector.

He climbed down and tried to ease his aching back and hips. He had never ridden a horse before joining the rebellion and after his first ride he'd realised that his body had long since grown inflexible and would never adapt to sitting astride anything so wide for long periods of time. He had barely recovered from the ride to and from the ambush and within a few minutes of his journey to Hector's camp all the same aches and pains had returned twofold.

Victor waited for half an hour before someone arrived to escort him inside. He had never been to Hector's encampment before. The five rebel fortresses were spread in a wide semicircle over several interconnected plateaus, the strategic intention being that they could support each other if they were attacked by Neravistas.

The layout of the camp was difficult to make out in the darkness but it seemed better designed to withstand attack than Sebastian's. Now that Victor was inside the perimeter he felt nervous and uncomfortable. The rebels he passed seemed to eye him suspiciously and not just because he was an outsider. Their looks felt almost accusatory. Victor wondered if Sebastian was right and that he had developed an overactive imagination that verged on paranoia.

The guide showed him to a large cabin, bigger than Sebastian's original quarters. He tied off his horse and looked around him. A group of armed men were gathered around a table illuminated by hurricane lamps. They watched him silently, their guns within easy reach. He was tempted to wave but decided against it. They looked a surly crew.

The guide pointed Victor towards the front door of the cabin but did not go near it himself.

Victor felt a sudden chill, not in the air but more like a warning from his heart. He told himself to calm down as he removed his hat, marched to the door and opened it.

Hector sat alone inside the comfortably furnished room, reading a document by the light from an elegant candelabrum. A small fire was burning in the grate.

He glanced at Victor before going back to his document. 'I thought they were mistaken when they told me you were here. Somehow I don't believe Sebastian sent you.'

'He did not.'

'Of course. Why would he?' Hector said sarcastically. 'I don't even understand what you're doing in this revolution, never mind second in command to a brigade. If there was ever an example of Sebastian's poor judgement it's you.'

Victor clenched his jaw and absorbed the abuse. 'I know you're angry with me, Hector. Perhaps you have every reason to be. I — '

'What are you doing here?' Hector interrupted rudely. 'I threatened your life the other day, yet here you are, alone in my camp.' He made a sudden pantomime of looking around. 'Maybe you have your Indians hidden somewhere,' he said, his sarcasm undiminished. 'Or perhaps you're feeling heroic after blowing up Chemora.'

Victor began to wonder if coming to the camp had been such a good idea. The man was already acting aggressively and Victor had not even said his piece. But he had come all this way and was not going to leave without telling Hector why. 'I

249

came to see you, Hector, because I'm afraid for the future of this struggle. I'm concerned that the reasons we started it have been lost. And I'm afraid for Sebastian.'

Hector chuckled. 'You're afraid for Sebastian? That's ridiculous. This revolution isn't about any one person. We're all expendable.'

'I think it would be a mistake to allow something to happen to him. He's still a great symbol to the people.'

'Why are you coming to me? Why not any of the other council members?'

'You are their voice.'

'I am a voice of reason that they agree with.'

'Someone tried to kill Sebastian.'

'Oh, so you think I had something to do with it?'

'I did not say that.'

'I have no control over those who did.'

'Then you know who they are.'

'Don't try and get smart with me,' Hector warned him.

Victor took heed and moderated his tone. 'This bad blood between you and Sebastian — perhaps it's sending the wrong message to some people. Maybe someone tried to get rid of Sebastian because they thought it's what you wanted.'

'You are amazing, Victor. You stand here in my house with your innuendos and ridiculous requests as if you were an equal or even someone of importance. I'm not interested in you or your opinions or anything else you have to say. Did you seriously think when you were daydreaming about coming here that I would put my arm around you and say, 'Sure, Victor, let's find a way to all live together, you're a great guy, Victor'? You have no importance to me or to anyone, actually, and that includes Sebastian.'

Desperation began to gnaw at Victor. His planned dialogue was falling apart at the seams. He had believed that being Sebastian's number two might count for something outside of his own commander's cabin but Hector's ridiculing was battering his self-confidence. He became flustered and started to lose the thread of his argument. All that was left was a suspicion he had developed about the attempt on Sebastian's life and, perhaps in desperation to be taken seriously, he could not help but blurt it out. 'I don't think it was a coincidence that the bomb in Sebastian's house detonated when it was known that Louisa would be out of the camp for several days.'

Hector stared at him with narrowed eyes. 'You go too far with your suggestions.'

Victor's blood was now up. Louisa was Hector's one obvious weakness and he decided to go for it. 'It's you who've gone too far,' he said. 'You've lost her heart to another because of your actions.'

Hector got to his feet, his face reddening. 'That is a personal insult. I should kill you where you stand but I will still observe a visitor's right — even yours — to safety.'

'She's no longer yours — if she ever was.'

Hector stared at him, his teeth bared. 'Who is he?'

'It doesn't matter, other than he shares Louisa's political convictions. But doesn't it even hint to you that you're wrong?'

'Get out of here,' Hector said, drawing his machete. 'One more word and I *will* kill you where you stand. I don't ever want to see your face again! Go!'

Victor stepped back at the vehemence in the other man's words, turned for the door and left the cabin.

He put on his hat as he marched to his horse and climbed onto it. He rode away looking back over his shoulder, uneasy that the threat to his life had not gone.

Hector stepped outside to see the Frenchman disappear into the darkness. He put his machete back in its sheath as he looked over at the group of men, focusing on one in particular. It was the one who had delivered the message to Louisa at the stables. The man responded to Hector's gesture of summons and hurried to his master. After a few brief words he walked away, at the same time alerting subordinates of his own who quickly followed him.

Hector went back inside his cabin and closed the door. Victor's words about Louisa had wounded him. He walked over to an ornately carved dresser, pulled open a drawer and removed something wrapped in a scarf. He smelled the material and even though the perfume that had once pervaded it was long gone the smell of the scarf itself prompted memories of her. He removed it to reveal the frame with Louisa's picture in it that he had stolen from Sebastian's house all those years ago. His jaw tightened as he studied her eyes, her slight smile and elegant poise. Over the years he had made it his picture. It was him she was looking at, even though she had not known him when it was taken. Something snapped inside of him at the thought of her heart going to another and he threw the frame and scarf into the fireplace.

Unable to watch the flames distort and burn her face into oblivion he turned his back on it and stepped through a door in the far wall into a smoke-filled room where Steel and Ventura were enjoying cigars and brandy.

They watched Hector as he poured himself a drink and downed it in one.

Ventura gave Steel a sideways glance and a knowing smile. 'Hector? If you don't mind. The way I see it now, you have two choices. You either remove Sebastian yourself, and soon, or you allow us to.'

'I told you I would take care of it,' Hector replied softly.

'Can I remind you,' Ventura continued, 'that there have been two significant occurrences since we last met that have greatly influenced current events. One, Chemora was killed by Sebastian. Two, an attempt on Sebastian's life failed.'

'Gentlemen,' Steel interjected diplomatically. 'If I may add a little flavour to this stew that you guys are cooking. My people are pleased with the peace proposals as presented by Neravista and agreed to by you, Hector.'

'There is no agreement yet,' Hector corrected

253

him in a tone that suggested he had said it a thousand times.

'Okay,' Steel acknowledged. 'A proposal that provides the foundations on which you and Neravista could possibly build an understanding.'

Hector shrugged to confirm that he considered the statement close enough.

'A speedy and sustainable end to the conflict is all that we — as in 'my people' — are concerned with at the moment,' Steel added.

'Sebastian's death could seriously upset this strategy, at least for some months,' Hector warned.

'Then why did you try to kill him?' Ventura asked.

'I didn't,' Hector insisted, looking at Steel.

Steel drew on his cigar before realising that both men were looking at him. 'Why're you lookin' at me?' he asked, unable to suppress a grin.

'I know that one of Julio's men planted the bomb,' Hector said. 'What did you promise him?'

Steel blew out smoke and shrugged, knowing when he was cornered. But it was no big deal to him. 'A US passport. But not to kill Sebastian. He arranged the booby trap in the weapons cache and was supposed to maintain the confusion.'

Hector shook his head in disappointment.

'It was Julio's idea,' Steel added.

'Julio has never had an idea of his own in his life,' Hector said accusingly.

'It sounds like Victor thinks it was you,' Steel said, sounding amused.

'Don't worry about Victor. He won't be telling anyone any of his suspicions after tonight,' Hector said.

The news did not faze the other two men.

'I appreciate the personal difficulties you might have in sanctioning Sebastian's death,' Ventura offered. 'Which is why I think it would be best if you did not have that burden.'

'You think that makes it any easier for me, letting you do it?'

'I am right, though, aren't I?' Ventura said, looking at Steel as if he was speaking to him. 'I don't believe the peace negotiations will be jeopardised by Sebastian's death. On the contrary. I believe it will speed the process.'

Hector took a sword from the wall and weighed it in his hand. 'They would not be jeopardised by your absence either, Ventura.'

Ventura gave him a piercing look, angered more by Hector's insolence than the physical threat.

'Gentlemen,' Steel said soothingly. 'We're allowing our emotions to run a little high. I agree with Hector that we must be sure about the effect any mishap that might befall Sebastian could have on the people. I also agree with him that the decision on how to proceed in that matter should come from the revolutionaries themselves. Surely they are best placed to decide on that subject and they are also the best people to absorb the repercussions. But, Hector, I must agree with Ventura that you are perhaps too

255

emotionally involved to make the best judgement call here. You do see that, don't you?'

Hector's silence seemed to indicate that he agreed, in principle at any rate.

'Well,' Steel announced, getting up from his seat and finishing off his brandy. 'I've gotta go.'

Ventura too got to his feet, placed his unfinished glass on the table and stubbed out his cigar. 'Me, too,' he agreed.

'Why don't you think about it, Hector?' Steel suggested. 'This is the perfect time to strike. Neravista is mighty pissed about losing his brother. You push your demands, back them up with an assurance that you'll take care of the man who killed Chemora and you just might get a good piece of what you want.'

Hector glanced at him. It was something that he had not considered.

'Thanks for your hospitality,' Steel said as he strode out of the room, followed by Ventura.

★ ★ ★

The two men left the cabin and walked into the night towards the main camp, its fires burning in the distance.

'That was clever,' Ventura said. 'I hope Hector is intelligent enough to see it.'

'Was it? It is an issue, though. How to get rid of a legend without the legend biting you in the ass at the same time.'

'Have the legend die at the hands of someone he trusts — or make it look like that, at least.'

Steel drew on his cigar. 'You mean Julio?'

256

'No. He's unreliable. What if Sebastian was killed by outsiders?' Ventura suggested.

'What would their purpose be?'

'What's yours?'

Steel smiled, glancing at Ventura. 'You mean, if the Americans were to be accused?'

'Why not? You have to pay a price at some time. Playing one side off against the other has not produced the results you wanted. You have big shoulders.'

Steel contemplated the idea. 'I would have to cover my own ass. I don't mind Uncle Sam getting the blame but I don't want to make it look personal.'

'Of course. What about the Englishman?'

Steel nodded. 'That's a possibility . . . You're a natural at this, Ventura. I'm going to have to watch you.'

Ventura was pleased by the flattery. 'How would we go about it?'

'It wouldn't be difficult. We don't have to alter our plans any.'

'There is one other issue,' Ventura said, looking a little uncomfortable.

'What's that?'

'The Nerugan gold mines. I saw the licensing proposal. How much of that syndicate do you control?'

Steel came to a stop and faced the government official. 'Are you ready to take the pebble?' he asked, holding out his hand, a threatening look in his eye.

Ventura looked into the open palm that had nothing in it. 'It wasn't a challenge,' he said, aware how dangerous Steel could be.

Steel closed his hand on the invisible stone. 'Good. Your battalion is on the highway, right?'

'Yes.'

'It's ready to move in on your command?'

'Yes.'

'This is now all about neutralising Sebastian's brigade and there's only one way you're gonna do it. You have to move between Hector's and Sebastian's encampments. Hector won't touch your back. He's got too much to lose. If he countered your attack it would only push him further from his dream of becoming a revolutionary leader. I'll make sure he knows that.'

Ventura nodded in agreement. 'We could begin to move into position during daylight tomorrow. Preparations could be complete by nightfall. We could attack the following morning.'

'Sounds perfect to me, my friend. It'll be over in a couple hours. Especially with those helicopters we gave you.'

'So what's the final story concerning Sebastian?' Ventura asked. 'How will the people eventually see it?'

'They'll see what they're given. The revolutionary council brokered a deal with the government but Sebastian stood in its way. Sebastian's outfit became a rogue terrorist organisation that murdered the head of the government's beloved brother. The revolutionary council tried to get rid of Sebastian but failed and found they were unable to deal with the situation themselves. So they paid a mercenary,

258

who happened to be training Sebastian's troops at the time, to kill him. Meanwhile, government troops arrived to arrest Sebastian for the murder of Chemora. A skirmish broke out. People were killed. The mercenary was never seen or heard from again. But everything turned out fine in the end. The revolutionaries, under their new leader Hector, brokered a deal with Neravista and everyone lived happily ever after. It'll get a short column on page five of the *New York Post*.'

Ventura smiled thinly at the story. 'It will work. And you will be rewarded for your efforts . . . by your own people?'

'I get a reputation among people who respect that kind of thing.'

'Then there's the gold mine,' Ventura said, his words this time accompanied by a friendly smirk.

Steel glanced at him long enough to see there was no intended malice. 'You still ain't ready to take that pebble, Ventura.'

'But I'm getting closer, no?'

Both men laughed as they walked into the night.

★　★　★

In the darkness Victor trotted along the track, with the niggling feeling that someone was following him. He slowed to a stop to look back and listen, but he could hear nothing. It was so dark that he could not see far beyond his horse's nose. The glow from the fires of Hector's encampment had already disappeared.

259

He trotted on, not looking forward to the ride or to getting back to the camp. Terrible suspicions about Hector haunted him. He felt something very bad was going to happen. But no one would listen to him, anyway.

Victor felt suddenly alone, and not just physically. He wondered if it was time to move on himself. The rebellion no longer felt like the one he had joined. Deep down he was not entirely against Hector's efforts to broker a peace deal. Victor hated violence and the prospect of more to come while Sebastian remained entrenched appalled him. He knew his thoughts were disloyal and that his reasons for wanting peace now were selfish. But it was how he felt and he could not ignore it.

An unfamiliar sound snapped him out of his thoughts.

He slowed down again, turned and listened. He couldn't see anything, yet the distant sound remained. He stopped altogether.

It was a rumbling sound and growing louder, like hooves rapidly striking the ground. That was it. Riders!

Victor's first thought was to step back into the undergrowth and let whoever it was pass. But that would have been too risky right now. He might not have had good enough reasons for his paranoia before he'd arrived at Hector's camp but he felt entirely justified by the time he had left it. If he was right and Hector had been prepared to kill Sebastian then the man would have no qualms about doing the same to him. Victor was suddenly filled with fear.

The pounding of hooves grew louder and Victor dug his heels into his horse's flanks so hard that the animal shot forward at a gallop. He lost his hat and raced along the track.

Panic gripped him. He felt a desperate need to escape. But he could barely see ahead — the cloud-covered sky and the trees lining the track made the blackness complete. A branch whacked him across the face, a stinging blow that drew blood. He crouched low against the horse's neck and spurred the animal on.

The sound of pursuit became fainter but it had only become lost in the noise of the thudding hooves of his own mount. Victor wanted to look back but did not dare allow his stare to stray from the way ahead. His horse swerved suddenly to take a bend in the track but it had come upon it too suddenly and its flank struck a branch. Victor felt a solid blow against his leg that must have hurt the horse too but the animal did not flinch and powered on.

They galloped into another tight turn and this time Victor almost lost his balance. As he sat up in the saddle a low branch came out of nowhere and slammed him in the shoulder. He stopped dead while his horse continued on. He somersaulted backwards and struck the ground brutally hard, rolling over several times before coming to a halt in the centre of the track.

The blow and the fall stunned Victor and he lay in the dirt, trying to regain his senses. He rolled onto his front and pulled his knees beneath him, feeling a searing pain in his chest. He realised that the sound of beating hooves came from his pursuers. They would soon reach the bend.

Victor rolled as fast as he could to the edge of the track and got there just as the beasts thrashed past him. He pushed himself up onto his knees where he balanced unsteadily. He had to get going — but which way? if he remained on the trail there was a chance of running into the riders again. He could not be absolutely certain that they had been pursuing him but he was not about to wait around and ask them. His only option was to make his way into the bush and somehow shadow the track until he could be certain where he was. He needed to cross a valley to the adjacent plateau on top of which was his own encampment. But at night, in this jungle, that was going to be easier said than done.

He got to his feet, put his back to the track and felt his way forward, immediately hitting an impenetrable thicket. He tried to explore a way around it but the sound of hooves froze him. The horsemen were returning, this time at the trot.

Victor dropped to his belly and like a rodent scurried deeper into the bush, dragging himself in as far as he could.

As the sound of trotting horses grew louder he went motionless, feeling as defenceless as a tortoise on its back.

A lone horse slightly ahead of the others slowed to a walk and a flashlight beam played along the track and into the bushes. The light passed over Victor but the rider continued on. Another horse followed a little way behind and stopped a few metres beyond him. A new beam came on and shone along the track. Victor practically stopped breathing.

This horse and its rider remained perfectly still as if listening. Victor was afraid they could hear his heart pounding in his chest.

The sound of more hooves announced other riders closing in. They came to a stop. 'I found his hat,' a man's voice said. 'He was wearing it when he left.'

Another pair of riders joined them. 'We saw his horse,' one of them said. 'There was no sign of him, though. He's ducked into the forest.'

The men fell silent. Victor stared at the feet of the horses that were almost within touching distance. Then: 'Victor!' a voice boomed. 'I know you can hear me. You're lying somewhere nearby in the dirt, scared to death and wondering if we will find you. You have every reason to be scared. If we find you we will slit your throat. I have a message for you from Hector. Don't go back to Sebastian's camp or you will die. If you value your life you'll leave this place, leave this country and never come back. That's not just a warning, Victor. That's a promise.'

The horses remained still for a moment before trotting away in the direction of Hector's encampment.

Victor lay where he was for a long time without moving, partly to ensure that the riders had gone and were not trying to trick him but mostly because he simply did not know what to do. The very question he had pondered earlier had been answered for him. His revolution had indeed come to an end.

All those years of fighting and sacrifice were suddenly history. Worse still, he was now an enemy of those he had once fought alongside. He had known it would end one day but not like this. Even his death, which he had contemplated on occasion, would now be meaningless and without glory. He would not see the end of the great struggle. For him, there would be no celebrations, no hugging of comrades, no emotional reunions.

He could, of course, ignore the threat. Sebastian might even give him protection if he ever forgave him for going to Hector's camp in the first place. But Victor did not think he could live with that threat hanging over him. The constant danger would be too much for him to bear.

An hour or more passed before he eventually crawled out from under the bush and got to his feet. He stood in the middle of the track, bruised and filthy, and looked in the direction of Hector's camp. His chest hurt like hell, particularly when he took a breath. His faced throbbed where the branch had struck him. But he was alive.

Where he was headed he had no idea. Home was the obvious choice. Back to France and his beautiful Pyrenees. Strangely, the idea did not fill him with joy as it had in the past. Enforced on him by the threat of death, his exit from the rebellion would be made under a shadow. No more the return of a valiant hero. It would be a private homecoming. His story, with its unflattering ending, would not be worth telling to anyone, not when he and any listener were sober, at least.

Victor turned his back on Hector's camp and walked on into the night.

★ ★ ★

As the first rays of light broke through the gaps in the straw roof, Louisa awoke in Stratton's arms. They had made love several times throughout the night, their lust for each other heightened by the knowledge that he would soon leave.

Stratton was on the edge of sleep and his eyes opened as he felt Louisa sit up. He watched her stand and walk to the top of the stairs where she stopped to look back at him. She smiled, sadness in her eyes, and walked down the stairs, her rich black hair cascading down her back.

He sat up. He could hear her getting dressed and when her boots sounded across the floor he went to the balcony to watch her leave. She blew him a kiss before opening the door and then she was gone. It struck him that he might never see her again.

Stratton tried to think how it would be to stay. The obvious question was for how long. Even if the revolution ended that week, what would he do? Follow her around like a puppy, hoping she might have a spare moment for him once in a while? Her path was set, or at least she had a plan and was the type to pursue it vigorously. Her political involvement would require work and dedication and mixing with similarly committed people. Having a soldier in tow, a lover from the fighting days, would be trying to live her life in two different worlds. It wasn't practical. It had no future. If it was so obvious to him it would be the same for her. Last night had been as much about goodbye as it had been about anything else.

Stratton rooted around the kitchen looking for any food he could take with him. He found some bread, cheese, dried meat and an apple which he distributed around his pockets.

He shouldered his parachute and pack, picked up his rifle, took a last look around and left the cabin.

Stratton cut across towards the defensive position at the foot of the slope leading up to the stables. He paused to look at Sebastian's cabin, the urge to knock on the door and see Louisa nearly overpowering him. He reminded himself once again that it was pointless and took a couple of steps away. But he stopped again. The pressure to see her was too great. It was almost painful. What was the harm, he reasoned. All he wanted was to see her face, a chance to touch her one last time. It was as if a part of him was willing him away while another tried to push him towards her.

A man ran down the slope calling his name. It was David. 'Victor's horse has returned without him,' he said, out of breath and looking extremely concerned.

They hurried together up the incline to the stables where Bernard had unsaddled the animal and was inspecting it.

'He has cuts on his face and flanks,' Bernard said, kneeling to inspect its legs. 'This horse has been run pretty hard through jungle.'

'Anyone know where Victor was going?' Stratton said.

There was no answer.

'Where're the Indians?' he asked.

'Mohesiwa was here when the horse arrived,' Bernard said. 'He left as soon as he discovered the animal was Victor's.'

Stratton thought of his last conversation with Victor. The man wanted to effect some kind of change somewhere that would take him the night to get there and back to. 'How far's Hector's camp from here?' he asked.

'Three hours,' David replied. 'Why would he go there?'

'I didn't say he did.'

'That road is dangerous,' David said, wondering if Stratton knew more than he was prepared to say. 'There have been reports of Neravistas on that path.'

'I'd like to look in that direction,' Stratton said, not really knowing what he would be looking for other than an unhorsed Victor lying injured somewhere.

'The patrol to relieve the northern outpost leaves soon,' Bernard said. 'It follows part of the route to Hector's camp. Maybe the outpost knows something.'

'Let's do it,' Stratton said.

'Give me those,' David said, taking Stratton's

pack and parachute. 'I'll leave them in the end stall for you.'

Stratton shouldered his rifle and magazine pouch and followed Bernard to the main entrance.

Half a dozen men equipped for their duty in the outpost were getting ready to leave the camp. The main entrance was busy with its usual traffic of burros bringing in food supplies, wood and water.

Bernard had a quick word with the patrol commander and came back to Stratton as the party headed out. 'We can go with them,' he reported as they followed the patrol through the entrance. 'They've not heard from the outpost this morning.'

'Is that unusual?' Stratton asked.

'No. The radios are old American HF sets and don't work very well.'

'How far is the outpost?'

'Less than an hour.'

Stratton looked back, thoughts of Louisa still lingering in his mind, hoping she might have heard about Victor's disappearance and come to see him. He could not see her in the crowd and within minutes the camp entrance was out of sight as they headed into the jungle.

The track was well travelled and easy underfoot, apart from a rocky section that was more of a climb than anything else. From the top Bernard pointed to a distant knoll, a kilometre or so away, where the outpost was located.

They trudged along, spread out in single file, Stratton near the rear with Bernard. As the head of the patrol approached a lone tree with the knoll beyond the lead man quickly signalled a halt, followed by another order to go to ground. Each man stepped off the track and dropped into a crouch, looking in every direction for signs of the enemy.

Bernard turned to Stratton. 'There's something wrong,' he said, looking around tensely. 'Someone from the outpost is usually waiting by that tree to meet the relief, but no one is there.'

Stratton found Bernard's unease alarming. The track traversed a long slope covered in long grass and patches of dense bush. They were exposed to the high ground, not the ideal place to hang around. 'We shouldn't stay here,' Stratton suggested.

Bernard understood and moved ahead. As he approached the front of the patrol the lead men were moving forward to the tree. Bernard signalled the others to move on.

One by one, each man walked past the tree, stepping between a group of large rocks and disappearing out of sight.

When Stratton reached the same spot he saw the others up ahead, standing around as if transfixed by something. As he approached he could hear the intense buzzing of thousands of flies. Lying on the ground in a small clearing were the six members of the rebel outpost, all dead, shot through their heads and torsos. One had had his throat slit.

One of the relief patrol moved away to throw his guts up. The rest stared unmoving at their fallen comrades with looks of horror and disgust.

269

Stratton found the situation curious insofar as the outpost crew had been shot out in the open rather than behind cover as one might expect in a firefight. He picked up one of the dead men's rifles and removed the magazine. It was full. He checked the man's magazine pouch which was also untouched. A similar inspection of another dead rebel's weapon and ammo pouch revealed the same. 'They didn't return fire,' he said.

He grew very uneasy with the location and looked to the high ground.

'What should we do?' Bernard asked.

'You need to keep this outpost open,' Stratton said. 'There's a reason someone wanted it wiped out. Set up the radio, inform your people and get reinforcements down here. Tell them to bring half a dozen claymores. This is what they were designed for.'

The radio operator removed his pack to set up communications, the patrol commander putting the headset over his ears.

'You?' Stratton said, getting the attention of one of the young men still transfixed by the dead. 'Cover the route we came in on. You? Cover in that direction. You and you. I want you to clear the high ground,' he said, indicating the area above the outpost. 'That whole area all the way to the top.'

The men obeyed.

Stratton went to the lookout position and studied the panorama. The knoll provided a dramatic view of the junction of three valleys, the main approaches to that side of the plateau. He scanned in all directions with his binoculars, hoping to see what the outpost had not been meant to report on. It didn't take him long to find something.

In the far distance, at the head of one of the valleys, what looked like a long line of soldiers and loaded burros was snaking its way in his direction. 'Bernard?'

The young man came to his side.

'When you get that radio working, tell them a large force of foot soldiers is heading this way. Three to four hundred, rough estimate. I also advise they check on the other outposts.'

The two men who'd been ordered to sweep the high ground mounted the rocks on the edge of the position to carry out their task. A couple of short bursts of high-velocity gunfire from the slope spat several rounds through both men, killing them before they hit the ground.

Other shots raked the position. One of the men covering the routes either side of the outpost was killed instantly, the other was seriously injured. Stratton, Bernard, the patrol commander and the radio operator dropped behind cover.

Stratton brought his weapon into his shoulder, waiting for a target. All he could think was that the outpost should never have been manned without a gun team on the high ground. Their only hope now was to defend themselves against an assault — there was no way that they could mount a counter-attack. They could not attempt a move with that gun covering their position.

A soft moan came from nearby and Stratton peered through the foliage to see Bernard

271

clutching at himself, obviously in pain.

'Where're you hit?' Stratton whispered.

Bernard tried to turn enough to see him. 'I'm okay,' he said, his voice quivering.

Stratton suspected otherwise.

'Drop your weapons or you will all die like your comrades!' a voice called out from the bushes. 'We have your position surrounded.'

Stratton remembered the men hanging by their necks in the jungle on the day he'd arrived. These attackers would be all too likely to mete out the same kind of retribution to anyone they captured.

'I have been ordered to take prisoners. Those others, they went for their guns. If you give yourselves up you will be allowed to live. If you fight, you will die.'

It was the kind of threat that the defenders wanted to hear but still could not really believe.

A man in civilian clothes rose from behind cover, his rifle aimed carefully at the rebel patrol's position. He was followed by another and then more, all of them in civilian clothes.

'I'm coming out,' shouted someone not far from Stratton. It was one of the rebels. 'I've dropped my gun. Don't shoot.' The radio operator did not waste any time as he got to his feet and stepped into the open, his arms raised in the customary surrender gesture.

The patrol commander followed him. They clearly realised the futility of resistance and were willing to take their chances by surrendering.

'What about you, Bernard?' Stratton asked.

'I . . . I can't fight,' he stammered.

Stratton exhaled heavily, his nerves on edge. A twinge of fear gripped him which he fought to hold at bay. It was one of those key moments of decision. He could go for it, come out blasting, take his chances on maybe creating a hole in the enemy's line and hope to get away. If he did, his escape routes were limited, to say the least. There was a steep drop from the view point behind him. He could jump and hope that he didn't break every bone in his body. Even then they could still pick him off. The other option was to stand up, surrender and take his chances. There were too many guns aimed at him for him to try and escape, he decided.

Stratton put down his weapon and got to his feet.

Bernard stood up painfully, holding his shoulder, blood seeping from a hole in the front and the exit point in his back.

The leader of the ambushers pushed his way forward and into the clearing. He was wearing a hat and carrying an AK47. He also had a pistol in a holster attached to his belt. He grinned at Stratton. His face was covered in a scruffy beard. 'Hello, Englishman,' he said stepping closer as his men closed in.

There were a dozen of them, all dishevelled and grubby.

The leader nodded to his men and several of them descended on the rebels to search their pockets and remove their webbing. One of them handed Stratton's belt to the leader who looked through the pouches with interest, inspecting the GPS. 'Tie their hands,' he barked.

His order was carried out swiftly. The other wounded rebel was dragged over and dropped to the ground alongside the others.

'I must now execute you all for crimes against the government of Neravista,' the bearded leader said casually. 'I'm sorry about the prisoner bit. I was lying. It's the law, as you know, that all terrorists are to be killed as soon as they are captured. I don't have time to find a suitable gallows so you will have to be shot.' The leader whispered something in the ear of his subordinate before stepping back. 'Carry on,' he said.

'Ready,' the subordinate called out. His men raised their rifles where they stood. 'Aim!' he shouted. The radio man began to cry and urine coursed down his legs. Bernard clenched his jaw and stared at his killers.

'Fire!'

Every rifle went off at once. Stratton flinched. The others dropped to the ground. Bernard and the radio operator died instantly, bullet holes in their heads and torsos. The patrol commander writhed in agony, a hole in his neck spouting blood several feet into the air, his arms motionless because his spine had been severed. One of the ambushers stepped closer, aimed his rifle, and shot the commander through his head. Then he adjusted his aim and put a round through the head of the wounded man who had been dumped on the ground, even though he looked to be already dead.

Stratton remained standing. He had winced when the shots were fired but otherwise had not moved.

The ambushers' leader chuckled. 'You don't like my sense of humour?' he asked. 'I'm sorry to disappoint you but all the patrols in this area were told not to kill the Englishman if they should come across you.' He shrugged. 'Maybe someone else wants that pleasure.'

He shouted a command and the group quickly made ready to go.

Stratton took a moment to come back to earth. For several seconds he had really believed his time had come, right up to and including an instant after the shots had been fired. He had felt the bullets striking Bernard who had been so close that he was almost touching him and he'd been splashed by the younger man's blood. But at that moment Stratton's brain could not grasp why he himself had felt no pain. The leader's laugh had come to him like a distant echo.

One of the men slammed him cruelly in the back with a rifle butt to get him going. He felt drained, as if his blood had left him. No amount of previous experience of the sight, sound and smell of death fully prepared one for it.

Stratton was placed in the middle of the group of ambushers. As he trudged along, his hands tied behind him, he could only wonder what fate had in store for him.

★ ★ ★

They walked along a track that led down into the valley and followed it until it entered another, larger valley, where they met the line of government soldiers in camouflaged clothing

275

who Stratton had previously spotted heading towards the rebel plateau. Each man carried a rifle and bulging backpack and looked equipped for a substantial campaign. They were accompanied by burros carrying ammunition boxes and machine guns.

Stratton's group veered onto a different track and continued for several kilometres before arriving at a large, flat area next to a precipitous rockface. A number of dark brown canvas tents and a large white marquee had been set up to form what was evidently a headquarters. It included a flagpole with the army's colours flapping at its top.

Stratton was made to halt in the open while the others headed for what looked like a field kitchen with a collection of tables outside. One of the men remained with him as a guard while the leader made his way to one of the brown tents.

The area beyond the HQ buzzed with activity. Dozens of horses were tethered in lines, their saddles and other accessories on racks beneath wood and canvas shelters. Burros carrying supplies trailed in from another direction. Soldiers grouped in companies, cleaning their weapons, chatting, smoking and generally hanging around. A whistle blew, accompanied by shouts, and one of the companies began to form up into a column.

A familiar noise began to drift above the general cacophony, the deep beating sound of rotors cutting through the air. It grew louder rapidly. The helicopters, unseen as yet, were closer than they sounded. Then the lead bird rounded the rockface, heading for the camp, a large artillery piece suspended beneath it on a long cable. A second was close behind. The noisy machines slowed as they approached the landing area, the rotors changing tone as their pitch altered. Some of the horses obviously resented the unfamiliar intrusion and a couple of the burros actually kicked out in fear.

The choppers came into the hover, kicking up a storm of dust, and men ran to the artillery pieces to disconnect them. Stratton noted the twin M60 machine guns mounted inside the doors. They were obviously combat-ready.

'They ain't new but they'll do the trick,' a voice shouted from behind him.

Stratton recognised Steel's drawl immediately but did not turn to acknowledge his presence.

The American stepped alongside him as the artillery pieces were disconnected, hitting the ground with rocking thumps. The lead chopper's turbines increased power and it ascended vertically before turning on its axis, lowering its nose and powering away. The second moved close to the HQ tents and eased itself to the ground. When it was completely down, several officers hurried to the cabin door as it opened. Two burly soldiers climbed out. Behind them another man in military garb eased himself from the cabin and onto the ground. The officers came to stiff attention and gave crisp salutes. More men clambered out behind him.

The entourage headed towards one of the large tents, past Stratton and Steel. 'In case you don't know, that is Neravista himself,' the American said.

Neravista was in his late fifties and fastidiously groomed from head to toe. He had a large, ugly face, with a bulbous nose and ears to match. His dark eyes flicked in Steel's direction and he gave a perceptible nod on seeing the American. Steel returned it. As Neravista passed he glanced at Stratton just long enough to notice the Englishman's tied hands. Stratton watched him until he entered the HQ tent.

'He is as charming as he looks,' Steel said. 'I wouldn't be surprised if his lifelong heroes were Hitler and Stalin. I'm sorry to see you like this,' Steel said.

'You don't show emotion easily.'

Steel chuckled as he bit into an apple. 'You made a mistake.'

'Yes. I never realised how much of an arsehole you were.'

Steel continued to smile. 'I meant after that. You got involved. You should know better, a man of your experience.'

'You're not working for the administration, are you?'

Steel looked round conspiratorially, as if he didn't want anyone else to hear. 'Keep your voice low, damn it. They don't know that.' He was clearly relishing his own sense of humour. 'Well, truth is I am a little and I'm not a little. I was officially sent to monitor the situation and then was given some latitude when it came to offering assistance to the revolutionaries. But this country has a lotta valuable resources. Here, look at this,'

278

he said, digging something out of a pocket. He held up a dull chunk of ore the size of a golf ball. 'Platinum,' he said. 'I could carry a fancy car's worth out of here in my pockets. A lot of private companies are interested in investing in this place,' Steel continued. 'Hell, some of 'em are downright chomping at the bit to get in here. But you can't bring in civilian contractors where there's a war going on. It's dangerous and expensive. So, yeah, I'm acting as point for a few of those companies, representing their interests.' Steel grinned. 'The sooner this place can get itself cleaned up, the sooner the investors'll start doing what they do best.'

'When did you switch from Sebastian to Neravista?'

'You mean did I know I was sending you in to help the losing side? Yeah, I did. But I wasn't clear how I was going to manage it. Switching sides was never gonna be easy since the Congressional funding was voted in to aid the revolutionaries, not Neravista. The trick was in reducing confidence in Sebastian and making him look more like a terrorist. That's the magic word these days. Changes everyone's perspective. We're just putting the final touches to that right now. Look, Neravista was the tougher guy in the end. The revolutionaries couldn't go the distance. They started squabbling. I had to take advantage of the situation as it presented itself. As long as Neravista can tone down the human rights abuses we should be fine. He may find that a lot easier now that his brother's dead,' Steel laughed. 'Good job, by the way. Nice hit.'

'Did you put the grenade in the weapons box?'

'Neravista's negotiator got a little pissed when he discovered how much ordnance you'd brought in. Shit, he went a little crazy. So I had to take some back. Sorry for any inconvenience caused.'

Stratton looked at him, doing his best to hide the venomous hatred he felt for the man. 'Why am I here?'

'I need you to kill Sebastian.'

Stratton just stared at him.

'Of course I know you won't do it. That'll be our little secret. But it'll get done and you'll get the blame. You did it for the money, you greedy little mercenary, you.'

Stratton realised the implications. 'What about Louisa?'

'Sweet kid, that one. If she makes it, fine. I hope she does. I like that gal. She's got oomph, you know? Great ass, too. I'm surprised you weren't all over that one. A little out of your league, maybe. Then again, I think she'd go for a guy like you.' Steel studied Stratton's expression for a moment, looking for any clue that he might have struck a nerve.

He could not find any and gave the ambushers' leader a nod. The man guarding Stratton came over to grip his arms, unaware of the pressure building in his prisoner. He gave Stratton a shove but the Englishman suddenly braced himself like a rock and would not move. The man was surprised and mustered his strength for greater effort. As he pushed again, Stratton bent away and then swung back, striking him in the face with his forehead with such force that the man's nose burst and he fell, poleaxed and almost unconscious. The bearded leader lunged forward but Stratton flattened his testicles with a knee to the groin. The strength went out of the man as he grabbed his crotch and dropped to the ground where he began to cry with the pain.

Stratton turned on Steel who whipped his pistol from its holster and levelled it at his face.

'You don't need to be alive for this next phase,' Steel said. 'It's just more convenient if you are. Which is it gonna be — dead or alive?'

Stratton did not doubt that Steel would shoot so he stopped in his tracks, glaring at the man. The other ambushers came running over, grabbed Stratton roughly and hauled him away.

'You keep a good eye on that boy,' Steel called out as he lowered his pistol. 'Tie 'im up good.' He grinned as he put his gun away and looked down at the two men on the ground, one of them sobbing in agony, the other still trying to figure out where he was. 'I told you,' Steel said, chuckling as he walked away. 'You gotta watch that boy.'

8

Stratton sat with his back against a tall, sturdy wooden pole fixed solidly into the earth, his hands bound securely behind it by a leather strap. His face and body were battered and bruised where the ambushers' leader had taken revenge once he'd eventually managed to stand up again. Dried blood was caked around the Englishman's face and on his chest, where it had dripped from his cuts. He had not moved for hours and had stirred only at the sound of Neravista's helicopter departing.

His captors had made a temporary camp on the edge of the broad clearing, their ponchos doing service as overhead covers above their bedding a stone's throw from Stratton. Nearby a company of soldiers lounged around, brewing coffee on small wood fires.

Stratton had been stripped of all his clothes and footwear except for his shorts. He was parched, having been denied water since his capture. But at least the sun had been hidden behind thick clouds all day and the temperature was lower than it could have been.

He had drifted into semi-consciousness during his beating and soon after coming round he gave up plotting any escape for which he would have to depend on his own resources. His bonds were secure and the pole was too high to loop the strap over. A brief effort to push against the pole proved he would never be able to break it or pull it out of the ground. His only chance would come if his captors gave him a window of opportunity. But the beating he had given the patrol commander and his subordinate had made them wary of him and they were keeping a close watch on him.

Stratton estimated the time at around four in the afternoon although it was difficult to judge without being able to see the sun. He could only hope that the clouds would burst soon so that he could ease his thirst with their rain.

He realised several soldiers were looking at him and it became obvious that he was the subject of their conversation. One of them walked over to talk with the ambushers' leader. Several of the others followed him. It attracted the attention of the rest of the ambushers and before long there was quite a gathering.

The bearded leader seemed to arrive at some kind of agreement with the soldier and together they walked over to Stratton, followed by the others. The leader and the first soldier stopped in front of the captive while the others surrounded him.

'Stand up,' the leader demanded.

The uniformed soldier stared intensely at Stratton, a grimace on his rugged face.

Stratton brought his feet under him and shuffled his arms up the pole as he straightened his legs. The ambushers' leader decided to lend a hand and grabbed him by the hair to help him up. The soldier stepped closer to square up to him, his face full of hatred.

'I'm told you are the one who blew up Chemora,' the soldier said.

Stratton couldn't see any reason to deny it. 'I had that pleasure,' he said. There was no point in being half-hearted about it, either.

'My brother was on that bridge. I could not find him when they asked me to look at the bodies. All I know is that he isn't here any more.'

Stratton could only stare at the man. But it didn't matter. The very sight of him seemed to enrage the soldier. He gritted his teeth, clenched his fist, drew it back and drove it deep into the pit of Stratton's stomach with all the strength he could muster. Stratton bent over as the wind left his lungs and he thought he was going to throw up despite having nothing in his stomach. But the soldier had not finished with him. He grabbed hold of Stratton's hair, yanked him upright and gave him a stinging blow across the face. Blood splashed those nearby as the wounds already on Stratton's lips reopened. He dropped forward again and his vision clouded. The soldier pulled his head up once again and delivered another savage blow to his body, following it up with another to his face.

'To hell with this,' the soldier said, taking a knife from his belt. 'I'm going to fillet him right here.'

He gripped Stratton by the throat and was about to shove the point of the long, sharp knife into the Englishman's gut when the ambushers' leader grabbed his arm. 'No, my friend,' he said, holding the soldier steadily. 'I'm sorry about your brother but this bastard's work is not done yet. My orders are to keep him alive . . . He dies tomorrow but not before.'

The soldier was far from satisfied but he did not force the issue.

The bearded leader seemed relieved that the soldier had backed down. 'If you're around at the time you can do it yourself. I'll look out for you.'

The soldier released Stratton and stepped back. He sheathed his knife but before leaving he hawked up a mouthful of phlegm and spat it in Stratton's face.

Then he walked away, his colleagues patting him on the back and consoling him.

'I lied to him,' the ambushers' leader said, watching the soldiers go. 'I'm going to kill you myself.'

As the bearded leader and his colleagues walked away Stratton slid back down the pole and slumped to the ground. His vision was still fuzzy and he felt nauseous. He dropped his head to one side, closed his eyes and drifted into unconsciousness.

★   ★   ★

Louisa stood in front of the stables, looking out across the jungle towards Hector's encampment. She had learned about the return of Victor's horse and Stratton's subsequent departure. It was late in the afternoon and the activity in the camp had greatly increased with the rumours of a Neravista attack. Reports that patrols from some of the outlying observation posts had not returned and their reliefs had failed to open up communications only increased the speculation.

Men headed to defensive locations throughout the camp. Sebastian had given the general order to stand to. The rebels' living quarters buzzed with preparations, the wiser ones among them gathering their possessions and packing them up in order to move quickly if they had to. Generally, confidence remained high that the combined guerrilla forces could repel a government attack.

Their leaders, however, had reason to be concerned. The other brigades had been unusually quiet, in particular their nearest neighbour, Hector. What messages they had received were vague. Their requests for intelligence on enemy troop activity had been met with inconsistent reports and even silence.

Sebastian had said very little about the matter. Some read this as evidence of calm confidence while others felt he had run out of ideas.

Louisa decided to give up waiting and headed back towards the cabin, looking over her shoulder one last time at the edge of the jungle behind her.

Men were preparing for combat in the courtyard in front of the cabins and on the open ground beyond. They were quiet as they speculated about the intentions of the Neravistas and the other rebel brigades.

Louisa entered her father's cabin where half a dozen officers surrounded the dining table, poring over diagrams of the camp and outlying area and discussing their defences.

Sebastian was not there. She crossed to his bedroom at the back and knocked gently on the door. 'It's me, father.'

She heard him reply and she opened the door. Sebastian stood by his wardrobe, holding a smart-looking uniform on a coat-hanger. He placed it on his bed with some reverence.

'What is that?' Louisa asked. She had not seen it before.

He looked strangely cheerful, as if the uniform gave him some kind of pleasure. 'It's a dress uniform. I had it made some years ago.'

'It's very regal,' she said, wondering why he was revealing it now. 'Is everything okay, father?'

Sebastian's expression became serious. 'I want you to leave, Louisa. Can you do that for me, without arguing?'

'No,' she answered lightly.

He looked tired. 'Why won't you do as I ask?'

'I have told you. It's my life now. It's no more complicated than that.'

Sebastian took a moment to consider his next words. 'If you are to pursue your ambitions, this is where we must part company. *I* must stay and finish what I started. *You* must go and begin your new life.'

'What are you saying?'

'This is over, Louisa. My dear girl, they mean to destroy us.'

'If that's true then why don't you just surrender, prevent all the bloodshed?'

'Neravista would hang us all anyway. He has already delivered his ultimatum. That would be the end of the revolution. Hector has betrayed me, but not what he believes in. So now I must do what I can to help him, to help what's left of our struggle. Hector is waiting for you on the road to his camp.'

The reality of what Sebastian was saying hit home and Louisa's lips quivered as she fought back tears.

'Will you go now?' he asked. 'Before it's too late.'

She shook her head. 'I would be deserting. That's not the reputation I want.'

'You're not a soldier.'

'Nor are the wives and children of those men out there.'

Sebastian looked at his daughter, the light of his life. Louisa would not leave because she was like him. He took her in his arms. She clung to him and buried her face against his shoulder, the tears rolling down her face.

He released her finally and walked out of the room, leaving her to face the painting of her great-grandfather charging across the Jarama Valley.

★ ★ ★

It was dark when the rain began to fall, hitting Stratton's upturned face. The gentle sting of the heavy droplets brought him out of his fog. He blinked heavily and opened his mouth, grateful for the water that fell on his dry lips.

As the liquid trickled down his throat he felt better. But it was not enough. The rain fell so hard that puddles formed around him. He stretched down against the bonds to touch the water with his lips and sucked. He coughed and nearly choked as the pain from the beatings returned, yet he exulted in the life that the rain was restoring and he stayed there, breathing, lapping up the water.

Someone grabbed the back of his neck brutally and a weight fell on him, forcing his face into the mud. He struggled desperately, his hands fast about the pole behind him. His attacker was determined to suffocate him.

Stratton mustered all his strength and fought to raise his head. He managed it just long enough to draw a breath. But his move only provoked his would-be slayer to double his own efforts. The assailant forced Stratton's face back into the mud.

Stratton was trapped between the man's weight and strength and the bonds holding his arms around the pole. His eyes began to bulge and his heart felt like it was about to burst. He had to make one last effort or drown in the mud.

He gathered his strength and gave an almighty heave while pulling against the pole at the same time. He lifted his face out of the mud but it was not enough to free himself. In a final act of desperation he lunged to one side. The attacker lost his balance and toppled over him. Stratton twisted his torso, raised a leg and brought it down with every ounce of force he could muster, striking the man on the side of his neck. The man was rocked by the blow and tried to roll away but Stratton hooked a heel over his head and held him in place, raising his other leg and bringing the heel crashing down on the man's throat. His body spasmed. Gripped by a wild frenzy, Stratton struck again and again and again in the same spot.

Stratton had crushed the man's larynx with the third blow but he did not stop until exhaustion eventually brought him to his senses. The man lay still, on his back, unmoving in the mud.

The rain continued to pelt down as Stratton sucked in air. He blinked heavily to help refocus his vision and looked around to check if anyone had seen him. Everyone was under cover, the fires extinguished, the darkness complete.

Stratton leaned forward to look at the man, wondering who it could be. He wore the camouflage fatigues of the Neravistas. His eyes and mouth were wide open. It was the soldier whose brother had died on the bridge.

Stratton remembered that the man had a knife and he quickly stretched out his legs, placed them over the body and dragged it towards him. Another effort brought it against Stratton's backside. He shuffled his back up the pole until he could stand and used his bare feet to move the man's jacket aside in search of the knife's sheath. He could feel it with his toes but, when he exposed it, to his horror it was empty.

The man must have had it in his hands.

The ground was covered in puddles, the mud disturbed by their struggle. Stratton swept his feet around the area where the man had been standing. His toe hit something — it was the knife. Stratton looked around once again to ensure he had not been seen. There was a flash of lightning followed by rolling thunder.

He curled his toes over the haft and dragged it close to the pole, turned around to sit back down and picked it up in his hands. He found the sharp edge, dug the tip into the wet earth against the pole, reached back so that the bindings were beyond the blade and slid them up and down it. The leather strap was severed in seconds.

In his peripheral vision he picked up movement. A figure climbed out from under a poncho. The man walked towards him through the mud and sheeting rain. Stratton moved his hands back behind the pole and felt for the knife.

The man stopped in front of Stratton, water cascading over the rim of his hat. Stratton looked up to see that it was the ambushers' leader. When the soldier saw the body his eyes widened and his stare flicked to Stratton's hands behind the pole. He crouched slowly beside the dead man to see who it was. Recognising the body, he flashed a look at Stratton again, his straggly soaked hair hanging out from under his hat. Closer now, he leaned to look at Stratton's hands — and saw the cut leather bindings in the splashing mud beside them. In that instant he knew he was in trouble.

He cried out as he turned to run away. But he slipped in the mud and fell to his knees. He reached for his pistol frantically as he looked back. Stratton was already coming for him. The man screamed but Stratton cut him short by driving the knife upwards into his throat. The man fired his pistol into the ground as Stratton forced the blade in all the way to the hilt and up into his brain. His last breath escaped as a gurgle through the hole in his throat, which quickly filled with blood.

Several men clambered from under their ponchos.

Stratton sprinted away.

He did not know in which direction to go nor did he particularly care as long as he got out of there. He slammed into a body under a poncho in the blackness, kicking it so that the man yelped in pain. Stratton sprawled in the mud, got up and kept on going. He saw the lights of the main tents ahead and veered away. Flashlights came on through the pouring rain and he ran from them too. A shout went up.

He heard loud bangs, saw muzzle flashes in the dark, but the gunshots were hopeless efforts. Someone was hit by a bullet meant for Stratton and screamed. Another man shouted abuse and yelled for the shooting to stop.

Stratton smashed into a soaking bush and ran straight through it. The thorny branches cut into his bare flesh but he felt nothing. He was running on pure adrenalin. Where the foliage was thick and he couldn't push through it he went under or around it, scrambling through the soupy mud, which was knee-deep in places.

The bushes gave way to a rocky incline but he did not slow down as he scrambled up it, careless of the jagged stones cutting the bare soles of his feet. His heart pounded in his chest, his lungs sucked in air, but he pushed on, finding hidden reserves of strength and will. He had his freedom back and he was not about to give it up again, knowing this was probably his last chance for escape.

As the ground levelled out Stratton found himself running through grass. He had gone a good distance from the camp and stopped to catch his breath and listen for pursuers. He put his hands on his knees and sucked in air. The rain made it difficult to hear much but that was to his advantage too.

He looked back and could just make out his deep muddy footprints in the soft ground. It reminded him that he could still be easily tracked and he set off once again, not as fast now but at a pace he felt he could maintain for several miles.

Stratton began to think where he should head for and how to work out where he was. He also thought about Louisa. Ideally he should look for his emergency stores. But without the GPS he was not confident that he could find the location in the darkness. He would have to aim in the direction of the camp and then, once he knew where he was, make his way back along the route to where the rebels had been hung. He doubted he could make it back to the camp by dawn, though.

Concern for Louisa now overshadowed his relief at escaping. He feared he might not get to her in time. The Neravistas had been moving into position all day and a dawn attack seemed most likely. Stratton pushed on with renewed determination.

In the HQ tent Steel, Ventura and several army officers were enjoying drinks and cigars. They had heard the shots and shouting and were waiting patiently, knowing that they would learn what the noise meant soon enough. Steel had a sudden uncomfortable feeling about it and got to his feet.

Before he reached the tent's entrance a young officer wearing a soaked poncho pushed aside the flap. 'The Englishman has escaped,' he said, out of breath, his face dripping wet.

'Goddamn it!' Steel shouted, losing his usual control. 'How the hell did he do that?'

'There are two dead men where he was tied up,' the officer replied. 'He fled into the jungle.'

'What are you standing here for?' the American shouted. 'Take that company of men out there sitting on their asses and go find him!'

The officer glanced at Ventura for confirmation. Ventura nodded.

Steel tossed his cigar to the floor. 'Son of a bitch!'

'Quite a resourceful individual,' Ventura said smoothly. 'I've never seen you this riled before.'

'That guy pisses me off, that's all. I should've killed him when I had the chance.'

'Does it really matter? He is insignificant. He's wearing nothing but his shorts. He probably won't even make it to the border.'

Steel reined in his anger. 'I like to keep things clean.' He slumped back into his chair and stared ahead thoughtfully.

'Why does he bother you so much?' Ventura asked, curious at Steel's reaction.

'He doesn't.'

Ventura was not convinced.

* * *

Stratton went at an easy jog through the jungle. As suddenly as it had begun the rain stopped and he could hear only his own breathing and his feet slapping on the mud. He caught another sound behind him, like a snapping stick in the distance. He stopped in his tracks and listened.

Stratton found it hard to believe that anyone had followed him this far but there was definitely something out there. He heard it again, in the same direction. And it was getting closer. It might have been an animal but that was unlikely. A jaguar, possibly. Either way, Stratton did not want to find out. He got going and increased his pace.

He ran as stealthily as he could but did not let up on his speed. After a couple of hundred metres he paused again to listen, trying to control his breathing.

There was nothing.

Just as he was beginning to think that he was not being followed, he heard the sound of feet running through wet mud. A bolt of fear shot through him. He was indeed being pursued.

Stratton broke into a hard run. The foliage thickened but he drove through it. He dodged between trees and leapt over fallen logs. The sound of something pushing through the undergrowth behind him revealed its presence. Stratton began to doubt he could shake it but he could not risk stopping to ambush whatever or whoever it was. If there were several armed men he would be screwed.

The ground dropped away and he ran downhill. He let gravity aid his speed, controlling it enough so as not to run headlong into a tree. He sidestepped obstacles nimbly in his bare feet.

The sound behind was constant now. They were gaining on him. Stratton burst through a thicket and the ground disappeared suddenly beneath his feet as he dropped onto a steep muddy slope. He fell onto his backside and slid downhill out of control, crashing through bushes like a runaway cart. He side-struck a tree, rolled onto his back and tumbled through some bushes to become airborne for a second before hitting water. His back struck the bottom of a shallow stream but he did not wait to check his surroundings. He was up and running through the knee-deep water as fast as he could. He searched both banks for an exit but thick bushes bordered the sides and they did not look easily penetrable.

The stream ran straight, a problem for Stratton if the pursuers reached it soon and had a rifle. A crash and splash behind warned him that his hunter had found the water. Stratton could feel the weapon's sights zeroed on his back as he ran. He had to get out of there and he dived for the bank, scrambling up it. But it was steep and as he clawed desperately he lost his footing and slid back down. He grabbed at anything to stop himself but the mud came away in his hands.

As he hit the stream again he caught a glimpse of a figure coming at him and heard the loud splashing of running feet. He grappled for anything he could fight with, grabbing a branch. The figure came at him relentlessly in the darkness. Stratton raised the branch and summoned all his strength. As he was about to lunge, the tip of a spear stopped an inch from his throat. Both men stopped dead in the stream, each one poised to strike.

It was Yoinakuwa.

The Indian lowered his spear and stood back, breathing heavily. It was the only time Stratton had ever seen him grin.

Stratton went limp and fell back into the water, dropping the branch. 'How the hell did you find me?' he asked, looking up at the Indian and not expecting an answer.

'I track,' Yoinakuwa said.

'You tracked me? How did you know I'd escaped?'

Yoinakuwa held his spear up like a rifle and made as if to fire it several times. Then he mimicked Stratton running right past him.

Stratton began to laugh, mostly in relief. He stretched out his hand. Yoinakuwa looked at it a moment, then took it. 'Thanks,' Stratton said, getting to his feet. 'It's good to see you.'

Yoinakuwa pointed in the direction the stream ran.

'Where are we going?' Stratton asked.

Yoinakuwa simply looked at him.

Stratton had no idea where they were or where they were headed but at least Yoinakuwa was not the enemy. 'Lead on,' he said, gesturing to indicate that the old man should go on ahead of him.

They went quickly but before they'd gone a kilometre Stratton had to stop to inspect the soles of his feet. They were badly cut in places. With his adrenalin gone, the discomfort was intense.

Yoinakuwa hacked two large leaves from a nearby plant and after trimming the ends he deftly wrapped and secured one around each of Stratton's feet. Stratton stood and tested them. They felt remarkably comfortable. What was more, the leaf seemed to have a cooling effect on his skin.

Yoinakuwa handed Stratton a couple more leaves, suggesting to him that the current ones would not last for ever, and off they went again.

The footwear lasted well on soft earth but rocky surfaces took their toll and after a couple of kilometres they needed replacing. By the time the leaves needed changing again Yoinakuwa had found some more.

As dawn broke, the general direction in which they were heading became more clear. But Stratton still had no idea where they were. Yoinakuwa marched decisively. Experience had taught Stratton in some situations not to ask and simply to follow. But his anxiety grew with every step. He had to get to the rebel camp and Louisa.

As they left the forest and the early-morning

light grew over the horizon the terrain became familiar. Stratton felt sure he had seen the hills before. They began to climb up a steep incline into another forest. Among the trees the ground was rocky and they crossed a track where he noticed some spent AK47 casings. They were shiny, indicating the possibility of a recent firefight.

As they went up the hill Stratton scanned around, trying to recall why he thought he had seen the place before. When he saw a shattered tree, its top half on the ground, he realised where they were. It was the site of the failed ambush, where they had found the hanging rebels.

Stratton ran past the rebels' ambush position to the top of the rise. He kept on going between the trees, leaving Yoinakuwa behind, to find where his emergency stores were hidden.

The tree with the mark cut into its bark was there and he reached between the roots at its base. He pulled away the earth and leaves and, to his immense relief, found his pack. He looked over at Yoinakuwa who was stone-faced. The old man had known about the pack all along.

Stratton opened it up, untied the waterproof bag and pulled out the pistol sitting on the top, a pair of trousers, shirt, underpants, socks, belt and camouflaged trainers. A side pocket contained a plastic bag with a passport and money, another a medical pack, GPS, compass, water-sterilising bottle, some food and matches.

Stratton took off his dirty underpants and quickly pulled on his clean clothes. As he laced up his footwear he heard movement through the wood. He glanced at Yoinakuwa who was clearly aware of it but had not responded. Stratton picked up his pistol and moved to where he could see the source. Kebowa and Mohesiwa were walking towards them. Behind them was Victor.

Stratton was pleased to see the Frenchman who looked no worse for wear than himself.

Victor grinned broadly on seeing Stratton. They hugged briefly in celebration of their survival.

'What happened to you?' Victor asked.

'I was looking for you when the wrong people found me. What about you?'

Victor sighed as he sat heavily on a fallen tree trunk to take the weight off his sore legs. 'I made the mistake of accusing Hector of trying to kill Sebastian.' Victor looked around, recognising the place himself. 'I wondered why they were bringing me here. Yoinakuwa and his boys seem to have everything worked out.'

Stratton threaded the belt through his trouser loops and attached the holster that his pistol fitted snugly into. A ray of light pierced the treetops as the sun rose over the distant hills. 'Neravista's soldiers are going to take out Sebastian's camp.'

'Hector has betrayed him.'

'Steel's the real manipulator.'

Victor nodded. 'I always suspected as much. What are your plans now? You want to take me along?'

'Sure,' Stratton said, pulling his small pack onto his back. 'You up to a brisk march?'

'Why brisk? We have all the time in the world.'

'They're going to attack today, Victor.'

Victor looked at Stratton, suddenly aware of his intentions. 'You're not going to the border, getting out of this country?'

Stratton realised they had been at cross-purposes and was somewhat disappointed in Victor. 'I'm going to the camp.'

'You're crazy! Neravista will hit Sebastian with everything he has. He'll kill everyone.'

'That's why I'm going.'

'They're probably attacking as we speak.'

'Then there's no time to waste.'

Victor felt confused. 'You're going to get Louisa.'

Stratton checked his compass. He was ready to go but stopped to look at Victor, understanding the Frenchman's dilemma. 'I don't expect you to come. It's over for you now. You take care of yourself,' Stratton said, offering his hand.

'You're not mad at me?' Victor asked.

'Why should I be? There's nothing you can do. Enjoy France — if that's where you're headed.' Stratton turned to go.

'Wait,' Victor called out. 'Wait. Just one moment.'

Stratton paused, impatient to go.

'I should go. I'm the brigade second in command.'

'There's nothing you can do.'

'Then why do I feel so damned guilty?'

Stratton had no answer for him. Victor watched him go.

9

A battery of four howitzers was lined up in the clearing where the Neravistas had their headquarters, the barrels angled for maximum trajectory. The sky had cleared but everything was still dripping wet. The battery commander glanced at his watch, as he had done every twenty seconds or so for the last few minutes. He stared at the second hand as it jerked its way closer to the top of the hour. He raised an arm and held it there. When the slender hand reached the number twelve he brought it down sharply and the valley shuddered with a thunderous boom as the number one gun fired, mud splashing up from its wheels as it recoiled.

Birds took to the air in every direction as the shell shot out of the clearing and into the sky on its journey away from the earth. It reached its maximum height ten seconds and five thousand metres from the end of the gun before levelling out.

Had the gunner been able to see through the nose of the shell he would have enjoyed a view of a large portion of his country: the interlacing valleys and lush green forests; rocky outcrops and steep ravines; streams and rivers flickering in the sunlight and patches of manicured agricultural squares. As the shell began its descent he would have seen the many snaking trails criss-crossing the countryside and the system of plateaus that was home to the rebel brigades. As the shell dropped closer to the ground he would have been able to make out Sebastian's camp, the cabins, the stables behind them, the patchwork of tents and campfires and the many tracks connecting them. He would have had to concentrate during the last few seconds because the image zoomed in rapidly as the shell seemed to accelerate towards an open piece of scrubland beyond the tented area.

It struck the ground where it exploded, kicking up a geyser of earth and sending fiery shrapnel in all directions, none of it harming a soul since nobody was within range of it.

Everyone in the camp heard the explosion and those on the outer defences looked back over their shoulders. They all had the same thought: the battle had begun. All rumours and speculations were resolved. The thought that followed immediately was whether anyone had been hurt. Those with family in the tented areas feared for them.

The men inside Sebastian's cabin hurried out to look in the direction of the explosion. Most of them ran off towards their posts.

Louisa came outside to see. Sebastian stood in the doorway and she looked back at him. He did not react. The blast merely signalled the start of the next chapter in a story whose ending he already knew.

★ ★ ★

On a high point beyond the camp perimeter, the site of a rebel lookout post before the rebels had pulled back, a group of Neravista army officers surveyed the view through binoculars. Their saddled horses were held in the background by soldiers, some of whom were setting up a machine-gun emplacement.

One of the officers took the handset from a soldier carrying a radio on his back, its ten-foot whip antenna sticking vertically out of its top. 'Drop five hundred,' he said into it. 'Right one hundred.'

Back at the artillery battery a radio operator relayed the message to the officer who passed it to his gun crew. The howitzer's dial sights were adjusted and they looked up to see the commander with his arm raised again. As he brought it down they fired.

'It's away!' the officer at the lookout post called out and the others watched intently for the landing point. The shell announced its arrival with an accelerating scream that came to an abrupt stop a split second before the boom of a crunching explosion.

In unison the officers aimed their binoculars at the detonation, like observers at a racetrack as the horses go by. The shell had landed somewhere beyond the stables and although they could not see the precise impact point the plume of white smoke was clearly visible as it rose into the sky.

'Up two hundred,' the officer said into the radio handset.

The next shell arrived thirty seconds later and

struck the centre of the tented camp, blowing a shack to smithereens. Seconds later women and children ran screaming from the camp's fringes.

'Mark that as centre,' the officer said casually into the radio. 'I want a random pattern four hundred metres radius of centre. Commence firing at will.'

Within a minute the shells had started to scream in one by one, peppering the encampment within the perimeter. One struck close to the cabins and Louisa, still outside, was caught in a rush to find cover. She ran into the heavily sandbagged square on the edge of the courtyard clearing outside the cabins, along with a couple of men on their way through. As the dust settled she recognised the man preparing the machine gun in the emplacement that would defend the approaches to the cabins from the camp entrance. It was David.

'It's going to be a busy day, I think,' David said as he helped his partner prepare the belts of ammunition.

The rebels who had taken cover with Louisa scrambled out and hurried on their way. Louisa peered over the top of the sandbags as the shells started landing everywhere.

* * *

Sebastian leaned on the table, looking down on the map of the encampment. He had made all the preparations he could think of. It was now up to his men to do the best they could. He expected the bombardment to continue for some time, hours perhaps. The Neravistas would soften up the place as much as possible. When they were satisfied that enough damage had been done, both physically and psychologically, they would send in the troops. The garrison's only hope was that enough men would survive to repel the assault. In the back of his mind Sebastian hoped that Hector and the other brigades might have a change of heart at the last moment and attack the enemy's rear. But deep down he feared it was a fantasy.

★ ★ ★

A group of riders galloped into the lookout position, Neravista's battle commanders, Steel and Ventura among them. The general himself dismounted along with his immediate entourage and joined the officers watching the scene through their binoculars. The subalterns saluted briskly and stepped back to allow the general to survey the scene.

'Some breakfast, I think,' the general said, scanning the panorama through his binoculars.

One of his officers hurried off to check on the preparations. The general had decided to make a display of his confidence and sophistication by including caterers in the advance party at the outpost. They arrived with burros laden with stores and the cooks and waiters began setting up chairs and tables, spreading white tablecloths and unpacking silverware and hampers.

Dozens of trays covered with a variety of culinary delights were placed on the tables

306

among plates and silverware, pots of coffee, overflowing bread baskets, bowls of fruit and platters of cheeses. Wine was served in silver goblets and a humidor offered a selection of fine cigars. Waiters fanned away the flies and provided service at the snap of a finger.

'Where's the band?' Steel quipped as he accepted a cup of coffee and a selection of canapés.

'There's your music,' Ventura replied, waving a hand as the artillery salvos maintained a continuous staccato of booms and crunches.

'I gotta hand it to you guys,' Steel said. 'You do war in style.'

Laughter and conversation continued as men stuffed food into their mouths, washed down with coffee and wine, in between aiming their binoculars at the rebel camp that was now dotted with plumes of smoke.

* * *

The roof of Sebastian's former cabin exploded and a wall collapsed as the inside caught fire. Another shell landed near the stables, frightening the animals. The white stallion reared up as it was led to its stall.

Shells pummelled the main accommodation areas where women and children lay dead and wounded. Some survivors huddled in groups while others sought shelter in the woods.

A direct hit on the ammunition store caused it to blow up, creating a fiery display and prompting a round of applause from the officers

307

at the lookout post.

Explosions peppered the perimeter and men lay in shell holes. A tree exploded, showering those below with deadly shrapnel and splintered branches. It seemed like there was no place to hide.

Rebel commanders moved down the line of men, calling for calm and telling them to prepare for the enemy's inevitable charge. Stretcher bearers removed the seriously injured while women made their way along the lines looking for the wounded, doing what they could with limited medical supplies. The dead were left where they fell.

* * *

Louisa heard crying and looked over her sandbag wall to see a woman and several children running across the courtyard desperately trying to find somewhere to hide. A shell landed nearby. She hurried towards them and grabbed two of the children, yelling for the woman to follow with the others.

Louisa brought them back into the sandbagged position and the whimpering family huddled in a corner behind the machine gun. Louisa held one of the children in her arms in an attempt to console her while covering her ears against the deafening noise of the explosions.

'How long will this go on for?' Louisa asked David.

'Could be hours,' he replied, as another shell

landed close to them, sending earth and shards of metal flying over their heads.

★ ★ ★

As Stratton walked fast along a goat track near the bottom of a valley he caught sight of movement on the ridge above him and dropped into the long grass.

He crawled carefully away and leaned up enough to take a look. Yoinakuwa was standing on a rock and looking down at him. 'What is it with that bloke?' Stratton muttered.

As Stratton got to his feet, Victor and the other Indians came into view. He could only wonder what they were doing.

Victor motioned for him to come up.

Stratton shook his head to himself and jogged up the slope.

'Yoinakuwa knows a more direct route,' Victor said as Stratton arrived a little out of breath.

It seemed that Victor had had a change of heart. 'I'll be honest with you. I think I'd be better on my own,' Stratton said.

'Great. You make me feel guilty so that I feel I have to come to the fight and then when I do you don't want me. Hell, I don't care. I'm going anyway.'

'What are you going to do when you get there?'

'Well, as my military guru once told me, I'll plan backwards from my aim.'

'What's your aim?'

'I haven't worked that out yet.'

The Indians had sensed something.

Stratton heard it too. The faint sound was like distant thunder. 'Artillery,' Stratton said and set off at a brisk pace.

Victor did his best to equal Stratton's speed. Kebowa and Mohesiwa ran ahead, past Stratton, to take the lead.

As they reached the top of the next rise not only had the sound of the shells exploding got louder but they could hear the screaming noise of their flight through the air.

By the time they reached the bottom of the plateau where there was a small brook they were breathing heavily.

'Please. Let me take a little water,' Victor begged, dropping to his knees and drinking thirstily.

The Indians did the same.

Stratton decided it was a good idea and took a quick mouthful and wet his hair to help himself cool down. The sun had fully risen now and was heating up the air, intensifying the humidity after the night's rains.

'The shelling could mean they've not started the main attack yet,' Stratton said. 'I doubt they're accurate enough for anything more complex. Let's go.'

He moved swiftly up the hill and the others followed, Victor wiping his face with a handkerchief that he had doused in the water.

The stream of shells screaming overhead seemed endless.

The group made good progress up the hill, pausing at every little rise to make sure that the enemy was not the other side. Stratton felt sure they were near the final rise before the perimeter. When he saw the Indians flatten themselves on the ground short of the next crest he hoped that was it.

He crept forward alongside them to take a look.

His hopes were rewarded. The camp perimeter was the other side of the dip in front of them. But there was no sign of the government forces he expected to see lined up ready to attack.

A shell landed just outside the camp perimeter. That was why the government troops were not yet in position. They had no confidence that the gunners could keep their deadly firepower aimed accurately so that their shells landed within the rebel camp.

'What do you think?' Victor asked as he crawled up beside Stratton.

'That's the perimeter there, right?' Stratton asked, making sure.

'Yes. That's it.'

Stratton looked all around to double-check for the presence of the enemy. 'You ready?'

'You want to go into that? Now?' Victor asked anxiously, as a shell exploded on the edge of the perimeter in front of them.

'When that stops the assault'll begin and that'll be even more dangerous for us.'

Stratton was about to get to his feet when Kebowa touched his shoulder and pointed to the extreme right of their position. Stratton had to move forward in order to see what he was indicating.

A line of government soldiers came into view, marching in single file along a track that ran parallel with and below the line of trees that concealed the rebel camp perimeter. Each man carried an assault rifle and had bulging ammunition pouches slung around his waist. Their number grew as they marched into view. By the time the column came to a halt Stratton estimated there were about two hundred of them. A runner made his way down the line and each soldier he passed turned and faced the slope that led up to the perimeter, stepped off the track and walked into the undergrowth for a few metres before sitting down.

'They're forming up,' Stratton decided. 'The shelling will stop soon.'

Another company appeared, marching in file along the same track. They carried out the same manoeuvre beyond the first company, with each man facing the rebel camp and moving a few metres off the track before getting down. Yet another company of soldiers appeared and marched past the second company to repeat the procedure.

'Have you seen enough?' Victor asked.

'Of what?' Stratton asked, studying the Neravistas.

'To put you off? You can't get through those men.'

'I told you, Victor. You don't need to come.'

Stratton's comment irritated the Frenchman. 'How do you expect me to join my brigade if I can't see how to get through those troops to them?' Victor hissed, allowing his fear and frustration to surface.

'I'm going to wait until they attack.'

'Then what? Follow them into the camp?'

'Something like that.'

'Excuse my ignorance but that sounds crazy, even for you.'

'It's not ideal, granted.'

'And you think you can see your plan working? You can see us getting through the Neravistas and joining our men — and then what?'

'Shhh!' Stratton ordered abruptly. 'You hear that?'

Victor listened. 'I don't hear anything.'

'Exactly. The shelling's stopped. They're going to attack.' Stratton realised the Indians were confused by what was happening. He went back down the slope a few feet. 'Victor,' he said, beckoning him.

Victor slid down beside him.

'I have my reasons for going into the camp. You have yours,' Stratton said. 'But you should tell your friends not to go any further. This is no place for bows and arrows.'

Victor looked at the Indians.

'I'm going to get a little closer,' Stratton said, making ready to go but pausing to look back at Victor. He squeezed the man's shoulder, expecting this would be their final farewell, slipped over the rise and moved down the slope in a crouching run.

The Indians looked at Victor inquiringly.

Victor stared back at them. The truth was that he had not given any thought to them taking part in this conflict because he had never really

313

expected to go into the camp during the battle. He wanted to tell the Indians that they were all leaving together for the border. But before he could say the words they jammed in his throat. He couldn't do it. This wasn't over for him. Not yet. That was his revolution the rebels were fighting for. But it was much more than that.

He crawled towards them. 'My friends,' he began, searching for the words. 'Listen to me. You cannot come where I must go this time. What I do now is not like any time before. You cannot come with me . . . It's time to say our goodbyes. Do you understand?' he asked.

Yoinakuwa looked at Victor thoughtfully.

'Please don't make this difficult for me,' Victor went on. 'We have had a long journey together. You have suffered more than anyone should. Your sons deserve their future.'

The old Indian read the sincerity in Victor's eyes and finally shrugged as if he accepted the Frenchman's words.

'Good,' Victor said. He held out his arms to each Indian in turn and embraced them awkwardly — he had never displayed such a level of affection towards them before. 'Right,' he said, feeling uncomfortable, almost as if he was deserting them. 'Good luck. It has been an honour to know you.'

Victor climbed over the rise and went down the slope in pursuit of Stratton, resisting the urge to look back.

★   ★   ★

Stratton reached the bottom of the slope and found himself on the same level as the Neravistas a hundred or so metres away. The undergrowth was thick enough to conceal him.

The shrill metallic sound of whistles suddenly filled the air. When Victor realised it was the enemy's signal to advance he broke into a shambling run to join Stratton.

The whistles were accompanied by shouted orders and every soldier got to his feet, rifle in hand.

'Fix bayonets!' an officer called out. The order was passed down the line.

The soldiers removed the blades from sheaths on their belts and attached them to the barrels of their weapons.

Victor dropped beside Stratton, out of breath. 'I have to be honest with you. I was about to leave you. But it dawned on me that, well, the entire meaning of my life lies in the next few hundred metres. I realised that I'm not going to the camp for my brigade. I can't help them. I'm going for myself. If I left now, the meaning of all these years would be lost. Does that make sense to you?'

'Yes. It does.'

'Good,' Victor said. 'I'm glad you think so.'

The order to advance echoed along the line and the Neravistas began to march forward, up the slope towards the trees.

'At the risk of pointing out something obvious,' Victor said, 'we don't have any rifles!'

'We'll have plenty to choose from in a while.'

The thought chilled Victor.

315

The vegetation grew taller as the Neravistas moved up the slope. Many of them disappeared within it, the swaying tops of the bushes the only indication of their continuing advance.

Stratton moved forward in short stages, then stopped as he pondered on the next phase of the battle.

'What is it?' Victor asked, sensing Stratton's concern.

'We're going to be in the line of fire when our guys open up.'

'I've noticed you have a habit of getting in the shit before you figure out the next move,' Victor said.

'Do you ever stop griping?'

'I like griping. This might be my last chance to gripe about anything.'

Sounds from behind made both men look back to see the Indians approaching at a crouching run.

'For God's sake, Yoinakuwa,' Victor hissed in exasperation. 'I made such a farewell speech. Why are you here?'

'Ask them,' Yoinakuwa said.

Kebowa and Mohesiwa stared at Victor and Stratton, gripping their bows.

Stratton shook his head and looked towards the Neravistas' advance.

★ ★ ★

When the shelling had ceased, the handful of experienced men among the rebels lining the perimeter shouted for the others to move into

316

their positions. 'The Neravistas will be coming,' was the cry.

Most of the men had survived the artillery barrage and now prepared to defend their camp against the frontal assault. Many were dazed or wounded, though, and some were badly disorientated. A cry for help came from a man trapped beneath a dead body that had landed on him. Bits of flesh and severed limbs lay scattered around. A man dragged himself forward into his firing position, ignoring his missing leg which had been blown away below the knee. A comrade applied a tourniquet to the stump so that he would not bleed to death before the fighting began. There were no more stretcher bearers on hand to ferry the wounded back. Every able-bodied rebel was now there to fight.

★　★　★

Louisa suspected that the end of the shelling was an ominous sign. A feeling of helplessness began to overwhelm her and she handed the little girl back to her mother.

'I have to go,' she said to David. She left the cover of the sandbags and ran across the courtyard and down the muddy track towards the only place she could think of where she might be of use.

As she approached the medical tent on the edge of the main living-quarters area Louisa slowed to a walk, an expression of utter horror on her face. The tent had received a direct hit. Bodies lay scattered everywhere. Many were

317

those of women and children. Hospitals had an aura of sanctuary about them and, in the absence of a church in the camp, when the shelling had started many non-combatants had tried to take cover around its canvas walls. Shattered structures lay burning and smouldering. Cots had been pulverised along with the bodies that lay in them. A handful of women were attempting to deal with the carnage but they were dazed, emotionally overwhelmed and unequipped.

The sprawling living quarters had been largely destroyed. Smoke billowed from fires and large, charred holes in the ground where homes had once stood. Moans and weeping filled the air. A piercing scream went up as a woman staggered from the smoking ruins carrying the limp body of a child.

Nothing in Louisa's young life had prepared her for such a spectacle. She thought she had seen enough death and destruction at the bridge to harden her but now that had been utterly eclipsed by what had happened here. She didn't know whether to cry or be sick or just drop to her knees and scream. But all she could manage was to watch in stunned silence.

Movement at her feet snapped her out of her trance and she looked down to see a little girl who was clasping her blood-streaked arm. The girl was not crying — she was simply looking up at Louisa as if to ask what it was all about. Louisa took a firm grip of herself and knelt in front of the child. 'You'll be okay. I'll fix your cut. Where's your mother?'

The little girl had no answer.

Louisa got to her feet. 'Stay there and don't move,' she said and hurried into the charred remains of the hospital tent looking for anything that was usable. She found a box of bandages and grabbed as many other items as she could.

She returned to the little girl and picked her up. 'Listen to me!' she called out to the others. 'Listen to me!' she repeated for those too dazed to hear her the first time. 'Bring all the children, bring the wounded and as many medical supplies as you can carry to the cabins. Get help. We must all help!'

She headed back along the track, calling out for others to follow. She hurried past various manned sandbag defences to the cabin used by Stratton and Victor and pushed open the door. She put the little girl in a chair and immediately set about preparing the room to accommodate the wounded.

Louisa threw wood on the smouldering fire, hung a pot of water on the cooking frame, cleared the table of pots and pans and took a moment to tend to the little girl's wound.

A strange noise began to filter in from outside and she paused to listen. It sounded like whistles and Louisa wondered what it could mean.

★ ★ ★

The rebel commanders moved along their defensive lines, moving men to fill any gaps they found, ensuring that bayonets were fitted and each fighter had ample ammunition. The strategy

319

from that point on was basic enough and everyone knew it. The Neravistas needed to punch a hole through the perimeter defence in order to stream into the camp and take it apart. The rebels' mission was simply to stop them any way they could. Many still hoped that Hector would arrive to assist them. It was the only thing keeping some of them from running away.

A 'beaten zone' of open ground had been cleared along the front of the entire perimeter, something the men had complained about while they'd been doing it and now thanked God for. The zone was the width of a tennis court and it meant that the enemy would be exposed for the time it took them to cross it. During any such charge that the Neravistas might make the rebels hoped to kill as many of them as possible.

The line of Neravistas advanced ever closer through the forest, which for some meant hacking a path through it with machetes. Their commanders could be heard shouting at those who were too slow to speed up and at those who were getting too far ahead to hold their positions and keep the line.

The rebels brought their guns into their shoulders, adjusted the sights for close range, checked the positioning of their spare magazines — and moistened their dry lips.

★ ★ ★

Stratton was waiting for the battle to get started before he headed for the perimeter. It was the only way to avoid getting cut down by the rebel

320

volleys. Another line of Neravistas appeared, running up the track, forty or fifty of them. They stopped to form up in several short lines, one behind the other, and the officers quickly ordered them to advance, one after the other, with a few metres' gap in between each line.

'That's our way in,' Stratton said.

'Why is that?' Victor asked.

'Those men are extra support to ensure they punch a hole through the perimeter at that point. They'll be doing that all along the line.'

Stratton made his way forward, keeping low, gauging his distance so as not to get too close. Victor followed. Unusually for them, the Indians brought up the rear.

★   ★   ★

Every rebel squatted behind his defensive position with his stare fixed on the foliage at the opposite side of the beaten zone. They could hear the Neravistas' progress and expected them to break through and charge at any second. Then it would be the rebels' turn to do some killing. The need to deliver a powerful blow at this point was paramount. 'Kill a dozen each and we win' were the words handed along the line.

Men fixed bayonets, tightened fingers on triggers and blinked their eyes behind rifle sights, waiting for a man to shoot and then move on to the next.

The rebels had placed M60 machine guns at intervals along the line, their ammunition belts laid out for quick usage, ammo boxes open around gunners and loaders.

Suddenly the Neravistas went silent, the sounds of their advance fading away. The government forces had stopped.

The tension soared.

'They're waiting to charge,' a rebel commander whispered to the men either side of him. 'Wait for them.' The words were passed down the line.

Beads of sweat rolled down faces. Trigger fingers quivered. Breathing was ragged.

A rebel turned his head to one side, vomited and quickly turned back without wiping his mouth to look through his rifle sights.

Another urinated in his pants without taking his stare from the killing zone.

★　★　★

The Neravistas' front line stood still in the forest, their comrades in the next wave kneeling a few metres behind them. They could see the rebel perimeter beyond the sunlit gap they had to cross. It was difficult to see the rebels themselves in the relative shade of their position but occasional movements reminded the government soldiers that they were there and waiting for them. Few had really believed their officers who had tried to convince them that the artillery bombardment would kill most of the enemy.

Those Neravistas in the front line were the most scared. They were the ones who would step into the light first. But they had one weapon to aid them, to give them some confidence, a surprise for the rebels that, as their officers had insisted, if they could use it to full advantage would mean they could make it to the rebel positions without a scratch.

A Neravista officer made his way along the rear of the lines, ducking between branches and over logs as he reassured the men. 'The grenades will clear the way,' he reminded them. 'Let your grenades do the work. They will clear what is left of the rebel line.'

Each man in the front line held a grenade tightly in one hand, his gun in the other. They had already pulled the rings and were holding the striker levers against the grenades' casings, ready for the order to throw.

A rebel veteran saw the foliage opposite him move. He knew the Neravistas were there, waiting for the order to charge. He saw something beyond the outer branches, a pair of legs in camouflage clothing. He pulled his rifle tightly against his shoulder and rested his finger on the trigger as he aimed.

The enemy's legs shifted position. The rebel was sure that the man was about to charge.

He adjusted his sights to where the man's chest should be and squeezed the trigger.

His gun went off. The Neravista dropped out of the bushes and fell face down into the dirt, dead.

'Hold your fire!' a rebel commander yelled.

An instant later the grenade the soldier had been holding slipped out of his hand, the lever flew off and after a few seconds it exploded.

Several Neravistas nearby were hit by shrapnel. One of them screamed in agony as he fell.

'They have grenades!' a rebel shouted. 'Grenades!'

The implications spread along the rebel line like wildfire.

The commander was unsure what to do at that second. He had made up his mind to fire only when the Neravistas charged. But now things were different.

The realisation of the new danger struck many of the rebels far more quickly. They knew that they had to act first.

'They have grenades!' one of them shouted again. 'FIRE!' he yelled and the rebel front line erupted in a thunder of guns.

Dozens of Neravistas were cut down inside the forest. Explosions shook the ground as the grenades they had been holding went off.

The government soldiers reacted in desperation and many in the front line threw their grenades. Many were shot as they emerged from cover to ensure that their devices flew freely into the rebel positions.

The Neravista officers realised they had lost the element of surprise and knew they had only one option left to them. 'Charge!' they yelled repeatedly, running behind the lines and firing their pistols into the ground behind the heels of their men.

The Neravistas burst into the open. Many were cut down immediately but a fair number of grenades were thrown and succeeded in silencing the rebel guns long enough for the government forces to cross the gap.

The Neravista soldiers screamed as they came, leaping over fallen comrades, rifles held out in front of them, the points of their bayonets leading the way. They pulled their triggers repeatedly, firing at anything and everything confronting them.

The rebels had the advantage of being defenders behind cover but although they killed an enormous number of Neravistas the far larger force overwhelmed them.

Rebels caught changing magazines were killed before they could reload. Bayonets plunged into throats and chests. The sound of metal upon metal joined the gunfire as men parried lunges and skewered bodies. Rifle butts slammed across faces. The screams of the impaled and of those doing the impaling joined the cacophony. Soldiers gouged eyes, sunk teeth into flesh. They smashed skulls and shot faces.

All along the rebel line, Neravistas charged through gaps.

'Fall back!' came the order from rebel commanders but for many it was too late.

The line of rebels began to thin. Gangs of Neravistas set upon individuals, who were stabbed and shot from all sides. They battered, slashed and blasted the wounded where they lay or crawled.

★　★　★

Stratton and the others had listened to it all. The sounds of death and battle had not helped their morale any. If Stratton had stayed behind the others would gladly have done the same.

They watched the last of the Neravistas head into action.

'Now,' Stratton said as he hurried forward.

Victor gritted his teeth and followed closely behind, feeling utterly vulnerable and not just because he had no weapon. This was madness, he thought.

The sound of gunfire grew louder as they made their way up the slope and into the undergrowth where visibility dropped to a few metres. The fighting seemed to rage all around them.

A bullet zinged through the air between Stratton and Victor, and more slapped into the leaves and branches above. Victor crouched as low as he could without actually crawling on his belly and stretched a hand out in front of him, almost touching Stratton as if afraid of losing contact with him.

Bullets raked the ground close by and Stratton checked behind to see if the others were okay. Kebowa had suffered a nick across an arm but otherwise the team seemed to be unscathed.

They came across their first dead body, a Neravista with most of his head blown away. Stratton snatched up the rifle beside him and cocked it to ensure it was loaded. A few metres further on lay another body and Stratton relieved the dead man of his magazine sack. Victor grabbed up his weapon, eyes wide as he looked ahead.

They pushed on at a steady pace, Stratton

aware that they had to avoid getting too close until the way was clear.

More bullets spat past them as they reached the cleared zone. Stratton crouched low and paused on the edge to take a look. Dead and injured Neravistas littered the sunlit ground. The main sound this far behind the battle line was the groaning of the wounded.

The sound of gunfire came from ahead. Stratton continued to wait, his gaze darting everywhere, his heart pounding in his chest.

The fighting seemed to move to the left and right of their front. It suggested that the Neravistas had successfully breached the perimeter at that point and were clearing the sides.

'The Neravistas have won through,' Stratton said as he turned to face Victor. 'From here on it's whatever your goal is. You know mine.'

Victor nodded. When he looked at Stratton the man was wearing a thin smile. Amid the madness that surrounded them, the flying bullets and the grotesque screams of dying men, the Englishman's expression had a calming effect on him. His fear remained but he could focus his thoughts.

'Thanks for everything,' Stratton said.

Victor wanted to say something but could not. This was a place where men said goodbye to life without a word.

Stratton looked at the Indians who understood he was saying farewell. He turned his back on them and ran across the clearing.

Victor watched him disappear into the foliage on the other side and when he was gone he felt a sudden relief. Stratton's single-mindedness had driven Victor to levels he could never have hoped to reach on his own. Mostly it had simply meant following the man but it had always seemed as if they were heading straight into hell. Now that he had gone the pressure was off. Victor felt free.

He faced his companions. 'Let's go,' he said, jutting his chin back the way they had come. 'We made it to the camp. How I don't know. We can go now.'

Kebowa and Mohesiwa indicated that Stratton had gone forward.

'He's got things he must do,' Victor explained. 'We go,' he said. 'I've come this far. It's enough. My conscience is clear. To be brutally honest with you, I don't want to see any more dead bodies, especially those of people I know.'

Victor started back down through the forest, followed by the others. Yoinakuwa made his way to the front, moving stealthily down the slope. But as they reached the point where the foliage began to thin out Yoinakuwa stopped and held his hand out behind him to indicate that the others should do the same.

He moved forward and crouched to look through the leaves.

Victor came to his side. 'Merde,' he muttered.

Trudging along the track was a fresh company of Neravistas. An officer yelled an order and they came to a halt. Another command and they faced towards Victor and the rebel perimeter and marched forward.

10

Stratton jumped through the rebel defences and over and between bodies as he made his way carefully towards the other side of the strip of jungle that formed the perimeter at that point.

He paused halfway through the strip to look ahead. Figures ran across in front of him in the field beyond. He could not make out which side they were from. Shots rang out — a distant machine gun. Some of the rounds entered the jungle and struck the trees above him.

Something grabbed his leg and he leapt back like a cat, his gun barrel traversing and ready to fire. It was a wounded rebel, lying on his back. Blood oozed from bullet holes and bayonet cuts around his chest and face. He tried to say something but the words would not come out. His eyes were filled with sadness as he reached out to Stratton for help.

It was the cruellest of choices for Stratton, but one to which he knew the answer immediately. Even if he could have saved the man, which did not look possible, he would not have done so. 'I'm sorry, mate,' he said. 'I'm sorry.'

Stratton hurried on, as much to get away from the man and the feeling of guilt as to pursue his goal.

He reached the edge of the jungle strip from where he could see the interior of the camp. He made out the roof of the stables a few hundred metres away. Smoke was everywhere. Gunfire raged to either side of him but directly ahead, towards the stables, it seemed to be quiet.

As he stood to better see the ground ahead he saw several dead Neravistas lying in the grass between him and the stables. There were a dozen or so of them, cut down while advancing across the open ground. Stratton remembered a machine-gun emplacement at that end of the stables and suspected it was the source of the gunfire that had killed them.

A loud explosion nearby made him duck behind a tree. It was too big to have been a grenade and smaller than the artillery ammunition that the Neravistas had been using. It had to have been a mortar shell. Having secured the perimeter, the Neravistas were preparing to carve up the camp interior. Stratton had no time to waste.

He concentrated on solving his immediate problem which was to get to the stables. He considered going further round the perimeter to approach from a different direction but it would waste time and the obstacles would probably be the same.

Stratton looked for a nearby dead rebel, one whose camouflage jacket was not too bloody, and quickly removed it. He pulled it on, found a rebel cap and moved back to the edge of the strip.

A helicopter screamed overhead, banking steeply, with another close on its tail. Stratton watched as they flew to the far end of the camp where they seemed to hover low. Troops leapt out of the side doors and the helicopters took to the air again.

He took a deep breath and headed across the field past the dead Neravistas and into the open.

★　★　★

Louisa, daubed in blood, applied pressure to a heavily bleeding wound in a young rebel's thigh. A woman came over to help and removed the young man's belt, looped it around his leg above his wound and, pushing a spoon under the loop, twisted it repeatedly until it tightened around the muscle. The man winced at the pain but the blood gradually stopped flowing from between Louisa's fingers.

A burst of machine-gun fire slammed across the outside of the house, several rounds smashing in through the window. Louisa and the woman dived to the floor. As Louisa lay there waiting for another burst she looked over at the crowd of women and children huddled at the back of the room.

Blood began to pour off the table onto the floor beside her and she sprang to her feet to reapply the tourniquet that had come undone. As she began to twist the blood-soaked belt she stopped in horror. A fresh bullet hole was visible in the young rebel's chest. He was dead.

Louisa put her shaking hands to her face, fighting to choke back her anger, and quickly turned her attentions to an injured soldier seated in a chair. Another burst struck the building and as Louisa flinched the front door flew open and a rebel fell into the room with a comrade in his arms. Louisa helped one of the women drag them out of the doorway so that the door could be closed. Then she inspected the soldiers. Both had been badly wounded. Louisa checked the pupils of the one who had been carried in, confirming her suspicions that he was dead. The other had a severe chest wound that was beyond Louisa's skills and she placed a dressing on it for no other reason than to give him hope. She put his hand on top of it to hold it in position and went to inspect another casualty.

A helicopter flew low overhead, the vibration of its engines rattling the building, and an explosion went off nearby.

Louisa's thoughts went to her father and she opened the door enough to look at his cabin that was partially obscured in smoke.

The sound of machine-gun fire came from across the courtyard. It was David, firing bursts from behind his sandbags.

Single rifle shots came from scattered rebels lying prone on the ground at the corners of buildings. The log table had been turned onto its side and men were lying behind it, shooting through the smoke at distant Neravistas closing in.

She looked back at Sebastian's cabin. The smoke had cleared just enough to reveal that the door was open and her father was walking around the front. She watched him, wondering what he was doing. He headed past the end cabin and up the slope in the direction of the stables.

'Father!' she called out.

Sebastian did not respond, unable to hear her above the noise of battle.

Louisa left the hut and as she stepped into the courtyard an explosion threw her to the ground.

She lay dazed for a few seconds before trying to get up, her vision out of focus. As she rose shakily to her knees a man was at her side, helping her.

'Stratton?' she asked, confused, looking into the face that was a blur.

'It's me, David,' a familiar voice replied.

Louisa's vision came back into focus. It was indeed David. Blood and black powder burns covered his hands and face. 'Are you okay? Are you hurt?'

'I . . . I think I'm okay,' she said, not really sure.

'Quickly!' he said, helping her to her feet. 'Come with me.'

He guided her across the courtyard to his sandbagged emplacement and they dropped to the ground as a burst of machine-gun fire raked the position.

David's machine-gunner was lying slumped over the ammunition boxes. Louisa reached to help him.

'He's dead,' David told her as he lifted up the feed tray from the M60 and placed a new belt of ammunition in it.

Louisa saw the bullet hole through the corpse's head and lowered her gaze despondently. 'Are they going to kill us all?' she asked.

David cocked the weapon. 'We should expect

that,' he said before firing several bursts. The noise hurt Louisa's ears.

The gun jammed and David pulled up the slide to clear it, only to discover a bullet stuck in the breech.

'Damn,' he cursed. Without bothering to try and remove the obstruction he struggled to twist off the M60's barrel while looking around the debris inside the emplacement. 'Hand me that other barrel,' he told Louisa.

She followed his gaze, saw what she assumed he was talking about, grabbed it up and held it out to him. Several enemy rounds struck nearby. David hardly flinched as he pulled the old barrel off, threw it to the floor, grabbed the spare from her grip, placed it in the bracket and in a few seconds was firing the machine gun again.

Louisa lay back against the sandbags, her hands over her ears, lost in hell.

★ ★ ★

A machine-gun emplacement at the top of the track near the side of the stables covered the approaches up from the cabins. Two young rebels manning it aimed their gun at the individual marching up through the wisps of smoke towards them. They recognised Sebastian as he walked at a brisk pace, seemingly unaware of the bullets flying around.

He was not wearing his usual civilian clothes. Instead, he had on the perfectly tailored officer's uniform that he had taken from his wardrobe earlier. His epaulettes were finished off with gold

334

braid, the brass buttons down the front of his jacket highly polished. The outfit was completed by a leather Sam Browne belt with its supporting strap passing over his shoulder to his waist. An ornate cavalry sword dangled at his side.

Sebastian passed the men in the emplacement with not so much as a nod and turned the corner of the building. He went to the first stall and opened the door to see his white stallion inside.

★   ★   ★

Stratton walked across the open ground towards the stables, his eyes focused on the rebel machine-gun emplacement tucked against the side of the building. He waved as he walked, holding his gun in the air, praying that those manning the position could see his rebel uniform through the smoke. He could see movement behind the sandbags and halted, ready to dive to the ground. To his relief a man stood up briefly and beckoned him to keep coming.

Stratton broke into a run towards the position and slid to the ground behind it. 'Thanks,' he said.

The two men in the emplacement were wide-eyed and anxious. 'What's happening?' the gunner asked.

The noise of battle was not as heavy as it had been, suggesting that the Neravistas were consolidating their positions. The mortar explosions continued at random.

'You have a radio?' Stratton asked.

The men shook their heads.

'The perimeter's been breached,' Stratton explained.

'We thought so,' the loader said, looking worried.

'What shall we do?' the gunner asked.

Stratton didn't know what to suggest that might reassure them. With some luck the Neravistas would call for a ceasefire and they would have to take it from there. But then again, perhaps not. But he had his own problems. 'Keep an eye on your flanks as well as to the front,' he told them. 'I'm heading down to the cabins. I'll tell your commanders you're okay and holding this position.'

They nodded but the fear remained in their eyes.

Stratton got ready to move on. 'Good luck,' he said.

'You too,' the gunner said, as Stratton headed to the corner of the building.

He stopped to look along the fronts of the stalls. He was about to move off when the door of the far stall opened and out strode the white stallion, saddled and bridled. Sebastian was riding it.

Stratton was stunned by the sight. Sebastian, his expression proud and commanding, sat stoically in the saddle as the powerful if slightly nervous animal moved in a tight circle.

A mortar exploded harmlessly at the other side of the corral and Sebastian calmed his horse with a pat and a few words. He realised he was being watched and looked over to see Stratton.

The two men stared at each other, the old

warrior and the new. Sebastian drew his sword from its scabbard and held it with the tip pointed skyward, the hilt at his waist, his back ramrod straight.

Stratton was not entirely sure what prompted him, since he had not made the gesture for a long time, but he came to attention and gave the old man a solemn salute.

Sebastian appreciated the gesture. He nodded to Stratton, turned the horse and trotted away towards the cabins.

Stratton made his way around to the other side of the stables and headed into the trees.

Sebastian broke into a canter as he reached the cabins and then into a full gallop through the courtyard. He tore past the rebels lying behind cover and firing, past the machine-gun emplacement without seeing Louisa there and rode on at full speed.

Louisa saw him race past. 'Father!' she cried, scrambling to her feet to run after him. David leapt from his position and grabbed her. He stared at their leader, stunned.

Sebastian straightened his sword arm, held the tip out in front of him and charged into battle. Bullets flew around him but he ignored them as if lost in another world, another time, perhaps even another battle.

★   ★   ★

A government officer at the lookout post who was watching the battle's progress through binoculars could not believe his eyes. 'Look at

337

this!' he cried. 'Sebastian rides! Sebastian rides!'

Ventura, Steel and the other officers scrambled to look.

Sebastian rode like the devil himself, seemingly invulnerable to everything that was fired at him. The powerful horse moved as though it was at one with its master.

A mortar shell exploded close to them but neither man nor beast flinched as dirt and shrapnel flew around them.

'I knew he was mad,' Ventura said dryly.

'By Jupiter!' Steel exclaimed, a look of genuine admiration in his eyes. 'Now *that*'s the way to die!'

Several officers grabbed their rifles and began to take pot shots at Sebastian. But it would have taken a supernaturally lucky shot with an AK47 at that distance.

The old fighter was, however, struck by rounds from somewhere. One hit him in the chest, another in his thigh, but he held his posture and charged on. He directed his steed towards the troops who had been dropped off by the helicopter and were manning a mortar. When the officer in charge first saw Sebastian he did not know what to make of him. But as the old man and the white stallion bore down on his position he realised the threat they posed.

The mortar team scrambled for their weapons heaped in a pile around the ammunition boxes. The officer drew his pistol and began to fire a rapid series of shots. But Sebastian was to have his final moment.

As he closed the gap between the Neravistas

and himself the thunder of his horse's hooves grew louder and the men who'd been going for their weapons changed their minds and tried to scatter. The officer had emptied his pistol clip and stood his ground while struggling to reload.

Sebastian leapt over the stack of mortar ammunition, at the same time thrusting down with his sword. A good portion of its blade disappeared into the neck of one of the soldiers and pierced down into his heart. As the horse landed Sebastian withdrew his blood-soaked blade and with the practised ease of a polo player swung it in a cartwheel motion and took away the side of the officer's face.

He rode on past the position and made a wide turn as the soldiers scrambled to pick up their weapons. As Sebastian lined up for another charge they opened fire, all their guns on full automatic. The bullets tore into both horse and rider. The horse died as it charged, collapsing instantly. Sebastian flew over its neck to crumple in the dirt in front of it. He did not move and his eyes stayed wide open.

Applause and laughter resounded from the lookout post.

Steel seemed oblivious to the celebration, lost for the moment in appreciation of the old man's final moment.

'Why, Steel,' Ventura said, interrupting the American's daydream. 'I do believe you're jealous of him.'

'I am. Right up until the part where he died,' Steel said.

The officers roared with laughter again.

'I think we should follow his lead, though, don't you?' Steel suggested. 'The battle is all but won. Let's take a ride and get some real sport.'

'Go down there?' Ventura asked, unsure. 'It's still a little busy.'

'Why else would we go there?' Steel replied, downing his drink and walking over to his horse. 'Come on, Ventura. Show me some of that upper-class disdain for danger that you think you have. You're not gonna let Sebastian outdo you, are you?'

Ventura felt contempt for Steel's immature challenge but shrugged and finished his drink. 'Why not?' he sighed.

Several others joined them in mounting their horses and the group rode off towards the rebel camp entrance.

★ ★ ★

Louisa watched her father die after David had practically dragged her back to the defensive position while the enemy took shots at them. She squatted at his feet in tears while he started firing again at a group of Neravistas.

'They're closing in,' he shouted, reaching the end of his ammo belt.

The number of rebels in the courtyard was getting smaller as they were gradually picked off.

David ripped open an ammunition box to dig out another belt. 'You must go, Louisa! You must escape! They'll kill you just like they did Sebastian.'

She stopped her sobbing but remained where

she was, apparently unmoved by David's warning. He reloaded the M60, glanced at her to see that she had not taken any notice of him and grabbed hold of her roughly. 'Listen to me! You must try and escape. You are our future. Do you understand?'

His words penetrated Louisa's anguish and she looked into his eyes to see the fire in them. A round slammed into the top of the sandbags near his head and David pulled her down further. 'You stay alive for us, not just for yourself!' he added as he got back to the business of shooting at the enemy. 'Go! Don't waste everything we have done here!'

His words inspired her but she was left confused. 'How can I escape?'

'The cliff. Your ropes. It's your only chance.'

'But the children . . . '

'You cannot take them. Save yourself and one day you can save others.'

Louisa believed him. He was right. She had little chance of getting out of there and she knew it. But she owed it to him, to all of them, to try.

She got ready to run, but then shook her head in frustration as bullets flew around them. 'Which way?' she yelled. 'Tell me where to go!'

'The stables,' David said. 'Ride!'

Louisa looked in that direction hopefully. The stables were just visible through the smoke. She looked at David. 'Come with me.'

'No. Go! Now! I'll cover you.'

Louisa understood. She touched him gently, knowing she would not see him again, and then she was off at the run.

341

David fired an extended burst, sweeping the M60 through a wide arc of fire.

★ ★ ★

Hector sat on his horse, two dozen of his rebels with him, all of them listening sombrely to the distant sound of battle. A group of riders came galloping down the track from the direction of Sebastian's camp.

Hector looked expectantly towards them. It was the reconnaissance patrol he had sent ahead to wait for Louisa. But he could see that she was not among them.

The patrol leader pulled his perspiring horse to a halt in front of Hector and, a grave expression on his face, shook his head. 'Sebastian is dead,' he said.

Hector had been prepared for that news but still it shocked him when he heard the words. The revolution had truly changed its course.

'They're being destroyed wholesale,' the patrol leader continued. 'No one will get out of there alive.'

Despite everything that had come between Louisa and him, Hector's heart felt as though it was going to break open. A cherished dream he had held close to his soul for years had vanished like a puff of smoke rising into the air.

He eased his horse's head around and walked the animal past his men, back towards his encampment.

★ ★ ★

Stratton had watched Sebastian's death from the high ground behind the stables. It had not come as a surprise after he'd seen the rebel leader ride away on his horse the way he had. But having just conversed with him, in a kind of way, it was nonetheless a strange feeling to see him die so soon after.

Stratton swiftly made his way down to the cabins and around to the front of the one used by Louisa.

He pushed open the door and went inside. 'Louisa!' he called out.

The place looked empty, as if it had been abandoned in a hurry. The table was covered in maps with drawings of troop locations and movements on them. When there was no answer Stratton hurried to the back room to find it empty too.

He went back to the front door to look outside. A machine gun was firing from the other side of the courtyard. A couple of rebels were holding out behind the upturned log table as were others concealed elsewhere around the courtyard. Corpses lay all around.

Bursts of fire from the patch of wood on the edge of the main encampment raked the wall of the cabin close to Stratton. He dropped to the ground, crawled a short distance, got to his feet and ran at the crouch to the cabin that he had shared with Victor.

He ducked inside the door as another burst barely missed him. He fell back against the wall and looked around the room.

Bodies both dead and alive littered the place.

Wounded rebels sprawled on the table, floor and chairs, some of them conscious. Flies buzzed hungrily around the blood and soiled dressings. Most disturbing for Stratton, a group of women and children huddled on the floor at the far end, some staring at him while others hid their faces in fear.

As he looked around his hopes of finding Louisa shrank. 'Louisa!' he called out again.

The only reply was the sobs and moans of the injured.

On the floor of the kitchen a woman dabbed the wounds of a rebel soldier who'd been caught in a mortar strike. His face and torso were covered in lacerations. Stratton moved to the woman but she appeared to be in a trance and did not notice him.

'Where is Louisa?' he asked.

She did not respond. Stratton repeated the question, this time reaching out to touch her shoulder gently.

She looked around at him, her eyes lifeless. 'She was here,' she said calmly, going back to her futile task.

'How long ago?' he asked.

The woman shrugged, lost in her own world.

Stratton went back to the front door and peered out at the machine-gunner across the courtyard who was firing short bursts. He felt a sense of foreboding, knowing that there was little time left for the remaining defenders.

He crawled out of the doorway and scurried to the log table that was by now riddled with shrapnel and bullet holes. The two men at either end of it who were firing single aimed shots barely glanced at him, preoccupied by the need to keep killing in order to survive.

Stratton gauged the distance to the sandbages and sprinted across the gap. His movement attracted some attention, bullets striking close by as he dived over the sandbag wall to hit the ground heavily.

David glanced over his shoulder and gave his visitor a double take.

Stratton was as surprised as the young rebel. 'David?'

The young man released his weapon and slumped down to grab a drink from a canteen. He was exhausted, his body covered in dust, but he managed a brief smile. 'What are you doing here?'

'You okay?' Stratton asked, looking him over.

'No one is,' David said, putting down his canteen and turning back to the machine gun.

Several more rounds struck near Stratton and he looked in the direction of fire to see two Neravistas running towards the end cabin. He shouldered his AK to engage them but David traversed the M60 and released a quick burst before Stratton could fire. In quick succession the men crumpled to the ground and did not move.

Stratton was impressed. 'Nice shooting.'

The young man ducked down as a bullet flew past his head.

'Have you seen Louisa?'

'She's gone to the cliffs.'

Stratton's first reaction was relief that she was

alive, or had been when David last saw her. 'When?'

'Not long ago,' David said, unable to think how long it actually had been. It felt like seconds. 'She went to the stables.'

'Before or after Sebastian died?'

'After.' He could remember that much.

Stratton looked in that direction, frustrated at how little time they must have missed each other by.

As David started to open a new box of ammunition Stratton put his hand on it. 'It's time to go, my friend.'

'I can't,' David said, pushing his hand away and pulling out another ammo belt. 'I have to stay with my gun,' He clipped the link to the short length sticking out of the gun tray.

Stratton took hold of his arm. 'You love it so much, bring it with you. I'll carry the ammo. You've done all you can here, David. It's time to fall back.'

David could not resist Stratton's offer. The brief exchange had brought him a little way out of his murderous trance. He nodded and grabbed up the weapon, folded the legs away and threw the remaining ammo belt over one shoulder and a canvas bag over the other.

Stratton poked his head round the side of the sandbags and cupped his hands around his mouth. 'You men! Listen! We're falling back to the stables! Fall back to the stables!'

The remaining handful of rebels appeared to have understood.

'I'll cover you,' Stratton said, placing his

weapon against his shoulder. 'Go! Go! Go!' he yelled as he raised his head above the top of the sandbag wall and fired quick bursts at the various enemy positions.

David ran for all he was worth out through the gap and up the track towards the stables. The other rebels left their positions and fired as they ran. One took a bullet through the chest and died before he hit the ground. Another was shot in the back and fell but continued to crawl forward.

Stratton emptied his AK47's magazine, ejected it, reloaded and fired another series of bursts. As the last unwounded rebel tore past him he reloaded, fired again, leapt the sandbags and charged up the slope.

Bullets traced their footsteps, zinging through the air. One of the rebels went down and did not move again. A bullet grazed David's leg and he winced. Stratton grabbed his arm and dragged him on.

The two rebels manning the defensive position at the top of the track saw their comrades emerge from the thin smoke and put down covering fire beyond them.

Stratton and David, out of breath, fell behind the sandbagged position. But there was not a second to spare — David got to his knees and set up his machine gun ready to fire.

Stratton inspected David's wound, tearing the cloth of his trouser leg to get a better look at it. 'How's it going, lads?' he asked the two rebels who looked not much more than sixteen years old. 'It's a busy fight, eh?'

The loader nodded and ripped open an ammunition box as his partner fired several bursts towards the courtyard.

David's wound was not deep but it was bloody. Stratton took his field dressing from the machine-gun butt where it was taped and wrapped it around the wound. 'You'll live,' he said, squeezing David's shoulder. 'I'll be back,' he promised, picking up his weapon and hurrying away.

Stratton reached the corral fence and crouched to look around. He set off again, following the outside of the fence around to the other side, putting him closer to the top of the hill. He dropped to his belly and craned to look down the slope towards the cliffs in the hope of seeing Louisa. There was a lot of open ground but he found her and knew that he would never catch her up. She was riding her horse, and going like the wind.

Yet instant relief flooded through him on seeing her alive. Even though she was far from safe Stratton could not help grinning. All he wanted now was to be with her and to take her to safety.

It suddenly occurred to him that if Louisa could do it, then so could he, and he ran to the stables and down the line of stalls. All of them were open and visibly empty except for the last, whose door was closed. He pushed it open, praying that a horse would be inside. No such luck. All he saw was his own pack and parachute hanging on a hook where David had put them the previous morning.

Stratton ran back to the corral. He scanned along the edge of the cliff. Even if Louisa had been standing and waving she would have been difficult to spot at that distance. Finally he saw the horse trotting along the cliff edge, but without its rider. He felt a sudden panic that she had been shot and had fallen off it. Yet since the horse was at the cliff he reassured himself that she had most likely dismounted and was now at one of the rope bundles.

As he strained to get a better look a burst of fire raked the fence close by and he dived to the ground. He rolled away to look for the source of the shooting and found it. Several Neravistas were running across the open ground from the far perimeter in a flanking attack. Stratton brought his gun up to his shoulder but most of the attackers were cut down by firing from the defensive position on the other side of the stables.

'Stratton!' David called out from the other defensive position.

Stratton raised his head enough to see him.

'They've taken the cabins!' David shouted.

Stratton looked quickly for Louisa again and considered making a run for it down the slope. He looked over at David and the others. They needed to get away before their position was overrun. This was now about their escape as well as Louisa's. Maybe there was a way of combining the two, Stratton thought.

A group of horsemen in the far distance beyond the tented camp caught his eye. They could only be Neravistas and they seemed to be heading around the inside of the perimeter. If they continued on that route they would move around the outside of the smouldering shanty-town encampment, down a finger of jungle and eventually to the cliff before heading up to the stables. If they stuck close to the cliff edge they might find Louisa.

Stratton looked again towards the cliff, this time trying to spot the rope bundles. He thought he saw movement by one of them. It had to be Louisa. It would take a while to lower enough rope to reach the bottom in order to climb down, time that she might not have.

Stratton had seen enough. He needed to get down there as soon as possible.

The machine gun on the far side of the stables opened up with a sustained burst of fire. They were under attack again.

A mortar shell exploded on the other side of the corral. The two M60s at David's position started firing towards the cabins.

An explosion at the furthest defensive machine-gun position silenced the gun. Single shots followed and Stratton knew they signalled an attack at that location.

He hurried to the stables, holding his rifle ready to fire. A Neravista appeared in the open field and Stratton dropped him with a single shot. Smoke rose from the sandbags of the furthest M60 position and the two rebels who had manned it lay dead across their defences.

A bullet struck the side of the stables and Stratton fired as he moved, killing two Neravistas coming across the open ground from the perimeter. He jumped behind the M60 and tried to get it firing again but it had been critically damaged.

More bullets whined around Stratton. He took up his rifle and shot one charging Neravista after another. Aware that he was running out of ammunition, he pulled another magazine from his pouch as he fired. When the *clunk* that signalled he was out of bullets came he deftly pressed the catch that released the magazine and pushed in a new one.

Sudden screams came from off to one side and he looked to see two Neravistas charging towards him, their bayonets pointing right at him.

Stratton fired, hitting one, but then his weapon jammed. As he stepped back to parry the inevitable bayonet thrust arrows flew into the attacker's neck and side and he dropped onto the sandbags, writhing in agony. A volley of rifle fire aimed at the Neravistas' flanking attack broke it and drove them back.

Victor, the Indians and a dozen rebels were tearing across the open ground towards Stratton. They reached the building and quickly deployed to defensive positions.

The Frenchman was out of breath but he managed a grin as he huddled down at the side of the building. 'Now *I* get to save *your* ass,' he said, clearly pleased with himself.

'What are you doing here?' Stratton asked as he cleared his jammed weapon.

'I couldn't leave you here alone.'

Stratton stared at Victor, unsure of his sincerity.

Victor shrugged. 'Plus hundreds more Neravistas moved in to cover the perimeter. I don't think they want anyone to get out of here alive.'

'Don't get too settled. You have more running to do . . . David!' Stratton called out, heading to the other side of the building.

A mortar shell landed close by and everyone hit the dirt as shrapnel splattered around. One of the rebels dropped to the ground, holding his face as blood flowed through his fingers. Someone went to help him.

'They're preparing to attack!' David shouted back.

Machine-gun fire came up the slope, raking the defensive position. Stratton hurried, crouching, to the corner to take a look for himself.

Victor followed. 'Tell me what's going on.'

'I think the cliffs may be our only way out of here,' Stratton said. 'But if we just try and run for it these guys'll cut us down before we get there.'

'Is this another one of those plans where you know the aim but not how to get there?' Victor asked.

'Yeah, one of those,' Stratton agreed.

'I'm beginning to hate that kind of plan.'

David handed his canvas bag to one of the young rebels and pointed to Stratton. He fired a burst from his machine gun to cover the man as he sprinted across the gap. The other gunner did the same. The young rebel slid to the ground beside Stratton and handed him the bag.

Stratton looked inside. It contained two claymore mines with all their accessories. His mind raced at the possibilities. 'This is good,' he muttered, emptying the bag and sorting through the extras that included the standard trip wires and trigger devices.

After a brief survey of the terrain he unwound part of a wire spool and fixed the end to the corner of the building low to the ground. 'Stay here,' he said to Victor as he put the contents back into the canvas bag. 'Don't let anyone touch the wire,' he ordered, placing the spool over the end of his gun barrel and setting off towards David's position, the spool unwinding as he ran.

Stratton flung himself down beside David and the other gunner and set about preparing the claymore. 'Both of you get ready to move to the high ground at the other side of the corral.'

'What are we doing?' David asked as he fired bursts from his machine gun.

'Running as fast as we can. I suggest you get yourself a lighter gun,' Stratton advised as he screwed the detonator into the mine. He put a hand on the shoulder of the other gunner, who turned to look at him. 'I want you to clip as many ammo belts together as you can.'

The young gunner looked at David.

'Do it,' David ordered and the young rebel quickly set about the task.

'Give me a burst,' Stratton requested and David obliged.

While David fired, Stratton leaned over the front of the sandbags and, holding the mine, pushed the forks that protruded from its base firmly into the ground. It took him several tense seconds to ensure the device was properly wired before he dropped back behind the sandbags.

'How many have you done?' he asked the young rebel who was clipping ammo belts together and laying them in loops so that they could feed the M60 easily.

'Five, six hundred rounds.'

'That's good. Join your friend. And keep away from the wire. Go!'

The rebel ran across the gap to the stables.

Stratton prepared the second claymore and when it was ready gathered himself for another sprint. 'Keep their heads down for another minute.'

David obeyed as Stratton pushed off to the corral fence and round to the far side of it. He knelt down and, aiming the mine at the top of the hill, he shoved the forks into the ground and rested the spool of wire beside it. 'Victor,' he shouted. 'Here!'

Victor ran over to him from the stables.

'Look down there,' Stratton said, pointing towards the cliffs.

Victor looked where Stratton was pointing as he gulped in some air. Just as he did so a mortar shell landed nearby and they hugged the ground as they were showered in dirt.

'Louisa's down there,' Stratton continued, spitting dirt from his mouth. 'That's where you're going. A dozen or so riders are heading that way and you're going to take them out. If you can get their horses you might be able to

354

punch your way through the perimeter.'

'I see,' Victor said, trying to evaluate all the possibilities and dangers. 'Sebastian?' he asked, suddenly wondering where his leader was.

Stratton shook his head. 'It's your only hope,' Stratton said. 'Stay spread out on your way down, keep shooting and moving and you'll get there.'

'And you?'

'I'm going to buy you the time.'

'You're going to stay here so we can escape? You'll die.'

'I'll give you the start you need . . . But I'll still beat you to the bottom.'

'How long a start?'

'You should be halfway down the hill before I follow.'

'Not even I'm that slow.'

'You want to bet?'

Victor looked around. 'You have a horse?'

'No.'

Victor was confused. 'You don't have anything to bet with.'

'A life of servitude to the other, whoever loses.'

'If you survive and I beat you to the bottom you'll be my manservant for life?'

'And vice versa.'

'Done.'

'Go get the others and be ready to move on my say.'

Victor ran to the stables and Stratton headed back to David.

'They're mustering to charge,' David said as he arrived. 'They have numbers.'

'Let's not disappoint them, then.'

'How do you always seem so confident?'

'It's a trick . . . you ready?'

'Yes.' David nodded.

'Go to the other side of the stables and lay down a blanket of fire, everything you've got. I need the Neravistas on that side to stall before they join the assault. Then, on my signal, you go. Victor knows where to head for.'

'I understand.'

'Good luck.'

David was about to go when he paused to hold out his hand.

'Get out of here,' Stratton said without taking it. 'I'll see you later.'

David got the message and ran.

Stratton went back to the M60, dragged a sandbag off the wall and placed it over the barrel to hold the gun in position. He checked the long length of ammo belts that the young rebel had prepared and ensured that they were folded in layers. He snapped a length of wire from the spool, threaded it through the trigger and around the trigger guard and drew the wire tight, pulling the trigger close to the guard. The weapon began to fire as he twisted the wire tight. The extended belt of ammunition was sucked into the weapon, the spent clips and casings ejecting into the air on the other side.

Stratton left the firing gun and ran towards the corral.

David was directing a long burst of fire from the far side of the stables. As Stratton ran past he signalled Victor to move.

Stratton reached the second claymore on the other side of the corral as Victor, David, the Indians and the remaining rebels left the cover of the stables. They charged for all they were worth past the corral, over the crest and down onto the wide-open slope that led to the cliffs, spreading out as they ran.

Stratton took the spool of wire connected to the claymore and raced across the open ground with it as far as it would go. He jammed the metal stake attached to the end of the wire into the earth and hurried back to the claymore to arm the trigger mechanism. Only when he had completed the task did he realise that his machine gun had stopped firing.

He checked the slope that led to the cliff to see the others running at full tilt, the incline contributing to their speed.

Another mortar shell landed nearby but Stratton ignored it and sprinted to the stables and the end stall. He grabbed his parachute pack off the nail and ran back towards the crest of the hill, jumping over the tripwire on his way.

Gunfire erupted from the track leading from the cabins. The Neravistas were coming.

As Stratton pulled his parachute onto his back the first government soldiers came into view. Many more followed behind them, encouraged to charge by unforgiving officers waving pistols.

The first soldiers to reach the gun emplacement fired into it. The rest stormed up the hill, shoulder to shoulder, bayonets at the ready and screaming their war cry.

One of the soldiers tripped the wire. The claymore exploded, sending hundreds of steel balls into the advancing Neravistas, severing limbs, shattering heads, pulverising torsos. The projectiles passed through the front rank and into the second and third rows. Those behind were showered with the blood of their colleagues and dropped to the ground, stunned by the carnage.

Stratton looped the AK 47 strap over his neck so that the weapon hung against his chest and jogged down the hill while buckling the leg straps of the parachute.

The Neravistas regrouped to charge again. A soldier in the front rank, whimpering in fear, refused to go any further. An officer quickly shot him through the brain and levelled the pistol at the next man. Then he yelled and charged himself. The others followed.

This time the assault was unchecked. They were joined by the charge that came around the other side of the stables, the soldiers shooting wildly into the stalls as they passed. The two groups met at the crest of the hill, searching around for their enemy, hungry for blood.

They saw Stratton running away, the others far ahead.

They aimed their rifles.

One of the Neravistas tripped the second wire.

The claymore, aimed at the top of the hill, detonated like a thunderclap, sending its hail of steel through the men, shattering them like dolls. Those who were not killed outright or wounded flung themselves to the ground, horrified at the destructive power of the weapon as pieces of flesh and bone fell around them.

★ ★ ★

At the sound of the explosion Victor looked back and thought he could see a figure heading down the hill below the pall of smoke. He could only pray that it was Stratton.

He looked ahead to the bottom of the field and the edge of the cliff where he could make out a figure that he hoped was Louisa. A glance to his side revealed the riders that Stratton had described. They were closing on the end of the finger of jungle which, if they rode around it, would lead them towards the cliff. At the rate Victor's group was going he calculated they would intercept them. He held on to his magazine pouch as he ran.

Several shots rang out from a distant line of trees. Rounds zipped between the men. The bullets were aimed shots and at that distance, with moving targets, any hit would be pure luck. And a lot of luck was what Victor knew they needed. 'Keep going!' he shouted. 'Keep going!'

★ ★ ★

Stratton fastened his chest strap as he ran, feeling the wind in his face, the slope building his momentum. He felt for the rip cord and pulled it. The back of the pack popped open and the pilot chute sprang away, dragging the deployment bag to the ground as the suspension

359

lines played out. The bright green chute slid from the bag and Stratton felt the tug on his shoulders. He grabbed the risers and shook them to help spread the chute.

It began to inflate as the nylon edges snatched at the air.

The leading cells opened as the wind crept along the tubes and the chute started to rise off the ground and take on its rectangular shape. When the slider appeared above Stratton's head he knew he was in business and the firm grip of the harness around his body told him that the chute was eager to take his weight.

He ran as fast as he could in order to keep the canopy inflated. The harness tightened around his thighs and the chute started to pull at him.

Seconds later Stratton rose up. The ground zoomed by feet below as he glided with majestic ease, the chute's harness creaking under his weight. The wind ruffled his hair and the exhilaration he felt at his success was immense.

When he looked for the spot where he hoped Louisa might be he realised he was not on track and eased down on one of the toggles to make a gentle turn, angling across the slope.

Stratton gradually gained height and his view of the field became that of a bird's, his men spread out below him, running as fast as they could. The noise of distant gunfire filtered to him through the sounds of the wind blowing past his ears and the flapping chute. He looked towards the finger of jungle to see the riders coming around it and heading towards the cliffs.

As Victor ran he glanced back once again, hoping to see Stratton, but there was no sign of him. He feared he had been shot and was lying somewhere on the slope.

He ran on, suppressing any thought of stopping to make sure of the Englishman's fate. Stratton had made his sacrifice to give Victor and the others a chance to get away and for them to get themselves killed or captured would make a mockery of it.

A shadow moved across Victor although the sky was cloudless and he heard a strange flapping sound coming from overhead. He turned to look, his gaze angling skyward. Something big hung just below the sun. He squinted, recognising what it was, and could not believe his eyes.

Stratton gave him an easy wave as he sailed past beneath the green chute with its red dragon emblazoned across it.

Victor was filled with emotion, not knowing whether to laugh or cry. He roared. 'Go, my eagle. Go!' he shouted as he laughed. 'I am your slave! I am your slave!'

David looked up and around at Stratton and was stunned.

The Indians did not know what to make of the spectacle, Mohesiwa tripping and falling on his face because he was so distracted.

As Victor watched Stratton sail on he suspected what he meant to do. The Frenchman saw the riders appear around the trees and gauged where they would all intersect. He also knew what he had to do.

The grim reality of their plight came home with a bang, literally, as a burst of machine-gun fire caught one of the young rebels and he fell dead. The group pressed on. A mortar shell landed close by, followed by another, and shrapnel flew among them. Kebowa was struck in his side by a piece. It caused him to stumble but he regained his balance and pressed on, blood pouring from the wound.

Another burst of machine-gun fire found its mark again, one of the rebels dropping and rolling to a stop.

'Down!' David shouted and the group dived to the ground to return fire.

Another mortar shell landed nearby and David knew they had to move on or die. He got back to his feet. 'Fire and move!' he shouted to the others. 'Fire and move!'

He ran several metres, dropped to the ground and fired at the enemy. 'Move!' he shouted.

Several of the others scrambled to their feet and ran on a few metres before dropping to the ground to open fire. As the rest of the group caught on they began to repeat the tactic.

★ ★ ★

The riders arrived at the cliff and raced along its edge. Stratton pulled his gun strap over his head, brought the weapon against his shoulder and fired several shots at them. David and the others also engaged the horsemen.

362

Steel had been concentrating on the cliff edge when the first rounds struck the group and unhorsed an officer ahead of him. The man hit the ground and tumbled off the edge, screaming.

Steel brought his horse to a sliding stop, as did the others, and he dismounted to hug the dirt. The horses scattered, leaving their riders.

Only then did Steel notice the parachute.

Stratton fired several more shots until he ran out of ammunition. He dropped the rifle to the ground and grabbed the chute's toggles. The edge of the cliff was coming up fast and he still had not seen Louisa.

Steel lay in the grass holding his pistol, transfixed by the sight of the parachute. A grin spread across his face. 'Does that guy ever give up? Jesus!'

Stratton found Louisa struggling with one of the rope bundles, pulling the line over the edge. Elation coursed through him once more when he saw her. 'Louisa!' he cried. But she was still too far away and too distracted to hear him.

Steel tried to line up Stratton in the sights of his pistol and, despite the ridiculous distance, fired a couple of shots, knowing very well that they would be in vain. He assumed the Englishman was headed for the cliff and safety and followed his track, wondering if he might risk intercepting him. Then he saw Louisa on the edge of the cliff, pulling at a line of rope.

'There!' Steel called out to Ventura and the officers around him. 'Shoot them!'

They followed his order and opened up on Louisa as well as Stratton.

Bullets snapped past Louisa and slammed into the pile of rope. She dropped to the ground and scrambled behind the bundle as more rounds hit it.

Victor saw Louisa and the government officers shooting at her. He was suddenly overcome with such anger that he abandoned any more fire-and-fall defensive moves and charged as he fired, racing ahead of the others and bellowing with rage.

The Indians followed, arrows in their bows. David and the remaining rebels joined the charge.

Kebowa stopped long enough to loose an arrow that struck an officer who was reloading his rifle in the back. But the officer beside him turned swiftly and shot Kebowa through the heart.

A shell landed among the rebels, a piece of shrapnel severing Yoinakuwa's hand. Victor saw his friend fall and went to his aid as the old Indian lay on his side in agony.

Mohesiwa released a torrent of arrows in revenge, one of them striking Ventura through the top of his shoulder as he lay, prone, penetrating deep into his chest cavity. Yoinakuwa watched Mohesiwa fall after several government bullets found their mark, killing him as he drew back his final arrow.

Victor dropped to the ground to fire some shots and to look around to assess their situation. There was only a handful of them left. His gaze fell on several of the officers' horses wandering nearby, confused by the explosions and gunfire surrounding them.

Stratton drew closer to Louisa by the second. His loosely drawn-up plan had been to land beside her and take things from there. But now that they were in the middle of a battle he had only one option left.

'Louisa!' he shouted.

She looked up at the sound of her name and froze, wide-eyed and stunned. It was *him*. At the last possible moment he had come for her. And in a way she could not have dreamed of.

A bullet struck close by, snapping Louisa out of her trance, and she dropped to the ground but stayed looking at Stratton. With him there was hope. Always.

Stratton pulled down gently on the chute's toggles to lose some height and steered directly towards her.

Steel fired a couple of shots from his pistol, more out of frustration than anything else. 'Christ, can't any of you guys shoot!' he shouted, glancing at Ventura to find him staring at him, his mouth open and his tongue hanging out. The orange fletching of an arrow protruded from his shoulder, the long, slender green tail feather of the quetzal bird attached to the nock by a line of gut.

The rebels' numbers had lessened and they were hugging the ground although they were still shooting. Steel scrambled forward, taking pot shots at them, and broke into a crouching run along the cliff edge towards Louisa.

Stratton was close enough to see the expression on her face. He released a toggle to reach down as low as he could.

Louisa had not thought about his intentions for a moment until then. Too much had been happening. But as she saw his outstretched hand it struck her what he planned to do. She glanced back at the edge of the cliff a few metres behind her, then back at him as he bore down on her. There was no time to worry about the madness of it.

'Take my hand!' Stratton shouted.

He was confident that he could hold her. He would grip her like a vice, drag her up to him and hold her tightly in his arms as they sailed over the edge. And he would not let go until they touched down far below.

Louisa focused on the hand, her heart filled with fear. But there was no time to consider the consequences. She would hold on to his hand with all her strength and he would hold her with all of his and never let go. He was Stratton and she would live.

She stood up from behind the rope bundle and reached up to him.

Victor was running with Yoinakuwa and glanced towards Louisa. For a second he saw the image: Stratton sailing towards her and reaching down, Louisa standing and reaching up. A bullet ripped open Victor's shoulder, splashing his face in blood, and he ran on as hard as he could towards the horses.

The distance between the two outstretched hands shrank by the second. As they touched fingertips it seemed the gods had not yet finished toying with them both because the wind coming up the side of the cliff caught the leading edge of Stratton's chute and the invisible wall of air lifted it. Their hands failed to grasp each other and he sailed over her and the world opened up beneath him.

Stratton could not believe it. It was not possible. He yelled in frustration. He had failed Louisa at the last second.

He twisted violently in his harness, pulling down hard on the toggle to look back at her. The wind continued to raise him up and as his chute made a tight turn he realised it was not yet over. He had another hand to play as he faced Louisa once again and headed back towards her at speed.

This time as Stratton reached the edge he pulled hard on the toggles to shut down the chute's cells. His feet hit the ground and the chute collapsed around them.

Louisa threw herself into his arms and he wrapped them tightly around her. For a fraction of a second there was nothing else in the world but them.

But that was long enough. Stratton looked quickly over his shoulder to see Steel running at them.

Steel aimed his pistol, his malevolent stare fixed on Stratton. He was about to pull the trigger when he suddenly noticed the ground disappear in front of him and stumbled to a halt as he reached the edge of the chine that cut across his path. He almost toppled into the abyss but managed to regain his balance and take a step back.

Stratton's hand reached for his pistol, but the holster was empty.

Louisa turned her head to look at Steel.

Now he was within easy range and, breathing heavily, he levelled his pistol at them.

Stratton wrapped his arms tightly around Louisa, gritted his teeth and dropped backwards off the cliff.

Steel fired quickly several times before they disappeared over the edge. He could not believe his eyes as he moved to the cliff to look down.

The chute flapped furiously around the couple as they plummeted.

Steel smirked. He had won. Stratton was dead.

Then his smile vanished and his mouth dropped open in utter disbelief.

The chute popped open with a flourish, forming into its rectangular shape, the red fire-breathing dragon snarling up at him. It soared away from the cliff and glided majestically above the river below.

Epilogue

Victor gazed into the glowing embers of the fire and breathed out heavily. Yoinakuwa sat on the floor, his back against the fireplace, staring at nothing.

The FBI man, Harris, sat back in his chair, watching Victor.

His assistant, Jacobs, leant forward, elbows on his knees like a kid full of expectation.

Victor remained silent.

Jacobs glanced at Harris, wondering why Victor had stopped. He wanted Harris to ask Victor a question but his boss seemed lost in his own thoughts.

Jacobs could not stand the suspense any longer. 'Well, what happened then?'

Victor shrugged. 'We made it to the horses. Only three of us escaped. David, Yoinakuwa and myself. The women and children, those who survived, were handed over to Hector's brigade. Besides us, not a single rebel fighter lived through that day. Hector never took full command as planned. He died a few months later. He was found hanging by his neck in his cabin. Some say his death was by his own hand. Some say he was murdered in revenge for Sebastian's betrayal.'

Jacobs was still frustrated. 'Louisa and Stratton?' he asked. 'What happened to them?'

'America, I think. I have never seen or spoken

to either of them since that day. Her political ambitions had been formed on the campuses of Boston and Cambridge but they could not stand the test of the realities of this country. I think of them as living happily ever after, somewhere.' Victor emptied the contents of his mug and went quiet again, lost in his thoughts.

Harris stirred and put his notebook into his pack. He took a deep breath and got to his feet, studying Victor. He seemed to be about to ask a question but changed his mind.

He walked to the door, opened it and left the cabin.

Jacobs watched him leave and looked back at Victor. He wanted to hear more but decided against asking anything else. He got to his feet, nodded a thanks to both men, neither of whom were looking at him, and went outside.

Harris stepped off the porch and stood on the damp earth, looking up at the cloudy sky with patches of blue breaking through. Water dripped off the porch and the leaves on the trees. The air outside was refreshing after the damp room and cigar smoke.

'What do you think?' Jacobs asked.

Harris glanced at his assistant. 'I think it was Victor's story, more than it was Stratton's . . . or Louisa's.'

'You don't believe him?'

Harris looked undecided. 'It was a good story. It's the end that wasn't true.'

'What do you mean?' Jacobs asked, anxious to know. 'What end?'

'She died. That's pretty obvious.'

'How do you know that?' Jacobs asked. A part of him didn't want to hear it but another part had to.

'That's why Stratton killed Steel, of course. It's the only reason he would have. He wouldn't have done it if they were together. And she would've come back, don't you think? She didn't sound the type to give up easily.'

'Why did Victor lie?'

'To protect Stratton.'

Jacobs considered the explanation. Despite his feelings, his wish for a happy ending, it made sense. 'What will happen to Stratton?'

'Steel acted outside his parameters. He broke US law as it applies to an overseas intelligence officer, for one thing. The CIA would be too embarrassed to acknowledge him. Stratton can't be charged with murdering someone who didn't exist.'

Jacobs looked back towards the cabin door. 'Maybe Victor doesn't know that Louisa died. Not if he never heard from them again. It's possible.'

'He knows.'

'How do you know that?'

'Look at the porch canopy.'

Jacobs looked up at the canopy flapping in the wind and his mouth opened in astonished realisation. The fabric was bright green, with a red fire-breathing dragon emblazoned on it. Stratton's parachute.

Harris shouldered his pack. 'Come on, Jacobs. We've got a long way to go,' he said, walking away. 'Goddamned waste of time, if you ask me.'

Jacobs grew sad as Victor's description of the couple's fall off the cliff came to life in his mind. As he stared at the parachute, flapping in the breeze, it suddenly went taut and the cells filled with the air flowing through them.

★ ★ ★

Stratton hung beneath the shadow of the canopy with Louisa in his arms. He held her tightly, as he had promised himself he would. Her head rested against him, her rich black hair flowing around them.

To begin with, her arms were tightly about him but then they began to lose their grip. Eventually they let go completely and hung loosely by her sides.

The ground grew ever closer and Stratton held Louisa firmly with one arm as he pulled down both toggles with the other. He stalled the fabric and touched down lightly, unclipping the risers from his shoulders to disconnect the chute, which floated away to roll onto the river bank.

Louisa's head dropped back in Stratton's arms and he saw that the light had gone from her eyes. His heart was filled with panic as he knelt down and lowered her onto her back. When he released his hand from around her waist it was covered in blood.

'Louisa,' he said, but he knew she was already gone.

Stratton made no effort to stop the tears rolling down his cheeks. They had both lost in the end.

He leant down and his lips touched hers gently. 'Safe journey, my love,' he said.

A distant shot sounded and a bullet struck the ground close by. Stratton did not flinch. He cared about nothing else at that moment. His world had been shattered and he didn't give a damn if he lived or died.

Another bullet struck the ground and he got to his feet and looked to the top of the cliff where the shooting was coming from. The tears fell as he stared up at the man who had destroyed the only thing in the world he had ever truly loved. The man he was going to kill if it took him the rest of his life.

★   ★   ★

Steel, his pistol in his hand, looked down at the tiny figure. He knew that he could never hit anything with his gun from that range.

Deep inside his heart he suddenly felt something — an unusual feeling for him. But he recognised it nonetheless. It was fear.

We do hope that you have enjoyed reading this large print book.

Did you know that all of our titles are available for purchase?

We publish a wide range of high quality large print books including:
Romances, Mysteries, Classics
General Fiction
Non Fiction and Westerns

Special interest titles available in large print are:
The Little Oxford Dictionary
Music Book
Song Book
Hymn Book
Service Book

Also available from us courtesy of Oxford University Press:
Young Readers' Dictionary
(large print edition)
Young Readers' Thesaurus
(large print edition)

For further information or a free brochure, please contact us at:
Ulverscroft Large Print Books Ltd.,
The Green, Bradgate Road, Anstey,
Leicester, LE7 7FU, England.
Tel: (00 44) 0116 236 4325
Fax: (00 44) 0116 234 0205

UNDERSEA PRISON

Duncan Falconer

When elite SBS operative John Stratton is given orders to retrieve a missing computer chip, he soon discovers that this mission could be his most dangerous yet. The chip is embedded beneath the skin of a fearless Taliban terrorist — who has been captured by the American military and placed inside the notorious Styx penitentiary. And the Styx is no ordinary prison. It is located 300 feet beneath the sea — more secure than either Guanténamo or Alcatraz. Even if a prisoner did manage to break free, the pressure of water as he rose to the surface would make his head explode. With murderous convicts, crooked guards and a kamikaze terrorist to contend with, it seems that Stratton may have signed his own death warrant . . .

THE PROTECTOR

Duncan Falconer

Disillusioned after serving in Iraq, Bernie Mallory left the Royal Marines. Now he's working in private security, safeguarding civilians and journalists in war zones. The job gives him the cover to return to Iraq and unearth a secret that has lain buried since he was last there, in a bombed-out graveyard near Fallujah. Jake Stanza is the journalist he's guarding. Stanza has his own mission: to find a kidnapped fellow American — for the kidnapped man has a story that could make his fortune. Abdul, their translator, is an Iraqi ex-policeman. Seemingly a nice, polite guy, war has left him scarred — physically and mentally. Mallory and Stanza trust their translator implicitly, but behind his smiling façade he is harbouring dark and potentially deadly secrets . . .